--- ★ ---

Over the hushed night sounds of traffic and surf he heard another sound, a high whining noise he didn't recognize. As it became louder, movement on the water caught his eye. A black shape crossed the rippled reflection from a shore light. It was a large model boat, perhaps two feet long, but with a strange outline. What the hell? There was a lens of some type on top, like a robot eye. Robot?

"Jessie! Get out!"

The explosion hit his back like a brick wall. He flew through the air into the empty slip next to his. Unconsciousness claimed him before the black water closed over him, but the water shocked him awake. A scream of pain and fear stabbed through the night. "Tommyyy!" A muffled whump from an exploding fuel tank cut the scream short. More flames hissed into the air.

--- ★ ---

DAVID BURTON

MANMADE FOR
MURDER

WORLDWIDE.

TORONTO • NEW YORK • LONDON
AMSTERDAM • PARIS • SYDNEY • HAMBURG
STOCKHOLM • ATHENS • TOKYO • MILAN
MADRID • WARSAW • BUDAPEST • AUCKLAND

MANMADE FOR MURDER

A Worldwide Mystery/March 2000

First published by Write Way Publishing, Inc.

ISBN 0-373-26342-2

Visit us at www.worldwidemystery.com

Printed in U.S.A.

Dedication

This book is dedicated to many people. To all those girls thirty years ago to whom I promised to dedicate my first book,

and

To my wife, Dee, the most supportive writer's widow on the planet. She took care of all the mundane, real-life things while I got to sit alone and have adventures. Thanks, cutie.

Acknowledgment

This book would not be what it is without: Leonard Adelman's creation of the first DNA computer; Sally Cook bringing it to my attention; Penpointers' valuable critiques; Dorrie O'Brien's editing, and the foundation of fiction writing and support from Elizabeth George.

To all the above, and all the unnamed who deserve it, thank you. Anything right with this novel is their fault. Anything wrong is mine.

Who says robots don't cry? They are made by man for the use of man. How can they not take on the attributes of man? Intelligence and emotion are inevitable. The infinite combinations of intelligence and emotion can be sublime or deadly, either way, too deep to change. Who says robots don't cry? Not I.

—*Anonymous*

PROLOGUE

FIVE MINUTES BEFORE he was murdered Brian Childress received a telephone call. He listened intently, nodding his head in a slow, thoughtful manner, a tight-lipped frown on his smooth, handsome face.

He said without enthusiasm, "Yeah, okay, I'll look it up. What is it again?"

He took a yellow Post-it notepad from a tidy stack in the front left corner of his desk's center drawer. From the inside pocket of his Brooks Brothers gray pinstripe suit he took a gold Cross pen and wrote as he listened, then said, "Hang on." He pushed the hold button with a manicured finger, then set the receiver precisely in its cradle. He dropped the note pad on top of the stack it came from. It landed half on, half off, leaning against the top edge of the stack. Brian noticed its crookedness as he closed the drawer. His lips pressed together with annoyance, but he was in a hurry, so he didn't line it up with the others. He pushed the thought of the pad lying untidy in his drawer out of his mind as he picked up his briefcase, left his office and turned right, through a set of heavy, metal swinging doors with small square windows set in them.

White-topped workbenches littered with electronic equipment ran along three, white concrete walls. Midway on the wall across from where he entered, tools hung patiently against a yellow peg board. The fourth wall, to Brian's left, was glass. Behind the glass stood three rows of mainframe computers, rectangular metal boxes filled with thousands of silicon chips into which he knew he could breathe life.

As Brian angled to the right, toward the far corner, a red light winked on underneath the clear plastic cover of the second computer from the end of the middle row. Reaching the corner, he smiled at the robot waiting there. "Hi DEX," he said. The robot did not respond. Brian set his briefcase on the workbench and reached for the third three-ring notebook in a row of eleven. He opened it, and finding what he wanted, picked up the receiver from the black telephone on the wall and pushed line one's blinking red button.

"Still there?" he asked. Receiving an affirmative answer, he leaned over the notebook and began reading off numbers. Fifteen seconds later he stood up straight, sensing movement behind him. Frozen for a second, he watched a hand crafted in shiny metal swing around from his left and push hard on his chest, pinning him against what he knew to be DEX's metal body.

From the right, another hand came into view. It swung underneath Brian's chin where the one-and-a-quarter inch diameter tube that formed the radius bone of the forearm contacted his throat. He struggled to free himself but the pressure on his chest increased. Breathing became difficult as the tension on his neck forced his head back. Despite rapidly failing vision he noticed a security camera high in the corner above him, patiently watching him die. A small orange light below the lens glowed unblinking and uncaring.

Before he died, Brian managed to whisper at the camera lens, "You bastard."

The room became still, lifeless. The camera remained focused on the scene, its small light unwavering. Then, slowly, almost gently, DEX laid the body, face up, on the workbench and went through the pockets one by one, extracting a wallet, some keys, a plane ticket and fifty-five cents in change.

That task accomplished, DEX moved away from the body. There was no movement for ten seconds, then his video eyes whirred out and in. Focused now, his head dropped and in utter stillness he stared at Brian like a faithful dog wondering why his master didn't wake up.

DEX picked up the body with a few jerky movements and wheeled toward a set of swinging doors opposite the ones Brian had entered. DEX wheeled through a work area and through another set of doors into a storage room. At the far side of the room, he stopped by a corrugated roll-up door and waited for it to open. He turned left through the opening and went down a ramp to a fenced area containing two battered dumpsters. Brian Chambers' body disappeared into the boxes and papers of the closest one. DEX peered into the dumpster, then, delicately, reached in, picked up a flattened cardboard box, and laid it over a protruding brown loafer.

DEX returned the way he had come. He picked up the brief-case, wallet and keys and placed them in a drawer of a tool box. The notebook was returned to its proper place. The fifty-five cents lay undisturbed.

Again the room was still. The security camera light blinked out, followed a few seconds later by the red light on the second computer from the end of the middle row.

ONE

HOT SEA WIND ruffled Tommy Case's unruly dark hair. The air felt heavy and thick against his tanned face as he maneuvered his sailboat up Newport Bay under a hazy, cloudless sky—the same boring summer weather as always. No wonder Southern California starts so many trends and fads, he thought, the weather never changes, something has to.

Sailing singlehanded, Tommy's movements were quick and sure. His hands, calloused and strong from years of sailing, lightly caressed the leather-covered wheel. He concentrated on the feel of the boat under his bare feet. His eyes, green like shallow tropical water, measured the distance to the sterns of the million-dollar yachts that lined the bay. At the last second he leaped into action, bringing his boat about under the critical eyes of watchful skippers.

As he guided his boat, under sail, toward his slip in the Leeward Marina he noticed a woman watching him from shore. He recognized his former secretary, Jessie Padeski, underneath a floppy sun hat and dark glasses. They had been on more or less amicable terms the last time they'd talked, eight months before, considering the argument they'd had about closing the office. But something about the way she leaned against the rail, motionless, silently watching—instead of waving and smiling—produced in him a strong urge to turn and sail off to the South Pacific three months earlier than planned.

The break in his concentration almost made him miss his slip. With a quick flip, he spun the wheel hard to port. The boat missed the concrete piling by inches, but held too much speed. Tommy threw the wheel hard to starboard, released the main sheet with a flick of the wrist and scrambled out of the cockpit. On the dock, he grabbed a line fixed to the port side of the boat, and with a practiced roll, whipped it around a dock cleat. The line stretched taut. The cleat groaned, but held. Bucking like a roped wild horse, the boat stopped within inches of the dock.

After a landing, Tommy usually faced the shore, spread his arms and said, "Tadaaa," to an imaginary audience. This time, disgusted with himself for such a sloppy job, he just shook his head and set about securing the boat. Down below, a few minutes later, he heard a knock on the deck. Knowing it would be Jessie, he shouted out, "Come aboard."

She came down the companionway ladder backwards like a landlubber. Tommy smiled as he watched her big feet descend the ladder, followed by trim legs that disappeared into snug white shorts. He had forgotten how big her feet were.

At the bottom of the ladder she turned to face him. Although she stood in shadow, he knew the lime green blouse tied up underneath her breasts matched her eyes. She took off her hat and sunglasses and laid them on the counter to her right. Tommy continued to look her over, remembering the auburn hair, now drawn back in a loose braid, that framed a round, pale, freckled face that didn't like the sun. Not approaching the pneumatic build of Lucy down the dock, Jessie had a quality about her that made men look twice without quite knowing why. Tommy hated to admit it, but that was one reason he had hired her.

Three years after he left the Sheriff's Department and had become a private investigator he was doing well enough to need a secretary. Jessie had been the first to apply, recommended by the wife of a cousin of somebody he didn't remember. Right out of Community College, she had little experience and so-so grades, but, he was busy; she was attractive; his marriage was on a downward spiral. She got the job.

"So, are you going to stand there with that shit-eating grin on your face or are you going to say hello?" she asked.

Startled, Tommy continued to stare; Jessie never swore. She had changed somehow. More aggressive, judging by the way she said that one sentence and the way she stood, inviting, as well as daring him to look at her. Before, her aggression index had been close to zero.

"I guess I'm going to stand here and look at you some more. You look great," he said, meaning it.

"Just goes to show what makeup can do. I feel like shit."

She moved to him, put her head against his chest and hugged him tight. Close up she didn't look quite so good. She looked tired, with dark circles under bloodshot eyes. Again, he had the sinking feeling this was not a social call; nevertheless, he returned her hug. Her familiar smell assaulted his senses, raising his heart rate a notch.

He asked, "Jessie, what's the matter? What's going on?"

Backing away, she rubbed her eyes as if wiping tears away. She sighed, laughed, shook her head. "Sorry. I don't know why I'm getting so upset. It really doesn't matter to me what happened to that son of a bitch."

"Jessie, come on. You've sworn more in five minutes than in the past five years. What's happened?"

Jessie paced to the companionway ladder and back. She squeezed past him and sat at the built-in table on the starboard side, across from the settee, a long bench seat that ran fore and aft. She looked him right in the eye and said, "I miss you, Tommy. I miss the office. I really liked that job, and I was good at it, too. Wasn't I?"

Uncomfortable, Tommy agreed. "Yeah, you were. The best."

"It really hurt when you quit. Everything was so right."

Rubbing his temples, Tommy said, "Jessie, I explained it before. I just couldn't take that leap to the next level. Everything was closing in on me. I mean, I've lived in this area for almost thirty years, but now there's just no space left. And there's too damn much traffic. You know how I like to drive. Well, all that traffic is crowding me and I don't have to take it. So I'm not."

Jessie sighed. "I do understand, Tommy. But I don't have to like it." She smiled to herself and said, "You've changed, you know. You used to like all that fast-lane stuff. People and parties, business."

Tommy shrugged, "Yeah, I know. But at the end it was a lot more people and parties than business. If it hadn't been for that Biodata job I'd be a guest of Betty Ford's by now."

"I'm not the woman you used to know, either."

"I can see that."

Jessie smiled sympathetically and said, "Meek little secretary Jessie is gone. The real me is here now."

"Oh? Where was the real Jessie five years ago?"

Jessie's smile took the sting from her words, "She was there, but at the time you were playing Mr. Righteous, trying to save a marriage that wasn't. Of course that didn't last long when it was all over, did it?"

Uncomfortable with the memories seeping out of the dark places in his brain, Tommy asked, "What happened to who?"

She frowned at the table top as the flame in her eyes died. "They found Brian. He's dead."

Brian? Who the hell was Brian? Her other strange words forgotten for the moment, he finally had to ask, "Brian?"

She watched her fidgeting hands click their fingernails together before saying, "Brian Childs. We got engaged right after the last time I saw you. You met him once, just before you..."—she looked daggers at him—"closed the office."

Tommy's mind went blank for a moment, then, "Yeah, tall, long brown hair, baby bottom skin, good looking as hell."

"Beautiful is what he was, although he didn't look so good Monday night when I saw him."

"Do you want something to drink?" he asked. His heart thumped as a smile barely bent the corners of her mouth. *Damn, she can still do that to me.*

"Are you still drinking that silly white wine with ice?"

"Yeah, but when I'm with the guys I put it in a beer mug. Much more macho that way."

"Very funny. I'll have some, without the ice."

Tommy poured the wine and sat down.

"What happened?" he asked again. "I didn't know you were engaged."

Leaning back, she twirled the glass between her fingers. "Do you believe it? Somebody good came into my life. I was so happy, we had everything taken care of, it was going to be great." She took a long drink. "Then about six months ago I came back to my apartment and there was a message on my answering machine I'll never forget. 'Jessie. I'm really sorry, but it can't work out for us right now. Maybe later when I've got what I want. I'm really sorry. Goodbye.'"

Tommy stared at her. "You're kidding. Why?"

"That's what I wanted to know. I tried to find him, but he just vanished. Later, I was so pissed off I didn't want to see him anyway, so I had a last good cry and stopped looking. I was over him, too, until Monday." She sipped her wine and stared unseeing into a corner. "Monday when I got home from work—I work at Tim's Gym in Huntington Beach now—there was a Sergeant Cartwell from the Sheriff's Department waiting. He was very polite and all, but there's no good way to tell somebody that a body found in the landfill had nothing in his pockets but your telephone number."

"Jesus," Tommy whispered. "That must have been a shock."

Jessie rolled her eyes and shook her head. "Christ. I guess. I didn't know what to say. He wanted me to look at the body to see if I could identify it and I figured I really didn't have much choice, so I went with him. I'd never seen a real dead body before and wasn't looking forward to it, believe me." She gulped her wine and continued. "When the guy pulled that sheet back I just about fainted. It was Brian. Do you believe it? Christ!"

Tommy refilled their glasses. Jessie relaxed a bit, flashed him a smile that reminded him of all the years he had denied to himself he wanted her. At first they had wanted each other, but for some reason he still didn't understand, he wanted to wait until his divorce was final. Maybe he hoped it would help him and Bonnie get together again. In any case, Jessie didn't wait. Thinking he was over her, for five years they had a friendly, if slightly distant, business relationship. Now, he knew the desire was still there, and he didn't like it. A complication like that, he didn't need.

"So what happened then?"

"I got the third degree, is what happened. I was surprised at how little I really knew about Brian. He came from back East and had a degree in computer science. He sold computers and seemed to know a lot about them. Anyway, this Cartwell wanted to know where I was last weekend and said not to leave town without telling him."

Jessie was quiet for a while, then seemed to come to a decision. She pursed her lips in a crooked way Tommy remembered fondly and said, "Tommy, I know it's silly, but I loved Brian, maybe the only man I ever really loved. He did a shitty thing to me and I'm still angry, but I'd like to know what happened to him. I deserve to know, don't I?" she said, eyes pleading.

A lump rose in his throat. "Sure, of course."

"Tommy, could you talk to this Sergeant Cartwell? He didn't seem very enthusiastic, you know. He treated it like a stolen bicycle instead of a murder."

"Murder?" Tommy said, looking up. "Well, yeah, I guess it would be murder if he was found at the dump. Not a likely place to commit suicide or have an accident. How did he die?"

Jessie shivered. "They told me his throat was crushed." She shrugged her shoulders with resignation. "Would you just talk to him? Maybe you could find out what Brian was doing? Please, for the old Jessie."

She leaned across the table and took Tommy's hands in her own, kneading them with a slow rhythm while she gazed directly into his eyes. *Oh boy,* he thought, closing his eyes slowly, in an attempt to shut out the look in her eyes. His insides tightened and twisted. He did not want to do it. Yet, he knew he would, even though he really did not want to get involved in any sort of investigation, especially a murder. That wasn't his field and besides, he liked his quiet, uninvolved, uncomplicated life while he waited to sail off to the South Pacific and beyond. He started to say no, but she lifted his hands to lips that were soft and moist and warm. Her tongue slid lightly over his fingers.

He opened his eyes and all those years of desire came back and instead of saying no, he said, "Okay, Jessie. I'll talk to him. I'll see what I can find out. But that's all. I owe you that much."

"Oh Tommy, thank you. You promise?"

He sighed, resigned. "I promise."

Jessie moved around the table and put her arms around his neck. "Thank you, Tommy. There might be hope for us yet." She kissed him, softly at first, then harder, then drew back. Breathing rapidly, voice hoarse, she said, "God, I've wanted you forever, Tommy." Jessie pulled him to her and kissed him again.

He returned her kiss eagerly, knowing he was being used, but not giving a damn.

Tommy asked, "Is this the old Jessie, or the new?"

"New to you," she said, breathless.

She stood up, pulled her blouse over her head and threw it on the table. Her small, pert breasts with upturned nipples, jiggled slightly as she helped Tommy pull off his shirt.

At first Tommy thought the noise he heard was the beat of his own pulse, then he realized somebody outside was pounding on the outside of the boat. They separated, looked at each other with wide-eyed surprise, chests heaving, arms stiff by their sides.

A man's angry voice called, "Jessie! Jessie are you in there? Jessie!"

To herself Jessie whispered, "Damn. George."

The boat heeled over as a heavy body stepped on deck.

Jessie grabbed her blouse and slipped it on. Tommy, just beginning to get his wits about him, struggled with his red Hawaiian shirt. He started aft to confront the untimely visitor, but Jessie's hand on his arm stopped him.

"Stay back, let me talk to him," she commanded.

Confused, Tommy stepped back. He gaped as the man dropped easily through the companionway hatch. The interior of the boat was too small for him; his sand-colored flattop skimmed the cabin support beams. That made him six foot three. His muscles filled the cabin, every lat, delt and pec conspicuous underneath a tight black T-shirt and smooth, bronzed skin. Despite the angry expression on the guy's face, directed at him, Tommy almost laughed aloud. The visitor stood slightly bow-legged, his shoulders hunched forward. His thick-jawed face reminded Tommy of Popeye. All he needed was a pipe and a sailor's hat.

Jessie spoke first, anger in her voice. "George, what the hell are you doing here?"

"Cindy told me where you went." His squinted eyes never left Tommy's face.

"That bitch," Jessie muttered.

"She said you'd gone to see an old boyfriend." He stuck a muscled finger in Tommy's direction. "And that must be you."

Before Tommy could react, George pounced. He lifted Tommy

by the throat with one hand and slammed him against the bulkhead. Wild eyes only inches from his face, George's fingers closed on Tommy's throat.

Fear surged through Tommy. He wasn't laughing now. He couldn't breathe. *Holy shit; he really is going to kill me.* The pressure on his throat cut off the blood flow to his brain. He struck at George to no effect. Bright flashes of light streaked across the insides of his eyes. His lungs screamed for air. Through the roar in his ears he heard Jessie yelling. Her fists beat ineffectually on George's massive back.

Then, as blackness descended over him, Tommy heard a sharp crack as Jessie slapped George full on the face. The pressure lifted from his throat. His feet felt like they were two miles away when they touched the floor. Chest heaving, he slid down against the bulkhead, sucking in fiery gulps of air.

After a few minutes his breathing slowed, his pulse fell back to almost normal. Jessie helped him stand, but he immediately had to sit again. She held a cool, wet towel to his burning face. George fidgeted meekly by the companionway ladder, like a naughty schoolboy.

"Jessie," Tommy croaked. "He tried to kill me."

"Tommy, I'm so sorry. He wouldn't have, really."

Yes, he would have, really, his foggy brain told him.

"He gets so jealous sometimes he can't control himself." She shot George an angry look.

"Who is he?" Tommy managed.

"George Stanis. He's the assistant manager at the gym. We go out together sometimes." She leaned close. "I guess he thinks I'm his girlfriend more than I think he's my boyfriend. Are you sure you're okay? I'm really sorry this happened." She whispered quickly in his ear, "At least he could have waited an hour or so."

Tommy had to smile. George didn't like seeing them smiling together, "Hey, what are you...?"

Eyes flashing, Jessie turned on him. "Stay away from him, George," she warned. "If you even think about touching him you'll never see me again, ever. Do you understand?"

Tommy watched with astonishment as George, a foot taller

and three times heavier than Jessie, backed down with almost a whimper. He stepped back to the ladder, but his dark unblinking eyes never left Jessie's back.

"Are you sure you're all right?" Jessie asked. Tommy grunted that he was. "I think we should go."

Tommy agreed. Popeye, lurking by the ladder, frightened him more than he cared to admit.

"Be careful of him," Tommy warned quietly.

"I'll be fine," she said. "You'll still talk to Sergeant Cartwell, won't you, and find out what you can?"

Tommy assured her he would, anxious for them to go, his quiet life interrupted enough. Tomorrow he would talk to Cartwell, who he knew from his time in the Sheriff's Department, and that would be that. He wanted a drink and something to eat, if he could swallow it, and to lie back and listen to some jazz and not think about anything.

With a flick of her hand, like to a dog to get into a car, Jessie motioned George up the ladder. The steps creaked with his weight. Jessie turned to Tommy, held his head in her hands and said, "Next time, no interruptions." She kissed him quick and hard. Then she was gone.

TWO

THE NEXT MORNING over English muffins smothered with peanut butter and raspberry jam, Tommy thought about Jessie. A year ago he would have laughed if anybody suggested Jessie would be cursing or coming on to him like that. Could she have been hiding another facet of her life all those years? Admittedly, he'd been more involved in work, and himself, than her when it became evident they weren't going to get together. And what about George? Tommy had no doubt of George's intent to kill him. He recognized the wild-eyed look that said the brain has been disengaged and emotion has taken over. Sorry afterwards, George's apology wouldn't have helped Tommy much.

Tommy had changed, too. As an MP in the Army, a Sheriff's Deputy and a private investigator, being involved in other people's problems had been his job, but for eight months now he had led a blissful life of no involvement and no responsibilities and he had no desire whatsoever to be involved or responsible again. However, sore throat or not, he had promised, so he would see Cartwell. The thought of Jessie keeping her implied promise was not unattractive either.

In the parking lot, Tommy met Wash, Leeward Marina's owner and dockmaster. Barrel-chested, solid as a rock, five-and-a-half-feet tall, he needed only an eye patch and a sword to be the classic image of a pirate. They had been boat friends for years and hoisted many a cup of grog together.

"I saw your landing yesterday," Wash greeted him. "Tsk tsk, not up to your usual standards, Tommy my man. You weren't distracted by that woman, were you? Who was she?" He nodded at Tommy's bruised neck. "She do that?"

Rubbing his throat, Tommy said, "That was Jessie Padeski. She was my secretary once. You've met her, but were too out of it to remember. Jack Tandy's boat launching party?"

"Oh yeah, I remember...vaguely. She's the one who pushed me in the water."

Tommy laughed. "She never did take kindly to comments about her feet."

Chagrined, Wash laughed through a lopsided grin. "Well, those big feet sure did the job, kicked me right in the ass and into that cold, dark water."

Their eyes met. Tommy knew what Wash was thinking. Not a good swimmer, and totally wasted, he had been going under for the last time when Tommy jumped in and saved him. Tommy shrugged off the deed, but Wash, sometimes even when he was sober, could get overly maudlin on the subject.

To avoid a sentimental scene, Tommy said, "Apparently, her ex-fiancé was murdered and she wants me to make sure the police don't forget their duty." He finished with a shrug and a throw-away motion of hands, "Or something."

All sentimentality gone, Wash replied with good-humored disbelief. "You, investigating a murder? You: Mr.-I'm-through-with-detective-work-forever? Mr. Tommy I'm-never-going-to-investigate-anything-more-than-what's-under-a-grass-skirt Case?" He pursed his lips. "Must have been an interesting meeting. If I had a buck for every time you said you were through with investigating, I'd be a rich man."

"You're already a rich man and I'm not investigating. I'm just going to talk to the detective. That's all. I have to go. Why don't you go do whatever it is dockmasters do. Count your money, or something."

Tommy got into his car, a black, two-year-old Mustang Cobra convertible with severely upgraded suspension and an engine tweaked past the Smog Check limit.

Wash's round, leering face appeared at the window. "You're cute when you blush," he said.

Muttering nasty things about his friend, Tommy smoked a hundred miles of rubber off his tires on the way out of the parking lot.

Ten miles inland, in Santa Ana, the temperature already stood over ninety-five. The parking lot by the Sheriff's Department Headquarters shimmered in the heat. At one-thirty he entered the

Orange County Sheriff's Department through a nondescript door and shivered in the sudden chill.

Investigator Hugh Cartwell had his Hushpuppy-clad feet on his desk. He read some papers held in one hand while the other scratched absently behind his ear, causing the bifocals resting on his short round nose to slip down. He pushed them up and went back to his ear scratching, repeating the cycle.

Unnoticed, Tommy observed several cycles before saying, 'Hello, Cartwell, scratching for fleas?''

Cartwell started, then stared over his glasses, trying to place Tommy. Tommy leaned against the door, a small smile fixed on his spare face, sun-bleached eyebrows raised in question. He was still in good shape, his body lean with broad shoulders, but his shorts, loud Hawaiian shirt and unkempt hair were a far cry from his old gray uniform.

After half a minute of silence, Cartwell laid his glasses on the desk and said, "Case. Tommy Case. I thought you'd show up sooner or later. What are you doing in this neighborhood? I hear you're mingling with the yacht club set these days."

He dropped his feet to the floor and stood up to shake Tommy's hand. Although he appeared to be out of shape—stomach protruding over his belt and a round, puffy face looking like it hadn't seen sun in years—his grip was firm and no nonsense. He pointed to a chair in the corner of his office.

Tommy slouched into it, long bare legs crossed at the ankles, hands clasped over his stomach. "Well, I'm just slumming, you know? Have to remind myself of what all those beautiful, rich yacht women are trying to make me forget. They try so much harder when I tell them of my sordid past."

"Right," Cartwell replied, dripping sarcasm. "Rich women don't go for quitters like you, Case."

Tommy's eyes flashed. His hands gripped the arms of the chair, body suddenly taut. After six years, being called a quitter still rankled. It had been for the good of the department. They didn't know that, and he couldn't, or wouldn't, tell them. He forced himself to relax.

Cartwell asked, "Why did you leave, Case? You were a damn good officer, as I recall."

"Personal reasons," Tommy said. The last thing he wanted to do was get into that. When his partner Jim Flores had died in his arms after an undercover assignment went wrong, Tommy had every intention of keeping his promise; somehow though, he never quite got around to telling anybody that Deputy Sheriff Bob Penny had released information, for his own political motives, that got Jim killed. Tommy carried that guilt for almost a year until, in an attempt at expiation, he'd quit the department.

He often speculated if he had done the right thing, especially during the first hard years when his marriage was ending. His marriage to Bonnie had always been shaky. What cop's marriage wasn't? Leaving the Department, and the regular paycheck that went with it was the final blow. Bonnie did have some attributes besides California beach girl good looks and partying, but living on a budget and standing by her man weren't among them.

He kept himself going doing miscellaneous security work: concerts, bodyguard, outside operative for investigators. Then he opened his own office. The first two years had been tough, and scary, with little money. The second two years had been the best. Plenty of work, but not too much. He put money in the bank every month and clients called him instead of the other way around. The last year he made the most money and enjoyed it the least. His clients were bigger and richer and so he had to appear bigger and richer himself.

A job with BioData was the turning point. The return of their stolen gene-combining formulas netted him over a hundred and fifty thousand dollars in billings, fees and bonuses. The time had come to seriously expand or get out. It was a particularly smoggy hot day when he left BioData, the traffic worse than usual. By the time he arrived at his office he had decided—*To hell with it, I'm going sailing.* Besides, the effort needed to take care of everybody's problems took a heavy toll. Sailing and solitude, the freedom of responsibility for everyone else's problems, beckoned like the Sirens.

He sighed, said, "What do you mean, you knew I'd show up sooner or later?"

Cartwell dropped his glasses on his cluttered desk, "The Childs case. Your ex-secretary thinks you're a hot-shot detective.

although she had some choice words about how she felt when you closed up shop. Of course, in the next breath she's saying you'd be happy to help her, and us, bring the culprit to justice."

"Ha. Frankly I'd be very happy to count myself out. I'm only here to find out for her what's going on, as a friend, not in any professional capacity." Tommy took a long deep breath, let it out slow. "She mentioned murder. Was it? I have to admit I'm a little curious, even if it is no concern of mine."

Cartwell rummaged around on his desk as Tommy spoke. He pulled a thin manila folder out from under a pile, set his feet on the desk, put his glasses on and leafed through the file. "The body was found by a bulldozer operator at the county landfill last Monday, the nineteenth. Padeski's phone number was found in his right front pants pocket. She identified the body as Brian Childs. There's been no missing persons report, no phone number listed or unlisted, no towed or registered cars under that name. A blank. A nobody. So far."

Cartwell closed the file he hadn't been reading anyway and continued his recital. "He'd been dead about two days. The apparent cause of death was strangulation by a round hard object. And that's about it. Maybe the autopsy report will give us something. All we can do is check out what little we have."

"That's not much to go on. Jessie told me he was a computer scientist. Have you checked out where he used to work? What about all those high-tech companies around here? Anything in the garbage?"

"We aren't totally incompetent, Case," Cartwell snapped, throwing the file on the desk where it blended in with the other files. "We do think of some things. Do you know how many computer, or computer-related, businesses there are in this county alone? Over two hundred. That means time to check them out and time is something we don't have much of these days." He shook his head in exasperation. "With all these damn gangbangers killing each other we have twice as many homicides as usual."

Cartwell leaned toward Tommy, warming to the subject. Tommy listened patiently; detectives always complained about how overworked they were, with good reason usually. Besides he was curious about what was going on.

"And the other ones we have going," Cartwell said, "are rea bitches. Speaking of which, there's that society lady from New port Beach that got herself stabbed in her Mercedes, out in th boonies. Everybody wants something done, but nobody's talking The only thing they'll say is they aren't surprised. It seems sh liked her sex in unconventional places and wasn't very discree about it. Shut the door."

He opened the right-hand drawer of the desk and brought ou a pack of Marlboros. He lit one with a cheap plastic lighter an took a long drag. Exhaling smoke he said, "Yeah, I know it' bad for me, for you, for everybody within a half mile, but shi if they don't like it they can stay away. That'll suit me fine.' He took another lungful of smoke. Tommy, who quit years ag and still fought it, made no comment.

The investigator continued with a smoky sigh, "Then we hav the more garden variety killings, two robbery homicides, thre illegal aliens dumped in a ditch, a drug pusher shot in the stree and assorted family members killed by the ones they love. An that's only in the unincorporated areas." He returned his feet t the corner of the desk. "So, Case, we'll investigate your Bria Childs, but frankly, with the county's financial situation, we'r spread damn thin and you know the powers above are not goin to give him top priority unless something solid turns up. An that's the way it is," he finished with a fatalistic smile. "As I'n sure you know."

They nodded in unison, both knowing the way things were.

Cartwell leaned back in his chair. "Ordinarily you private guy are a pain in the ass, but to tell the truth I could use some un official help. You'd have access to what information I have, o which you already know as much as I do, anyway. Just findin out where this guy lived or worked would be a big help. I, an Ms. Padeski, would appreciate it, because we just don't have th manpower at the moment to do a proper job of it. What do yo think?"

Tommy sat up straight and punctuated his words with a finge poking into the air. "I think you don't want Jessie Padeski al over your ass about finding out why her poor Brian got himself dumped in the garbage. That's what I think.''

"Hey, take it easy.'' Cartwell said. "You didn't think much of this guy, did you?''

"Hell, I never knew him. Sounds like an asshole to me. Did she tell you how he dumped her? Now she calls me out of the blue and wants me to help find out what happened and you want me to help you find out what happened, and I don't want to do either." He slumped into his seat. "The thing is, I know I'm going to do it. And that pisses me off.''

Cartwell fiddled with a pen for a minute while Tommy cooled down. Then said, "Yes, she did tell me what happened and I have to admit I can understand her wanting to know why he left. I'll also admit I don't need anybody on my ass at the moment.'' He checked his watch and stood up. "Now, I'm busy, which means I have things to do and places to go. So, what are you going to do?''

"What I'd like to do is forget all this and go sailing. I'm no expert in murder investigations." But, what the hell. He really didn't have anything else to do. "Can I see the file? What about the autopsy? What about the garbage around him?''

Telephone already at his ear, Cartwell mumbled a question then hung up and said, "The autopsy report is on its way. The area is marked off at the dump, if you want to see it. There are pictures in the file and a sample of the garbage in the lab.'' He reached for his coat. "Look, I have to go. The autopsy report will be here in a minute and I'll leave word you can see the stuff in the lab if you want. I appreciate it, Case.'' He paused at the door. "If you find out anything I should know, you'll contact me immediately, right?''

"Yes Sir! Sergeant Cartwell, Sir!'' Tommy replied, beaming an exaggerated grin.

Cartwell spoke a few words to a uniformed secretary and stomped away. Tommy, after a long look in the direction of the drawer with the cigarettes in it, put his feet on the desk and read through the file. The autopsy report arrived and he read that, too.

An hour later, Tommy walked out of the building into heat that took his breath away. He opened both doors to allow the stifling heat to escape, turned on the air-conditioning and thought over what he'd just read.

The case and autopsy reports hadn't told him much more than he already knew. Brian Child's throat had been crushed by a smooth, inch-and-a-quarter-diameter metal pipe or bar. The interesting thing was that there had been no hard blow to the neck, but the damage was more than any but the most powerful man could have inflicted. Minor wounds were consistent with having been bulldozed with the garbage after death. Time of death was sometime Friday night or Saturday morning. The only other item of interest was a trace of light, high-quality machine oil found in the wound. The sample bag of garbage was just garbage. Tommy decided he might as well end a perfect afternoon with a look at the dump. As a consolation, it would be a chance to open up the Mustang on the road out to the landfill site.

The narrow, two-lane paved road wound through open scrub brush toward the foothills of the Santa Ana Mountains. He ran the road at speed, running a slalom course marked by garbage trucks. The Mustang's suspension was close to race car quality and Tommy took full advantage of it. Two years of amateur racing after the Army and years of watching races on ESPN saw to that. Hands at three and nine o'clock on the leather-covered steering wheel, he took the turns at the ragged edge of adhesion, braking hard for the corners—downshifting—engine screaming in delight. Hard right. Hard left. On the gas. Up hill, wheels catching air over the crest. Brake hard for a fast turn before the pavement ended.

Tommy relaxed his grip and settled back into the contoured driving seat. He hadn't felt this good in weeks. He loved to drive twisty, turny roads. It wasn't the speed he liked so much as the feeling of control, of being able to take a turn at the very limit of adhesion. If he hadn't decided to sail off in search of uncrowded space, he'd probably race cars again.

At the landfill gate, the guard directed him to the middle of the dump line and a fifty-foot square cordoned off with yellow police-line tape. The heat and stink pressed on him, making it hard to breathe. A fair breeze blew, brewing up occasional dust devils that spun across the wide gray access area. Flies buzzed and single sheets of newspaper tumbled silently across mounds of garbage. Seagulls squawked and fought over choice tidbits. In the distance, a brown haze covered any trace of civilization. A truck raced its engine to dump its load at the far end of the dump line.

"A hell of a place to die, Brian. A hell of a place," Tommy said to the wind.

He stepped over bulging green plastic bags, broken toys, cardboard boxes and soggy paper to get to the yellow tape. In the middle, wood stakes connected by red tape outlined where the body was found.

Inside the police line he traversed the area with his eyes. Nothing. Next he walked the area slowly. Still nothing. Finally, with a resigned sigh, he crouched down and looked close, shifting debris with a broken broom handle, half expecting something mean and hungry to jump out at him. Fifteen minutes later, he reached out a bit too far beyond the yellow tape. He slipped and landed flat on his face. His left hand slid into a hot, sticky, green mass that might once have been somebody's expensive dinner.

"Shit!" he yelped, scrambling to his feet. He grabbed a rag that looked relatively clean and wiped his hand. Under the cloth hid a small pile of electronic components that looked like insects spilling out of a small cardboard box. He recognized computer chips. An interesting item to find near a dead computer scientist, he thought. Gathering up the components, he looked around, said, "The hell with it," and stomped back to his car, carrying the box.

Using paper towels from a roll in the trunk, he cleaned himself off. He threw the used towels in the air and watched them float away on the hot wind. Sometimes it was satisfying to just throw something away and not worry about the scenic landscape or the environment. Probably some genetic defect humans picked up along the evolutionary way.

He listened to the silence for a minute, imagining himself high up on a tropical island while the trade winds etched moving patterns on a sparkling sea below. But it didn't last. The stench of garbage cooking under the white hot sun overrode any imaginings. *Only three more months,* he thought. The hurricane season would be over and he wouldn't have to imagine tropical islands, he'd be heading for the real thing. He grinned and drove slowly toward the gate, leaving a plume of dust behind him.

THREE

THE DRIVE BACK TO the marina with the top down cleared the garbage stink from his nose. While he cooled off under the marina showers he thought it unlikely Brian had been killed at the dump. It was guarded twenty-four hours a day and they kept a close watch. Most likely he had been dumped, probably from a trash truck that picked up the body in a dumpster. Cartwell hadn't found any trace of a Brian Childs. So, he had either changed his name or maybe gone back to his real one. Brian was supposed to be a computer scientist from back East. He'd have to have a degree from some place, but where? Unless that was fake, too? The only lead he had was a box of computer chips found near the body of a supposed computer expert.

Back on board his boat, *Nomorr (No More Rat Race)*, Tommy poured a large glass of wine and stretched out on the settee. He punched a number on his cordless telephone.

"Fumio," Tommy said. "How's it going, Mr. Wizard? Still wasting the taxpayers' money?"

"Tommy-san, how can you call it a waste when you fine taxpayers are paying me to play with state-of-the-art computers and other electronic gadgets and teach others in search of the 'gift' how to use them? Think of the benefits to come for all humankind."

"Just what the world needs, another video game."

"Please, Tommy," Fumio replied, pretending to be offended. "I am way beyond video games. I have not played in at least two weeks. Virtual reality is happening now. It's like playing a video game from the inside. Remember the movie *Tron?* So, what can I do for you, Sherlock?"

"I found a box of computer chips out at the county dump. Any chance you could look at them and tell me where they came from or what they do?"

"At the dump? What the hell were you doing out there?"

"Don't ask. I've had enough of it for today. I'll tell you later."

A knock on the deck interrupted him. A woman's voice called out, "Hello. Anybody aboard?"

Tommy recognized the voice and yelled, "Yeah, come aboard Lucy." To Fumio he said, "Well, here comes just the person to take that stink away. What do you think? Can you look at these things for me?"

"No problem. Bring them by the school tomorrow at lunch time. You are buying."

Tommy hung up and looked at Lucy, standing easily by the companionway, wearing shorts and a halter top. "Jesus, Lucy, you shouldn't drop in on me looking like that. I could bust a zipper and hurt myself."

Lucy dazzled him with a thousand-amp smile and said, "Why Tommy, you sweet talker, you."

Tommy let his gaze take in the most perfect body he'd ever seen. A couple of inches less than his own six feet, Lucy was built like the proverbial brick shithouse: long, strong legs, wide hips, narrow waist and full breasts. "How could anybody talk anything but sweet to you?"

A flicker of something dark dimmed her smile for an instant before she said, "Tommy, if you're feeling sweet and horny, there's only two ways to fix that condition. Death or screwing."

"So shoot me."

"Your gun is in your car under the front seat." She shrugged. "So I can't shoot you..."

They laughed with the ease of friends and sometime lovers who did not need to pretend they had not just agreed to spend the night together.

"Some wine?" Tommy asked. She nodded assent and made a point of not moving out of the way so he had to slide against her to get to the galley. The smell and touch of her made him shiver and his eyes lose focus. He busied himself with the wine, though she remained prominent in his mind's eye—light brown hair pulled back into its usual ponytail, huge brown eyes, a sharp nose and a full mouth that crinkled at the corners when she smiled. She lived by herself on a thirty-two-foot sloop down the dock and worked around the bay varnishing some of the area's biggest and most expensive yachts. Tommy knew she had other money; every once in a while Lucy would drop a comment about her past life—the Life, as she referred to it—which Tommy took to mean she'd once been a high-priced call girl, or maybe even owned her own establishment, but he didn't feel he should ask her straight out about it. He hoped she'd one day tell him on her own.

"Was that Fumio?" she asked. "That funny Japanese guy from the university with computers on the brain? He said he wanted to hook me up to one of his machines and record me so he could play with me anytime." She laughed. "I've heard some lines before, but that's one of the best. Tell him I'm still considering it."

"I'll tell him tomorrow. I'm sure it'll do his chips good." He handed her a glass and they sat on the long settee, one at each end, facing each other. "So, what have you been doing? I haven't seen you for a while."

"The usual," she said, "I'm working on a big power boat over at Newport Tides Marina. Four million bucks if it's a dime. It's beautiful." She sipped the wine and shook her head bemusedly before continuing. "You know, it's crazy. The county is broke, not to mention the whole state in general, and this owner is spending thousands, like he does twice a year, to varnish a boat he never uses."

"The very rich live in a different reality than the rest of us. They always have more money than they know what to do with."

"Yes, I know that," Lucy said, more to herself than to Tommy. She shook off her momentary mood and said, "I talked to Wash this morning. He said Jessie, your ex-secretary came by yesterday and you didn't seem too happy about it, so I thought I'd be nosy and come by to cheer you up." She raised her eyebrows in question. A sly, crooked smile stole over her lips. "So tell me everything," Lucy insisted. "What did she want? What happened? I have to know what I'm cheering you up from, don't I?"

"Yes, I guess you do," he said and realized he did want to

tell her everything. Not only about Jessie and George's visit, but about hiring Jessie and everything afterwards.

Tommy cooked dinner in an absentminded way. Lucy just listened, prompting him with a question when he needed it. She already knew much of the story, but let him ramble on, sensing, in her empathic way, he wanted to talk about it.

Later, as they sat together in the cockpit drinking a second cup of coffee, he suddenly stopped talking.

"Ah, Lucy, I'm sorry, I didn't mean to babble on for so long about myself. Even though it's been eight months, contact with that past life upset me more than I thought. I never realized I'd come to dislike it so much." He paused to sip his coffee. "On the other hand, I have to admit I'm intrigued about what happened to Brian Childs. It'd be a challenge, which I haven't had for a while."

He laid his head back and stared at the few stars visible in the sky not washed out by a billion city lights.

"I don't think it's the detecting part I don't like," he said. "I think it's the business part, dealing with clients, paperwork, advertising. Having to do it. Having to take a case because the rent is due."

Lucy swung her legs over his lap. "And Jessie?"

"I'll have to think about that. I have a feeling something's going on she's not telling me." He ran a hand through his tangled, sun-bleached hair. "There's an attraction, I won't deny it, but I don't think anything will come of it."

He turned to her and, reaching up, rubbed the back of her neck. She snuggled her head against his hand, lips forming a dreamy smile. Her hand caressed his cheek as she purred, "You won't call me Jessie tonight, will you?"

TOMMY ROLLED OUT OF his bunk in *Nomorr*'s bow at ten o'clock. Lucy had risen hours earlier. He'd watched with half awake eyes while, naked, she'd made herself coffee and toast. His last vision before drifting back to sleep was of her perfect face lit by early morning sunlight that highlighted wisps of hair gone astray during the night.

The early morning marine layer had burnt off and it was a

clear day, indistinguishable from the last fifteen or twenty. Tommy headed south on Coast Highway. Top down, radio up, he cruised past expensive harbor-side restaurants, yacht brokers and condos, to MacArthur Boulevard. He turned inland toward the University of California at Irvine. Twenty minutes later he entered the computer science building. He walked down the hall to the last door on the right. He entered without knocking.

"Fumio! Time to do some work for a change. Put it back in your pants and let's get to it."

Fumio raised his head from his computer monitor. Sounds of gunfire and death came from the speakers. Voice still carrying traces of his Japanese boyhood, he said, "Damn! I almost beat my record." He tapped a final key and turned to his friend. "You're in a good mood today. You must have gotten rid of that stink you had yesterday."

"Smelling like a rose, my man. Smelling like a rose."

Tommy sat on the only other chair in the tiny, cluttered office. Setting the box with the computer chips in front of Fumio, Tommy said, "Lucy says she's still thinking about letting you record her."

Fumio leaned back in his chair; the smile formed by his small mouth showed perfect, white teeth. Five-foot-seven and chubby, his only exercise was punching a keyboard, which he did with amazing speed. Officially, he was an assistant professor but he rarely taught a class, being the computer science section's jack-of-all-trades. If help with hardware, software or special programming was needed, Fumio was the one to call. A mostly reformed hacker, computers were his life's blood, computer problems, his oxygen.

He put his hands behind his head, intertwining his fingers around a ponytail of glossy black hair he unconsciously bobbed up and down when he talked.

"Virtual reality and Lucy. Now that's a million-dollar idea if I ever heard one." The ponytail bobbed faster. "So what's up, Hercule? Are these the mysterious chips?"

He leaned forward and looked into the box, then dumped them on the desk and examined each one, nine in all.

"What, exactly are you...we looking for?"

Tommy gave him a brief rundown. At the mention of murder Fumio's eyes grew big, but he said nothing until Tommy finished.

"So what you want to know," Fumio said, "is, do these chips contain any clues to where your man came from."

"Right."

Fumio picked up one brown, inch-and-a-half long by a half-inch wide rectangle. It had fifteen silvery legs on each long side and a round window in the center showing the actual embedded chip.

"These are EPROM chips; they can be erased with ultra-violet light and reprogrammed. Handy for software development. They are used when you want to program the chips with your own program. To burn in your own program can be tricky. Failures occur or the chips burn out. I assume these are one or the other. Or, they may be obsolete." His chair squeaked as he leaned back. Bobbing his ponytail again, he continued, "That won't help you much because there might be fifty companies in this area that use them. What we have to find out is what the programs do."

"Can you do that?"

"Maybe. There's only one way to find out." Fumio scooped up the chips. "Follow me Charlie Chan."

Fumio was out the door before Tommy could stand up. At the third floor, they went through double glass doors carrying the ubiquitous legend, Authorized Personnel Only, in large red letters.

Inside, Tommy stopped and stared, feeling like he had walked into a mad scientist's laboratory. Electronic equipment filled the room. Stacked on shelves, workbenches and floor were terminals, monitors, oscilloscopes, and banks and boards of meters, dials and switches. Circuit boards, electronic machines' viscera, were exposed throughout the room, their ceramic components islands of color on the white countertops. Thick, black wires snaked along walls and dropped from holes in the ceiling. Tangles of tiny, brightly colored wires blossomed randomly from the ends of gray-sheathed bundles, thick as fingers. Only journeymen in the electronic arts could be comfortable in that room; the uninitiated were lost.

Fumio sat at a terminal, ignoring his friend. Tommy decided he didn't understand what went on in the room and wasn't going to try. He sat patiently, watching Fumio coax secrets out of the chips.

Half an hour later, Fumio pushed back from the terminal and said, "Lunch time."

He didn't say anything about what he'd found until they were seated at a table in the snack bar with their cellophane-wrapped sandwiches. Fumio waved away Tommy's questions with an airy wave of his hand. Tommy, familiar with Fumio's ways, refused to beg.

Finally Fumio said, "I was right. They are burned-out chips. Possibly test versions. One of them is partially readable, but is very complicated stuff. Some of the language is new to me, with parts that are unusually elegant. There's one subroutine that is very intriguing. It has a—"

"Fumio, wait. I hate to interrupt you on your favorite subject, but is there anything there I can use?"

Fumio took a bite of his sandwich and pondered the question. "I don't know whose chips they were and I don't know exactly what the program is for, except that it seems to be a program that controls a machine or a piece of equipment of some kind. A sophisticated machine, something optimized for speed with extensive I-O for sensor feedback, a spacecraft for example. Or maybe a robot."

"So where do I look?"

The computer man poked inside the box of components with a short finger, like a cat playing with a bug. "Assuming they came from the same place your man came from, I would look into either aerospace or robotics companies. Look for somebody who uses an embedded controller like the Motorola or the Intel type. That should narrow it down to about twenty or twenty-five companies. Whoever wrote that program is brilliant, so I would start at the top and work down. Does that help any?"

Tommy stared into the box. He cocked his head to one side and said, "Well, twenty-five is a lot better than two hundred. I don't know if there's any connection, but it's the only lead I have." He thought for a moment. "Do those electronics companies keep tabs on who's working where? Would one company know who the hotshots at another company were, even if they weren't direct competitors?"

"Well, yes and no. Everybody is always on the lookout for top talent and a certain amount of networking goes on. But, they also have their secrets and do not necessarily advertise whom they hire."

"Hmm. Maybe I'll go see Steve Langdon. Remember him? The car electronics guy we went to the races with."

"The one who married his son's girlfriend?"

"That's him. Between him and Suzanne they probably know everybody in the electronics industry around here." Steve and Suzanne were his best friends, though he hadn't seen them in months. Tommy took a picture from his pocket and handed it to Fumio. "Have you ever seen this guy?"

The snapshot, taken by Jessie, showed a boyish, handsome man in his early thirties, shoulder-length brown hair combed straight back from a low forehead with a pronounced widow's peak. A square face with perfectly tanned skin showed a flawless smile.

"No. I've never seen him. He looks too good to be true. Maybe that is why he is dead?"

"Maybe," Tommy said, taking the picture back. "Maybe."

FOUR

AT TWO O'CLOCK, Tommy stopped at a 7-11 for a drink and a Reese's Peanut Butter Cup to get the after taste of the plastic-wrapped tuna sandwich out of his mouth. He called the Langdon's house from a pay phone. Ramona, the housekeeper, told him Mrs. Langdon would be back at three and Mr. Langdon at four.

The beach in Corona Del Mar is on the east side of the entrance to Newport Bay. Tommy walked out onto the stone jetty and found a vantage point on the rocks to watch the boats tacking toward open water or running downwind back into the bay. He gazed longingly at the open water. He decided that, after learning what he could about Brian, hurricane season or not, he'd start down the Baja coast. The sooner the better.

Thoughts far away, Tommy trudged through the sand toward his car. He passed a woman, naked but for a tiny patch of fluorescent orange over her smooth rear. With her long blond hair swept to one side so as not to cover her bare, bronzed back, she reminded him of Suzanne Langdon. Suzanne's body was all soft curves, but her face consisted of hard angles and flat planes. She had the thin lips, high cheek bones and blue eyes of a classic beauty, but the way they were put together the best she could hope for was plain. Intelligent, though uneducated, Suzanne had made the transition from bimbo to wife of a rich man, unscarred. Tommy valued her friendship highly.

Steve Langdon had hired Tommy to find his twenty-one-year-old son Harry, who had disappeared with his father's Ferrari Testarossa and a major credit card. It didn't take long to track Harry to Las Vegas where he was having a big time living large and playing the high roller for the benefit of twenty-two-year-old Suzanne. When Steve Langdon arrived he left Harry with enough money for a bus ticket and a hamburger, then drove home with Suzanne. Three months later they were married.

At four o'clock, Tommy drove through stone gate posts and parked at the far end of a four-car garage connected to a white Spanish adobe-style house. The garage held a speed-freak's dream combo: Steve's Ferrari F-50, a Mercedes S600, and a Land Rover. Desert landscaping—aloes, ice plants, cactus and a tall Joshua Tree—bordered the short concrete driveway. The premium for land was too high on the hillside overlooking the harbor and the ocean to waste it on large front yards. Tommy knew the pool area in back more than made up for any deficiencies of the front.

The bleached-wood front door opened before he could ring the doorbell. Ramona, the live-in housekeeper, stood in the shadow of the doorway, a broad smile on her handsome face. A thin Mexican woman who at first sight looked frail, she was in excellent health, as the immaculate four bedroom house and her numerous boyfriends could testify.

"Buenos tardes, Tomas. Como esta?" Ramona was the only person who did not call Tommy, Tommy.

"Muy bien, Ramona. Y usted?"

"I am well, Tomas. It has been a long time since you visited us. You will stay for dinner? I am preparing my tacos for you tonight."

Tommy knew an order when he heard one and agreed to stay. Ramona's tacos were the best.

He followed her through the cool, open, southwestern-style interior. The off-white walls and flowing pastel colors were easy on the eyes and the furniture was simple and comfortable. He had spent many hot summer afternoons dozing on the big couch in the den.

The Langdons sat together in the shade of an oak tree by the pool. Ramona announced Tommy and retreated to her kitchen. Suzanne greeted him with a kiss and a hug.

As usual, Steve Langdon looked as if he had just stepped out of the pages of *GQ*. Italian leather shoes, gray, perfectly creased pants and custom-made striped blue shirt with a silk tie knotted, just so. A Movado watch peeked out from under a gold cufflinked shirt sleeve; blond hair swept back from his forehead and hung neatly trimmed a half inch over his collar.

Steve would be fifty soon. Ten years ago he had been in debt with a start-up company and happily married. His wife, Miranda, died suddenly, only weeks before his first success that led to Autotronics becoming a multi-million dollar company. Sometimes, after a few drinks, he raged at fate for taking her from him before the success became a reality. She had always been poor and for her to die so close to the life they had both worked so hard for devastated him. Steve didn't talk about his own childhood. His parents hadn't been well off and were now dead. Tommy assumed they were not missed.

While Steve and Tommy greeted each other, Suzanne poured him a glass of chablis on ice. The three of them stretched out on padded pool chairs and talked about the things that friends talk about after a long separation.

As they talked, Tommy became aware of the precise way Steve set down his drink, Cutty Sark on the rocks. Steve joked in what seemed to be his usual, casual way, but when he set his glass down it was as if the glass would explode if not placed exactly right. Suzanne watched, too, gripping her own glass with both hands. They were both on edge and, to a stranger, hiding it well.

Tommy was just getting around to asking about Brian Childs when Ramona announced dinner. He handed the picture to Suzanne. Steve, distracted by Ramona, missed Suzanne's reaction. Tommy didn't. Her eyes went wide and she sucked in a short breath. Hand halfway to her mouth, she quickly returned it to her lap. It only took a fraction of a second, but it surprised Tommy. Before he could say anything, Suzanne recovered herself and handed the picture to her husband. Almost whispering, she said, "Haven't we seen him around? A friend of Sylvia Von Joss', I think."

Steve took the picture and scrutinized it intently. If Tommy hadn't known better he would have thought his friend was trying very hard not to show his astonishment, too.

After long seconds Steve said casually, "Yes, with his looks I don't doubt he was a friend of Sylvia's. But I think he works for Niles. His name isn't Childs, though. Childers? Childress? Something like that.''

"Are you sure?" Tommy asked.

Steve looked at the photograph again, shrugged and said, "Fairly sure. You'll have to check with Niles."

"Who's Niles?"

"Niles Ernst Von Joss. Of the Munich Von Josses, supposedly," Suzanne said with close to her usual humor, although her face seemed paler than a few minutes before. "About whom, horror of horrors, nobody knows anything. It's surprising they're even allowed to live here. After all, you can't expect to be friends with somebody without knowing who his great-grandfather was screwing, now can you?"

"Suzanne," Steve said, his voice a mixture of amusement and parental admonishment.

"Sorry," she said, not sounding one bit apologetic. "You know how I feel about all that old family crap."

"Yes, I certainly do," Steve replied, rolling his eyes.

"Anyway," Suzanne continued, "Niles owns Electrobotics Corporation. They do research, make electronic gadgets and robots and things."

Tommy thought she looked like she was going cry. Steve didn't seem to notice.

"Now that's interesting," Tommy said into the silence. "Brian—whatever his name is—was supposed to be a computer scientist. He disappears and, if you're right, turns up at Electrobotics, which I believe has a reputation for hiring brains." He looked at Suzanne. "How well did Brian, assuming we're talking about the man in this picture, know Sylvia?"

She hesitated, getting back in gear, it seemed to Tommy. Where had her thoughts been?

"Well, I don't know for sure, but the hair salon gossips had them as quite an item."

"An 'affair' type item?"

"Oh, yes."

"Were the rumors true?" he asked.

"I don't know. She never mentioned it to me, but—"

"It wouldn't surprise you if they were true."

"No," she said in a small voice.

Ramona called them again. Obediently the three headed for the informal dining room off the patio. After they settled down at the round glass table, Tommy asked, "Did Niles know about Brian and his wife?"

Steve answered. "Niles is something of a workaholic and has no interest in gossip."

Tommy looked at Suzanne, who just nodded in agreement. He turned back to Steve. "You don't sound as if you approve of workaholics. I remember when you used to put in eighty- or ninety-hour weeks."

"Sure, when it's necessary," Steve said, turning his eyes to his wife, who returned his gaze, cold eye to cold eye. She did not return his smile. "But there are other things to enjoy besides work. Don't you agree, Suzanne?"

An I-know-something-you-don't smile crept across her thin lips. "Yes I do, Steve."

Tommy, pretending not to notice his friends' odd behavior, asked, "Would it be possible to talk with Sylvia? And Niles?"

"Well, you're in luck," Steve answered. "We just happen to be going to a party at their house tomorrow afternoon. Their daughter and her husband just moved back to Newport, from Boston, I think. Why don't you come? That would be all right, wouldn't it, Suzanne?"

"Oh. Yes. Fine," she said, not sounding at all certain it would be.

A RED-VESTED KID took Tommy's car in exchange for a yellow ticket. He wondered where the kid was going to park it. Parking on Linda Isle was scarce at best; most people who could afford the million-dollar-plus homes, jammed together like row houses, preferred to park in their three- or four-car garages. Street parking was discouraged.

The Von Joss house stood on the bay side of the island, separated from the houses on either side by almost twenty feet. A brick wall stood in the middle of these gaps, taking up a precious foot of space. Tommy went down a brick walk on the right-hand side of the house.

Tommy had dressed up for the occasion. He wore his best pair of Topsiders, a clean pair of L.L. Bean khaki pants, a blue, button-down shirt and a light-weight tan jacket. His preference was Hawaiian shirts, shorts and sandals, but he didn't think he could get away with that kind of attire on his first visit.

Tommy surveyed the gathering from the corner of the house. The guests were scattered over the flagstone terrace and the lawn that sloped a hundred feet to the seawall. About fifty people were present. Young and old, all dressed in expensive, brightly colored, casual clothes. A few of the men wore ties, and red, green or yellow socks were popular. The women favored elegant pantsuits, usually of some slinky, shimmery fabric, or cocktail dresses with plunging fronts and/or backs for the women who could wear them and, unfortunately, some who couldn't, to more conservative, but fashionable dresses for those with taste.

Tommy wandered over to the bar set out on long tables covered with white tablecloths. Spotting Suzanne by the seawall with a wizened old man, he went to join them.

"Tommy, I was wondering where you were. You look awfully spiffy. I haven't seen you this dressed up since Steve's and my wedding." She kissed him on the cheek, laughing.

"Well, once every four years I guess I can handle it."

Suzanne seemed in much better spirits today, he noticed. Maybe the martinis had something to do with it?

"Tommy, this is Jonathan Avery. A friend and neighbor of ours. He's an old sea dog just like you want to be."

The old man's face was burnt a deep mahogany from years in the sun. Wrinkles like worn crevasses radiated from twinkling blue eyes that never wavered. His firm handshake caught Tommy by surprise.

"You're a sailor are you, young man?" Avery asked, his voice rough, but strong, no doubt from yelling orders in the middle of typhoons.

"Yes sir. I live on a sailboat and plan to sail to the South Pacific this fall."

Tommy spent the next half hour enjoying Avery's sea stories until a hand on his shoulder brought him back to shore. It was Steve Langdon, one of the tie wearers.

"Sorry to interrupt you two, but Sylvia happened to ask me who that incredibly handsome young man with Jonathan was, so, I felt it my duty to make introductions."

Regretfully, Tommy took leave of the old sailor. After introductions, Tommy escorted Sylvia Von Joss to a corner of the lawn by the sea wall, away from other guests.

"Steve said you wanted to talk to me, Mr. Case," Sylvia stated.

"Yes, I do," he said. "I'm looking for a man named Brian Childs." He handed the picture to her. "Have you seen this man before?" He watched her study the picture.

According to Suzanne, Sylvia Von Joss was fifty-nine years old. She looked forty-five. She wore her dark shoulder-length hair pulled back behind ears with two pierced earrings each, a small plain diamond and dangly silver things that looked like fishing lures. Her full figure was shown off nicely by a slinky silver dress that matched the larger earrings. Half her right little finger was missing.

She froze still as stone before saying, "I know this man, but not by the name of Brian Childs. Brian Childress is his name. He works for my husband."

Tommy wanted to ask if she had had an affair with Brian, but instead he asked, "Do you happen to have his address or telephone number?"

She handed back the photograph, keeping sharp gray eyes on it until it disappeared into his jacket pocket. Her stare shifted to Tommy. "No, Mr. Case, I don't have any of that information. You'll have to go to the lab on Monday and talk with my husband. Why are you looking for him?"

Tommy ignored the frost in her voice and said, "I'd rather not say until I've talked with your husband. Is he here? Maybe I can talk to him now and not have to disturb him at his office?"

"He isn't here. He had to go to St. Louis and won't be back 'til late tomorrow night. I'll tell him to expect you."

"Thank you. I'd appreciate that." Tommy took a sip of wine and looked out over the water. In a casual tone he asked, "Do you know Brian well? I was wondering about the last name,

Childs and Childress are pretty close. Did he ever mention anything about changing his name?"

Sylvia sipped her drink, looking out over the water, also. A smile formed on her lips. "No, I don't know him well. I met him at the yacht club. New Year's Eve, I believe. He's a charming, handsome, intelligent young man. He knew quite a lot about computers, so I introduced him to my husband and Niles gave him a job. I assume Niles checked him out. As far as I know his name is Brian Childress and always has been. When you see him you can ask him. Is that what you wanted to know, Mr. Case?"

Tommy hoped he looked as good when he approached sixty; she must have been a real beauty when she was younger. Her smile was a killer, but cold. The smile of a calculating woman who kept her guard up and got what she wanted and let nothing show she did not want to show—except when she saw Brian's photograph.

"Yes, it is. I appreciate your time, Mrs. Von Joss. I'll check at the lab on Monday. Thank you for the drink. I'd like to say goodbye to Mr. Avery and I'll be on my way."

"Nonsense, Mr. Case," Sylvia said, back to the gracious hostess. "A friend of Steve and Suzanne's is always welcome. Please stay and enjoy yourself." She turned and went into the house, back held rigid, looking neither left nor right.

He exchanged his glass for a full one from a silver tray offered by a white-coated waiter. He watched the party from the seawall and saw Steve Langdon standing with a group of men. One man was obviously telling a joke, but Steve's focus seemed to be on Suzanne, standing with her back to him, across the yard. His face had the faint twisted expression it got when he committed occasional petty cruelties against insolent waiters or clerks.

Tommy turned away and pretended to study the big sportfisher tied to the dock in front of him.

"She's beautiful, isn't she?"

Tommy barely looked at the woman who appeared beside him. "Yes, it is. Not much you couldn't catch from that."

"I meant the sailboat on the other side."

He studied the sailboat half hidden behind the bulk of the sportfisher. It was long and low and had to be fast. "Sorry, I didn't notice her. Well, I did, but it takes a while to get past that," he said, pointing at the fishing boat with his wine glass. "She looks like a custom design. Who built her?"

"It's a Barefoot Fifty-One built up in Costa Mesa. It belongs to my husband and me. Well, mostly me," she laughed. "He gets seasick. Would you like to see her?"

Without waiting for an answer she walked to the dock ramp. Tommy grabbed another full glass and followed.

Now who was this? He hadn't gotten a good look at her, but he approved of what he did see. Nape of the neck-length shiny brown hair, with long bangs that hung down to irreverent brown eyes. A tight, white silk jumpsuit that jumped in the right places as she descended the ramp. At the bottom, she turned left and he couldn't help but notice the jumpsuit's zipper down almost to her navel, and the hint of a breast visible through the gap.

She kicked off her shoes and stepped aboard. Tommy followed. In the cockpit, she turned to him and said, "I'm Anne Sexton. This is my party. Suzanne told me you're trying to find Brian Childress and that you're a sailor. I thought you were admiring my boat, so naturally I had to come and accept compliments."

As she talked, Tommy compared her to Lucy. Lucy represented girl-next-door wholesome sexiness while Anne Sexton with her lanky frame—Tommy imagined he could see every one of her ribs—seemed to embody the idea of sex for sex's sake. After two minutes Tommy was sure she would deliver, husband or no husband, on any promise her body made.

"Your boat certainly deserves compliments, Mrs. Sexton. Did...do you know Brian Childress?"

"Call me Anne."

She smiled a little half smile that sent a thrill right to his crotch and Tommy wondered what kind of aphrodisiac was in the excellent wine.

"I'm Tommy."

"So, business before pleasure? You sound like my husband," she said with a sigh. "I never actually met Brian. He was good-looking and sexy, had brains but no common sense. What more could you ask for? Also a phoney, tons of charm, but with no natural social grace. He could bewitch the older ladies, like my mother, but not the younger women, not that some of them didn't sample what he had to offer.''

"Do you think your mother might have had an affair with him?" Tommy asked carefully.

Anne laughed. "Probably. It wouldn't be the first time, either. My mother can still appreciate what a young man has to offer. Brian was rather free with his cock and didn't discriminate because of age, especially if it was somebody who could do something good for him.''

"Like a job at a big electronics company?"

"Exactly. Daddy probably never checked him out. If Brian knew his stuff Daddy wouldn't care where he learned it or where he came from.''

"I'm going to his office on Monday, I'll ask him. Do you think he knew about Brian and your mother?"

She paused to think before answering. She sat on the bridge deck, feet resting on the port side cockpit seat. Tommy sat on the starboard seat trying, with little luck, not to get too fascinated with the simple but exciting curve of her left breast that kept peeking at him from behind the zipper.

"I don't know. I wouldn't be surprised. People think of him as a workaholic who doesn't notice anything not made of wires and silicon, but he's sharp and doesn't miss much." She tossed off the rest of her drink. "I love my dad, he's always there when I need him, but he can be very calculating. He didn't get where he is by not knowing who was doing what to whom. People underestimate him and it costs them. A word to the wise, Tommy.''

She took his glass and led him below. "So what do you think of my beautiful boat?"

AN HOUR LATER Tommy retrieved his car from valet limbo and drove unsteadily to the marina. He had already forgotten half of what they'd talked about, but did remember a promise to go sailing.

At the marina, Tommy ran into Wash, who had little trouble persuading him to have a few drinks at the Blind Grape Saloon on the beach by the Newport Pier. They had plenty of company, women attracted by Tommy's beach boy good looks, and staying because of Wash's ribald humor and deep pockets.

Tommy kept comparing the women to Anne Sexton. The wine he'd been drinking all afternoon kept her fixed in his mind. About midnight, convinced there was something in the wine making him think of her, he switched to scotch. That did the trick, but he also forgot his name and his manners.

At two-thirty that morning Wash guided him down the dock. Laughing and yelling, "Honey, I'm home," to his empty boat, Tommy stumbled down the companionway ladder and flopped onto the settee. Immediately the inside of the boat started to spin. "Wash," Tommy cried, "we're in a fuggin whirlpool, man. All is lost." He started a laugh that ended up a moan.

Like all people who live on boats, Tommy had grown accustomed to the normal motions a boat makes and unconsciously recognized and ignored them. But, let someone unexpected step aboard, and even deep in an alcoholic stupor, mental alarms go off.

Tommy's eyes and mind snapped open, the rest of his body paralyzed except for his churning stomach. A shadowy figure dropped silently through the companionway. Tommy, not yet sure where he was, opened his mouth, but no words came out. The intruder looked around, then stepped into the galley and drew a knife out of a wooden block fixed to the counter. Adrenaline began to break through the fog surrounding Tommy's brain. Knife in a raised fist, the figure crept into the main salon. Shock broke Tommy's paralysis when the approaching figure moved into the light from a porthole and he saw a girl's pale, frightened face. The girl sucked in a sharp breath when she spied Tommy watching her, but didn't hesitate to raise the knife and plunge it toward his chest.

FIVE

INSTINCTIVELY, Tommy threw up his right arm for protection. A blanket hampered his movements. The knife ripped through the blanket and he felt the sting as it sliced into the flesh under his forearm. The girl raised the knife for another try. Tommy kicked and landed a solid blow against her ribs. She stumbled hard against the table. The knife clattered to the floorboards. With a breathless cry that could have been a sob, she crouched, grabbed the weapon, and swept it in an underhanded arc towards Tommy's neck. Now sitting up, he lashed out with his fist and connected with her cheek at the same time the blade grazed his shoulder. The girl fell to the floor. Their eyes met. Only the whites were visible in the semi-darkness but Tommy recognized the fear there. Before he could speak, she scrambled to her feet and vanished out the companionway as silently as she had come.

Danger gone, the alcohol took over and after five minutes of vomiting and five more of dry heaves he dropped onto the settee and just managed to pull the blanket over himself before unconsciousness took him.

BY THE MIDDLE OF Sunday afternoon he had almost convinced himself the attack had only been a nightmare. He remembered nothing clearly after downing his second scotch and water the night before, but the cuts on his arm and shoulder, though minor, were real enough and a knife was missing. Cartwell's reaction, however, was not unexpected.

"Case, lay off the booze. You don't really expect me to believe a teenage girl snuck into your boat and tried to kill you with your own knife, do you?"

Tommy held his throbbing head. "Yes. It happened."

"Bullshit. Okay, assuming it did happen, why? I thought you had enough sense to stay away from jailbait."

"Maybe I'm getting close to finding out who Brian Childs was."

"And your mystery girl killed him?"

"I don't know."

"Well, when you do, tell me, okay? Why don't you take a bottle of aspirin, go back to bed and don't bother me with your whiskey fantasies?"

Tommy managed a shower and a meal and a call to Jessie with no answer. In bed at nine o'clock Sunday night, he swore never to drink again and was asleep by nine-ten.

WITH THE MUSTANG'S top down, Spyro Gyra's first album on the tape deck and light traffic, Tommy felt good. Sunday's misery was over, today he would find out about Brian Childs/Childress, tell the cops, tell Jessie and begin final preparations to sail off for paradise.

He cruised up Newport Boulevard, through Costa Mesa. A brown layer of smog obscured the concrete landscape for any distance. Electrobotics Corporation in Irvine consisted of two three-story silver-green glass buildings connected by two covered walkways at the second floor. He parked in a large parking lot shared with the company next door and followed two people wearing white lab coats into the right-hand building. The guard at the desk inside pointed to the elevator and said, "Second floor," when he asked for Mr. Von Joss.

Tommy exited into the reception area and almost tripped on the plush gray carpet. Behind a modern wood desk an efficient-looking young receptionist wearing a white blouse with ruffles down the front ignored him, perhaps because she was not used to people in green Hawaiian shirts asking for the president of the company. She finally condescended to point to her left and returned to her paperwork.

A short hall decorated with blowups of ads for various Electrobotics products led to another equally efficient-looking woman, older, with curly salt and pepper hair. A nameplate announced her name as Sarah Formly. Before she could speak, Tommy said that Mr. Von Joss was expecting him, but he did not have an appointment. She seemed miffed he had gotten in the first word, but announced him anyway.

Niles Von Joss' office was a working office with two floor-to-ceiling glass walls, which on a rare smogless day would have a view all the way to Mount Baldy to the north. Filing cabinets and a drafting board lined one of the solid walls. A large U-shaped desk with a computer screen on each wing took up most of the other. Technical drawings and photographs of computers and robots covered the walls. Several precisely detailed boat models were enclosed in glass cases. In the glass corner two leather-covered wingback chairs faced each other. Between them sat a beautifully carved, richly finished, cherry coffee table, the whole ensemble looking as if it should be in an English duke's private library.

Niles Von Joss rose up from behind his desk. He was the same height as Tommy, but more powerfully built, and hard blue eyes looked out from under bushy white eyebrows. His manicured hand engulfed Tommy's as they introduced themselves. Tommy sensed the controlled power of the man and reminded himself to be careful. The plastic pocket protector with colored pens caught his eye. He wondered if anybody had ever called Niles Von Joss a nerd and lived to tell about it.

"So, Mr. Case, my wife tells me you are interested in finding Brian Childress," Niles said, as they both sat. Tommy detected a slight trace of a German accent in the man's precise speech. "May I ask why you are inquiring about him?"

So much for the amenities. Tommy pulled out the picture of Brian and placed it on the desk. "Is this the Brian Childress that works for you?" Tommy asked.

Von Joss didn't pick it up. "Yes. It is."

"Have you seen him in the last week or so?"

Von Joss studied Tommy for a full minute before answering. "The last time I saw him was a week ago Friday. Here, in this room, at three o'clock in the afternoon. He was leaving that night for a week-long conference at the Santa Fe Institute in New Mexico. He should be here today, but so far he is not. I have not heard from him in that time, and I should have. Perhaps you can tell me why?"

Uncomfortable under the old man's steady glare, Tommy said, "Mr. Von Joss, I'm sorry to tell you this, but he's in the morgue in Santa Ana where he's been since last Monday when his body was discovered in the county landfill. The coroner says he was killed Friday night or Saturday morning. He didn't make it to the conference."

The older man didn't move. Sadness crept over his broad face. "What happened to him? How did he die?"

"He was murdered. His throat crushed."

"I see. I was troubled not to hear from him. The conference was important to him...and the company." He looked out at the smog. "If he was found Monday why did it take a week to contact us? And why you, not the police?"

Tommy gave him the whole run down as he knew it. He left out Jessie's name. "He was probably dumped in a dumpster, which was picked up Saturday morning. Is there any way to tell if he left here Friday?"

Von Joss thought for a moment then replied, "If he was here after five o'clock he had to sign out with the guard. Before that, he would not have to sign out, but he would have to go out the front door past the security guard. The only other exit is the delivery door at the opposite end of the building, which is alarmed and must be opened from the guard station."

Von Joss leaned back in his chair and gazed at the ceiling. Tommy sat back and watched him.

"The connecting doors to the other building are locked at five o'clock and need a key and the correct code to be opened. In the restricted area where Childress worked, an electronically imprinted ID badge and a retinal scan are needed for entry and exit. A record is kept in the security computer."

He turned toward the keyboard on his left and started tapping keys. In a few minutes, he said, "He entered the restricted area at eight-ten a.m. and last left at four forty-six p.m. on Friday the seventeenth. He did not return."

Tommy frowned. He had been sure Childress was killed here. Of course he had no proof, or reason to think so, but it felt right.

"Was he working on anything secret? For the government maybe? Could he have been stealing information that somebody might have killed for? How about other employees? I hear that he was a bit of a ladies man."

Tommy tried to look innocent while asking the questions. Would Von Joss rise to the ladies man remark? A slight widening of the eyes at the mention of ladies man. Surprise or knowledge? Eyes as blue and cold as a winter mountain sky held Tommy motionless. *This man is intelligent and dangerous if he chooses to be my enemy,* he told himself. Anne Sexton thought him a loving father, but warned him to be careful. He believed it.

Von Joss came to a decision. He sighed and said, "I will tell you about Brian Childress. First, his real name is Brian Chambers. He was a natural at mathematics and computer programming. He attended MIT and stayed at the top of his class until the end of his junior year. He became involved with a woman student who was also a prostitute at a local, well-known brothel. His grades suffered badly as a result." The older man's eyes turned to the glass wall, though he did not seem to be enjoying the view. "So when this woman suggested that he steal test questions, which were kept in a computer file, he agreed. He was caught, of course, and expelled. The woman disappeared."

"Do you know who she was?" Tommy asked.

"No. I saw no reason to pursue that line of inquiry."

Tommy nodded in agreement. Niles Von Joss continued.

"No big school would take him, and his mother would have nothing more to do with him. She apparently took his father for all his money and ran out on him years before. Brian finally graduated from a small college in Pennsylvania. Things did not go well for him. A brilliant career over before it started." Von Joss' expression softened. "Are you married?"

"No."

"Divorced?"

"Yes."

"Money? Another man? Or a woman?"

"Another man with more money."

"Ah yes. Money. Two years ago Brian left Columbus, Ohio, having just been divorced by a greedy wife who finally realized that his brilliance did not include ambition. A year and a half ago he arrived in Newport Beach and found a job selling computers."

Von Joss frowned at his desk top. "Somehow he attended some private functions and met my wife, who introduced him to me. I talked to him, liked his ideas and had him checked out. He confirmed what I have just told you. All he wanted to do was put his intelligence to work, so I hired him and have no reason to regret it."

"Do you think he was happy working here? Any problems with other employees?"

"Brian Chambers was finally doing what he was born to do, Mr Case. In that he was happy. In his private life, I do not know. As for his relationship with other employees, you will have to ask them."

"You said the conference was important."

"He believed he was close to a major breakthrough. At the conference he was to meet with Doctor Alberto Cammillo of MIT. If he confirmed Brian's work, the implications would have worldwide significance."

"I assume that means a lot of money."

"Billions, Mr. Case. Billions."

"What was this breakthrough?"

Von Joss hesitated. His eyes bored into Tommy's as if he could see inside his brain and determine his trustworthiness and need to know. Tommy wanted out from under those hard eyes, but knew that if he turned away he would lose face with the older man and for no reason he could name it seemed important for that not to happen.

"A billion dollars," Tommy said, "is a hell of a motive for murder. The police will need to know who might gain from Brian's death."

Von Joss nodded slowly, then finally turned his eyes away. A feeling almost like glee filled Tommy's chest at his release from that penetrating stare. He hadn't won, but he hadn't backed down either and after Cartwell's remark about quitters that was unfamiliarly important to him.

"What do you know about artificial intelligence?" Von Joss asked.

"Well, a computer that could learn from experience, that could make real-world decisions from sketchy information. Oh yeah, the Turing Test. If it can pass for human in an on-screen conversation. Something like that."

"Close enough. Heard of a DNA computer?"

"Seen a couple articles. Pretty new stuff. A mega-supercomputer in a test tube. Very fast, lots of memory, but hard to get the answer out of the soup."

"Very good, Mr. Case. In nineteen ninety-three or -four, a scientist in California named Adleman came up with the idea. It's not right for all types of computations and, you are right, getting the information out quickly has been a problem."

"Has been?"

The excitement of discovery lit up Von Joss's face. He rocked back in his leather desk chair, then rocked forward, resting his arms on the desk. The intensity of his voice matched the intensity of his expression. He held pink hands with long thick fingers up as if holding what he was saying between them.

"I believe, Mr. Case, that Brian has solved the problem of information extraction from the DNA and furthermore, has discovered how to connect the DNA with a silicon-based supercomputer to achieve true artificial intelligence."

He slumped back in his chair as if just speaking of the discovery was a totally draining experience. His head shook with the wonder of it all. "The implications are staggering. Space exploration, ocean floor exploration, medical diagnostics, criminal investigation, not to mention robotics in its role in all of the above."

"Not to mention world domination by a computer gone mad," Tommy added with a wry smile to show Von Joss he was only half joking.

"You've been reading too many old science fiction novels, Mr. Case."

"The Internet gives world wide access."

"True," Von Joss admitted. "Your concern is well-founded. Safeguards will have to be implemented, obviously. I don't think insane computers will be the most dangerous problem. An unscrupulous individual using this discovery for personal gain, however, could be a problem.''

"Who else knows about this discovery? What about this Dr. Cammillo?''

Von Joss pressed his palms together under his square chin. His lips formed a tight frown as he thought. "Dr. Cammillo knows of the general theory. Not specifics. Several others here know the full extent of the research.''

"Have you actually built this super-biocomputer?''

The older man seemed preoccupied and took a half minute before he responded offhandedly, "Preliminary experiments only. Brian had no doubts it would work though, and wanted to apply his theory in full application.''

They were silent for a time while Tommy digested the news. He could understand how a man like Brian Chambers—finally a real name—would be bitter about what happened to him. One relatively minor mistake should not ruin a life forever. Unfortunately the academic world is very unforgiving of activities such as cheating. It must have been a dream come true to find himself in a place where his intelligence was appreciated.

But where did Jessie fit in? Why her number in his pocket? Tommy definitely wanted to talk with her again.

"Mr. Case.'' Tommy looked up from his reflections. "I am a busy man, and will be more so now that Brian is dead. He was very important to this company. With him gone some decisions will have to be made. If there is nothing further?''

Tommy stood up. "I'd like to get Brian's address, see where he worked and talk to the people he worked with.''

"All right. Keep it brief.'' Von Joss strode to the door and yanked it open. Back to business. "Sarah, print out for Mr. Case, Brian Chambers', that is, Childress', personnel file, use special code "Boston" when it asks. Get Dr. Jackson and Dr. Madding up here. Get Mr. Case a visitor's pass to the restricted area.'' He turned to Tommy, stuck out his hand. "Mr. Case. I hear you are a sailor. Have anything against powerboats?''

Caught off guard, Tommy took the proffered hand and said, "Ah, yes, I am a sailor and no, I have nothing against powerboats as long as they watch their wake.''

"Good. Do you fish? We will have to go sometime. The marlin are running."

Without waiting for a reply Niles Von Joss turned, re-entered his office and shut the door.

SIX

TOMMY STOOD BY Sarah Formly's desk and watched a puzzled frown appear on her pale purple lips as she read what came up on her screen. She cast a quizzical look in his direction when she laid the printout on the edge of her desk. The intercom interrupted her before she could ask any questions, allowing Tommy to retreat to a U-shaped chair, covered with smooth, pastel pink fabric.

He looked at the address—Newport Beach. He knew the area, houses built tall and thin within five feet of each other between Pacific Coast Highway and the beach at the north end of town. The first section of the file contained the Childress section, for public viewing. The second, longer part, consisted of reports from the investigators Von Joss hired. In more detail it said essentially what Von Joss had told him.

A plain woman wearing a white lab coat approached Sarah, who told her to go right into Von Joss' office. Next, a thin man carrying a clipboard and also wearing a white lab coat approached, glared at Tommy and, without knocking, entered the office.

"Who was that?" Tommy asked.

"That's Dr. Nicholas Madding," Sarah said, with reverence. "He's our head of research. A genius in the field of robotics and computers." It was obvious that Sarah Formly believed Dr. Madding was the best thing since sliced silicon. In the few seconds he saw him, Tommy got the feeling Dr. Madding thought so, too.

"What's going on?" she asked. She looked pointedly at the paper Tommy held. "Is it about Mr. Childress?"

"Yes, I'm afraid it is," he answered slowly, unsure if he should reveal the news of Brian Childress' death. However, you could tell a lot by people's reactions to news, good or bad, and he was still investigating. "He was found dead a week ago."

She drew in a sharp breath and both hands flew to her face. "Do you know any reason why somebody might want to kill him?"

She started to say something, hesitated, then slowly shook her head. "No. No. He was a nice, polite young man. Everybody liked him…as far as I know." Tommy watched her head swivel on her thick neck to stare at Von Joss' office door. Their eyes met and locked for an instant as Sarah turned back to stare blankly at her monitor screen.

Fifteen minutes later the two scientists exited the office, looking grim. Dr. Madding put a solicitous arm around the woman's shoulders. Tommy thought she flinched just a bit when the man's long, bony fingers grasped her shoulder.

Tommy rose and went to meet them. "Dr. Madding, Dr. Jackson…?" he said to the woman, who nodded yes. "I'm Tommy Case. I'm sorry about Brian."

Dr. Madding regarded Tommy with squinted eyes as if looking at dog shit found on the new living room carpet, but he said nothing.

Dr. Jackson responded, "Thank you, Mr. Case. Brian was a good man. I hope you can find whoever did such a terrible thing." To Dr. Madding she said, "Thank you, Nicholas. I'm okay."

Madding nodded to her and, still without a word, walked away.

"Friendly guy," Tommy commented.

"This came as a shock to us, Mr Case. Brian was an important part of our team. I'll miss him," she said, emphasizing the I. She wiped her nose with a tissue and swept her short blond hair behind her ear. Equaling Tommy's six-foot height, she stood with her head slightly hunched down between her shoulders, as if trying to make herself shorter. She took a deep breath, extended her hand and said with a shaky smile, "What would you like to see?"

Dr. Jackson inserted her ID card into a slot at the door leading into the restricted area, then looked into a rubber-cupped eyepiece. A few seconds later the door buzzed open. She motioned for Tommy to insert his card and look into the eyepiece.

"All cards must be scanned before entering or an alarm sounds," she told him. "That eye-piece is a retinal scanner, the retina being as unique as fingerprints. Both the card and the pattern must agree to the person's identity for the door to open. A record of each entry and exit is kept so they know who went where and when. This area is quite secure.''

She led him down a wide, thinly carpeted hallway with smooth white walls. The hall had a hush broken only by the clack of computer keyboards and a voice that said, "Oh my God, not Brian." Bad news travelling fast. Doors on each side led into offices filled with desks, drafting tables, file cabinets and computers, five offices on each side. They entered the last door on the right.

Larger than Fumio's hole in the wall, Brian's office was also orders of magnitude neater.

"This is his office, Mr. Case. What exactly are you looking for?''

She leaned a shoulder against a gray metal filing cabinet, her arms crossed over her chest. Despite the lab coat over the black T-shirt and jeans she wore, Tommy couldn't help but notice that Dr. Jackson would look very good in a bikini. Immediately, he turned his concentration to the rest of the room. Now was not the time for that.

He inspected the books in the case next to the file cabinet—thick professional tomes with words like neural net, algorithm, cybernetics and L-Systems in their titles. One shelf had books on biology: biotechnology, biochemistry, cell structure, protein structure, DNA. He knew they were all filled with totally incomprehensible formulas and jargon.

Tommy sat in the leather desk chair, hands flat on the desk top. On the right were stacked long, green-and-white striped printouts. On the left, a low table held a keyboard, monitor and printer. In the exact center sat a mug from Orange Coast College filled with pens and pencils. A new yellow legal pad lay precisely in line with the mug.

"I don't know what I'm looking for. Was his office always this neat? Does anything look different? Anything missing?" He flashed her his best ingratiating smile. "And call me Tommy."

"He always kept things neat and tidy. We kidded him about it. You should see the mess in the other offices." She forced a smile while she looked around the room. "I don't see anything different. All his notebooks are here. Those are the important things. And I'm Caroline."

She took one of four black three-ring notebooks from it's perfectly in-line position on top of a file cabinet and riffled through it.

"Are you sure all the notebooks are complete?"

While Caroline looked through the remaining notebooks Tommy held the legal pad up to his eye. The page was perfectly smooth. The center drawer contained only miscellaneous desk things: rubber bands, stapler, paper clips, erasers, Post-it note pads. He replaced one of the note pads that had slipped off its stack. Much better, he told himself, then shivered at the thought of so much neatness. The saying, "A tidy desk is the sign of a sick mind," came to him and he wondered if that applied in this case.

In the bottom side drawer of the desk he found empty file folders and a simple brass picture frame turned face down. Tommy turned it over and looked at a picture of Jessie and Brian, their arms around each other, smiling big toothy grins.

"Damn, Brian. What are you doing with this?"

"What is it?" Caroline asked, leaning close to see.

"A photograph of Brian and a woman he broke up with seven months ago. Have you seen her before?"

"No. She's pretty, though. Why did he break up with her?"

"I don't know." He shrugged, returned the photograph to the drawer.

Caroline returned the last notebook to its proper place.

"Well," she said, eyes roaming the room, "these notebooks look complete to me. We'll have to go through them page by page, though, and even then not be absolutely sure. They're Brian's notes, not mine."

A puzzled frown came over her thin lips. Her eyes darted around the room.

"What is it?" Tommy asked.

"Did you see a spiral-bound notebook in the desk? The kind students use, thick, with a purple cover?"

"I don't think so," Tommy said, looking through the drawers again. "What is it?"

Caroline searched quickly through the rest of the office.

"His working notebook. He used it to write down ideas, questions, doodles, whatever." She stood in front of the filing cabinets, staring at them, then turned to Tommy. "Mr. Case, I don't know what Mr. Von Joss told you, but Brian was sure he'd reached a breakthrough that would make artificial intelligence viable. Do you know what that means? A genuine learning, thinking, reasoning computer. The implications are staggering." Face flushed with excitement, she leaned over the desk. "The Japanese have a seven-hundred-million dollar, ten-year project to develop the sixth generation computer, a neuro-computer. Brian's work would leapfrog right over that effort. Seventh, maybe eighth generation—a biocomputer. If his theories are right, and I know they are, that notebook is priceless, Mr. Case. Priceless."

She turned to the files and yanked on one of the drawers. It was locked. "Damn it!"

While she fumbled through a jumble of keys, Tommy thought about what she'd said. When Fumio had a few beers he tended to teach, so Tommy couldn't help but pick up something about neural networks. Neural Nets were supposed to work like the human brain processing input in parallel instead of in series, whatever that meant. In their own way, they could learn from previous experiences, drawing conclusions from random data like people do. He remembered Fumio explaining expert systems and pattern recognition which might lead to being able to talk to your computer, like Star Trek. In fact, he'd read that voice recognition was already possible.

"Dr. Jackson, uh, Caroline, what makes a so-called DNA computer so much better than regular computers?"

She continued to search the files while she answered him, slamming one drawer shut and yanking open the next. "Capacity, Mr. Case. A cupful of DNA has as much memory capacity as all the computers ever built. It can do orders of magnitude more simultaneous parallel operations than silicon-based computers." Caroline banged the last drawer closed. "It's not here."

Tommy went to her, gripped her arms. "Caroline, relax.

We've only just started to look for it. Could he have taken it home with him?'' She nodded. ''Then that's probably where it is. Let's not worry yet.''

Caroline took some deep breaths. ''You're right. It's probably there. It has to be. But you don't understand. These other notebooks are background material. Absolutely necessary, some new thinking, yes, but that purple notebook is where the real theory is.'' She looked away as her eyes turned glassy with tears. ''Without that book, and Brian, it will take years for others to make the incredible leaps he did.''

''When I leave here, I'll go look for it, okay?'' She nodded again. He pointed to the keys she held. ''Do you have the keys to all the file cabinets?''

''Oh. No. Just mine and Brian's. We worked together a lot; it was just easier to have my own.'' She quickly dropped them into her pocket.

With a smile to lessen the bite, he said, ''I thought all you computer geeks put everything in the computer. Wouldn't he have a private, encrypted file somewhere?''

''Brian wasn't your ordinary computer geek. Sure, he knew the hardware and all the basic programs, but he didn't use computers just for all the cool things they can do. He knew computers. I know it sounds silly, but he was one with them.''

She swept her hair back and leaned a shoulder against the file cabinet. A small, wistful smile turned up the ends of her full lips.

''Sometimes I'd see him staring at a program scrolling up the screen. Though he sat absolutely still, you could just tell that his whole body was alive. You know ALIVE! with capital letters and an exclamation point.'' She fished a tissue out of her pocket and wiped her already red nose. She tossed the tissue and forced a smile. ''Besides, Brian didn't trust computer security. He said if someone can put it in, someone else can take it out. There's probably a disk with the notebook, but what we're looking for won't be in any of our data banks.''

''Surely he made a copy down at the local You-Print-It store,'' Tommy said.

''God, I hope so.''

''Where else did he work?''

Caroline's eyes lit up. "Of course. That's where it is."

She brushed past him and taking out her keys, opened a door at the back of the office. The room he entered was the same size as the other offices but drastically different and not what he had expected.

"Jesus, this looks like a high school biology lab. Or an electronics lab, or chemistry."

While Caroline began searching, Tommy inspected the room. The outside work benches, actually folding tables with laminated plywood added for tops, were covered with a mixture of electronic equipment and test tubes and laboratory glassware. He was drawn to a sturdy, stainless steel table in the middle of the room. Wires from around the room led to it.

A low, Plexiglas cube sat in the center of the table, insulated on three sides with a fan box on the other. Inside were hundreds of two-inch long glass tubes filled with a clear liquid. Two thin wires ran from each tube. Exiting together, the thick bundle of wires snaked across the floor and disappeared into black boxes.

"Your computer?"

"Part of it, but we weren't going to do any full tests for at least another month. He did this on his own."

"Is it turned on?" Tommy asked, fascinated but skeptical.

"I don't know." She checked the back of the box. "The temperature control is working." She surveyed the rest of the equipment. "Nothing else seems to be on. Though..."

Tommy had the same feeling. "Though, not to be melodramatic about it," he said, "it feels like somebody else is here."

"Yes," Caroline agreed uncertainly, continuing to inspect the room.

"You didn't know about the DNA?"

"No. I haven't been in here since the Wednesday before Brian...died. It wasn't here then."

"Another mystery. No notebook?"

"No."

"Any place else he worked?"

"What? Oh, yes."

Tommy waited as Caroline continued to examine the room. A few times she started to push a button on some mysterious piece of equipment, but then drew her finger back as if not to disturb a sleeping beast.

Tommy followed Caroline into the hallway and through heavy, double swinging doors with small windows set in them. They entered a large room with white walls and workbenches on three sides and another set of double doors opposite. To his left the wall was all glass with a door at each end. Computers filled the room behind the glass, tall rectangles four or five feet high with whirling reels of tape and blinking lights. Several white-coated people huddled together inside, one man leaning casually against a million dollars worth of wires and chips and switches.

Caroline led the way to the far corner, where a robot waited.

"Tommy, meet DEX Four," Caroline said proudly. "Dexterity Experiment Number Four."

DEX 4 stood a bit taller than Tommy. Its base was a metal rectangular box that seemed to float a couple of inches above the floor. A shiny metal tube, about ten inches in diameter, rose from the center of the box. An oval metal structure, similar to a man's chest, blossomed from the top of the tube. From the "shoulders" hung two skeleton arms, a two-inch diameter tube for the humerus in the upper arm and two smaller, twisted tubes for the radius and ulna of the lower arm. Attached to the arm by a complicated "wrist" hung a replica of a human hand, four fingers and a thumb with all the bones and joints of a flesh-and-blood hand. Tommy saw tiny wires and tubes through holes in the back of the hands. The head was a square, with video lenses for eyes, and an oval speaker for a mouth. A half circle of metal cupped an ear hole on each side. DEX gleamed and stood tall like a Marine at attention. At first glance, DEX-4 looked like a prop from a B Sci-fi movie. But as Tommy continued to look he had the feeling that DEX was proud of what he was.

"I'm impressed. Does it work?"

"Absolutely." Again, Tommy heard the pride in her voice. "The hands are what the experiment was all about. DEX's hands are fully articulating. DEX will duplicate exactly what the human hand does, with a special sensor net on a human arm, right down to writing longhand and playing the piano."

"I'm still impressed. What did Brian do for DEX?"

"Developing the hand was the original project. We played around with virtual reality, that's where the sensor net came from, then we wanted to make him respond to visual and aural stimuli. That led to AI, but we weren't having much luck 'til Brian came along."

"I see. I think. I'm sure DEX will make Isaac Asimov proud. What do you do?"

"Basically, I test the programs. If something doesn't work, I have to tell the programmers why and I also help integrate the soft and hardware."

"Who designed it...him, Von Joss?"

"Oh no. Mr. Von Joss owns the company, but Dr. Madding runs the research lab. He designed DEX. Nicholas is really quite brilliant, if a bit hard to get along with sometimes. But," she added quickly, "he can be nice when he knows you and even sympathetic, sometimes."

"How did he and Brian get along?"

She shrugged, bit her lip and turned away. She regained control of herself and turned back, a forced smile on her pale face. She pushed hair behind her ear. "Sorry, Brian was a good friend." She pulled a tissue from her coat pocket and used it. "I don't have many friends," she said unnecessarily.

Tommy felt uncomfortable watching Caroline. He wanted, if he could admit it to himself, to put his arm around her and comfort her, but since the death of his older sister as a teenager, grief was not something he would allow others to see.

"When Brian first came here he was very quiet," she said. "He seemed in awe of the place, actually. After a few weeks he started to question the way some things were done and he and Nicholas had some real shouting matches. I don't know why, but in the last month or so they've gotten along and worked together and we've made some real progress because of it. Do you want to see the rest of the lab?"

"Maybe a quick tour. I don't want to take up your time. The police will ask you the same questions, anyway."

"It's okay. Without Brian it'll take awhile to get reorganized."

Tommy stood directly in front of DEX 4 and put his hand flat on the robot's chest. He pushed and felt a little give, like a human.

"So if this artificial intelligence theory works out," he said. "I guess DEX here will be one smart robot?"

"The smartest."

Tommy put his face inches from DEX's and looked deep into its video eyes. He had the uncomfortable feeling that something was looking back at him.

He followed Caroline through the second set of double doors into another hallway. On the left was a "clean room" where miniature electronic parts were assembled in a dust-free environment, to the right a meticulously clean machine shop. Fifty feet farther on another set of swinging doors led to storerooms. A metal roll-up door was set in the rear wall. A numerical keypad with a slot above hung next to it.

"This can only be opened from the security desk. Is that right?" Tommy asked after inspecting the doors and open area.

"That's right. You insert your card, then punch in your own code number. The guard will verify you have a reason to open it, then he opens it for you. He watches everything through big brother up there." She pointed to a security camera on the opposite wall.

"Can it be opened from outside?"

"No. There's no number pad outside."

Tommy and Caroline were back in Brian's office when Dr. Madding entered, carrying a clipboard against his chest. He seemed a bit friendlier than before.

"Mr. Case. I'm Dr. Nicholas Madding. Brian Childress was on one of my teams." They shook hands. Dr. Madding's hand was clammy, his grip weak, like shaking hands with cold liver. Tommy unconsciously wiped his hand on his pant's leg.

"Dr. Madding, Dr. Jackson tells me you designed DEX Four. I don't know much about robots and all, but I'm impressed. Was Brian—"

"Chambers, Mr. Case, Brian Chambers. Niles told me all about him. I thought there was something wrong about him from the start, as if he were pretending to be a scientist. And of course, I was right. He had no real credentials after all. Niles said to use him, so I did. I must admit once I got him on the correct path he did contribute to his team's objectives.''

"So he did make a contribution in the time he was here?''

"Yes, he did,'' Dr. Madding admitted grudgingly.

Tommy glanced at Caroline, who leaned against the desk with her arms crossed, a tight frown on her face.

"However, now that he has left us, we must get back on track without delay.'' Madding's tone clearly suggested he felt it was Brian's fault for getting himself killed and slowing down work. Tommy wanted to shake the pompous scientist and tell him he hoped he had killed Brian just so he, Tommy, could have the pleasure of catching him. Madding consulted a list of handwritten notes with little dashes filling one margin. He stood up to his full six-foot-plus and said, with a pointed look at Dr. Jackson from icy blue eyes, "We all have things to do, Mr. Case. We're busy here.'' He turned and left.

Tommy turned to Caroline, who hadn't moved. "Shouldn't you tell him about the notebook?''

She shrugged one shoulder, swept her hair back. "You'll probably find it at Brian's place. I'll tell Mr. Von Joss.''

Tommy leaned against the desk close to the unhappy woman. "Does Dr. Madding know about the notebook?''

Again the half shrug. "I don't know.''

Surprised, but not surprised, Tommy asked her to explain.

"From the time Brian started here Nicholas put him down. He tore his work apart, questioned everything, never gave him any credit. Brian would never have told Nicholas anything he didn't have to.''

"So Dr. Madding may not know the real extent of Brian's theory? That it was complete, written down?''

"Maybe not.''

"He told Von Joss, though.''

"Oh, yes. Brian was extremely grateful to Niles for giving him a chance. He told him everything and Niles always encouraged him.''

"So you don't think that Brian might have thought about selling his discovery?''

"No way,'' Caroline said, then repeated for emphasis, "no

way. Brian was completely loyal to Niles. About a month ago, somebody offered him a another job for a lot of money. He didn't say how much, but he turned it down flat. He would never sell Niles out.''

''Who offered him the job?''

''He didn't say.''

Tommy turned in his visitors ID card at the security desk. After thanking Caroline for the tour he asked her, ''Do you remember if Brian stayed late on the Friday before last? Or arrived late that morning? Or anything unusual that day?''

''I don't know. I...I left about four-thirty with Dr. Madding. Brian was still here then, finishing up things because he was going to be gone for a week. He might have left right after us. I don't know.''

''You left with Dr. Madding? I wouldn't have thought he was the kind to leave early. After all, the whole place might fall apart if he wasn't here.''

''We,'' Caroline said looking into the distance, ''were going to a concert at the Music Center that night, so we left early.'' As if in defense, she added, ''He had an extra ticket.''

She obviously didn't want to talk about it, so Tommy asked, ''Do you know what kind of car Brian drove?''

She turned toward him, a quizzical look on her face. ''No, I don't. It was new, though. He was excited about it,'' she said with a whimsical smile. ''He'd only had it a week or so and liked talking about it.''

''Ah, excuse me, Mr. Case. It was a Toyota Supra, a beautiful metallic blue.'' Tommy turned to the security guard who had spoken.

''You're sure?''

''Oh yes, sir. He parked it right out front there one day. I watched him turn around and look at it with a big grin on his face before he came through the door. He was real proud of that car, you could tell.''

''You didn't happen to see a license plate number?''

''No license plate. New car.''

''Yeah, that's right. Were you here Friday before last? Did you see him arrive or leave?''

"Yes sir, I was here. I saw him arrive a little before nine that morning. I remember because he was hardly ever late. He just walked in and said his usual 'Morning, John' and went on into the security area. I never saw him leave."

"Thanks, John. I appreciate the information."

"Anything I can do to help, sir. I liked Mr. Childress, ah, I guess that's Mr. Chambers, isn't it?"

Tommy rolled his eyes at how fast bad news travels. He nodded to the guard and turned to Caroline. "Thanks again. I'm afraid the police will be asking the same questions pretty soon. I've done my bit, so—"

"Dr. Jackson! If you are finished?"

"Yes, I'm coming." She turned to Tommy. "My master's voice. Nice to meet you, Tommy. Goodbye."

They shook hands and Caroline followed Dr. Madding into the restricted area.

Tommy waved to John the guard and went out into the heat. The Electrobotics parking lot adjoined the lot of the business next door. He hadn't noticed the name, but it looked and sounded like a manufacturing plant of some sort. Maybe, if it ran two or three shifts, a car parked for a long time wouldn't be noticed. If Brian had been late, he might have parked over there.

He spotted the Toyota in the middle of the row closest to Electrobotics between a beat-up pickup truck and a sharp little Yugo with red stripes. Dust coated it, but otherwise it still looked new. Tommy copied the numbers from the temporary registration. He wondered what would happen to the car. Back to the finance company, probably.

With a sigh he left the Toyota and returned to his Mustang by the long route around the back of the two Electrobotics buildings. Then he headed back toward the beach and Brian's apartment and, with any luck, the priceless purple notebook.

SEVEN

IT WOULD, of course, be illegal to enter Brian's apartment, but he figured he could get Cartwell to cover for him if necessary. He didn't really think he would find anything there worth the risk, except satisfaction for his curiosity. He doubted the notebook would be there. Of course, he might not be able to get in; he was not that good at picking locks. Play it by ear, he decided, put off a decision until circumstances force you to act.

The house was right on the beach, a two-story gray building with an open deck on the beach and a balcony off the second floor. Large windows looked out on the ocean.

A wooden stairway in need of paint rose along the right side of the house. The name on the mailbox was Brian Childress. Tommy rang the doorbell. Nobody paid him any attention. He was trying to decide which pick to use when the door swung open.

Dumbfounded, mouth open, Tommy stared at the woman in the doorway. She slowly lowered her gaze to the leather lockpick pouch in his hand. She raised her head to look Tommy square in the eye, blond eyebrows raised in question. He felt like a kid caught ringing the neighborhood grouch's doorbell.

The woman stood casually, one hand holding a white, terry-cloth dressing gown closed at the neck, the other hidden in a large front pocket. She was tall, slim, lightly tanned. A white towel covered her head, except for a few strands of blonde hair waving lazily in the sea breeze. The scent of bath soap surrounded her.

She stood relaxed and confident, showing no fear at discovering a strange man about to break into her apartment. Tommy, as he began to recover from the surprise, thought she looked amused by his predicament, enjoying his embarrassment.

After a minute it became obvious she was not going to speak

first. Finally, he had to laugh at the situation. "Well, I don't know what I expected to find, but it certainly wasn't you." He thought for a second. "This is Brian Childress's apartment, isn't it?"

"What if I said it wasn't?" she asked, a hint of the east, and the south, in her voice.

"I wouldn't believe you, because I'm pretty sure it is."

"And you are?" She nodded her head at the pouch still in his hand. Quickly he slipped it into his pocket. "Not a friend, I assume."

"Ah. Well, no. I don't really know Brian. Are you a friend of his? I wasn't really expecting anybody to be here."

"I'll bet you weren't. I'm Brian's sister."

Sister? He didn't recall any mention of a sister in Von Joss' report, but he could have missed it.

"My name is Tommy Case. May I talk to you for a few minutes? It's about your brother."

Her face closed down, amusement gone. The hand holding her dressing gown clenched tighter. "What about him?"

She was not going to move until he told her and there was no easy way so he just said, "Brian is dead. He died a little over a week ago."

"TELL ME," she said. They were seated across from each other in the sparsely furnished, immaculately clean apartment. He sat in a black leather armchair, she curled on a matching loveseat across from a black lacquer coffeetable. The furniture was spare and simple, mostly solid colors, black, white, red, gray, the kind bought in Scandinavian furniture stores. A plain white desk was in a corner, covered with computer equipment. Computer printouts lay neatly on the desk and on the floor. Cheap white bookcases held magazines with titles like *AI Expert, Dr. Dobbs' Journal, Mondo 2000* and *Wired,* each title even and in order. Books about chaos, robotics, nanotechnology, virtual reality and biology and other equally obscure subjects written by Rucker, Asimov, Minsky, Gleick and others were lined up, tallest on the left. The purple notebook was nowhere in sight.

He gave the woman an abbreviated account, mentioning the

notebook but downplaying its importance. She said she hadn't seen it. Expression grim, she listened without interruption. She wore glasses with thin black frames. Reflection from the window hid her eyes.

When he finished she asked in a flat, no nonsense voice, "Who do you think did it?"

No false sentimentality here, Tommy thought. Of course, he didn't really know if she was Brian's sister, or even her name, yet.

"Well, ah— What is your name by the way?"

"Salina."

"Well, if he was killed inside the building, which is what I think happened, then it would have to be one of the people he worked with, of whom I've only met three." He held up one finger. "Niles Von Joss, the owner and chairman of the company. He's the one who hired Brian and found out about him. If Brian's breakthrough is real, it's definitely not to his advantage to kill him. On the other hand, he's a ruthless businessman and I wouldn't doubt that he could kill, if he felt it was necessary. Brian was having an affair with his wife, or so the gossip goes."

Two fingers. "Dr. Nicholas Madding is the head of research. All ego and brains. Not a very pleasant combination, but after a rocky start they seemed to be getting along without injuries. According to Doctor Caroline Jackson, Brian didn't tell him about the notebook."

Three fingers. "Dr. Jackson has plenty of brains and not enough ego. An interesting woman, I think. I got the feeling there might be something between the two doctors, but I don't know what it might be. Love would not be my first guess. She wouldn't be Brian's type, so I don't see any connection as far as a jealous boyfriend or the like. If he was killed outside, I have no idea."

"I see," she said. He couldn't see her eyes, but felt them studying him.

"In any case, it's the police's problem now or will be as soon as I get back to my boat and call Sergeant Cartwell. I'm sure he'll want to talk with you."

Salina stared out the window, one corner of her mouth curled up. "Shit," she muttered. She sighed and stood up. "Thank you,

Tommy, for telling me about Brian. I'll have to decide what to do.''

They shook hands and he turned to go. She said to his back. "Are you really going to drop out now and leave the rest of the investigation to the police? It doesn't sound as if they'll give it the attention it deserves. You've done well so far. I could pay you, if necessary.''

"Thanks for the offer, but I don't need the money and I'm retired. I told Brian's friend Jessie, and Sergeant Cartwell, that I'd try to find out where Brian worked and maybe what he'd been doing the last six months. The cops are working on it; they can handle it from here.'' He took a deep breath, looked at the ocean. "I admit there was an element of challenge, which I enjoyed, but I'm not up for a murder investigation. Let the professionals handle it.'' His hands dropped to his side. He looked into Salina's eyes and saw anger and contempt there. "Look, I'm sorry. I'm sorry about Brian; I'm sorry you didn't see him; I'm sorry I can't help you any more.''

"You mean you won't help.''

"Right. I've done what I can. I just want to resume my nice, quiet life and go sailing.''

Tommy walked toward the door; turning midway to say goodbye, he watched Salina unwrap the towel from her head and start drying her hair. *Not much of a figure,* he thought, *but attractive enough. Might be a dancer the way she moves without effort.*

She glanced up at him and said, scorn thick in her raspy voice. "Is that what you do? Just stand around and stare at women all day and never get involved in anything? What did Jessie have to do, promise to sleep with you before you'd help her?'' Tommy stiffened at the near truth of the remark. "Would you help me if I paid you and slept with you? Or would that be too much to handle? Too involving?'' She struck a mock sexy pose, with both hands on her hips. Whipping off her glasses she shook them at him. "Well, I'm not going to do either one. I'll find out what I need to know without you. Just go back to your little boat and hide away.'' They glared at each other for a long moment. Tommy stalked to the door and wrenched it open. "Oh, by the way,'' Salina said with false humor, "I won't tell the police you were going to break in here." She moved toward the back of the apartment and said over her shoulder, "Don't let the door hit your quiet, boring ass on the way out."

Tommy swung around to face Salina. "What the hell do you want from me? I did what I said I would do. What's the difference, especially to you, why I did it? I did it. That's what counts." His eyes narrowed. "I don't see you out investigating any murders of people you don't know and probably wouldn't like if you did. If it wasn't for me you'd be sitting here for a hell of a long time waiting for Brian to show up, so don't give me any shit." He stepped toward her. "I don't even know you. You could be some bimbo off the beach for all I know. Maybe you broke in here yourself and don't even know who Brian is. I don't know who you are and frankly I don't care."

As he turned to leave, a yellow paper on a table by the door caught his eye. A Federal Express receipt. The addressee was Dr. Alberto Cammillo, Massachusetts Institute of Technology.

EIGHT

WHILE HE WAITED to squeeze into the summer traffic on Pacific Coast Highway, Tommy defended himself to himself. He *had* gotten involved. He had spoken with Cartwell; he had tracked down Brian and his past. And, he would have done it without the promise of sleeping with Jessie. Salina, even if she was Brian's sister, had no call to give him grief. What did she know about him anyway?

Tommy fumed for about three minutes, then had to smile at the thought of Salina opening the door. *Christ, I must have looked like a total idiot standing there with lockpicks in my hand and my mouth hanging open.* Something about her reaction, or lack of reaction, bothered him still. She had not been the least bit frightened. As he pictured her standing so calm and sure of herself the thought crossed his mind that the hand in the pocket of her robe may not have been empty.

At a stop light, he propped the Electrobotics printout against the steering wheel and looked for mention of Salina. When the light changed, the car behind him had to honk twice to get his attention. Muttering general curses, he threw the report down and chirped the tires in his hurry to move. Later, in *Nomorr*, he settled on the settee with a big glass of wine, the file unopened on his chest. The stereo played softly. An oscillating fan attempted to circulate the hot, humid air.

Tommy found himself reluctant to call Cartwell. Salina had asked him if he could really just drop the case and he had replied that he just wanted to resume his nice, quiet life. But did he? To Lucy he said he liked the challenge of detective work, but not the business of detective work. Maybe he should follow in Travis MaGee's footsteps? Live on his boat and let the occasional client come to him.

On the other hand, he had been dreaming of sailing off into

the sunset for a long time. It was a dream many people have, but few see through to fruition. When he thought of the trip his insides twisted with anticipation and impatience. It would be a hard dream to let go.

He opened the file. It didn't take long to find her. Salina Chambers was twenty-nine years old, four years younger than Brian. She graduated from the University of Maryland with honors in 1982 with a degree in electrical engineering. The rest of the report filled in some details, but did not tell him anything new. The last entry was for 1985.

He closed the file and looked at the ship's clock. He had to call Cartwell but there was one other call to make first. It took three tries to track down Dr. Cammillo, working late in his office. Identifying himself as writing a special report on Brian's work for Niles Von Joss of Electrobotics, Tommy asked about Brian's theory. Cammillo was eager to talk about the theory, but hesitant to speak to a stranger. Tommy threw enough jargon at him to convince the scientist he already knew all about the theory. Cammillo's enthusiasm easily overcame his reluctance.

The scientist's high voice had a marked, but understandable Italian accent. "Mr. Case, the notes Childress sent me are either absolute genius or total gibberish." Tommy recognized confusion in the man's voice. "Sometimes I think I understand what he's doing and it makes a wonderful sublime sense. Other times, I feel a complete imbecile. I very much wanted to meet him at the conference last week to discuss his incredible ideas. Why was he not there?"

Instead of answering, Tommy asked, "Dr. Cammillo, do you think Brian's ideas will work? And if they do, how important would that be, and, to come right down to it, how valuable?"

A half minute of silence followed Tommy's question. Then the scientist said, "There is much work and experimentation to do of course, but yes, I think they will work. If they do, Brian Childress will be like God. He will have created a new species. As for value, Mr. Case, how much is changing the course of humanity in the universe worth?" When Tommy didn't answer right away, Cammillo added, "Why didn't you answer my question about why he was not at the conference?"

"Brian Childress is dead."

"No! That cannot be." Tommy assured him it was and explained the situation. Cammillo had no trouble understanding what the missing notebook meant. "*I* have the only copy of his work?"

"Seems so," Tommy answered. "Except, of course, if he was killed for that notebook."

"You think I am in danger?"

"If you were the killer would you want somebody else to have what you killed for?"

"I see. What do you suggest? It is possible, you know, that nobody but Brian will ever be able to understand what he has written."

"You don't really believe that, do you Doctor?"

Cammillo hesitated, then finally admitted, "No, I don't."

"I think you should contact Niles Von Joss and make arrangements to return the papers to him. I assume they belong to him; he paid for them."

After he hung up, Tommy refilled his glass and called Cartwell. He relayed his information and finished with, "And that's the report, chief. You know everything I know. The sister, I would imagine, is waiting for your call. She seemed surprised he was dead, but not particularly sad about it. More like an 'Oh hell, now I'll have to change my plans,' type of thing. Anyway, all I have to do is tell Jessie what poor old Brian was up to and I'm out of it. Off into the sunset."

Free of responsibility again, he lay still for five minutes, mind blank, watching condensation run off the glass he held on his stomach with both hands. Presently, he lifted the phone and dialed Jessie's number. No answer. He sniffed as he put down the phone. She was probably out lifting weights with Popeye. He tried to picture them together. His jaw clenched and a flush warmed his cheeks. This is not something I should be thinking about, he told himself. He cranked the stereo up, rummaged for something to eat and began making a mental list of things to do before he slipped away from the dock for the last time.

He fell asleep later, surrounded by sailing magazines, their glossy pages open to postcard pictures of tropical anchorages. The empty wineglass lay by his upturned hand.

LATE TUESDAY AFTERNOON Cartwell called to tell Tommy they'd found no trace of Salina Chambers in Brian's apartment, no sign that anybody had even been there. Somebody had done a thorough cleaning job. Could Tommy add anything to what he said the night before? Tommy couldn't.

THE NEXT DAY Cartwell called with a grimmer request—to meet him at the morgue.

"Nice place for a date, Cartwell," Tommy said to the waiting investigator. "What's up?"

"Can you identify the girl you say tried to kill you Saturday night?"

As the implications of the question hit home, Tommy's mind was back in his boat, seeing a ghostly face pass through a beam of light. Thin, wide-eyed and scared, framed by dark hair, he knew the face was forever imbedded in his memory.

"You think she's in there?" He asked Cartwell at the morgue.

"You tell me," Cartwell said, leading the way.

Tommy had seen dead people before, but didn't like it. He fought the urge to turn away when the attendant pulled back the sheet. Her face was as he remembered it, pale and unblemished, except for a dark bruise on her right cheek. "That's her." He could not stop himself from brushing his fingertips against the bruise he had given her. "She was pretty, wasn't she?" he said sadly.

Back in Cartwell's office Tommy asked, "What happened?"

The other man sighed heavily, "I always wanted a daughter." He shrugged. "No kids at all. Don't know why. Just as well, I guess."

For a minute both men sat with their own thoughts, then Cartwell said, "She was found yesterday out by Rattlesnake Reservoir. She'd probably been there since Sunday; her head was caught up in some brush, so it's in a lot better shape than the rest of the body—the insects and sun hadn't got to it yet."

He handed Tommy a file. After the first two photographs Tommy closed the cover and handed it back. He wasn't sure his stomach could take any more.

"How was she killed?"

"Strangled by hand. Coroner says she had sex just before or during death. He doesn't think it was rape, but can't say for sure."

"Shit," Tommy whispered. "Why'd you call me?"

"Bruise on the right cheek, bruise on the right side ribs—you cracked two of them by the way—and a long bruise on the back like from a table top."

Tommy just grunted, then said, "So she was probably killed because she didn't kill me. But who the hell put her up to it?"

They discussed motives for about a half an hour, but the only viable theory they came up with was that Tommy had found out, or was about to find out, something about Brian Chambers' death. Cartwell asked if he had any particular suspects in mind. After a long pause he said unconvincingly, "No." Cartwell stared at him for a long minute, but let it go.

During the next couple of days he didn't sleep well and could not contact Jessie. He got no answer at her apartment; no answering machine with a cute message, saying she couldn't come to the phone. Tim's Gym had not heard from her, or George, since the past Friday morning when Jessie had called to tell them a good friend had died and she was taking a few days off. A good friend? More likely muscleman George had slipped his leash and slapped her around a little and she didn't want to be seen with a couple of black eyes.

On Friday afternoon she left a message on his machine that she would be at the boat at seven that evening.

At five after seven, he sat in the cockpit under a dark blue awning, his feet propped up on the opposite seat cushion. He swirled the ice in his glass as she approached. She wore khaki shorts with big outside pockets and a gray knit shirt with a polo player on the pocket. Her hair, loosely braided, ended with a red ribbon and she had a fresh, scrubbed look like she had just stepped out of a long hot bath. They looked at one another, as if sizing up an opponent. Her lopsided grin said "Well, here I am big boy; are you ready for this?'' Finally, she actually said, ''Well, may I come aboard, Captain?''

When she was settled in the cockpit Tommy said, ''I've been calling you since Monday night. Was it a nice funeral for your 'good friend'?''

''Sorry about that, Tommy, really. After what happened last week, or maybe I should say what almost happened, George needed some calming down—he does get awfully jealous sometimes—so we went to Las Vegas for a few days. I'd been hoping to take some time off anyway. Then on Sunday I won five thousand dollars in a slot machine, do you believe it? So I said what the hell and we stayed until yesterday. I still have most of the money, too, if you can believe that.''

They sat on opposite sides of the cockpit with their feet up, legs touching. Absently, Jessie ran her hand lightly over the fine hair on his legs.

''They told me you'd called. Have you found anything?''

''Yes, I have,'' he said, keeping his eyes on the slow movement of her hand. ''I don't know who killed Brian. I think I know where he was killed, but I can't begin to prove it. I do know, more or less, what he was doing since he left you and I think I know why.''

He looked up at her. She looked back, no emotion showing, expression blank. She shrugged her shoulders and said, ''So, tell me.''

He told her everything he knew, from Brian's expulsion from MIT to his arrival in Newport Beach and his sudden acceptance into society. He did not mention that that part bothered him. You don't just show up at a garden party and be accepted, especially when you don't have a pedigree. Like a championship show dog, you have to have your papers to prove you belong; even Brian with his looks and charm would need an introduction. Who was Brian's sponsor?

''I think he left you when he found out what Sylvia Von Joss could do for him. He wouldn't jeopardize a chance for a job at Electrobotics for anything. According to Niles Von Joss he just wanted to work with computers. Brian was just a nerd at heart, but his luck had been bad for a long time because, in his mind anyway, of women. So he learned to use them to get to where he felt he should be.''

Her hand lay motionless on his leg. She looked past him, out over the bay. He had the feeling she wasn't paying any attention to what he said. When he moved his leg, she jumped as if he'd awakened her.

"Anyway, I think he really did love you. He had your picture in his desk. He was probably going to call you now that he was settled into his new life.''

She smiled an I've-got-a-secret smile and patted his leg. "You're sweet, Tommy. I know you're trying to make me feel better about what he did but it really doesn't matter anymore. I'm over it now. Even if he had called, I wouldn't have been interested. Things are great for me now and going to get better.''

She stood up and stretched, pushing her arms straight over her head. Her breasts pressed against the thin fabric of her shirt and his mind's eye remembered what they looked like—perfectly symmetrical, the pale skin dotted with freckles around small nipples. Their imprint showed clearly as she knelt on the seat, straddling his hips.

"I do appreciate what you've done Tommy, but I really don't care about him anymore. I never should have come to see you. Still, it's nice to know that maybe he really did love me.'' She clasped her hands around his neck. "I know how reluctant you were to do any investigating, so I won't ask you to continue with it. The police can do what they want.'' Snuggling her hips against his, voice husky, she said, "Now, you didn't let me down, it's time to finish what we started.''

She kissed him, lightly at first, then harder, forcing her tongue deep into his mouth. Pulling her to him, he had a brief thought that he shouldn't be doing this, but couldn't think why. Then he remembered.

"What about George?''

She leaned over him. Ran her tongue around his ear and whispered, "Don't worry about him. You're safe with me. Just...stay...close.''

HOURS LATER Tommy came awake and rolled silently out of the bunk. With one foot on the companionway ladder he looked back at Jessie lying uncovered, hips and face turned toward him. Shore lights coming through the hatch illuminated her pale skin with an eerie glow. She seemed to float above the sheets. Tommy felt limp all over, used up. Jessie made love as if she knew it was her last time and she had better make the most of the opportunity. But then, what she'd said...

Earlier, during a pause to catch their breath, Jessie said, "I'm glad we got to get it on at least once. This is the last chance we'll have."

"Why's that?" he asked.

"That's a secret, but I'm happy we did it." She sipped from a shared wineglass. "Do you ever wonder what we'd be doing if you hadn't been so silly about your divorce?"

"If tonight is any indication, I'd probably be in a wheelchair by now."

Over the hushed night sounds of traffic and surf he heard another sound, a high whining noise he didn't quite recognize. As it became louder, movement on the water caught his eye. A black shape crossed the rippled reflection from a shore light. Just before it went out of sight behind the stern he caught a good look at it. It was a large model boat, perhaps two feet long, but with a strange outline. Tommy moved to the starboard side to get a better look. The model turned into the three foot space between the dock finger and his boat, becoming clearly visible. What the hell? There was a lens of some type on top, like a robot eye. Robot? Something in his brain clicked. *Of course, the robot did it.* Then he saw what the lens was strapped to.

"Jessie! Get out!"

The explosion hit his back like a brick wall. He flew through the air into the empty slip next to his. Unconsciousness claimed him before the black water closed over him, but the water shocked him awake. Within seconds he surfaced, gasping for air. *Nomorr*'s awning and mainsail were engulfed in flames. A scream of pain and fear stabbed through the night, "Tommy-yyy!" A muffled whump from an exploding fuel tank cut the scream short. More flames hissed into the air.

"Jessie!" Tommy cried. He started to call out again but the

mast, with nothing left to hold it up, was falling. Flaming against the night sky, it dropped in slow motion, the spreader aimed directly at him. His eyes fixed on the mast. Followed it down. The tip of the spreader, growing huge in the firelight, pierced the water inches from his head. The heavy rigging wire whipped across his shoulder, forcing him under. The top of the mast crashed onto the opposite dock, almost cutting it in two. The center of the mast bounced to a rest inches above the surface where Tommy's head had been.

Screams sounded from shore and running feet thudded on the wooden docks. Only a few flames remained; *Nomorr* had sunk. Hands tugged at him. He relaxed and let himself be pulled onto the dock.

A distant siren wailed. Questions came from far away.

A voice cried out, "There's somebody else!"

Tommy struggled to sit up. "Jessie," he moaned, as her limp, blackened body was pulled from the water.

Then, for him, there was nothing.

NINE

TOMMY FELT nothing as consciousness returned. He floated in a void inhabited by visions of the blast, dark water, flames, screaming, Jessie's limp body. His own body twitched as he relived the scenes. Suddenly, pain slapped his backside. He cried out once, then clenched his teeth and tried not to move, not to breathe.

He heard a voice from a thousand miles away. "Mr. Case? Are you awake?"

Opening his eyes, he stared into a lovely face, below which was a nurse's uniform. She smiled. "Are you in pain, Mr. Case?"

He wanted to scream *Yesssss!* but he couldn't bring himself to speak. Instead he managed a slight nod and a roll of his eyes. The face said, "Yeah, I know. Stupid question," then went away. Minutes, hours, later, a warm liquid feeling flowed through him and the pain slid away, followed by unconsciousness.

Tommy woke. He lay still, remembering the pain. Gingerly he moved toes and fingers, then worked through the rest of his body. The pain was there, but he could stand it if he moved slowly and carefully. It was daylight, the usual blue sky visible through an opening in the curtains. In a chair, feet up on the window sill, lounged a familiar figure.

"Hey. Who's looking after my boat?" He meant his voice to sound strong but it came out a coarse whisper.

Wash jumped at the sudden sound. Standing by the bed, he spoke, but Tommy heard only an unintelligible drone.

"I can't hear you," he interrupted.

Wash sat down and leaned close. "You had us worried for a while, my man, but you'll be okay, if a little sore."

"Sore? Shit. My backside feels like it's been beaten with a baseball bat." He took a breath. "Jessie?"

Wash shrugged his thick shoulders, "Well, she's alive. But

just barely. She's in pretty bad shape, seventy per cent burns, broken bones, scrambled insides and her lungs were full of water. You know how dirty that bay is; I guess there's a big risk of infection. As weak as she is..." He shrugged again. "It's just the machines keeping her going now. Jesus, Tommy, what the hell happened?"

Tommy's thoughts drifted around might-have-beens about Jessie, but there was no solace in any of them.

"I don't suppose there's much left of my boat, is there? No more *Nomorr*." He sniffed a laugh through his nose then hissed against the pain.

Wash just shook his head. "The police had divers on it yesterday. They said half the starboard side was gone. I talked to Jeff Worth, your insurance guy, he says there'll be an investigation but there shouldn't be any problem paying off. There are other boats."

"Yesterday? How long have I been out?"

"Almost two days. It's Sunday afternoon. We're going to raise the boat tomorrow and take it to the shipyard. If it's okay with you and Jeff, we'll strip what can be salvaged and store it for you." Wash leaned toward him. "What the hell happened, Tommy? The Newport Police, the Harbor Patrol, the Coast Guard, a Detective Cartwell from the Sheriff's Department, among others, would like to know. They'll be all over you when they know you're awake."

Tommy looked straight up at the ceiling and said, "It was blown up on purpose, Wash. A damn little model boat loaded with explosives and a video camera. Can you believe it? Hell, Jessie used to say that."

"What are you talking about? Somebody blew up your boat on purpose? Why?"

"They were after me. Remember, I told you about Brian Chambers, Jessie's friend, being murdered? I found out where he worked. Somebody must be mad at me for snooping around."

"But you were finished with that, weren't you?"

"Yeah, but I guess I never really told anybody at Electrobotics. What other reason? For Christ's sake, a radio-controlled boat with a video camera on it would be a piece of cake for any of those people." Tommy turned toward Wash, pointed a finger at him, his anger overcoming his pain for a moment. "And it wasn't an accident, either. That boat steered right at me. I saw it. If I'd watched it a few seconds longer my head would've ended up in Long Beach." He fell back on the pillows, suddenly very tired.

Tommy broke a long silence, his voice quivering with emotion. "Shit, Wash. She's gone. My boat is gone. I know I should be thinking of Jessie or that someone wants to kill me, but my boat is gone, damn it. I was going to leave early. A couple weeks and I'd have been gone. Now what do I do? The boat was ready, I was ready. Now there's nothing."

Gently, Wash laid a hand on his friend's shoulder, his eyes glistening. He thought Tommy was sleeping again so he got up quietly and went toward the door, but Tommy's voice stopped him. "Wash, thanks for being here. I'm going to get the son of a bitch. You know that, don't you?"

"Yeah, Tommy. I know."

"I'm going to get the son of a bitch." Tommy's voice faded at the end, but Wash understood. He didn't wait to see the tears on Tommy's cheeks.

TOMMY WOKE EARLY the next day and spent the hours before breakfast thinking. The pain of the loss of his dream still lingered, occasionally clutching at his throat. He had been ready to let the police take over Brian Chambers' murder investigation. He had been ready to sail off. This person or persons unknown had wrecked his boat, wrecked his dream and wrecked Jessie. Now, it was Tommy's turn. He had nothing to lose and revenge to gain.

Cartwell walked into Tommy's room at seven forty-five, just in time to watch him eat breakfast. Cartwell told him the investigation at Electrobotics was not going well. There were no serious suspects. The security records confirmed when everybody left, including Chambers. They figured he was killed outside, which unfortunately greatly increased, or decreased the number of suspects, depending on how one looked at it.

Tommy shook his head, sure the murder had taken place inside. Frowning, he tried to remember something that supported his idea. What was it? He stared at the ceiling, searching for a clue. What was it? His eyes roamed the room until they came on Cartwell, quiet, still, watching him. Like a statue...or a robot. Yes! He sat up quickly, winced as pain shot up his back.

"DEX Four did it!"

"What the hell are you talking about, Case?"

Tommy explained about the size of DEX 4's arms being the same size as the pipe that killed Brian, the light oil in the wound could be the same as used in machining his parts, the strength needed to do it, a place to do it. Cartwell had told him earlier the trash was picked up on Saturday mornings and the driver was pretty sure he dumped his load in the same area the body was found. Tommy went on to say there was access from inside the building to the dumpster, the gates around the loading area were locked and the dumpster was too far from the fence for the body to be shoved over and in. He held up a hand to stop Cartwell's protest.

"I admit he could have been snatched in the parking lot; it would only take a few seconds. But why? If it was a common mugging why not just dump the body anywhere? You haven't found him to be involved in any nefarious schemes, have you? Or hanging out with bad guys or anything like that?" Cartwell shook his head no. "I didn't think so. And I'll bet you haven't found any witnesses who actually saw him leave."

"Again, no."

Tommy lay back on the pillows. Spreading his hands out, he said, "So, am I right or am I right?" Before Cartwell could respond Tommy added, "And that was his car in the parking lot, wasn't it?"

Hugh Cartwell didn't share Tommy's enthusiasm for the theory, but couldn't come up with a good argument against it, either. With a straight face he said, "So you think DEX Four was taken over by a space alien, who killed Chambers."

"Very funny. Obviously somebody would have to control the robot. Hell, hook it up to a joystick and any ten-year-old kid could do the job."

"Do you have any ten-year-old kids in mind?"

"Well, not really. Anybody in that lab is capable. What about the notebook?"

"Nothing yet. We've been looking into Jessie Padeski and her boyfriend George Stanis. A very interesting couple. As a sideline he deals steroids and pills to bodybuilders and athletes. The word is he's looking to move up and needs cash." Cartwell sat down by the window. "Now the interesting thing is that Brian Chambers had a life insurance policy with Jessie Padeski as sole beneficiary of fifty thousand dollars."

"What the hell are you talking about? She never said anything about any insurance. Son of a bitch."

"I thought you'd be interested in that. She filed a claim the day after identifying his body. Insurance company did their own investigation and found out he's definitely dead. Both Padeski and Stanis have alibis, good ones unfortunately, from Friday afternoon to late Saturday morning. He's dead, she didn't do it, they paid off." The detective paused for effect, enjoying Tommy's discomfort. "Guess when she picked up the check?"

Tommy's head shook from side to side, a puzzled expression on his face that meant he didn't believe a word of it. "When? Never mind. Friday probably."

"Right. We don't know yet what she did with it, but we will today, once we talk to the banks. If she got cash for it, there's fifty grand floating around somewhere." Cartwell looked far away out the window. "That'd be a nice find for somebody, wouldn't it? I'd love to ask Stanis about it, but he hasn't been seen since Friday morning. Did I mention that?"

"No," Tommy said with a sigh, "you didn't. The next thing you're going to say is that Stanis blew up the boat to kill Jessie because she didn't want to share."

"I was going to say that in her car we found a one-way, first-class ticket to Paris, leaving Saturday afternoon. She missed her flight."

Tommy muttered to himself, "What the hell is going on?" Now he knew what she meant by it being their last chance. "When did she buy the ticket?"

"The original reservation, for Wednesday, the twenty-eighth, was made a week before Chambers was killed. On Monday, the insurance company told her the check would be ready on Friday, so she changed the flight to Saturday, the thirty-first. For an extra fifty grand I'd wait a few days, too."

"Where'd she get that kind of money? It sounds like she was planning to stay gone. What about George?"

"No reservation in his name and he didn't try to get on the plane under another name. We'd definitely like to talk to him about Friday night. Maybe he found out she was taking off and thought it was with you. I hear he has a temper."

Tommy agreed to that. He could still feel George's fingers around his neck. "Maybe, but I doubt it," Tommy said. "Blowing up a boat by remote control is much too subtle for big George. He'd just come into the boat and strangle us with his bare hands and be done with it. What about the other dealers? Maybe somebody didn't want any competition and did away with Jessie as a warning." He shook his head. "There's all sorts of ways to figure it, but you find the person who controlled the robot, you'll find the person who tried to blow me to Tijuana. Jessie's luck just ran out."

Cartwell stood and stretched. Leaning against the wall, he stared out the window and said with disinterest, "We're looking into all those angles, too." He frowned. "By the way, we ID'd the girl. Kim Freeland, a runaway from Ohio. Been missing four months. She spent time at Safe House, a place for runaways in Santa Ana. Three weeks ago she told some of the other kids she'd met some kinky old guy who was going to take care of her."

"Stupid runaways. Always thinking it's going to be so great somewhere else."

"Going to be hot today," Cartwell said, "A hundred degrees inland. Lucky you, getting to lie around in a nice cool room all day and play grab ass with the nurses."

"Right," Tommy said, dripping sarcasm. "You should be so lucky to get blown up so you can lie around in pain all day." Looking straight ahead, expressionless, he added, "I'm going to get whoever did this to me. With or without your help."

Cartwell seemed not to have heard, still staring out the window, but said, "Yeah, I know." He turned towards Tommy. "There's something else you'll be interested in."

"What?" Tommy sighed.

"Salina Chambers. We aren't the only people who'd like to talk with her. It seems she has a nasty habit of mingling with the local rich and famous, then when they're all at some charity bash, she rips off their jewelry, paintings and whatever. Hits two or three places in one night. The police in Richmond, Virginia, especially, would like to have a serious talk with her. Seems some rich old boy became attached to her, then ate his twelve gauge when she disappeared with a truck load of his expensive knick-knacks. She's an expert with sophisticated security systems. Needless to say, if you see her again we'd like to know about it."

Christ, Tommy thought, isn't anybody what they seem to be? He wasn't really surprised to hear Salina was a sophisticated burglar, she had the moves; the term "Cat Burglar" could've been coined just for her.

Cartwell left soon after, leaving Tommy to his thoughts and his visitors. The day was busy for Tommy. With the help of pain pills he could sit up in reasonable comfort. He spent the day telling various officials the same story. When asked about who he thought might have done it he referred them to Cartwell. The doctor examined him that afternoon and told him he could go home the next day if he felt up to it, but preferred he stay another day. Tommy said he was leaving and called Wash to make arrangements to stay at his house until he figured out what to do.

Steve and Suzanne Langdon visited him late in the day. Tommy wanted to talk to Suzanne alone about her reaction to Brian's picture, but with Steve there it wasn't possible. Steve seemed preoccupied, avoiding Tommy's eyes and letting Suzanne do most of the talking.

Innocently, Suzanne asked what he was going to do now and offered him a place to stay as long as he wanted. Without warning, the anger he'd been holding back burst out of him. His fists beat on the bed.

"I don't want to stay with you," he said through clenched teeth. His face turned red and he lost all control. "Goddamnit-goddamnitgoddamnit. Son of a bitch took my boat." Cursing wildly, he tossed his pillows across the room. He swept the bedside roller table clean. Kicked at it until it crashed over, and then hurled the water pitcher at the wall. "I don't want to stay with anybody," he cried. "I want my boat back. I just want my boat back."

The nurse burst into the room. As quick as the anger came, it went. Tommy sat on the edge of the bed listlessly beating the mattress. Suzanne stood against the wall, arms hanging at her side and a frown on her face. The nurse brushed passed Suzanne and made Tommy lie down. He struggled, but the rage was gone. He didn't listen to the nurse's words, but took comfort from her soothing voice. She wiped the tears from his face and somehow things didn't seem so bad.

Tommy opened his eyes and through the blur saw Steve staring at him, the unfamiliar expression on his face completely unreadable.

"What?" Tommy asked.

Steve blinked once and said, "Nothing. I'm sorry about your boat, Tommy."

Tommy sniffed and wiped his nose. "That's okay. You didn't do anything."

His hearing returned to normal that evening; his muscles were stiff and his backside sported colorful bruises, but he could move okay and was anxious to get out of the hospital. Despite telling anybody who listened how good he felt, by nine o'clock he was sound asleep and didn't stir until the next morning, despite dreams of shadowy hands around Kim Freeland's throat.

TEN

ON WEDNESDAY MORNING, a nurse wheeled him to the main entrance to meet Wash. On the way, they stopped at the ICU to see Jessie. The right side of her face was unmarked, skin pale and slack. She looked dead, and without the machines, would be. The doctors couldn't say if or when she would come out of the coma.

Tommy watched her, thinking maybe now she would wake and live. During the silence he promised Jessie he would find whoever had hurt her.

Wash had at least five cars, but he only brought out the 1967 Thunderbird on special occasions. The ride to his house was short and silent on Tommy's part. Wash lived in a comfortable two bedroom house on the cliffs overlooking Newport Bay and the Pacific Ocean. His view took in all the marinas at the north end of the bay, including Leeward. The sound and flash of the explosion had woken him and his companion. He had arrived on the docks just in time to see Jessie's limp body pulled out of the water. Wash participated in the efforts to keep Jessie alive, but now wondered out loud if it might have been better to let her go. Life in a coma was no life at all.

Tommy only half listened to Wash ramble on about what was left of his boat. He felt listless and unsure. In the hospital room he'd felt safe, people were nice to him and cared for him; it seemed an easy task to go after the person responsible for his being there. He didn't know if he was still in danger. Would there be other attempts on his life? Was Wash in danger? What about George? Did he have anything to do with this? Was the bomb really meant for Jessie? Was it really meant for him? What was that insurance all about? He needed to talk to Suzanne, too; she'd reacted to Brian's picture too strongly for there not to be something he needed to know.

In Wash's house, he sat at the polished table in the dining area of the combination living-dining room, and stared out the picture window, sinking deeper into a blue funk. Wash roused him out of his mood. He had to get back to the marina and did Tommy want to go down to the marina with him and get his car?

Tommy drove sedately back to Wash's house. He watched to see if anybody followed him, he had to start being careful, but there were no suspicious characters in sight. With a glass of wine, he stretched out on the sofa to think, and quickly dozed off.

A continuous pounding shook the house, waking him. Still muzzy with sleep, he shuffled to the door yelling, "I'm coming. I'm coming. Hold your water."

The front door contained a diamond-shaped, wrinkled glass window now completely blocked by the person outside. It took a few seconds for Tommy's fuzzy mind to realize who it had to be. "Oh shit," he muttered. Just then the door burst open and he was face to chest with a furious George Stanis. He still looked like Popeye, but was not amusing as he growled, "Where's my money, Case?"

There were two doors in the entrance hall, one to a coat closet, one to the guest bedroom. George slammed them open, glancing quickly through each one, then advanced on Tommy, who retreated into the living room.

"What are you talking about?" Tommy asked, voice weaker than he liked. "I don't have your money. What money?"

"Don't bullshit me, you bastard. You have my two hundred thousand dollars and I need it back. Now!"

Two hundred thousand? "Look, I don't have your money. Why are you asking me?"

Tommy kept the sofa between him and George, the picture window at his back. To his left a door led to a wood deck along the front of the house. If he could get to it—

George stumbled over his words in his hurry to get them out. "Jessie had the money on Friday. She was supposed to meet me. Instead she was with you. I searched her place Sunday and it wasn't there. Where the fuck is my money? I need it now."

George's huge chest heaved as he gulped in ragged breaths. Face purple, neck straining, he fought to control his rage. Behind the sofa was a narrow table with framed pictures, books, and two small bronze figures. George swept the table clean, held it over his head and threw it. The smaller table crashed into the corner by the dining table, overturning several chairs. A framed poster of a stylized sailboat dropped off the wall. Glass shattered, sending silver slivers sparkling over the floor.

"George," Tommy snapped, trying to break through to the man. Then, as calmly as he could, he said, "The only money I know about is the fifty thousand dollars insurance money. I don't know anything about your money. I don't have it. I have no idea where it is."

It took a few seconds for Tommy's words to sink in.

"What fifty thousand dollars?" George asked, suddenly very calm. "What insurance?"

Tommy regretted bringing up the subject, but said, "Brian Chambers' life insurance. She got the money Friday."

"Brian Chambers?"

"How about Brian Childs?"

"Him? She got fifty grand from him? That bitch! Where is it?"

George's fists struck out at the sofa, knocking it over. Then he turned to Tommy, murder in his eyes.

Recognizing the look, Tommy said quickly, "George, goddammit, I don't know where any of the money is. Jessie had nothing with her when she came to see me. Not even a purse, only what she was wearing. I don't—"

Oh shit. Tommy knew he shouldn't have said that as soon as he said it. He knew first hand what form George's jealousy took.

George's eyes bulged, his voice strained. "And I bet you had them off damn fast too, you son of a bitch."

Tommy dashed for the door. George leaped over the sofa. Tommy got a hand on the door knob, twisted it, but a crushing grip closed on his right arm and spun him around like a rag doll. The pain in his back covered the pain of the huge fist that flashed against his cheek. Another blow grazed his ear. Fear turned to anger. Tommy struck out with his free hand, hitting George square on the chest with as much effect as punching a bronze statue. Suddenly, he found himself flying through the air. In the fraction of a second it took to pass the large window he thought inanely: *Looks like a nice breeze on the water today.*

He landed rolling along the carpet into the overturned chairs. His left arm came down hard on the shattered glass. Immediately, blood oozed from his arm. When he lifted it, slivers of glass hung like bloody wind chimes. He cursed, shaking the arm to dislodge the larger pieces.

An adrenaline rush allowed him to stand up and face Stanis.

"Stop, damn it! I don't have your goddamn money and I don't know where the hell it is. It's not your money, anyway. It's Jessie's. You want to know where it is, ask her." They stood facing each other, chests heaving, blood pounding. For a few seconds, at the sound of Jessie's name, Tommy thought George was going to cry. When George looked up, though, anger still glistened in his eyes. Tommy prepared for another charge.

Stanis took two steps and stopped. His eyes unfocused, then a new expression came over his face—fear.

"I need that money Case," he pleaded. "She got it for me. I have to have it. I ought to kill you for what you did to her, but I need that money. If you give it to me now I'll walk away. Forget everything."

Tommy stood at the end of the room by the counter separating the kitchen. He wrapped towels around his arm and puzzled over the change in George. Was he really as scared as he looked? He shook his head to clear his mind, but it only made him dizzy. He leaned against the wall for support.

George didn't move.

"What are you so scared of?" Tommy asked. "You're a big man. Who'd mess with you? And what do you mean, what I did to her? I figured you tried to kill her so you could take the fifty thousand."

Hearing the accusation, Stanis stared hard at Tommy, but remained still.

Encouraged, Tommy continued, "Look, I don't have the money. I'd like to know how she got it, though. Tell me what was going on. Maybe, maybe, I can help. Tell me what you meant when you said she got it for you."

George considered the suggestion for a minute, then his shoulders slumped, he let his head fall back and he took several deep, slow breaths. He righted the sofa and sat on the arm. Tommy slid down the wall to sit on the floor.

Voice devoid of emotion, George said, "I need two hundred grand to expand my business. Jessie said she might know a way to get it, something about an old friend who might do her a favor. She promised the money Friday night. I know she had it." He shrugged in resignation. "They said if I didn't have the rest of the money by yesterday, I was finished. I thought she had crossed me, that you and her were going to take off with the money."

Tommy thought it best to get off that subject. "Who do you owe the money to?"

George shook his head.

"I can guess." Tommy hurt all over. He tasted blood, felt it thickening on his face, smelled his own sweat and fear. He wanted to put his head back and sleep. "Look, I'm in no shape to help anybody at the moment. My advice is, go tell the police. What have you got to lose? They might be able to protect you if you tell them enough. Either that, or run."

George stood up. "You said you'd help me."

"I said maybe. Shit. I'm sorry man, really, but the last people I want to get involved with are anybody you owe money to; that's way over my head. You can either run or talk. That's all the help I have."

"You said you'd help me, Case, you lying bastard." The color of George's face deepened, his body bulged. "I'm going to kill you. I should have done it the first time."

George started toward Tommy. Tommy just looked at him through half-closed eyes. He had no strength left to help George, or himself.

A new voice stopped George in mid-step.

"Hold it, Stanis. You aren't going to kill anybody."

ELEVEN

GEORGE WHIRLED AROUND. "What the—"

Tommy looked up. An arm holding a large black pistol in a leather-gloved hand extended from the entrance hall. It pointed unwaveringly at George's chest. Above the arm Tommy could only see one unblinking, dark eye shaded by a dark blue cap.

The voice, when it sounded again, was higher than Tommy would have expected from behind what he thought was a .45 with a silencer attached. It was all the more frightening because of its lack of emotion or accent, the voice of a killer, accustomed to generating fear.

"You've become a problem, George," the voice stated. The gun was rock steady. "And problems need to be solved. There's a third solution besides talking or running."

George started to speak, but never got it out. The gun jumped once, twice. Instantly, the back of George's shirt turned to bloody tatters. A spray of blood and flesh spattered the wall and Tommy. Already dead, the body crashed to the floor next to him. Blood seeped from two holes in its chest. Tommy sat stunned, mouth open, until a movement caught his eye. The gun was now pointed at him.

Tommy had been in fear of his life before but usually he could do something to help his chances of survival, or things were happening so fast there wasn't time to be scared. Now, though, there was absolutely nothing he could do to save himself. His life rested on a few millimeters' movement of a finger. Unconsciousness tugged at him, but his eyes were held by the black hole at the end of the gun like a small animal at the mercy of a big snake.

The gun relaxed and moved a few inches to the side. The voice seemed almost friendly now. "We have no quarrel with you, Case. Leave this alone and there won't be any problems." The gun flicked toward the body. "If you find his money, keep it. I know about your boat. You could probably use a couple hundred grand about now." The gun pointed at Tommy again. "Don't move," the voice commanded, then the gun disappeared.

Tommy blurted out, "Who blew up my boat?"

The eye and cap appeared at the corner and stared at Tommy for a few seconds before the voice said, "I don't know. If I hear anything I'll pass it along." Then the eye, the cap and the voice were gone and there was quiet except for the shushing of cars on Coast Highway and a dog barking in the distance.

Tommy closed his eyes, laid his head back and let the darkness take him.

THE SAME NURSE wheeled Tommy out the hospital's main entrance into summer heat. He scanned the three-page bill in his hand and said, "I'm sure glad I kept my health insurance paid up. Your services don't come cheap."

She laughed, a delightful, deep laugh that made Tommy grin even as he stared at the obscene number at the end of the bill.

Wash waited at the curb with the Leeward Marina's pick-up truck. He wanted Tommy to stay at his house again, but Tommy was adamantly against the idea. Whether Jessie and George were involved in Brian's death, he didn't know, but with two dead, one almost dead, a quarter of a million dollars and a sister missing and a professional killer hanging around somewhere, he wanted to put as much distance between himself and his friends as possible.

David Anthony, a grateful past client who lived in Los Angeles and had something to do with the movies, had already offered Tommy the use of the Stephens powerboat he kept at the Leeward Marina.

"She's thirty years old and looks fifty, but she's sound, I think, and well insured, so if she explodes, it's okay," he'd said, adding quickly, "unless you're on board, of course."

Tommy hadn't thought it was as funny as David had, but he'd gratefully accepted the offer. He could tell Wash was miffed he wouldn't stay with him again, so on the silent ride to the marina he thought over what some of his visitors had said during his short stay in the hospital.

Hugh Cartwell, for once, had been in a jovial mood. "Well, Case, the way I hear it, you're lucky to be alive. Now, if you were really lucky you'd find the missing two hundred and fifty thousand."

Tommy's brain found it slow going through all the medication. "Two hundred fifty thousand?"

Cartwell's smile disappeared for an instant. "Fifty grand from the insurance, plus Stanis' two hundred."

"Right," Tommy said. "The money Jessie was supposed to have. You didn't find it?"

"Not a trace. We have a witness who saw her leave her apartment with nothing but a small purse, which we found in her car, containing two hundred and eighty-six dollars. It looks like your little miss ex-secretary stashed the money so Stanis couldn't get his muscle-bound paws on it before she left him. And speaking of lucky, we didn't find your name on any airline reservation to Paris. That would have been interesting, don't you think?"

Fumio had stopped by and Tommy'd told him his killer robot theory. Isaac Asimov's three Laws of Robotics notwithstanding, Fumio allowed it was possible, but difficult to prove. Tommy swore Fumio to secrecy and told him about the missing notebook. Fumio's eyes had glistened with excitement as he'd quizzed Tommy about the nature of Brian's ideas, using terms like fuzzy logic, bionet, hypercube and teraflop that gave Tommy a headache.

Lucy visited and in her own inimitable way had offered to help him "relax" to help speed his recovery. A few weeks ago he would have accepted her offer, but now, his whole body hurt and he doubted he could survive her enthusiasm.

On Wednesday evening, Tommy had called his father.

"Do you want me to come down?" David Case asked.

"I'll be fine, Dad. I'm getting out tomorrow anyway."

"You be careful, Tommy. You're the only the family I have left now." After a short silence Tommy's father asked, "What are you going to do when it's over? Still go cruising?"

"I don't know. I've been thinking a lot about Colorado the last few days."

"You always did like the mountains. We had some good vacations there, didn't we?"

"We sure did," Tommy said, meaning it. "If I go, maybe we could do some fishing. That one big trout is probably still laughing at us."

"I'll bet he is. You say the word, I'll be there. I wish your mother could be there, too; those trout won't taste the same with either of us cooking. Anyway, if you see Jessie's parents tell them how sorry I am. She sure was a cute girl."

"Yeah, she was cute all right. In more ways than one, it looks like."

"What does that mean?"

"Nothing. I'll call you."

"Be careful, son. I love you."

"I love you too, Dad."

Tommy had stopped in to see Jessie again. Her condition was unchanged. Her parents, a solid man with jet black hair and liquid brown eyes and a handsome Irish woman who still showed the beauty of her youth, had been there. He had tried to talk with them about Jessie, her childhood, the two Jessies she talked about, but he hadn't been able to break through their stoic grief. Though, when he asked if she had any friends she kept in touch with, they answered simultaneously, "She didn't have many friends." When he asked about any that might have given her two hundred thousand dollars, they stared at him in bewilderment, then turned away. Tommy hadn't felt any better for them saying they didn't blame him for what happened. He believed they did, if unconsciously; it strengthened his resolve to find the person behind the explosion.

AFTER TAKING A MINUTE to unpack—he only had one change of clothes Lucy had bought for him—and ten minutes to familiarize himself with the boat, he sat down at the peeling mahogany table to figure out how to proceed. He had to assume the Sheriff's Department had assigned a low priority to the Brian Chambers murder. Cartwell, who was in charge of the investigation insisted they were "looking into it," though they had just caught a break in another case. Tommy told him of the "few friends" remarks and reminded him of the one generous friend.

The boat explosion was old news. The authorities were more interested in George Stanis' death, at the moment. So, Tommy would assume he was on his own and any help from the authorities would be gravy. His body was stiff and his arm tender under the bandages, but he felt good after his two-day rest and ready to take on the investigation in earnest.

He used the phone on the boat to call Suzanne. When she asked where he was staying he almost told her, then just said he was staying at a friend's place. It bothered him he didn't trust one of his best friends, but better safe than sorry and all that crap. With Wash not speaking to him, he wondered if, besides losing his boat and his dream, he was going lose his friends, too? Suzanne told him Steve would be playing tennis in the morning so why didn't he come over for brunch the next day?

He called Jim Lincoln of the County Bomb Squad. "C-Four," Jim said. "No doubt about it. I'd say about a pound. The delivery system's a new one on me, though. Probably an amateur. With that amount of stuff a pro would've left nothing but sawdust."

"Maybe," Tommy said dryly, "but believe me, the bang was big enough. Where would you get that stuff around here?"

"Oh, discreet inquiries at gun shops or gun shows would probably turn up somebody with something to sell. Stolen from the military, most likely."

"Thanks. If you come up with anything else tell Cartwell, okay?"

"I will if he's still here."

"What do you mean?"

"The rumor is he's thinking of retiring."

"Retiring? Now?"

"It's just a rumor. Hell, he's been here forever."

How strange, like, out of the blue, the guy wants to retire? Tommy thought.

What he really needed was to find out more about Electrobotics and the people there. He connected with Fumio at his office.

"Fumio! Don't you ever go home? They're going to charge you rent pretty soon."

"Ah, Sam Spade. You sound in good spirits. Are you out of the hospital? What's up?"

"Well, I sound better than I feel, but, yes I'm out and as usual I need a favor."

"As usual."

"I need to talk with somebody from the Electrobotics Research Lab not involved with Brian Chambers, but who knows all the people there. You wouldn't happen to know somebody who knows somebody, would you?"

"You don't want much, do you? Knowing you, I assume you want to talk to this person yesterday."

"Of course. And Fumio, if possible, try not to use my name. I'd just as soon stay out of sight and out of mind as much as possible."

"I'll do what I can. Watch the shadows."

By the time he finished his calls Tommy's rumbling stomach reminded him he hadn't eaten since breakfast in the hospital. A search of the galley turned up a large stock of liquor, but nothing edible. He had a hundred dollars Lucy lent him so lunch came next.

The usual afternoon breeze carried the thick smell of the ocean. The wind blew steadily and it was quite pleasant as he sauntered to Coast Highway and down a few blocks to the Buccaneer Restaurant. Though he bitched about the sameness of the weather, the wind reassured him. Some things didn't change. He read the latest issue of the *San Diego Log,* a free boating newspaper for the Southern California area. There was no mention of the explosion, for which he was grateful.

He couldn't help but think of sailing again as he sat in the cool restaurant on a hot summer afternoon dressed comfortably in sandals, shorts and a blue Hawaiian shirt. The pull of the sea was persistent. In the back of his mind he knew it would always be with him. He stared at a classified ad looking for crew to sail to the South Pacific and fought an intense urge to call the number and offer his services.

The longing was strong, but memories of the flames and Jessie's limp body slid down between him and the desire to get up, walk out and disappear. Slowly his grip relaxed. He set the crumpled paper aside and tried to keep his mind blank while he ate. Back on the boat, he lay down in the salon where the breeze blew cool and tried to form a plan to find Brian's murderer, but he soon dozed off.

He woke with a start to the annoying electronic warbling of the telephone, unsure for a moment where he was. Groggy, he reached for the phone.

"Hey, Sherlock, Dr. Watson comes through again. I have just the man you are looking for," Fumio said in his best Japanese-tinged British accent. "Leon Flakee. He knows everybody who is anybody at Electrobotics, and many who aren't." After a short pause he added, "There is one problem. If you want to talk with him before Monday night it has to be tonight."

"Tonight? Okay. Sure. When? Where?"

"Well, that is another problem. He is going to the sprint car races tonight; you will have to go with him. He is leaving at six o'clock."

Tommy, a little more awake, said, "Well, if I have to, I have to. Actually, I haven't seen the sprint cars run for over a year; it might be fun. Tell him I'll buy the tickets."

"One thing, Tommy. Leon is what I think you call a 'good old boy.' Blue jeans and T-shirts are his style, but he has degrees from Stanford and Cal Tech; he is as sharp as they come. Don't underestimate him because he looks like a redneck."

"Thanks for the warning. I'll be in front of Zack's on PCH at six."

THE SMELL FROM the restaurant reminded Tommy that beer and hotdogs were a first priority at the track. A line had formed outside, so he stood separate from the waiting diners. After a few minutes he felt a prickly sensation on the back of his neck. He turned around slowly but didn't notice anybody paying any particular attention to him. Ah, paranoia sets in. It *was* a bit dumb to be standing out on Coast Highway on a Friday evening when he should be keeping out of sight. A minute later that strange feeling of eyeballs resting on the back of his neck returned. He spun around, thought he saw a face duck back around the corner. He walked toward the line of waiting diners, eyes intent.

Before he reached the corner a horn blasted and a voice yelled, "Hey, you Tommy? Let's go, man."

Tommy saw a figure wave at him from a shiny red and black four-wheel-drive Ford pickup. The truck sported pin-striping and plenty of polished chrome, including a huge rollbar with four rectangular lights and oversized tires that looked like they should be churning up a mudhole out in the middle of nowhere. As he climbed up into the cab he glanced back. Was that a faintly familiar face that pulled back from the corner?

The truck leaped forward with a roar. Tommy looked back through the window but there was nothing to see. He turned to meet Leon Flakee.

Leon was in his late twenties, clean shaven but with unfashionably long black hair flowing from underneath a red Budweiser cap. They were about the same height but Leon had a heavier build. He had a wide face with a squinty look to it like a person used to wearing glasses when they aren't wearing them. The first thing Leon said was, "Fasten that seat belt. I wouldn't want you flying through my windshield and making a mess, ya know."

Tommy buckled up and asked, "You are Leon, aren't you? I'd hate to jump into the wrong truck."

Leon laughed. "That would be a bitch, wouldn't it? Yeah, I'm Leon. I assume you're Tommy Case. Nice to meet ya. Fumio says you're a race fan. You follow the sprint cars at all?"

"Not too much. Roadracing is more my interest. Sports cars mostly, IMSA, Trans Am."

"Don't like the open wheel cars so much, huh?"

"They're okay. I went to a driving school up north and did a couple years of club racing. I have to admit I prefer my wheels tucked into some sheet metal rather than hanging out there waiting for somebody to knock them off."

"Well, ya got a point there. They do get in the way sometimes. A guy I know is really into roadracing. He owns Autotronics, the car electronics company. A lot of the big teams use his stuff. Steve Langdon, you know him?"

Surprised, Tommy answered, "Steve? Yeah, I do. He and his

wife, Suzanne, are good friends. I know he knows your boss, but I didn't know he did business with you guys.''

"Oh yeah. We've done some design and testing work for him. Nothing big. He and Niles are good buddies, so I imagine they have some deal worked out.'' Leon threw a hand in the air as if pointing to the lab. "He's over there once or twice a month checking on something. Goofing off, if you ask me. He spends fifteen minutes on business and half an hour yakking about cars. Niles probably talks about fishing. Von Joss is big on fishing and boats, he even has some remote-controlled models. Have you seen the boat he's got in back of his house? It's something, isn't it? Of course, I'd rather get my fish already cooked on a plate, you know?''

Tommy only half listened as Leon rambled on about any subject that caught his fancy. Tommy didn't know Steve had done business with Electrobotics. Why hadn't Steve mentioned it when Tommy first asked about Brian? If he was over there that much he must have known him. And what about Von Joss and his model boats? The police couldn't have missed that connection, could they?

Leon stood on the brakes to avoid running over some jerk weaving all over the road. Tommy took advantage of the break to ask, "Do you know if Steve knows any of the people working on the robot project? Would he be allowed in there to see it?''

Leon laughed, "I wondered when you'd get to that subject. I'd say he must know most of those guys down there. I know he knows Doctor Carol, that's Caroline Jackson.'' He smiled. "She's pretty nice for a nerd lady. I can't say the same for Nick the Nuke, though. That is,'' he stuck his nose in the air and exaggerated each syllable, "Doctor Nicholas T—for tightass— Madding to you. He may be a genius with robots and all, I'll grant you that, but his little tyrant style of management doesn't impress me.''

"Nick the Nuke?'' Tommy asked.

"Yeah, he can reach critical mass in two nanoseconds. Definitely an unstable compound, if you ask me. When Childress first arrived, if he questioned anything Madding said, Nick the Nuke just went berserk. He never hit Childress, but you could sure tell he wanted to. I only saw him lose it once, and man, it was scary, but the last few weeks, I don't know what happened, things were peaches and cream between them.''

"Did he ever get that way with any of the other people?''

"Oh, he yells at everybody," Leon said shaking his head. "But nothing like with Childress."

Leon shook a cigarette from a soft Winston pack and lit it from the truck's lighter. He offered one to Tommy, then shook his head when he declined. "I bet you eat lots of fiber, too. Let's see, you might ask Tom Landis or David Kosow. I think they did most of the work on Steve's stuff." He paused while he entered the freeway. "This is strictly rumor you understand, but I did hear that Steve seems to be very interested in Tina Booker." He looked at Tommy with raised eyebrows and rolled his eyes. "For which I don't blame him one bit. She's one beautiful little woman. And I do mean little. I think she's about twenty-eight but looks like she should be in junior high. She complains that kids on bicycles are always trying to pick her up. She's smart as a whip, though."

"So you think he's had access to the security area where the robot is?" Tommy asked.

"Oh sure. I've seen him come out of there myself. Now that I think of it Dr. Carol mentioned Steve was real interested in DEX Four and how he worked, but then everybody is. And by the way, the so-called Restricted Area isn't all that restricted. Almost all you have to do is ask and you can get in. Hell, one of the secretaries took her boyfriend and her ten-year-old daughter in to see DEX." He chuckled. "From what I heard the kid knew a hell of a lot more about how he works them either of the other two."

"What about if you weren't let in?"

"You mean if somebody wanted to break in?" Tommy nodded. "That would be tough, I think. For an outsider to get in undetected would be hard. The place is secure in that way. What are you getting at? You think somebody broke in and killed Brian?"

Tommy sighed, "I don't know what I'm getting at. The evidence so far shows he left the lab Friday afternoon and was killed that night. I think he was killed in the lab, by—''

He had been about to say "by DEX Four" when he remembered he had known Leon for less than fifteen minutes. No sense in telling everything he knew or thought he knew, though his instincts, which could of course be wrong, said Leon was not a killer.

The serious tone of Leon's voice broke in on Tommy's thoughts. "You were about to say you thought DEX Four killed Brian when the thought crossed your mind maybe I was the killer and you had better shut up before you gave away what you knew. Right?''

With a sheepish look on his face Tommy said, "Something like that.''

"Well, I didn't kill him and I don't know who did. I didn't know him that well, he was software and I'm hardware, but he seemed like an okay guy. Of course, there're probably a few boyfriends and husbands who wouldn't agree with me. That old boy charmed the pants off more than one woman from what I hear. I don't think he discriminated against married women, either. I suppose that's where I'd look for a motive. How do you figure DEX did it?''

Tommy explained his theory to Leon. He saw no reaction to Jessie's name. As they walked to the ticket office he could hear the thunder of engines in the evening air. His heart beat a little faster; his steps came a little quicker; a grin appeared on his face. As they approached the entrance he had to force himself not to run.

Leon was a real fan. He gave Tommy a running commentary on the drivers and cars. After half an hour Tommy was able to put aside thoughts of murder and enjoy the racing. He matched cheers and jeers with Leon, urging on the cars Leon cursed just for the fun of it. They ate foot long hot dogs, drank beer and had a good time.

They fell silent on the trip back to Newport, small smiles on their faces. The traffic was light for a change, so they cruised along at sixty-five, enjoying the cool night air. They discussed avenues of investigation, Leon eager to help. Tommy warned him that after the first murder the killer had little to lose by a second. "Be discreet," Tommy warned. Leon promised he would be. He had a job he liked for which he was paid an outrageous salary, a nice house and a girlfriend who didn't want to get married. As a favorite with the gossip set at the lab he could ask about jealous boyfriends without too much trouble.

Tommy walked back to the boat after Leon dropped him off. He boarded the boat cautiously, checking for surprises. He jumped as an unfamiliar floorboard creaked. Unconsciously he listened for the buzz of little boats. It took a long time to drift into a restless sleep, disturbed by dream fragments of Suzanne Langdon, naked and inviting but with a long knife held behind her back.

TWELVE

TOMMY SLEPT LATE. The unfamiliar noises of a strange boat and the snatches of even stranger dreams had kept his nerves jumping until dawn. He had heard dark intruders in every creak and felt dangerous boarders in every unfamiliar movement.

He looked at the clock with sleepy eyes. Damn, ten o'clock; he was supposed to be at Suzanne's. Standing naked in the middle of the cabin, he tried to stretch the sleep out of his bones but pain sparked through him from head to heels. A few spots of blood stained his arm bandages. He found coffee but was too tired to figure out how to make it in an unfamiliar galley. He downed four aspirins with some stale bottled water from the refrigerator, relishing the cold as it spread through his stomach.

At his car, he heard somebody call his name. He watched Mark and Janet Dowling, acquaintances who had a sailboat in the marina, approach.

"Tommy, we're so sorry about your boat," Janet said. "How is the woman?"

"Not good. She probably won't make it."

"Oh god, how awful."

"She was a fine boat, Tommy," Mark said. "Where are you living? With Wash? The reason I'm asking is that somebody asked us last night."

Immediately alert, Tommy asked, "Oh, who was it?"

Janet looked at Mark, her sheepish expression matching his. "Well, we don't know, really. We were celebrating last night, our tenth anniversary, and had had a fair amount of champagne and, ah, were sort of in a hurry to get back to the boat." She blushed and looked at Mark, who also blushed. Tommy tried, unsuccessfully, to keep a straight face. Janet blushed more, and said "Well anyway, it was about ten and this guy called down to us from the railing just as we got to the boat, asking if we knew where you were. We said, no we didn't, we hadn't seen you since before the explosion. He just walked away.''

"What did he look like? Would you know him again?"

They both shook their heads. Mark said, "He wore a cap. One of those longbilled fishing ones. His face was shadowed, but I'm pretty sure he had a big mustache. Couldn't tell you what age, thirty to sixty as opposed to zero to thirty if I had to guess. Not fat, not thin, that's about all."

Janet nodded agreement. "I'm sorry, Tommy. We really weren't paying much attention. Was it important?"

After offering congratulations, Tommy drove off wondering where was he going to stay now. After what Mark and Janet said, he didn't feel safe staying on the boat anymore. He thought about staying at the Langdons, but there were too many questions there and besides, it would be best to be someplace where nobody knew him.

Ramona opened the door at the Langdon's. Speaking rapidly in Spanish and English she told him how happy she was he was all right, how sorry she was about his boat and scolded him for not coming to the house sooner.

Tommy was ravenous. Both Suzanne and Ramona remarked on how thin he was. They looked on with approval as he attacked the breakfast Ramona served: fresh orange juice, platefuls of Ramona's lightly spiced scrambled eggs, bacon, sausage, sourdough toast covered with thick strawberry jam, fresh fruit, cold milk and rich, freshly ground coffee. As usual when Tommy ate Ramona's cooking, he asked her to marry him and as usual she declined, saying he would chain her in the kitchen and soon he would be fat and she didn't like fat men.

Now that he was with Suzanne, Tommy was a little reluctant to question her and not sure he would like the answers. But, after breakfast, while sipping Ramona's coffee, he came straight out and said, "When I showed you Brian's picture, it really surprised you. Why?"

Suzanne stared toward the ocean, thin lips pressed together in a small frown, hands resting in her lap. Tommy waited a minute and said, "Suzanne, if at all possible I won't mention anything to the police, or Steve. Your silence tells me there's something.

I don't want to hurt you, you know that, but I really need to know what you know about Brian."

Suzanne seemed to deflate when she took a big breath and let it out long and slow. "I thought when you showed me that picture it would probably come out sometime," she said distantly. "I had an affair with Brian, well, not an affair, really, only a few hours."

She wouldn't look at him; her perfectly polished fingernails clicked as she absently tapped her fingers together.

Tommy kept his face blank and sipped lukewarm coffee.

"About a year ago," she continued, "Steve and I had a fight. We were supposed to go to a charity affair I worked hard to help organize. It was very important to me. He called late that afternoon to say he had to go out of town to a race somewhere. Things had been a little bit rough for awhile anyway so I screamed at him and he yelled at me and we said things we both knew weren't true and finally hung up on each other. Jesus, it made me so mad I didn't get to hang up on him first. Anyway, I was furious, and a few stiff drinks didn't make it any better. I didn't even go to my own party." She watched her fingernails go tick, tick, tick. "I ended up in one of those Newport bars where everybody's on the make and met Brian. He was handsome and charming and a good listener. He listened to my tale of woe and then I took him home and screwed his brains out."

Tommy could not have spoken if he wanted to. A breeze blew strands of fine blonde hair against Suzanne's square face. She ignored the hair and continued, "I fell asleep and when I woke up, he was gone; he didn't even steal anything. Last December he called me. He wanted me to introduce him to some of my friends."

"Like the Von Josses."

"Yes, or he'd mention our few hours of bliss to Steve. He just wanted an invitation to one or two private parties and some introductions to get him going."

Suzanne became animated. She turned to face the breeze and brushed the hair away from her face. Square jaw thrust out like the figurehead on an old-time sailing ship, she said, "I knew it was blackmail and told him right off if he wanted money he would have to ask Steve himself, but if all he wanted was to mingle with the society folk, I guessed I could arrange something. A week later I got him into a cocktail party, like the one we went to a couple of weeks ago. I introduced him to a few of the ladies, and that was it. He was a charmer, I have to admit. I even found myself jealous of the women he talked to.''

"What happened then?" Tommy asked.

Suzanne shook her head and sipped her now cold coffee. With a casual flip of her hand she continued. "A couple of months later he started working for Niles and I never saw him again. I really was shocked when you showed me that picture. I thought the next time I heard of him he'd be president of his own company or something. Not dead.''

They were quiet for a while. The haze over the Pacific began to clear, revealing the dull outline of Catalina Island on the horizon. Sailboats with bright white sails and powerboats streaming white wakes headed out to deep blue water through the jetty. Tiny figures with fishing poles could be seen hopping along the rocks. In the shade of the patio the breeze was still cool and carried the smell of sea air and freshly watered flowers.

Tommy was relieved by Suzanne's story—almost. A quick one night stand done in anger was not as serious as some scenarios he'd imagined and was nothing compared to some situations he'd seen. He felt disappointment that his friends' marriage was not as perfect as he wanted it to be. But few are, he knew, remembering his own marriage, which had started out so perfect until his wife's greed led to lies, adultery and finally bitter dissolution.

And he believed Suzanne. He had not really considered her a suspect; she did not have the expertise or access to kill somebody, using DEX 4. He now knew she had a motive, but unless Brian had been asking for money, it was very weak. Just to make sure, he asked her where she and Steve were the Friday night Brian was killed.

"Tommy!" she said, realizing what he meant.

"Suzanne, it's just for form's sake. I need to know everything. The police already asked you, didn't they?"

A puzzled look crossed Suzanne's face. "No, nobody has asked us anything about it. Why should they?"

"I told Cartwell how I found out about Brian. I thought somebody would call you just to check. I guess not. So were you guys here?"

Suzanne thought for a minute, one finger in the air counting on an invisible calendar while she figured back three weeks. Finally she said, "I was here 'til about seven-thirty, then I went to a party at the Yacht Club. Ramona was here helping me decide what to wear." She shook her head. "Silly isn't it? Ten thousand dresses and I can't decide what to wear without help. Anyway, Steve wasn't here; he went to a race back East. He left late that afternoon."

"Did you see him go? Take him out to the airport?"

"No, he drove himself like he always does. Exactly what are you getting at?"

"Did Steve know about you and Brian? Do you have any reason to think he might have found out elsewhere?"

"No, I'm sure he didn't know. I didn't tell him. Frankly it meant nothing and there was no sense in hurting Steve."

"Tommy, you're here?"

Startled, they jumped up.

Suzanne blurted, "Steve!"

Steve took a few steps toward them, still dressed in his tennis whites, racket in his hand, a red and blue sweatband decorating his right wrist. Suzanne folded her arms across her chest and moved a few steps away, facing the pool.

Steve looked from one to the other.

"What's going on?"

Without turning around Suzanne said, "Oh nothing. Tommy was just accusing you of murdering Brian. That was after he accused me, of course."

As calmly as he could, Tommy explained, "I wasn't accusing anybody. I just have to ask so I can eliminate people from the investigation. Suzanne says you left that Friday for the east coast. Can you prove you left on the plane?"

"Jesus, Tommy, you sound like a TV cop," Steve said smoothly. "Charlie Alister, the crew chief for Danner Racing, picked me up at the airport in Boston. Will that do? Why would I want to kill somebody I didn't know?"

"You spend a lot of time at Electrobotics. I know you know Doctor Jackson, are interested in DEX Four and have spent time in the Restricted Area. I find it hard to believe you didn't know Brian Chambers. His office was right there. You had to at least have seen him and know he worked there. Why did you lie to me when I asked before?"

Steve's usual composure slipped. His mouth opened and closed, gasping for an answer. Tommy knew before Steve said anything he was going to lie. He heard Suzanne turn around.

"Sure, I saw him there," Steve said. "I just didn't recognize him in the picture. I didn't know him that well."

"Steve!" Tommy said sharply. He heard Steve's teeth clamp shut. "Come on man. I can find out easily enough. Just ask Tom Landis or David Kosow, or—" Tommy knew he shouldn't say it, but he had to see Steve's reaction, had to know, "Tina Booker?"

Steve froze. Emotions smoldered in his eyes; fear, rage, surprise, pain. The breeze blew stronger across the patio now, ruffling hair. A gust blew a white linen napkin off the table and it fell onto the flagstone floor with a sough. An unbalanced spoon tinkled against a china plate.

"What the hell do you mean by that?" Steve finally asked. "You sound like you're accusing me of something else. First murder and now, what, an affair?" He shook his head. "Don't be ridiculous, Tommy. You know I wouldn't do that."

Voice tinged with sadness, Tommy said. "Not anymore, I don't. Anybody can have an affair." Against his will, he glanced at Suzanne. She glared at him, eyes and mouth wide open. Turning away, he felt her disgust. Hating himself he said, "Maybe you knew of something he did and killed him."

"Tommy!" Suzanne cried.

"You son of a bitch." Steve strode up to Tommy. His face livid, his breathing quick, shallow. "I don't know what you're trying to do, Tommy. Pull everybody down to your level? You lost your precious damn boat and now your life is screwed up so you're trying to screw up our life, too? Shit. Do you think I killed Brian because he slept with my wife? You're crazy. I'm not sorry he's dead, but I didn't kill him. Our marriage is stronger than that." Steve whirled away.

Tommy looked at Suzanne. Her hands covered her mouth; her face crumpled. She whispered, "Oh, god. Oh, god."

Without looking at Tommy, Steve said, "Too bad our friendship isn't as strong." He gestured with one hand. "Get out, Tommy. Investigate whatever you like, just stay away from us." Tommy watched Steve take Suzanne in his arms. He walked slowly through the house trying to impress it on his memory, sure he would never see it again. He took a last look at his friends. The weird idea came into his head that they were actors on a stage, waiting for the curtain to come down.

THIRTEEN

DANNER RACING TEAM headquartered in Torrance, south of Los Angeles. They ran an Indy car, big brothers of the sprint cars, in the PPG Indy Car Championship Series. Tommy had been to the shop before with Steve. He still remembered the thrill of sitting in a full-on racing machine.

Charlie Alister started out building dragsters and worked his way up to crew chief of Scott Danner's Indy car race team. The team wasn't doing very well and rumors were he might be replaced next season. At fifty-four, with a checkered history full of unsubstantiated rumors of various types of misconduct, being replaced would be the end of his career in big-time racing.

"So, what can I do for you, Tommy?" asked Charlie as he set his thin, almost emaciated, body down at his cluttered desk. He spoke in the light southern accent so prevalent in racing. "Something about Steve Langdon?"

"Yes," Tommy said, coming right to the point. "Did you pick up Steve at the Boston airport on Friday night, August sixteenth?"

"Yeah, sure."

"What time?"

"I don't know. Somewhere around nine o'clock. What's this about?"

Tommy laughed without humor. "I'm sure you know, Charlie. Where did you go from the airport?"

Charlie hesitated a bit too long and wouldn't look Tommy in the eye. "We drove up to Louden, New Hampshire, and went to the hotel by the track."

"Did he have his own room there?"

"No, he stayed in my room."

"Then where did you go?"

"We went to the track. He had new parts with him and I needed to know if they would do the fix."

"And some of the other crew will swear you arrived when you say you did? Which was when?"

Charlie shrugged his bony shoulders and kept his eyes anyplace but on Tommy. "About eleven or so. None of the guys were there. We were the only ones in the garage."

Tommy leaned forward in his chair, eyes intent on a very uncomfortable crew chief.

"What about security guards? Surely you can't just walk into the garages where quarter million dollar race cars are kept without somebody seeing you? Without checking in somewhere? If I talked with the security people at the track do you think they would say that was possible? Would they say you and Steve were there at that time? Or did you go someplace else?"

Charlie's clenched hands shook, but he answered, "I don't know what they would say. We were there, if the guards don't know about it I can't help that."

Tommy stood up, putting both hands flat on the worn brown desk. "Cut the shit, Charlie. You're lying and we both know it." He was silent for a few seconds then said, "Look. I don't like being a son of a bitch, but this seems to be my day for it. In the last few weeks I've been beaten up a couple of times, had my boat blown out from under me, a woman I know is in the hospital and probably won't live, I've lost some of my best friends and a man was murdered right in front of me."

He paused, eyes locked on Charlie's, putting as much menace into his voice as he could. He hoped he wasn't making a fool of himself, although part of him hoped he was.

"This is a murder investigation, Charlie. If you withhold information, you can be an accessory to murder. They don't race many cars in prison. Tell me what you did, where you went."

Tommy watched Charlie's jaw muscles working, saw his hands turn into fists. Then Charlie's anger vanished. Suddenly he turned into an old man, slumped in his chair, head bowed, beaten. For a moment, Tommy felt sadness for the man, who only a few years ago could have, and would have, thrown him out without a moment's thought.

"Steve is my friend," Charlie said. "You're asking me to betray him."

"He's my friend, too, Charlie. Look, if at all possible whatever you tell me won't go any further. Even Steve doesn't need to know."

"Sure, great. That'll be almost like I didn't let him down at all, won't it?" The comment hit home. There was a little bit of life left in the man yet. Charlie leaned forward; his voice cutting sharply through the air, "Okay, I'm going to tell this once, then this conversation never happened. That night, before we drove north, your friend was in a whorehouse sitting naked in a big armchair watching two girls having sex with each other while their 'Big Sister' went down on him, saying what a great 'Daddy' he was."

"Bullshit. I don't believe it." Although, he did.

"Believe it. And that wasn't the first time."

Tommy wasn't sure what he expected to hear but this damn sure wasn't it. A wealthy, intelligent man like Steve Langdon, in a whorehouse. Buying it, even with a luscious wife at home. He tried to ask where this place was, how often Steve went there, how did he find it, but full sentences wouldn't come out.

Charlie watched Tommy's confusion and shock with no compassion; his expression said *"Don't ask if you're not prepared to know."* In answer to Tommy's questions he just said, "You don't need to know, but *he* took *me* there." Charlie stood up, leaned over his desk and said, "Now get the hell out of here. You can do whatever you like with that information, but like I said, this conversation never happened."

He held the door for Tommy and slammed it behind him.

TOMMY BROUGHT the Mustang to a slow stop at his usual space in the marina parking lot. As he drove back to Orange County, his feelings about Steve changed by the minute, anger that a friend of his would stoop so low, cheat on his wife like that, to relief that he wasn't a murderer. He even questioned which was worse.

Sitting in the parking lot, engine running, he looked at his empty slip and for the first time it hit him—he had no place to go. Despair and loneliness clamped over his mind, eliminating rational thought and letting emotions flow unchecked. He pushed against the wheel with both hands, trying to think, to find a way out from under his low thoughts.

A tap on his window interrupted his self-pity. Guiltily, he snapped his head around. Lucy. Her smile vanished when she saw Tommy's expression. He turned away when she opened the door and didn't reply when she asked, "Tommy, what's wrong?"

He tried to ignore her insistent questioning, but she persisted. She led him down to her boat, a thirty-two foot Ericson sloop with an interior similar to Tommy's. Sitting him down on one side of the table, she poured a large glass of wine and sat down opposite him.

Lucy cocked one eyebrow and asked again, "What's wrong?"

Tommy told her about Steve and Suzanne and what Charlie had told him. About how lost he felt when he realized he had no place to go. As usual, she listened to him without criticism or judgement. Another glass of wine later, he fell silent. Drained, he waited. He could make no decisions of his own at the moment.

Lucy broke the quiet between them. "Was Steve a good person before today?"

Surprised at the question, Tommy mumbled, "Ah. Well. Yes. No. I don't understand what you mean."

"Yesterday, if someone had asked, you would have said Steve was one of your best friends. Right?" He nodded assent. "Now you think he's a creep. You're wondering if you should tell Suzanne." Tommy started to protest but Lucy went on. "You feel like you couldn't possibly keep up your friendship because of this unfortunate quirk in his nature. You're wondering whether you should turn him in, try to close down the house."

"No. No. That's not true. I was...did think some of those things but I couldn't...wouldn't turn him in."

"Do you think he killed anybody?"

With a sigh he said, "No. I don't know. I guess that maybe I'm not positive. There are some things... Shit, when I was a cop—"

"You're not a cop now," Lucy interrupted.

"I know. I just don't know what to do. There've been too many changes. Too much happening too fast. I wish I could just sit in the middle of the ocean for a month and come back and have everything like it was. Or better yet, not come back at all."

Tommy sat with head in hands. Lucy moved around behind him. Her strong fingers massaged his shoulders.

"Look, Tommy, no offense, but stop whining. You've got it better than ninety-nine percent of the people on this planet. You're in a rough patch right now. You'll get over it. You can't run from your life. If you run away, life won't forget and someday it'll come back and bite you right on your ass."

"I know," he said with a sigh.

They were quiet for awhile. Tommy hunched over the table, head down and Lucy slowly kneaded his neck and shoulders, her fingers working to the rhythm of the water lapping against the hull.

Suddenly she stood up. "Damn, Tommy, I've felt softer shoulders on a wooden Indian. Get up," she commanded. He stood, a puzzled expression on his face, but did as he was told. He climbed onto the bunk and lay on his stomach. Lucy straddled him and went to work on his wooden shoulders.

Images of the last days and weeks meandered through Tommy's mind. He tried to make some sense of events, but there was none to be had. He began to relax. The faint harbor sounds, the warm afternoon breeze drifting through the deck hatch and Lucy's hands on his back calmed his emotions. After a while, he drifted off to sleep.

FOURTEEN

A LITTLE AFTER NINE, Tommy and Lucy sat in the cockpit watching the last indigo glow of sunset fade into the dark of night. The aroma of dinner—thick hamburgers grilled on a small stainless steel barbecue hanging from the stern rail, macaroni and cheese from a box and fresh French bread from a bakery a short walk from the marina—hung in the still air.

The afternoon's despair receded behind a flimsy door in Tommy's mind and he had to be careful of his thoughts lest the door swing wide and allow depression to overwhelm him. For the moment he felt good, content to sit in the warm night air in friendly silence with Lucy.

From the cockpit, he stared at the hospital, sitting tall above the bay. He thought about Jessie and Cartwell and money. He thought he knew what happened to the money, but did that have any bearing on Jessie or Brian? He didn't think so. Still...

"May I use your phone?"

"Of course. I'm going to the head."

By the time Lucy returned, Tommy had made three calls. He gave Lucy a long hug and left for the hospital.

Jessie lay quiet in her coma. Tommy watched her for awhile, then went to a separate waiting room and waited. About ten-thirty, an opening door disturbed the waiting room stillness. Hugh Cartwell stood uncertainly by the door, face pale, eyes darting about the room. White shirt, dark slacks, tan jacket as always, but he wore no tie and the Hushpuppies had been replaced by new hundred-fifty dollar Nikes.

Cartwell walked over to the coffee machine, poured himself a cup and turned to Tommy, "So what do you want, Case? What was all that crap on the phone about my retirement?"

Tommy stood up, shoved his hands in his pockets and said with false friendliness, "Well, Hugh, it's about how you can afford to retire. What's your pension worth these days? Assuming the county has any money to pay it. Or do you have a job as a security guard line up? Nice sneakers, by the way.''

"What the hell are you getting at, Case? My reasons for leaving are none of your business. I'm only thinking about it anyway." Color began to show on his cheeks.

"Oh, I can think of two hundred and fifty thousand reasons why it's my business, Hugh."

Tommy watched Cartwell closely. At the mention of the money he saw the truth in his eyes and the color drain from his face. Tommy knew he was right about Cartwell, but he wasn't happy about it.

Cartwell waited half a minute before replying "What are you saying, Case? That I took the money? Don't be ridiculous. A whole team searched the woman's apartment. There was no money there."

Disgusted, Tommy said, "Come on, Hugh. One day you're in my hospital room crying the blues, saying what a nice find that money would be and the next thing I know the money is missing and you're talking about retiring. You probably figured Jessie cashed the check, so you went and made an unofficial search of your own, thinking you might help yourself to the fifty grand. I bet you pissed in your pants when you found a quarter of a million instead."

Tommy watched Cartwell in a matter-of-fact way, lips pursed in a crooked smile. The detective didn't reply but dropped into a chair, cocked his head to one side and without expression, looked at Tommy.

"Look," Tommy said. "I can't say I blame you. I can't guarantee I wouldn't do the same thing, especially with drug money. But Internal Affairs probably wouldn't look at it like that. Don't forget, George Stanis was killed because he didn't have that money. The headhunters would be all over your ass, if they aren't already. And you know it."

Cartwell sighed and shrank into his chair. He said, "Assuming this bullshit you're spouting is true, what do you want from me? A share?"

Tommy stood in front of Cartwell. He leaned over and tapped

the investigator's chest with a finger. "I want you to work on this case, not sit behind a desk until your papers come through like you've been doing. Get out and work this investigation, get your men on it. I checked on the way here, this is still your case, and you haven't been doing shit with it. I want full access to information, full cooperation. I want a thorough, top priority, kick ass job done."

"I'll be happy to give you the kick ass part, Case. We're working on it, and you know it; it's getting all the attention it deserves."

"Not as much I think it deserves. Hell, nobody's even talked to the Langdons, for Christ's sake. They knew Chambers. If it wasn't for them I might not have found out where he worked and you guys'd still be sitting at the donut shop with your thumb up your ass." Tommy turned away, raised his arms and stretched. "Of course, at the moment it might have been better if I hadn't done your job for you in the first place. Did you find that notebook yet?"

Cartwell glared. "You're so smart. You find it."

"I will if I have to and you can read about it while you get your degree in license plates."

"You can't prove anything."

"I don't have to. Internal Affairs will be happy to do it for me. It's up to you. As far as I'm concerned after we get this bastard you can go down to Mexico, or wherever, and drink beer, lay in the sun and get skin cancer." Tommy walked to a wall and leaned against it, "Besides, even if you don't have the money, which you do, wouldn't it be better to go out a hero instead of a loser?"

Cartwell stared at the worn carpet. Suddenly Tommy didn't care what the detective did. The day had been an emotional rollercoaster and was catching up fast. Cartwell was silent so long Tommy almost fell asleep standing up. He caught himself nodding off and jerked awake.

"Cartwell, I'm too tired to deal with this anymore. Do what you want. Maybe somebody will find out about the money and maybe they won't. George Stanis paid with his life for that money and even if he was a drug dealing scumbag you owe him something. And Jessie, you need to pay her, too. Do it the right way.''

Tommy slumped onto the couch. Cartwell stared at the floor for a long minute before standing up. Their eyes locked, then the sheriff's investigator left without a word.

FIFTEEN

TOMMY WOKE UP slowly. He pried open one eye and looked around. It took him a few seconds to recognize the waiting room; it looked less depressing lit with sunlight. Someone had covered him with a blanket. He splashed water on his face in the bathroom and went to check on Jessie.

Her bed was empty. He asked the nurse on duty where she'd been moved to and by the professionally neutral expression that came over her face he knew what she would say. She consulted a clip board, then announced in a matter-of-fact voice that Jessie Padeski had passed away at five fifty-two that morning.

He dropped into a chair in a deserted corner and stared unseeing out the window. Her death wasn't unexpected, of course, and it seemed evident she had some secrets he needed to know, but the fact of her death left a void he would not have thought possible.

Tommy drove back to the marina and parked in his usual place in the Leeward Marina parking lot. The habit of heading toward the marina was hard to break, but he had no where else to go. He would have to get an anonymous motel room somewhere that night, and sleep in a real bed. Shutting out thoughts of Jessie, he made a mental list of things to do: eat, call Cartwell, get some clothes, go to Electrobotics, find a room, sleep.

After a long shower Tommy walked down the street to the Buccaneer. Lucy appeared a few minutes later and they spent an hour eating and talking. Lucy offered the use of her phone and to go shopping with him. Gratefully, he accepted Lucy's offer of cheery company. He did not really want to be alone.

Lucy left him alone while he spent three minutes on hold before Cartwell, his attitude no nonsense, answered.

"Cartwell, here."

"Yeah, this is Tommy. Jessie Padeski died this morning."

"Shit. I guess it wasn't unexpected, though, was it? Did she regain consciousness at all? Say anything?"

"No, she never woke up. Even the machines couldn't keep her alive any longer."

There was a silence finally broken by Cartwell. Cautious, he said, "You know, if what Stanis said is true she might have been the start of all this. I'd like to know who that 'friend' he mentioned is. If there is one. Since you called, we've been checking, but she really didn't have many friends. She was plain 'weird,' according to more than one old acquaintance."

"I can believe that, now. If she was the start, that would also imply she knew about Brian. Then why come to me?"

"Maybe she knew where he was but not what he'd been doing or why he left her. Just like she said."

"Hell, I don't know," Tommy said. "This is getting confusing and I need some rest. Maybe in my dreams it'll all come together."

"Right," Cartwell said. "Look, Case, you know more about this than anybody. I'm pulling all the files and trying to get up to speed. We need to meet and go over what we have so far. There's a meeting with the brass tomorrow afternoon and I'd like to seem as if I know what I'm talking about." He paused for a second and said, "You know, I just thought of something." Tommy could imagine him nodding thoughtfully to himself. "I'll have to check it out, though; it may or may not be relevant. See you tomorrow morning?"

"Late. You can buy me lunch."

When he finished, Lucy grabbed his hand and led him up to the parking lot and her car, a burgundy Alfa Romeo Spyder. While she put the top down she told him cheerily, "When the going gets tough, the tough go shopping."

She took Tommy to his bank and told him to get lots of cash. She prattled on about shopping experiences she'd had and how much more fun it was to spend cash instead of using "plastic." They stopped at K-Mart first for basic underwear, cheap shirts and shorts. Lucy made him change into his new clothes in the car. The top was down and she was greatly amused as he struggled to get his shorts on before a pair of prim looking women reached their car next to Lucy's. Despite himself, Tommy couldn't help laughing.

By the time they entered South Coast Plaza they were having a good time. They giggled and joked their way through the ritzy, designer stores, acting like teenagers with free cash.

For a few hours Tommy forgot his and the world's troubles. He had planned to go out to Electrobotics that afternoon, but that, too, was forgotten. Lucy decided she had to match Tommy blouse for shirt and pants for pants and despite sore feet and more packages than they could reasonably handle, Tommy had to admit he enjoyed himself.

On the trip back to the marina they sang along with the oldies on the radio. Not the kind of music Tommy preferred, but it was the right music for the situation. After separating their bags, Lucy asked Tommy if he wanted to stay with her that night.

Tommy replied, "I never thought I'd ever hear myself say this but, thanks, but no thanks. I really need to just sleep tonight. In a real bed. Alone."

Her mouth a tight frown, Lucy followed his eyes as he looked wistfully up at the hospital. "I understand. Where'll you go?"

"I'm not telling. My secret," he said seriously. "It might not be a bad idea for you to stay somewhere else, too. If this guy knows about you he could come after you."

Lucy shrugged slightly. "Maybe, but I can take care of myself. Trust me."

Tommy helped her carry her new clothes to the boat. He turned to leave, but stopped when she played a message left on her answering machine. The voice was electronically altered, but the message was clear. "Beautiful Lucy, tell your friend Tommy Case to stop investigating and go sailing. It will be safer for him, and those close to him."

They played the tape several times, Tommy growing angrier each time. He tried to talk Lucy into spending the night else-where, but she refused. She went forward and reached under her mattress, pulling out a chrome .45 semi-automatic pistol with pearl handles. Expertly, she checked the clip.

"I know how to use this thing, Tommy. I can take care of myself. I'm not leaving."

After more warnings and instructions about what to do in case of trouble, Lucy kissed him on the cheek and said, "Thanks Dad. I'll be fine. You go off and have a good sleep."

TOMMY DROVE to Jessie's apartment, a three-story building on Beach Boulevard not far from the beach. He wasn't in the mood to hassle with reluctant managers, so he took his lockpicks and actually managed to open the door with some finesse.

The one-bedroom place was relatively neat despite the police search. It only took him a minute to realize that there was nothing in the apartment to distinguish it as Jessie's: no personal pictures, no magazine labels, no clothes or books or junk mail. The CDs by the stereo were in two stacks, one light jazz, pop and new age, the other hard rock. The videos in a cardboard box were generic porn not even slanted to one particular type of kinkiness.

The bedroom had a king-size bed with frilly pillows and a black comforter. An open suitcase lay on the bed, surrounded by sloppily-folded clothes.

Tommy sat on the bed and idly fingered a green silk blouse. Who was Jessie? It saddened him that he really had no idea.

"Hello?" A pretty woman about thirty stood in the front door. "Oh, hi," she said pleasantly. "I saw the door open and thought maybe Jessie was back."

"No. I'm sorry. Jessie died this morning."

"Oh, lord." The woman crossed herself. "Oh lord, the poor soul."

Tommy stood in the middle of the living room. He had no desire to share her grief. "Did you know her well?"

"No, not really. When she first moved in she asked me if I wanted to go to a bar and check out the men." Her shoulders moved with a little uncomfortable shrug. "That's not really my thing. She was always pleasant after that, but never mentioned it again."

"Did you know her boyfriend, George?"

"That big man? He was scary. We were never introduced. I'm sorry, I must go—I have a plane to catch; I'm going to Hawaii for a week. Please tell her father how sorry I am. She's with God now."

"You knew her father?"

"She called him her Daddy. I thought that was so cute. I just saw him a couple times from a distance. He stayed with her when he was in town on business."

Tommy approached the woman. She backed up a step. "What did he look like?" he asked.

"Look like? Light hair, maybe six feet tall, about fifty. Look, I really have to go."

Tommy called after her, "Would you recognize him again?"

"No," she called back, and hurried down the steps.

Tommy let his gaze wander around the apartment. That description could fit a lot of men, but not Mr. Padeski. No, he really didn't know Jessie. Who did?

TOMMY TOOK the 405 Freeway north. It was rush hour traffic but he didn't mind; for once he wasn't in a hurry. He took a room at a Motel Six and parked his car where it couldn't be seen from the street. The room was clean and simple, bed, chair, table, and television.

After a tasteless dinner at the coffee shop next door, Tommy watched television for a bit, but fell asleep wondering how safe he really was in his little air-conditioned hideaway. At some point he jerked awake, thinking he was being watched. The window curtain rippled slowly above the air-conditioner. Was that a man outside the window? With a gun? Tommy rolled out of bed. Back pressed to the wall, he peeked behind the curtain, through the window. Nobody was visible, but he felt desperate eyes out there searching for him.

SIXTEEN

TOMMY ARRIVED AT the Electrobotics laboratory at nine-thirty Monday morning, eager, but not rested. Still alive in the morning, he had enjoyed the luxury of lying in bed dozing, trying to make sense of what had happened in the last days. Sometimes that transition time between wakefulness and sleep yielded answers, but no solutions came to him, only more questions.

John, the security guard remembered him. "Good morning, Mr. Case. How are you today?" He pointed to Tommy's still bandaged arm. "How's the arm? Must have been terrible seeing a guy killed like that."

At a loss for a moment, Tommy wondered how he knew about George. A folded newspaper reminded him he hadn't seen a newspaper or heard any news for days. He had no idea what was going on in the world.

"Yes, it was. It's not something I'll forget soon, as much as I'd like to." As if mocking him, his memory replayed the scene, the gun's jump, George's back exploding, his long, slow fall.

"Are you here to see Mr. Von Joss?" John asked pleasantly, unaware of the vision he interrupted.

"No. Actually I want to see Leon Flakee."

John laughed. "Nice guy, Leon, ain't he? If you want to know what's going on around here he's the man to see. He could get that robot in there to gossip, if it had anything to say. Third floor, room three-ten. I'll tell him you're here." Tommy thanked him and turned to the elevator, thinking that DEX-4 might have a lot to say if he had the chance.

Leon's office was bigger than Fumio's, but just as cluttered. A single metal desk sat in one corner of the long narrow room. Next to it were three computer monitors and keyboards surrounded by esoteric-looking computer gadgets connected by a tangle of wires. Work tables held more wires and what looked like exploded electronic equipment. The walls were hung with schematics and blueprints, but pride of place, high up in the middle of the long wall, was accorded to a poster of a mostly naked cowgirl looking back over her bare bottom and smiling a sexy smile from under a white hat. The sight of that bountiful bottom reminded Tommy of Lucy, but he quickly turned his attention to Leon hunched over a huge drafting table and making minute marks on a large schematic.

"Hey," Leon said with his cheerful, good old boy drawl. "You caught me." He looked down at the drawing on the table, then back to Tommy. "Yes, even us geniuses have to do it the old-fashioned way sometimes. All that CAD stuff is great"—he flipped a hand towards the computers at the other end of the room—"but the ol' personal touch still has its place. So what's happening? How's the arm?"

"Sore," Tommy said. "Any news on the grapevine?"

Leon stretched and slid off the stool. "You want some coffee?" Tommy declined. Leon left the room, returning in a minute with a large steaming cup that read I'M A GENIUS, WHAT'S YOUR EXCUSE? He sat at his desk, put his sneaker-clad feet up and indicated a chair for Tommy.

"Well, I did talk with one girl who admitted to sampling Brian's charms," Leon began. "Her boyfriend has a temper and made some threats. Apparently, they had a hell of a fight but now they're getting married. Besides, the guy has trouble plugging in a radio let alone manipulating a robot, so I don't think he's the one made DEX Four a murderer."

"Well, he'll have to be checked out, but you're probably right. He doesn't sound like our man..."

Leon cocked his head to one side. "Yes? It sounded like there was a 'but' coming next."

"No buts. Anything else?" Tommy had really been thinking "man or woman" but that would make Dr. Jackson a prime suspect and he wasn't sure about their relationship.

Leon smiled and shook his head. "There's a rumor that Niles Von Joss is a Nazi war criminal, butcher of Auschwitz or some-damnthing. I find that a little hard to believe, seeing as Niles would have been around fifteen at the time."

"Where the hell did you pick that up?"

"Oh, from impeccable sources—a friend of a friend's cousin whose best friend's boyfriend worked for an old guy who knew somebody who knew Niles when he was just a lad. Still," Leon continued, "a lot of rumors have a basis in fact."

"Which rumors are those? The ones that say you do some work around here occasionally?" a new voice said.

Leon turned to the door. "Dr. Carol. Imagine meeting you here, where the major work of this company is done."

"You wish," Dr. Jackson said with a straight face. She turned to Tommy. "I didn't know you knew Leon. Is he telling you all the company gossip? I'm sorry about your boat. You lived on it, didn't you?"

"Yes, I did," Tommy answered flatly.

"Where are you living now?"

Tommy, not expecting that question, almost blurted out, "Oh, in a Motel Six in Westminster," but caught himself and said, "Oh, here and there." Changing the subject he said, "We were just talking about the rumor—"

"From impeccable sources," Leon interrupted with a grin.

"—that Niles Von Joss is a Nazi war criminal. What do you think?"

Tommy expected her to scoff at the idea but she considered it seriously for a few seconds. In her white lab coat, jeans and low cut Reeboks with a spot of orange on them she looked like a frazzled student who had just pulled an all-nighter.

She swept her short tangled hair behind her left ear and said, "Well, I've heard something like that, too. You know, they did have those youth groups, Young Germans for Germany, or something."

"But not in the camps, for Christ's sake," Leon protested.

"No. I wouldn't think so," she replied. "Most likely it was somebody else named Von Joss. I don't think I've ever heard anybody mention his childhood."

Tommy said, "I have some friends who know him and they say nobody they know really knows where he came from, either."

"You might have to check it out," Dr. Jackson said, "but I don't believe it."

"But does this have anything to do with Brian's death?" Leon asked. "I can't see how Brian's death would be advantageous to him. I hear he made some big hush-hush breakthrough. Is that true?"

Caroline, leaning against the door jamb, arms crossed, checked the hall, then looked Leon in the eye and said with complete conviction, "Yes, Leon, I believe it's true."

Catching her seriousness, his eyes grew wide. "He was working on artificial intelligence, wasn't he? Do you think he really cracked it?"

She sighed and looked at her shoes. "I know he thought he did. Not totally, of course. It was only a theory. There's a lot of testing and experimentation to do, but he felt that a DNA computer interfaced with a silicon-based neural net with artificial life programming could learn on its own and build on that learning."

"Holy shit. True learning, that's the key."

"That's what Dr. Cammillo said," Tommy offered.

"From MIT?" Leon asked.

"Yes," Caroline answered. "Brian was going to discuss his theory with him at the conference. Tommy, how do you know about him?"

"I saw the receipt from when Brian sent him a copy of the notebook. I called him. He agreed with what you said and was going to send it back to Von Joss."

Leon dropped his feet to the floor and leaned toward the others.

"Jesus, Caroline, didn't he realize the risk he was taking? What a temptation that would be, even to someone like Cammillo? If Brian's theory works can you imagine the money and power and perhaps more important, the prestige, involved? People kill for a lot less. Am I right, Tommy?"

Tommy shrugged agreement and becoming concerned, asked Caroline, "Von Joss did get the notes back from Cammillo, didn't he?"

Becoming concerned herself, Caroline bit her lip and swept her hair back. "Mr. Von Joss and I have talked about the notebook. He's never mentioned Dr. Cammillo or getting anything back.''

The feeling that he might have made a colossal mistake gripped his stomach as if he'd been punched. If Cammillo thought the theory worked and knew that he might have the only copy and that the originator was dead, what would he do? Four days from their conversation to the explosion, plenty of time to find Tommy and set up a surprise boat visit.

"Caroline," he asked, "can you talk to Von Joss and explain what I just said so we know just where we are?"

"Sure," she said. Tommy and Leon sat silently while she talked low into a phone at the other end of the office. "He's coming up," she said.

Immediately Von Joss entered the room Tommy noticed new lines on his face. He seemed to have aged since they first met. Von Joss greeted his employees with a nod.

"Caroline, Leon. Case, what's this all about?" Tommy explained. "I have never met or talked to Dr. Cammillo," Von Joss said. "Perhaps it is time I do." He spent five minutes on the phone, mostly waiting.

He frowned as he stood over them. "Dr. Cammillo is dead. He died in a fire at his home two weeks ago."

"Whoa," Leon said.

"Oh my God," Caroline said.

"I don't believe it," Tommy said, again feeling as if he'd been punched in the stomach.

"Well," Leon said, "if one had a suspicious bend of mind, this new development presents some new questions."

"Can I use your phone?" Tommy asked. He called Cartwell and asked him to find out what he could. Tommy rejoined the group and said, "Cartwell from the Sheriff's Department is checking it out. Could Brian really have made this big breakthrough by himself? I mean, could he have stolen it from somebody else?"

"Mr. Case," Von Joss answered. "I know it may seem unlikely, but I believe he could and did work it out by himself. I think Brian was an idiot savant, without the idiot. When I first mentioned AI his face came to life and he said, 'I think I might be good at that.'"

"He was sure right," Caroline said. "The first day, we made more progress than we had the month before."

"He read everything about artificial intelligence—neural nets, fuzzy logic, expert systems—and understood it immediately, without question."

Caroline said, "It was so simple to him, no, so obvious, he didn't realize it wasn't so obvious to us. He thought we were kidding him because he was the new guy."

"Brian had the extremely rare gift of insight and intuition," Von Joss said. "He could see right to the heart of a problem, then intuit the next step." A smile of wonder took away all the extra years he had accumulated in the last month. "When he found Alife he said to me, 'Mr. Von Joss, I think Alife is it. Can we get a teraflop computer?' Just like a kid asking for a toy. I think he already had his theory then. He just didn't know it."

Tommy asked, "Alife?"

"Artificial Life," Caroline offered.

"Which is?"

She looked sideways at the ceiling for a moment and said, "Computer programs that evolve. Like real life forms do."

She looked at him as if waiting for the inevitable request for an explanation but Tommy just shrugged and said, "Okay. How about teraflop computer?"

"A computer that can perform one trillion calculations per second. But then he came upon DNA. It has the speed and capacity, if the extraction of the information could be solved...?"

"Which I believe he did," Von Joss added.

"Man, real AI," Leon said. "Have you done any experiments yet? I'd sure like to be involved, sir, if there's a place I can help."

Caroline and Von Joss traded glances. The old man nodded noncommittally at Leon and said, "We'll see."

"Okay," Tommy said. "Brian did it. How did Dr. Madding feel about Brian? It was his project, wasn't it?" Leon and Caroline stared at the floor. Von Joss stared intently at Tommy and didn't speak. Tommy said to him, "Mr. Von Joss, I have only my intuition, but I believe there's more than one death involved here. I know you and Dr. Madding have been together a long time. Anything you can tell me might help find Brian's killer—and maybe get his notebook back.''

The older man glared. "I resent that last remark, Mr. Case, but Nicholas did not like Brian. He was hard on the boy from the beginning. I don't know why; Brian was no threat to his position.''

"What happens to the project now?''

Von Joss and Caroline traded looks again. "It's on hold, for the moment. Without Brian, or the notebook, there is no progress. The others will be reassigned.'' Caroline nodded agreement, her lips crinkling at the corners in thought. "Nicholas is a wonderful engineer,'' he continued. "Brilliant in his own way, but I fear he does not have the grasp of the, shall we say, more esoteric new areas of research.'' He laid a thick hand on Caroline's shoulder. "Caroline, I want you to gather up what you can of his work. Determine to what areas his experiments are proceeding.''

She smiled fondly at him and said, "I'll do my best, sir.''

"I know you will. Let me know what you find, soon. And thank you for being his friend, he needed it.''

After Von Joss left, they discussed Cammillo's death. If it wasn't an accident, who were the suspects? Nicholas, obviously, but what did he gain? Tommy mentioned Von Joss.

"Ridiculous,'' Caroline said with certainty. "He lost big time when Brian died. He spent millions and has little to show for it.''

Tommy raised his eyes from the floor and said, "Rumor has it that Brian had an affair with Mrs. Von Joss. That's how he met Niles and got this job. One of the oldest motives in the book.''

The others stared at him, incredulous.

"Ridiculous,'' Caroline repeated.

"I agree,'' Leon said. "Niles is a tough ol' bird, a hell of a businessman. He might kill Sylvia, but never Brian.'' He rested his feet back on his desk, "Funny you should mention Sylvia, one of Dr. Carol's favorite people.'' Leon ignored her glare. "Did any of you know that Sylvia Von Joss was an up and coming heavyweight in the design of computers back in the 'fifties? She has degrees in marketing and mathematics and was a vice president of a small computer manufacturer, much of which she designed herself. That's how she met Niles.''

"Bullshit," Caroline told him.

Leon shrugged. "I had no idea she knew anything about computers myself until a couple days ago. Apparently she was very ambitious and resented Niles' success while she got demoted to housewife, mother and hostess. If Brian's theory worked out Niles stood to make it big time—long held, deep-seated resentments come to the fore, and Brian is dead.''

"Do you think she would know enough to operate DEX Four?'' Tommy asked.

Caroline stared daggers at Leon.

"She did seem quite interested in our work with DEX. It never occurred to me she really understood my explanations.'' She pressed her lips together in distaste. "What do you mean does she know enough to operate DEX?''

"Tommy thinks DEX killed Brian,'' Leon said.

"What?'' She stared at Tommy. "Are you sure?''

"Ah. Yes and no.''

"Which means?''

Tommy took a deep breath and let it out in one whoosh. "It means I'm sure that's how Brian was killed, but I have no proof. And, unless DEX is, or was, possessed by some malign alien intelligence, somebody had to operate the robot to do the job, but nobody was here.'' The frustration was evident in his voice. "Your security system even says Brian wasn't here, so I'm having a hard time winning the police over to my opinion. They think he was killed someplace else, even though I did find his car out in your parking lot.''

Dr. Jackson pulled a chair from under a workbench and set it in front of Tommy. She closed the door and sat down. "This is interesting; tell us what you think happened and what you want us to do.''

Tommy looked to Leon who shrugged assent. "Dr. Jackson, I certainly appreciate your time, but I don't want to keep you from your work.''

"Call me Caroline and don't worry about it." She looked at her watch. "But don't take all day."

In fifteen minutes he explained how he got involved in the case and what he had found out, not much, and what questions he needed to have answered—many. He kept his explanation concise and to the point, keeping all his personal baggage out. He did tell them about Jessie's death and that there was at least one other death attributed to the same person. He wanted them to know this was deadly business.

Finally, he said, "So what I, we, need most is to figure out how the killer used DEX to kill Brian when he wasn't here. If we know how, then we might know who and then maybe why. A jealous boyfriend or husband just doesn't fit."

The hush of the air conditioner was the only sound while they digested Tommy's words. Caroline spoke first. "That friend of Jessie's seems too much of a coincidence. George needs money. Jessie says she has a friend who might be able to help. Brian gets killed and just happens to have forgotten a fifty thousand dollar insurance policy with Jessie as beneficiary. That's too much. And where did the two hundred thousand dollars come from?"

"I don't know about the money, but I agree," said Leon. "That jealous husband thing won't work. I think you should be finding out if Jessie had any friends working here."

"Who have access to DEX," Caroline added.

"How many people would have that access?" Tommy asked.

"Altogether? From Von Joss on down, about twenty-five."

"Terrific," Tommy said. "The police can handle that part."

"I suppose that means they'll be here, disrupting things again," Leon complained.

"I'm afraid so. Maybe I can get them to take it easy on you. I'm meeting Cartwell later; maybe I can use my incredible influence on him to see that you all are treated with the respect you deserve."

"Oh, great. They'll have the rubber hoses out for sure."

"Which reminds me, I have things to do," Caroline said. She stood up, wrapping her lab coat tight around her. "I'll see what I can come up with."

"Oh yeah. What do rubber hoses remind you that you have to do?" Leon teased.

Caroline looked at Leon like a mother looks at an exasperating child. "Nobody likes a smart ass, Leon."

Tommy stood up also. "You know, I've been assuming that DEX Four did it, but could he really do it? I mean is he physically strong enough? Have you done experiments or whatever?"

Caroline laughed. "Don't worry, Tommy. DEX is at least twice as strong as a strong man." She turned to go, then stopped at the door. "Oh, by the way those chips you found, I'd like to see them."

"No problem. Fumio can bring them over. He knows a thing or two about computers, maybe you guys can come up with some ideas. Besides, he's dying to see your setup here."

Neither Von Joss nor Caroline had mentioned the beakers of DNA. Tommy followed their lead and kept it to himself, but, by their knowing glances, they had not forgotten it.

Hesitant, he asked Caroline, "Would it be possible to see Brian's office again? Or has someone taken it over? And also would David Kosow, Tom Landis or..." he chanced a quick glance at Leon who smiled and nodded knowingly, "Tina Booker, be here today?"

Caroline looked quizzically at Tommy and said, "Tina Booker, huh?"

Leon laughed. Tommy started to explain why he wanted to see Tina, but figured it was better to keep quiet.

Caroline said, "No, his office isn't occupied. Nobody has been allowed in. We've been going through Brian's official notes, with no luck, obviously. Nicholas thinks it's a waste of time, that the breakthrough was fake, but Mr. Von Joss wants us to look."

"What do you think?" Tommy said.

"I think the breakthrough was real and that we won't find it until we find the notebook."

"Maybe Nicholas stole the notebook," Leo offered. "Hey, maybe Nicholas was Jessie's friend. Brian told Jessie about his theory. She told Nicholas and out of professional and personal jealousy he does in Brian. How's that sound?"

"Leon, give it a rest," Caroline said.

"That's a big stretch, don't you think?" Tommy said. "Jessie was twenty-seven. Madding must be pushing sixty."

"Fifty."

"What?"

"He's fifty," Caroline said.

"Fifty? Christ, he looks at least sixty. A bad sixty."

"He does seem to have aged quite a bit recently," Caroline admitted, frowning.

"Like since Brian arrived?" Tommy asked.

Caroline just shrugged.

"Well," Leon said, "I didn't know Jessie, but I can't see Nicholas as friends with anybody."

Caroline glared at Leon. "You don't know what the hell you're talking about." She turned to Tommy. "If you want to see the office it has to be now." To Leon she said. "Haven't I told you not to call me Dr. Carol?" She turned and stalked out the door.

Tommy asked Leon, "What was that all about?" Then with a playful smile. "I think she likes you."

Leon shook his head and smiled a smile, that if Tommy had thought about it, meant that Leon knew something he didn't. "She's not quite my type," Leon said. He pointed at the cowgirl on the wall and nodded his head with a smirky grin. "That's my type."

Without a word Caroline let Tommy into Brian's office, and standing back, gestured for him to enter. "I'll see who can talk to you." She turned to go.

Tommy gently stopped her with his hand on her shoulder. "Caroline, wait. What about the DNA in there? You and Von Joss were hardly subtle with your little surreptitious eye contacts. What have you found out?"

She looked into his eyes and thought about it for a few seconds, then closed the door after checking if anybody was lurking outside. She leaned against the door, swept her hair back, thrust hands into her lab jacket pockets, and puffed out her cheeks with a big breath.

"Nothing, everything, we just don't know," she said, her expression one of total perplexity. "Mr. Von Joss and I have been trying to figure out exactly what Brian was trying to do. As far as we can tell the DNA is still alive, if that's the word. Brian isolated one of the mainframes in the computer room. There's information going back and forth between the two, but we can't make any sense of it. And some of the other equipment has come on." She flashed Tommy a sheepish grin. "We seem to be locked out of the loop, so to speak."

"So you might have artificial intelligence in there, but you don't really know, is that right?"

"Pretty much."

They both stared at the door that now had a deadbolt lock on it.

"Jesus. It's not going to take over the world is it?"

"Don't get paranoid, Tommy. The circuit is totally isolated."

Tommy detected a pinch of uncertainty in her voice and in the way she stared at the door. As if she was attempting to convince herself it was true.

"You could always pull the plug."

She looked at him then, eyes wide with alarm. "My god, we might lose everything." Her head swung back and forth at the thought. "We don't know what Brian did. And without the notebook we might never get it back." Her alarm turned to awe. "What's happening in there could be the discovery of the century. Two centuries. My god."

"What does Dr. Madding think?"

She wouldn't meet his eyes.

"He doesn't know about it," she said, voice almost a whisper.

It was Tommy's turn to puff out his cheeks. "Do you mean that the head of research doesn't know what's in there?"

Caroline shook her head and mouthed the one word: no.

"Why?"

Caroline pulled her hands out of the lab coat pockets. She didn't know what to do with them and finally crossed them tightly over her chest. "Brian set up the DNA experiment on his own. Mr. Von Joss thought it best Nicholas didn't know. He wouldn't really understand it, or approve." She moved away from the door. "You haven't told anybody about this, have you?"

"Nobody who can't keep their mouth shut."

"Good. Well, I have a hundred things to do. I'll see who can talk with you."

Tommy inspected the desk after she left. It hadn't been disturbed much, as far as he could tell. The books and printouts were in their place, but the yellow pad was gone and the top of the desk was not as neat as before. A quick look through the drawers revealed nothing new. The picture of Jessie still lay face down. For long seconds, Tommy looked at it lying there but didn't pick it up. Everything was still nice and neat in the center drawer. He checked especially to make sure the yellow Post-it note pad still rested in its proper place. It did.

He slumped in the desk chair and wondered what to do next. The room just wasn't telling him anything. His frown grew deeper as he looked for clues that weren't there.

The doors to the main work room burst open and suddenly there were two more people in the room. Two young men stood in front of the desk, ignoring Tommy, and carrying on a completely unintelligible conversation consisting of words like sigmoidal activation function, back propagation algorithm and Carlision end point position. Tommy observed the two men. He had no doubt that in front of him stood David Kosow and Tom Landis.

Kosow, he assumed, was the Asian. His oriental features had been blended with something else but fortunately the mix worked; dark almond eyes looked out intelligently from behind large rimless glasses, broad shoulders exaggerated his thin body and slender hands. His black flattop just reached the other man's chest.

His companion stood at least six and a half feet tall. Gawky as a teenager, his thin head and beaked nose bobbed up and down as he spoke to the top of the Asian's head. They both wore white lab coats with pens in the pockets. Tommy couldn't help but smile at the unlikely pair.

He cleared his throat. The two turned toward him as if he had just materialized from thin air. Then with a guilty laugh that sounded to Tommy awful close to a yuk-yuk laugh from a cartoon, the tall one said, "Oh, Tommy Case, right? Sorry. We get carried away sometimes when Tom here"—*So much for my powers of deduction,* Tommy thought—"won't listen to reason."

"Ha!" Interjected the shorter man. "Slim here may be long on body but he can be short on brains sometimes."

"He only says that when I don't agree with him, of course." David Kosow put a huge hand on top of Tom's head. "But I will admit that mini-brain here does have a good idea every once in a while."

Tom Landis swiped the hand off of his head. With a roll of his black eyes, he said with a slight British accent, "More than once in a while, thin brain." To Tommy he said, "Dr. Jackson says you want to talk to us about Brian?"

"Yes, I do. But first, what were you talking about when you came in? I couldn't understand a word of it."

David Kosow smiled and said, "Neural networks."

Tom Landis added, "Computers that can learn."

"Like the human brain."

"Brian wanted to hook DEX up to one."

"If we had one."

"They're quite expensive."

"You see they have many layers through which a..."

"Stop!" Tommy cried. "I get enough lectures from Fumio."

"Who?"

"Never mind." Tommy spread his hands out on the desk. "I assume the police have talked to you about Brian's death." They nodded. "So I wanted to know if you've thought of anything else since then." He hesitated for a few seconds then figured what the hell, put the idea out and see what happens, he wasn't getting very far by being secretive. "Also, there's a theory that possibly DEX Four was used to kill Brian. What do you think of that idea?"

Instead of laughing at the idea their brows wrinkled in thought as they considered the idea. Well, why not? If they laughed at every new idea, no matter how strange, they'd be sweeping floors at the Flat Earth Museum. Scientists were turning out to be more open-minded than Tommy thought.

David Kosow was the first to speak. "His throat was crushed

by a pipe, I think. Is that right?'' He stared without seeing at the wall behind Tommy.

"Yes."

"DEX Four is strong enough," Tom said, lost in thought.

"It would be tricky to work from the booth," David said.

"But it could be done."

"You'd have to take him by surprise."

"DEX isn't fast enough otherwise."

"If he was distracted..."

"If it was set up right..."

"It could work."

David moved behind the shorter man and acted like a robot, arms held out and moving with a slow, smooth motion. He brought his left arm around and tried to catch Tom around the neck with his forearm. Tom easily slipped free to the right. They looked at each other for a few seconds then without a word got back into position. This time David put his left hand on his victim's chest and pulled back. The right arm came around under his chin and Tom was caught. They tried several variations of the maneuver but the hand on the chest was the most effective.

"With the remote sensors on your arm it'd be a piece of cake," declared Tom.

"Who was here when he was killed?" asked David. "Not many have access to that equipment."

"As far as I can tell, nobody was here. Not even Brian."

"Puts a bit of a damper on that theory, doesn't it?" asked Tom.

"Yes, it does," Tommy sighed. "Well, if you think of anything, let me know. Got any other theories? What did you guys think of Brian?"

"He was all right," answered Tom.

"We actually didn't work with him much," stated David.

"Just knew him around the lab."

"Seemed like a nice guy."

"A bit of a ladies man."

"And not all of the ladies were single either."

"From what we've heard."

"And he and Dr. Madding didn't get along."

"Until the last month or so."

"Other than that."

"Nothing."

The three of them looked at each other, shaking their heads. Tommy said, "Nobody seems to like Dr. Madding much. Except maybe Dr. Jackson. Is he really so bad?"

The two scientists rolled their eyes and shook their heads together as if they'd been practicing that particular move for years. For once Tom Landis did the talking. David leaned against the wall and nodded agreement.

"Dr. Madding is a genius. His IQ, for what it's worth, is around a hundred and eighty. In electronics and robotics he's one of the best. His designs are at once elegant, yet simple; esoteric, yet practical."

"However, it's all based on existing technology," David added.

Tom paused, thinking, "Unfortunately, he can be so difficult to work with that he's working here instead of a major university or government research lab. He is unbending; everything must be done his way. His temper is legendary. He's quite wealthy and has a house up in Anaheim Hills, I think, but nobody we know has ever been there. He can be quite nice, actually, but he's got a hair trigger. We think he's just unbalanced, goes from nice to nuke too easily."

"I've heard about Nick the Nuke. How is he with neural networks and artificial intelligence and stuff like that?"

Tom sighed, glanced at his friend and said, "He understands them as well as anybody, but he'll never be an original thinker in those areas."

David added, "And he knows it."

"And doesn't like it."

"What about Dr. Jackson?"

"She's a nice lady. Almost as brilliant as Dr. Madding, in most people's opinion."

"But a lot saner," David added.

"Yes," agreed Tom. "She seems to be the only one who can talk to him without getting yelled at." Tom glanced at his partner. "There has been considerable rumor-mongering about something going on between them, however."

A thought came to Tommy. "You know, everybody says that about a month before Brian was killed, he and Dr. Madding suddenly seemed to be getting along just fine. It's been assumed they came to some sort of understanding, but what was it? Any ideas?"

The two other men, after a moment's thought, shrugged their shoulders—negative. Tom Landis looked at his watch and abruptly said, "We have to go."

David Kosow unleaned himself from the wall and stuck out his long fingered hand at Tommy. "Nice to talk with you, Mr. Case. Are you serious about DEX Four?"

Tommy had to lean back to look the man in the eye. With a shrug, he said, "Yes. If we can figure out how it was done, we'll know who."

"We'll think about it, Mr. Case. Good luck."

"Hey," Tommy called after the pair. "Be careful. This is a murderer we're looking for. He's killed at least once, maybe more. Two more won't make any difference."

The two looked at each other, then at Tommy, "Yeah, we know."

After they left, Tommy sat for a couple of minutes going over what they'd said. At least they seemed to think DEX could have done it—with proper supervision.

A voice in the hallway mentioned lunch and he realized he would be late meeting Cartwell. Leaving the office he looked through the glass of the double doors. In the far corner stood DEX 4, arms hanging down from slumped shoulders, his "face" pointed slightly down, looking sad and lonely. Tommy resisted the urge to go to DEX and reassure him that he hadn't been forgotten.

Caroline left her office, two doors down, just as Tommy turned from the doors. "Tommy, I was just coming to find you." Her eyes wouldn't meet his. She nervously swept her hair back. "Visitors aren't supposed to be unsupervised." Still fidgeting with her hair she said, "And, I wanted to apologize for the way I acted before. Nicholas...helped me, once. It was a rough time and he was there with a shoulder to lean on. He does have a good side, really.'' She looked up at Tommy with the pain of that rough time still in her pale brown eyes.

Tommy liked Caroline and didn't want to cause her any more discomfort, but he needed to know about her and Nicholas. In his mind Dr. Nicholas Madding had become a major suspect.

Reaching out for Dr. Jackson's arm, his voice quiet but insistent, he said, ''Caroline, we need to talk about you and Dr. Madding. I'm glad he was kind to you, but he's a suspect in a murder investigation. If he's innocent, that's great, the less suspects the better. If he isn't, friend or no friend, he needs to pay.''

Caroline's wide eyes looked hard into Tommy's for a few seconds. Looking away, she nodded once, resigned.

Tommy said, ''I know you're busy and I have to leave now, anyway. Can we meet after work? Have dinner and talk?''

They made arrangements to meet at the Coco's restaurant on Bristol Street at six o'clock that evening. While turning in his pass he asked her, ''Has anybody here done any work with explosives?''

''Explosives?''

''In the lab here or at other jobs or in the service? Demolition work? Research?''

Before she could answer a voice behind him said. ''Mr. Case, Dr. Jackson has work to do.''

Tommy turned to see Nicholas Madding and his clipboard only a few feet behind him.

Caroline took this as an order and with a glance at Tommy walked quickly away.

Tommy, using his friendliest smile, waved at her and said, ''See ya. Thanks.''

Madding's glower was not friendly as he ran a hand through his thinning black hair. ''I assume you're still asking questions about Chambers' death.'' Tommy nodded but the other man was busy cleaning his already clean glasses. ''Have you found out anything? Any good suspects?''

''Everybody's a suspect,'' Tommy said.

''Even me?''

"Even you," Tommy replied in a manner that really said *especially you.*

The scientist smiled. All innocence and light. "Well, you can investigate me all you want. I didn't kill him." His voice turned bitter. "Because of him dying my project has been canceled." Anger now. "At least that fraud didn't get what he wanted."

"And what did he want?"

Nicholas glared at Tommy. His voice was tight, restrained, menace just below the surface. "He wanted to control my project. He wanted to steal the credit from me. From me. He was an uneducated fool and got what he deserved." His dark clouded eyes continued to stare for a few seconds and then, like a switch being touched, he was back to the usual Dr. Madding everybody liked to dislike. He shook the clipboard at Tommy. "Let the police handle it, Mr. Case. I don't want you bothering my people again." Abruptly, he turned to go, then turned back. "If you must continue with this, where can I contact you in case I think of something that might help?"

On guard, Tommy said, "I'm homeless at the moment. You can call Sergeant Hugh Cartwell at the Sheriff's Department if you have any information."

Madding gave a curt nod and left. Tommy stared after him with a puzzled frown.

Then he turned to John, the security guard. They looked at each other with blank expressions. After a few seconds John said what Tommy had been thinking, "Nuts."

Tommy agreed. But nuts enough to murder? He thought over what had just happened. Could that be what this was all about, professional jealousy? It was hard to believe a scientist of Madding's stature could be jealous of someone like Brian, no matter how good he was at intuitive leaps. Contrasting that image with the kind and caring person that Dr. Jackson described made it even harder to believe. Maybe dinner with her would make everything crystal clear and he could go back to figuring out what he was going to do with the rest of his life.

SEVENTEEN

THROUGH LUCK and a lead foot Tommy arrived only ten minutes late for his meeting with Cartwell. He found him with his Hush-puppied feet on his file-covered desk and still having trouble keeping his glasses where he wanted them. Tommy knocked as he entered and sat down.

"You're late," the Sergeant said.

"Well, if I didn't have to worry about speeding tickets I'd have been here sooner."

"Forget it. Speeding tickets I can't help you with. Killing someone, maybe. You haven't killed anyone lately, have you?"

"Never. But I might if I catch this son of bitch."

"You catch him, you can kill him—as long as there aren't any witnesses."

Tommy took from the investigator's grim expression that Cartwell was serious. He was sure he could kill in self-defense, but despite his words, not at all sure he could kill in cold blood, even a crazy like they were dealing with. It was nice to know he had Cartwell's permission, however, for whatever it was worth, which was nothing.

Cartwell continued, "So what do you have? I have shit. Do you still think he was killed inside by the robot?" Without waiting for a reply, he got out of his chair and went to the door. "Ham and cheese on rye okay?" He opened the door and yelled at somebody to bring sandwiches.

Tommy ran down the suspects. Niles and Sylvia Von Joss, Nicholas Madding, Caroline Jackson (a long shot) and, reluctantly, Steve Langdon. He told Cartwell that Steve did have an alibi, but lied about knowing Brian. Feeling that he was letting a friend down, he mentioned Suzanne's brief affair and Brian's blackmail. He also reminded Cartwell of the friend of Jessie theory which was part of where did the two hundred thousand come from?

"The main thing, I think," Tommy concluded. "Is how it was done. I know DEX was the murder weapon. Nothing else makes any sense. Chambers' car was there. If he left, he must have gone back in somehow. If he was killed outside, what do we have?" He answered his own question. "Zip. That's what."

"Well, the traces of oil in Chambers' wound matches samples from the robot, so you're probably right. You have any ideas on finding out how it was done?" Cartwell asked. He had been busy scribbling notes as Tommy talked. He didn't look up.

"Dr. Jackson and some of the other people there are trying to figure that out. I'll bet it's something simple, if we can just think of it." He grabbed a handful of air and stared at it, trying to see the answer in his empty fist.

"So you think the same person who killed Chambers blew up your boat? Why?"

Exasperated, Tommy said, "We've been over this before."

"Go over it again. For me." Cartwell smiled his best ingratiating smile.

"Somebody at Electrobotics knew I was investigating Brian's death. Maybe they thought they'd gotten away with it and blamed me for finding out about the murder, so they tried to kill me."

An inner shudder flashed through Tommy at the thought that someone was really trying to kill him. He had been through enough lately, though, that the idea only bothered him for an instant.

Tommy sank back in his chair and continued, "Anyway, why else would somebody go to all the trouble? And the people at Electrobotics were the only ones who knew I was working on the case. And they were the only ones who would have thought I was still on the case. As far as I was concerned, it was over."

"What about Padeski?"

"Well, yes, she knew, but she didn't know I had found him or where or if I was even doing anything. I doubt she would tell anyone, especially George. And if she wanted me out of it, all she had to do was say so. And she did."

"Could the boat have been blown to get the woman?"

"I don't see how. She didn't call 'til late that morning. A remote control boat would take awhile to set up, I would think. Plus, it's a bit sophisticated for the drug crowd she was involved with. They would've just blown her, or us, away. Simple and direct. By the way, any leads on where the explosives came from?"

Cartwell spread his hands, negative.

They ate their sandwiches in silence for a few minutes. Tommy remembered, but didn't miss, the many times he had eaten day-old sandwiches wrapped in cellophane. They hadn't changed a soggy, stale bit.

"Remote control."

"What?" Tommy asked, his mouth full.

"Remote control," Cartwell said. "The robot was operated by remote control, from outside."

Tommy's face lit up. Why not? Yes, it could be. Then his face fell in disappointment. "A great idea, but it wouldn't work. Caroline, Dr. Jackson to you, told me the walls are shielded against outside interference, remote control waves or whatever they use included. Besides, how could they see?"

They finished their lunch in silence. Cartwell's feet hit the floor with a slap.

"Now I've got something for you." He took a brown file off a stack of brown files and dropped it in front of Tommy. "I saved this 'til after you'd eaten."

Tommy opened it and looked at the glossy black and white photos. "Jesus!" He looked away, glanced at the detective's blank face then looked again, turning the photographs over one by one, touching only the white borders.

The photographs showed a woman's naked body lying on the front seat of a Mercedes Benz sedan. Her legs hung out of the passenger side, her polished toenails inches from the dusty ground. She had been a very attractive woman. Her thick, dark hair splayed out around her head, like a mermaid's drifting in the sea. Blood seeped from stab wounds running in parallel lines from knees to breasts. Her throat gaped open in an obscene grin.

When Tommy finished with the photographs he gathered them up, made a neat stack and returned them to the folder, slowly closing the cover. Incredulous, Tommy looked across the desk at the other man, "I don't get it. Who is she?"

"Lucia Smyth. A rich divorcée from Newport. Best known for having sex, not very discreetly, with smart people."

"Smart people?"

"She only slept with brains. Ph.D.'s, professors…scientists. Nerds to celebrities, if Lucia Smyth slept with you, you were tops in the intelligence department."

Tommy shook his head in wonder. "Bizarre. Looks like her smarts ran out. Any ideas what happened?"

"Not really. Lover's spat, maybe. Anyway, apparently this Lucia Smythe had a new lover, a mysterious friend, but nobody knew who it was. For a change, she'd been very secretive about it, and it drove her friends nuts trying to figure out who it was. She'd had sex, but the coroner doesn't think she was raped. They found no semen or useful fingerprints, skin or hair samples. Some footprints, but no matches. No good leads. No nothing."

Puzzled, Tommy stared blankly across the desk. "So?"

"So, she hung out with the same crowd we're dealing with now, the Von Josses, the Langdons. Among the people who didn't have an alibi at the time were Nicholas Madding and Sylvia Von Joss."

"Madding? Jesus. Did he sleep with her?"

"He says no. They only met a couple of times. We couldn't come up with a hint of a motive. Those lines of stab wounds are awfully precise, though, and Madding is a precise kind of guy."

Tommy looked at the photos again. "Is the case still open, then?"

"Sure, but it's pretty well stalled."

"When did this happen?"

"About three months ago."

"Is there a connection here?" Tommy asked, still puzzled.

Cartwell flipped open the file for a few seconds and let it fall closed. "Most people go through life never being involved in a murder investigation. This is the second time in three months for these people. I guess it depends on how you feel about coincidences." Cartwell threw a folder down in front of Tommy. "Everything you want to know about Brian Chambers and family.

Nothing helpful that I can see.'' He put a hand on another stack. "These are statements from all the employees of Electrobotics." Another stack. "These are from others who knew Brian." Another. "These have to do with you and Jessie and George. You may not believe it, but we have been working on the case."

"Yeah, generating paperwork, it looks like."

Cartwell stood up, put on his tan jacket, picked up his notes and said, "I have to go pretend I know what's going on. Why don't you look through these files and see if they help." Tommy's eyes followed the detective out the door then returned to the brown stacks. He sighed, picked one up and started to read.

AN HOUR LATER, blurry-eyed and head crammed with facts that seemed to confuse rather than help, and the nagging feeling that he'd just missed something, Tommy stepped into the intense, bright heat. The sunlight burned the top of his head; he started to sweat ten steps from the door.

He made his way to the 55 freeway, heading back to Newport Beach. The traffic, as usual, was horrendous. He was, as usual, amazed by how quickly tall, modern office buildings were being built. All those new buildings brought more people and more traffic to the area, on streets and freeways that had long been inadequate. Some of the high-rises were quite striking, he had to admit, he just wished they were someplace else. Or better yet, he wished he was someplace else.

Tommy arrived at the restaurant. Caroline arrived. The plump uniformed hostess seated them in a booth in the non-smoking section. He had a good view of the entrance and the large square aquarium in the middle of the room. This was the first time Tommy had seen Caroline without a white lab coat on. She wore a dark blue, cotton blouse and tan pants. A little makeup gave her cheeks some color and hid some of the lines around her eyes. She wore a hint of perfume. Still plain, but much better.

They ordered white wine, no ice for her, and made small talk while waiting for the waitress to take their orders. They complained about the traffic and the parking and the heat. Caroline said they were expecting Santa Ana conditions. Tommy thought about the classic opening of Raymond Chandler's story, *Red Heat,* which gave the best explanation of how those dry desert winds can make you feel.

After they ordered, red snapper for Tommy and Chinese stir-fry for Caroline, Tommy asked, "Have you come up with any ideas about DEX Four yet?"

Beginning to relax, Caroline leaned back and watched the condensation sparkle on her glass. "It's only been a few hours, Tommy. I haven't had much chance to think about it. It'll take some time to come up with some ideas."

Slightly disappointed Tommy said, "There may not be much time. If I'm right, this guy has killed three, maybe four, people so far. I know he'd like to kill me, too, so you can see why I'd like everybody to devote full time to the investigation."

"Three people? I didn't realize...I mean Brian was bad enough, but three people?" She hunched her shoulders for a second as she thought of it and swept the hair back over her ear. "I'll think about it tonight. Who were they, the victims, I mean?"

"Well, Brian, of course—oh, by the way, I called Fumio this afternoon. He's going to call you tomorrow morning about those chips. He knows all about what's going on and what the problem is."

The waitress passed and Tommy ordered two more glasses of wine. They were quiet for a few minutes. Caroline, frowning, stared into her empty glass; Tommy watched the fish laze around the aquarium. The drinks arrived.

He said, "You told me Nicholas helped you through a rough time."

She swept her hair back, shifted her gaze to a far corner, the pain evident in her hesitant speech. "A few months ago a friend died suddenly. We were very close. She was special to me. I fell apart and...Nicholas was there. He seemed to understand. He came over to my place and...took care of me." She glanced at Tommy's impassive face. "He was a friend when I needed one. Away from the lab, he still is."

"But at the lab?" Tommy prompted.

She showed a shaky smile. "I'm just one of the boys."

"Why is that?"

"I don't know. It's strange the way he can turn on and off like that. It's a little disconcerting, but I can usually calm him down when he blows up. He trusts me, I think."

"Do you go out with him often?"

"Sometimes he takes me to a concert; he knows quite a bit about classical music."

"Ah, 'Music hath charms to soothe the savage beast.'"

"I think that's savage—"

"Breast! Savage breast," Tommy said a bit too loud. Several diners scowled at them. They both laughed. "Well, two years of Community College you can't expect too much."

Caroline patted his hand. "It's all right Tommy. I'm impressed. Nobody's ever quoted anything except scientific stuff to me."

"Hence, the sorry state of the world," Tommy pronounced.

"Why Mr. Case, you'll make me swoon," Caroline said with a flutter of eyes, appreciating the compliment.

The waitress brought their food. After a few minutes Tommy said, "You were with Nicholas the night Brian was killed, weren't you?"

"Yes, at the Music Center. I don't know what we heard. I like the music but I don't know the names."

"You left with him, from the lab I mean. Were you with him the whole night?"

Caroline shot him a sharp look that meant *don't be ridiculous.* She said, "We left the lab at about four forty-five. My car was getting fixed so he took me home and left about six. He picked me up at seven-thirty and I was with him until almost midnight. I told the police all this before."

"I know. There's an hour and a half when he could have gone back to the lab and killed Brian. Unfortunately there are witnesses who saw him at his house about six-thirty." He puffed out his cheeks as he exhaled a big breath. "There's no way he could go to the lab, go to his house and pick you up in that time."

"You'd like Nicholas to be this guy, wouldn't you?"

"Well, I'll have to admit from what I've heard and seen of him, Nicholas is not my favorite person, and I'll also admit, he's my favorite suspect. However, besides the fact that most everyone thinks he's crazy, there just doesn't seem to be much in the way of evidence against him.''

They ate for a few minutes in silence then Caroline said, ''You didn't answer before. Who were the three or four people?''

Tommy sat back and counted on his fingers. ''Brian, Jessie, a young girl and possibly''—a familiar figure across the room caught Tommy's eye—''a woman named Lucia Smyth.''

Tommy's attention focused on the woman walking toward the door. She wore faded blue jeans and a green blouse of some filmy material that flowed with the smooth rhythm of her walk. He knew that walk, the fluid way she moved over the floor, like a cat. At the door, the woman looked over her shoulder, right into his eyes. To his amazement Salina Chambers winked a slow wink, and was gone.

By the time he got to the door she had disappeared. He scanned the parking lot and the street, but she was gone. ''Son of a bitch,'' he muttered. ''What was that all about?'' He did not know if she was following him or if it was coincidence, but a chill flowed through him despite the warm summer night. Could Salina be the man with the cap?

Tommy didn't think she killed her brother. Her surprise had been genuine, but blowing up his boat could definitely be her handiwork. She was angry when he left because he wasn't going to investigate Brian's death anymore, so she blows the boat to make him mad enough to continue and Jessie was an unfortunate accident. Weak. Real weak. Salina was smart and experienced enough to find him without resorting to such extreme measures. Oh well, if Salina had a reason for letting herself be seen he'd find out soon enough.

When he returned to the table he immediately noticed Caroline's eyes were red and she had lost her color. She wore a sad frown like a lost and lonely little girl.

''Are you okay?'' he asked.

She managed a weak smile and said, ''I'm fine. Just tired. I don't usually drink.''

''You did drink that wine pretty fast. It'll get you if you're not used to it. I'm sorry I jumped up like that. I saw somebody who might be involved in all this, but I missed her.''

After dessert and coffee Tommy walked Caroline to her car. She assured him she could drive herself home. Standing by the open door, she asked Tommy, ''That woman you mentioned, Lucia Smyth. How is she connected to this?''

''The Langdons, Von Josses and Madding were involved in that investigation, too. Why? Did you know her?''

''No. No. The name sounded familiar. I must have read about it.'' She got into her car. ''Thanks for the dinner, Tommy. It was nice. I don't go out much these days and I'm sorry I didn't help, but I'll think about the DEX problem.''

He watched Caroline drive away. Concerned, he wondered if he should worry about her safety. That glimpse of Salina had strengthened his feeling of anticipation. For no discernible reason he felt that whatever happened wasn't going to be good.

EIGHTEEN

TOMMY HEADED SOUTH on Bristol Street, passed sprawling South Coast Plaza Mall and entered the 405 Freeway north. He cruised in the slow lane just keeping pace with the thinning traffic. If anyone was following him they were lost among the thousands of cars behind him, just like he was behind thousands more.

He exited and entered the 405 twice, doubling back to the Garden Grove Freeway, to be sure nobody followed him back to the motel. Refreshed after a long, cool shower, Tommy lay on the bed, a damp towel wrapped around his waist. He stared at the television screen without seeing it while his brain tried to figure out what Salina was up to. One foot kept time to an unheard tune.

He heard three light taps, so soft he wasn't sure if they came from the door or the TV. The tap, tap, tap sounded again, more insistent. Tommy rolled off the bed, went to the window and peeked through the curtains.

He opened the door.

"Well, I'm surprised you knocked. I thought big-time cat burglars only came in through the window after midnight."

Salina slipped through the door. Her scent hung in the air, an exotic aroma, reminding him he wore only a small towel. She turned to him and with a pointed look at the towel said, "Waiting for friendly company? I can come back later if you'd like."

"How did you find me here?"

"I followed you."

"Tonight?"

"Yesterday. From the marina." In one fluid movement she sat on one of the two thinly padded chairs covered with a dark fabric flecked with orange. "I'm surprised you didn't stay with Lucy. She's really quite beautiful, in a natural kind of way."

"You make natural sound like an insult."

"Ha. It's only an insult from women who don't have what she has and can't get it no matter how much they spend on cosmetics, surgery or self-help books."

"And of course, you're not one of those women."

Salina shrugged. Her smug grin had a condescending quality that irritated Tommy. He did realize she didn't have to give much away to other women. She was smart, good-looking and apparently a talented thief; she was independent, which he admired and he had no doubt she could be charming and sophisticated, if necessary. Unfortunately, she used her good qualities to build up trust and friendship with her victims. From his pile of new clothes, he picked out boxer shorts, khaki pants and a burgundy, short sleeve cotton shirt and disappeared into the bathroom to dress.

When he emerged, Salina looked him over with cool gray eyes. She indicated the new clothes with her chin. "Lucy has good taste."

Annoyed she might think he cared for her approval, Tommy started to say something, then didn't. He dropped his old clothes in a heap on the floor. Then, not being able to think of anything else to do, got a drink of water from the bathroom. Still annoyed, he said, "Lucy has nothing to do with this. Leave her out of it. Why are you following me?"

"It should be obvious," Salina replied calmly. "I want to know who killed my brother. The police don't seem to be getting anywhere, so I thought I'd keep an eye on you. Maybe I can help." She grinned. "I must say it hasn't been very hard keeping track of you. You seem to have been in the hospital most of the time."

"I don't suppose," his voice accusing as he pronounced each word slowly, "that you had anything to do with that?"

Salina dropped her feet off the table and turned to fix Tommy with a hard stare. "You can think what you want of me, Case, I don't care, but I don't kill people...or blow up boats." Tense, their eyes locked until Salina leaned back in her chair and relaxed her fists. She closed her eyes and Tommy watched her relax part by part—neck, shoulders, arms, on down to her feet.

She opened her eyes slowly, like a cat waking from a nap, and said pleasantly, changing the subject, "You've got a lot of balls asking a hitter like that if he knew who blew up your boat."

"How the hell did you know about that?"

Nonchalant, she replied, "One hears things. The word is that when you were a cop, you'd give a guy a fair break. You may have friends you don't know about." She looked at him with grudging admiration. "It took guts to ask that question in that situation."

"Jesus. Who do you hang out with? Do you know who shot Stanis?"

Salina ignored the first question. To the second she said, "No. And I don't want to know. And neither do you. Forget that. I have a lead on who sold the explosives to your man with the cap."

"Shit, you know about that, too?" Tommy just shook his head in wonder. "So what's your lead?"

"Guy named Michael. Owns a gun shop in Anaheim." With no discernible effort, she stood up. "He's waiting."

As he grabbed a jacket and followed Salina out the door, Tommy thought to himself *Come Watson, the game's afoot.*

They took Salina's car, a nondescript, black Pontiac Trans Am. The paint was faded and it had a rusty dent in the right rear fender. In the semi-darkness of the parking lot, Tommy did notice the tires were new Goodyear Eagles, with the highest speed rating.

Salina drove. Not that she didn't trust him, she said in a way that meant she didn't, quite, but if anything went wrong she preferred to depend on herself to get away. She had a lot more to lose than he did.

As soon as she started the engine, Tommy knew this wasn't some old beater she'd picked up from a used car lot. He could feel the power through the seat of his pants, hear the low rumble of a well-tuned exhaust. He doubted if the car would pass a smog check. When Salina wheeled it onto the street the stiffness of the suspension told him it had been reworked to match the engine.

They cruised up Beach Boulevard with the windows down and the radio up, taking their time. As a teenager in Los Angeles, Tommy had cruised with his friends on similar summer nights.

The relative coolness of the soft night-time air caressing their faces had filled them with energy and the expectation of romance and adventure.

The heady, sweet scent of night-blooming jasmine drifted in the window. It only lasted a few seconds but brought the memory of a Florida vacation with warm and sultry nights, and walks on the beach with a girl whose name he didn't remember, but would like to.

Caroline was right. The Santa Ana had begun; the dry desert winds were already stirring up dust, charging the air. Tommy's heart beat a little faster and his fingers beat a staccato rhythm on the rooftop.

Salina drove with one hand. Her left elbow was propped against the window sill, her fingers resting against her cheek. The wind through the open window blew strands of blond hair against her face, forming an ever-changing mask. She flashed him an inviting and mischievous smile. Tommy's brain kicked in and asked: *What the hell is she up to?*

In a slightly run-down area of small businesses on Lincoln Avenue, they came to Mike's Guns and Ammo. The one-story stucco building stood alone. To the left was a two-story building of offices and small stores, all closed. On the right, it shared a parking lot with a foreign car repair shop whose battered metal door rumbled shut with a tinny crash as Salina parked the Trans-Am beside the gun shop.

They entered through a glass door in the middle of the store front, flanked by two barred display windows. Inside were free-standing racks of shooting accessories. The right wall was covered with books and magazines and the counter toward the back contained glass display cases filled with handguns. The middle of the back wall held diamond-shaped bins filled with green, red and yellow boxes of shotgun shells. On either side of the bins were racks of polished blue-black shotguns and rifles. At the end of the counter to the left was a half-open door with a red and white sign that read KEEP OUT. No light showed behind it.

A tall, fortyish-looking man with a long face and dark hair cut short on the sides, military style, stood by the register in the middle of the glass counter. He needed a haircut, and the beginnings of a belly were evident underneath his olive drab shirt. He waited without expression for Tommy and Salina to make their way from the door.

Salina spoke first. "Are you Michael?"

The man nodded.

"We were told you might have some information for us."

"Told by who?" Michael's face remained passive.

Salina looked at Tommy for a second with cold eyes that said *forget this name.* "Pat," she said.

Michael visibly relaxed. He set the .45 he had been holding out of sight, on the counter. "I've been waiting. What do you want to know?"

"We're looking for a guy," Tommy answered, "who might have bought some C-Four explosive about three weeks ago. Might have been wearing a long billed cap and a fake mustache."

Michael looked down at the cash register in front of him. "Well, that does sound a little familiar," he said in an uncertain way that fooled no one. "But I'm not sure."

Salina's hand slapped the counter with two fifty-dollar bills. Michael looked at the money, looked at Salina, then looked at the money again. He took hold of the bills, but Salina kept pressure on them. "How familiar does it sound?"

"Very familiar." The bills disappeared. "I sold him some stuff. Three one-pound blocks of C-Four, plus some detonators. He was a real amateur; I had to show him how to set it up, but he caught on fast, I'll give him that."

"Would you recognize him?" Tommy asked.

"Maybe. He had on that hat and a fake mustache. Like I said, real amateur night. He stood about your height," pointing to Tommy, "and had a medium build, well dressed."

"What about his voice or walk or anything peculiar or different you might have noticed about him?"

Michael thought, said, "Well, there was one thing—"

Salina stood to Tommy's left, facing away from the half-open back door. Tommy, eyes on Michael, noticed movement in the dark portion of the doorway. He stiffened. The others noticed, turning to follow Tommy's stare. Michael reached for his gun as he turned, but was way too late. His head disappeared in an explosion of blood, brains and bone.

The concussion reached Tommy's ears, packing air against his ear drums with a huge noise. In slow motion, he brushed away a sliver of bone stuck in his arm, as, also in slow motion, Michael's headless body vanished behind the blood-spattered display case. Salina whirled about and headed for the door. Tommy followed one step behind when a tug on his left arm sent him sprawling. He sucked in a quick hissing breath as his wounded arm hit the floor. Again he felt the compression. Still in slow motion, he watched Salina's feet turn back toward him. Boom! The glass in the door disintegrated in a shower of sparkling, spinning shards.

Tommy's eye followed Salina's shoes. When they stopped beside him his head kept turning until he faced the figure behind the counter. He saw the cap's long bill jut out over yellow tinted glasses and a black handlebar mustache with one drooping tip. Mouth and chin were hidden by the 30.06 bolt action rifle pointed right between Tommy's eyes. For the second time, he stared into the deep, black hole at the end of a gun and wondered if he'd see the bullet that killed him.

NINETEEN

THE TOP OF the cash register shattered and pieces flew backwards, hitting the gunman in the chest. A puff of smoke appeared at the muzzle of the rifle and Tommy felt the heat as the bullet buzzed by his ear. The heavy odor of spent gunpowder hung thick in the smoke-filled store.

Salina fired again and the man dropped out of sight behind the glass display case which crumbled slowly inward as she fired again.

"Tommy! God damn it. Get up. Get out of here."

He looked up at Salina as she tugged at him with one hand. The other hand held a black semi-automatic pistol. Her voice wrenched him back to real time. He scrambled to his feet and headed for the door. With one step to go, the rifle boomed again. He heard the solid thunk of the bullet imbed itself in the wooden door frame at the same time he heard Salina's surprised grunt. Her gun slid to a stop against his foot.

On instinct, he grabbed the gun and fired a shot at the back wall. Salina struggled to get up. He grabbed her and propelled her through the broken door. She stumbled. Tommy fired two quick shots into the store, grasped her arm and raced to the car.

Blood soaked Salina's left side.

He dumped her into the passenger seat, jumped behind the wheel and reached for the ignition key. It wasn't there.

"Where're the keys? Where're the goddamn keys?"

"Pocket," Salina managed, her voice gritty with pain.

Tommy leaned across her and retrieved the keys from her pocket. The Trans-Am started with a roar. Tires screeching, he backed up but instead of turning toward the street he headed for the alley behind the store.

"What are you doing?" Salina screamed.

"Going after him."

"No! Get out of here."

Tommy reached the alley thinking he would see taillights speeding away. But there were no lights, only a dark car parked in the shadows behind the gun shop. Beside the car stood an indistinct figure. In the reflected glow of the headlights Tommy saw a rifle being raised.

"Oh shit!"

"Punch it! Punch it!" Salina cried.

Tommy punched it. The car swung around in a cloud of tire smoke and fishtailed out of the lot. As the car hit the street the inside of the driver's door erupted inward and an outgoing hole appeared in the passenger door, inches from Salina's slumped body.

Tommy took the first right, then the first left he came to before he forced himself to slow down. They were on a quiet, tree-lined residential street. He parked along the curb in front of a single-story house with a television's flickering glow showing in the front window. He took a minute's worth of deep breaths before turning to Salina. His mouth was dry and the cloying smell of fear and fresh blood assaulted his nose. A streetlight illuminated her blood-soaked blouse. The black seat fabric glistened red.

"How bad is it?" he asked.

"Not good," she replied weakly. "It's beginning to hurt."

"You need to get to a hospital."

"No. No hospitals. Back to your place."

"Don't be stupid. You're going to bleed to death."

"Don't you be stupid," she responded angrily. She reached out a blood-drenched hand and clutched his arm. "They'll call the police." Her hand clenched at a spasm of pain. "Promise me you won't let the police get me. Please, Tommy. Promise?"

"Okay, but if you fucking die, don't blame me."

Back on Beach Boulevard he spotted a drugstore, wheeled in and parked. Under the front seat he found a roll of paper towels he used to wipe blood off his face and hands. He pulled off his shirt, tore a long strip from it and tied it around the groove the bullet had cut in his arm. Breathing noisily through a clenched jaw, he pulled on his jacket.

Inside the store be threw bandages, tape and a large bottle of hydrogen peroxide into a red plastic basket. He passed by a shelf of towels and threw some of them in, too. At the checkout counter there was one customer ahead of him, a hefty old lady with unattractive brown hair and a mustache. The gumchewing checkout girl gave Tommy a look of exasperation when the lady said, "Oh, I have to write a check."

The women fumbled in a cavernous purse for her checkbook, then her pen didn't work, then she didn't know the date, then she had to be reminded of the total, then... Tommy didn't feel well. His head swam and he could feel a trickle of blood approach his wrist. Tommy dropped two twenties in front of the startled checker. "Keep the change," he said, and with a few quick strides vanished out the door.

A few minutes later he passed a police car waiting on a side street for traffic to pass. Tommy watched it in the mirror as it turned in his direction. Just before he reached the next light the police car's flashers came on and the wail of a siren drifted in the window with the hot, dry wind.

"Shit." He turned right, and put his foot on it. The car was halfway down the long block when the flashing lights appeared. "Damn it! Damn it!" he muttered.

Tommy looked over at Salina. She was curled up against the door, hands holding her side. Her head hung down but she was conscious, he saw the whites of her eyes behind the matted hair hanging in tangles. She watched him, like a caged, wild animal whose freedom was in his hands.

"Hell. Hang on," he said.

Tommy snapped a left turn in front of oncoming traffic. By the time the police car got to the same turn, the Pontiac was long gone.

With the car parked at the bottom of the steps it only took a few seconds to carry Salina's limp body up to his second-floor room. After moving the car out of sight from the street, he put Salina's pistol in with the bandages and hurried back to the room.

He worked quickly, pressing towels against Salina's wound. Bleeding stopped for the moment, he picked up the phone and dialed a number from a list in a small notebook. After two rings he heard a click, then another ring. Tommy's heart jumped; it sounded like an answering machine, what he wanted to hear. When the receiver was lifted on the other end, however, he heard the unmistakable, live voice of Nicholas Madding, calm and casual. Damn it, Tommy almost blurted out loud. He wanted the shooter to be Madding, but there was no way Nicholas could have gone from the gun shop to his house in Anaheim Hills so quickly. He hung up.

He dialed another number. Three rings again and a woman answered. "Hello," he said. "Is Niles Von Joss there?"

"No, he's not here right now. Can I take a message?"

Tommy hesitated. He wanted to talk to Von Joss anyway, so what the hell. "This is Tommy Case. Is this Mrs. Von Joss?" She said yes. "I wanted to talk to him, but I'll try him tomorrow. Do you know when he will be back tonight?"

"Oh, Mr. Case, the detective, right?" She didn't stop for him to answer. "He's at a business meeting. I have no idea when he'll return. May I help you in some way?"

Tommy wanted to talk with her also but Salina moaned, so he said, "No, thank you. I'll call him tomorrow."

Quickly, he dialed another number. Caroline Jackson's sleepy voice answered. He hung up, glad she was there. There was one other call he had thought of making, but didn't. Steve Langdon was a crack shot. Years ago he had been on the Olympic Free Pistol shooting team and been runner-up. If Steve had been doing the shooting in that shop all three of them would have been dead in the first five seconds. Michael had been right, the guy was strictly an amateur. He called the Langdons' number anyway. Busy.

He peeled off Salina's blood-soaked clothes and threw them into the sink. With a wet towel he washed around the wound trying to be gentle but her moans told him he wasn't succeeding. Just above the hip bone, the wound was the size of a nickel going in and half a dollar bill going out. An inch or two to the right and she would have left some of her guts on the gun shop floor.

Her body jerked and she sucked in a long breath when the hydrogen peroxide bubbled into the hole. Overcoming his nausea, Tommy put the flaps of skin back in place and taped large squares of gauze over the exit hole. He did the same for the entrance hole then pressed a clean towel, as hard as he dared, against both wounds. Her skin had gone pale and cold, her breathing irregular and shallow. He put a pillow under her feet and covered her with a blanket.

"Salina. Salina," Tommy said into her ear. He wasn't sure she heard him. "You need more help than I can give you. I have to call help."

"No," she moaned. "Call Pat. Call Pat."

"Who's Pat? Salina. Who's Pat? Call where?" He shook her. "Salina, don't pass out on me now. Who the hell is Pat? Give me a number. Another name. Something." Salina whispered unintelligible words, then numbers, her voice so faint Tommy had to put his ear to her cold, pale lips. She mumbled numbers but they made no sense, held no patterns, no connections. Her rasping breath obscured her words. She kept on and Tommy listened and finally a repeat sequence emerged.

Tommy dialed the number while keeping one hand on the bloody towel. After three rings a man answered.

Tommy said in a hurry, "I'm calling for Pat. Is that you?"

The man replied slowly, suspicious. "No, I'm not Pat. Who are you?"

"My name is Tommy Case. I'm with Salina Chambers. She's been shot and needs help, now. Is Pat there or not?"

"Wait," the man said.

Tommy waited, a frown on his face as he listened to Salina's labored breathing. A woman's voice, full of authority, came through the receiver. "This is Pat. What happened?"

He told her, briefly.

The woman's voice replied, "Ten minutes."

Nine and a half minutes later he heard a knock on the door. Tommy picked up the pistol and looked through the peephole. A woman stood there—beautiful, severe, ice, even from his fisheye view. He opened the door, keeping the gun hidden. The ice cracked for an instant when she saw him. He wore no shirt and blood covered his left arm, spots of it dappled the rest of him. Dried blood in his tangled hair gave him a wild-man look that complemented his gaunt, haunted expression.

She stepped quickly into the room, followed by a young man

dressed in an expensive gray suit. His curly hair and good looks could have come off the stage of any TV soap opera. He carried a black, soft leather suitcase by a strap over his shoulder. By the time Tommy closed the door, the man had knelt down by Salina's still body. The woman stood over him, concern softening her chiseled features.

She turned to Tommy, "Thank you for calling me, Mr. Case. Are you all right?"

"More or less," he said wearily. The tiny room grew close. His head swam and he had to step back and lean against the small dresser. Pat turned back to the doctor.

Tommy said, "She saved my life. I was dead, on the floor, one second from losing my head…like Michael." A shudder swept through him. "Christ, remind me to throw up later."

Another knock sounded and Pat moved swiftly to the door. She looked through the peephole, then opened the door a few inches. After a quick exchange she turned to Tommy and said, "The keys?"

He put down the pistol, pulled the keys from his pocket and tossed them to her, the blood on them flashing red in the dim sixty-watt light. Pat went to the bedside and asked the young man, "How is she?"

Without stopping what he was doing, he replied, "She's lucky, there's minimal internal damage. But there's shock, loss of blood. Fifty-fifty chance right now. I can't do any more here, she has to be moved."

"Dangerous for her?"

"Yes, but better than staying here." The man turned and locked eyes with Pat. "It's the only way."

"Oh, Sal," Pat said quietly to herself. Then, "Get her ready. I'll get the van." She stopped in front of Tommy. "Sal is a good friend. You could have turned her in or let her die. You didn't. I owe you one. Keep that phone number to yourself, but call if you need anything."

After she left, the doctor, having wrapped Salina in a blanket he took from his bag, approached Tommy. "That the only bad one?" he asked, indicating the groove in Tommy's arm now encrusted with dried blood.

"Yeah."

The doctor looked at it closely for a few seconds. "Keep it clean, dry and covered. It'll be okay." He set an orange plastic pill bottle on the nightstand. "When it hurts, take a couple of these." Slinging his bag over his shoulder the man picked up Salina as if she were only a sleepy child. "See if the van is there, will you?"

Cautiously, Tommy downed a couple of the pills, then opened the door. A black van with its side door open waited at the bottom of the stairs. Nobody was close. He stepped back and nodded to the man. Without a word he left with his burden and within seconds the van moved out onto the street and vanished. A quick glance told Tommy the Pontiac was gone, too.

The adrenaline had worn off and now that everybody was gone he could barely keep his eyes open. He knew he should leave the room, but fatigue overtook him. He forced himself to pick up the bloody towels and clothes and put them into the wastebasket. After a quick shower to scrub off the blood, sweat and stink, he wrapped himself in a blanket, then fell into an exhausted sleep.

The Santa Ana blew up in dusty gusts, like it sometimes does, blowing in fits and starts and occasionally howling around corners and rattling windows like a hungry banshee searching for prey, but Tommy heard nothing that disturbed his dreamless sleep and so, for the moment, he felt safe.

A door slammed.

Tommy woke with a start. He lay still, feeling the pain and trying to remember where he was and why he hurt. Ten minutes later he was still sorting through the events of the night before, his muzzy mind searching for a plan of action, but the only solid idea he came up with was to get out of the room.

On the second of January, the second day after he'd ceased being a working private investigator, he'd pawned his watch for twenty-five dollars and until recently never missed it. For Tommy, to be free of time seemed an achievement worth striving for. Few people in Southern California agreed with him. A bank sign yielded the time, 6:55 a.m.

Tommy headed south on the 405, breakfast his first chore. He exited at Harbor Boulevard in Costa Mesa and headed for PrimeBurger. Their breakfast special was high in calories, cholesterol, fat, sodium and taste, but low in price and waiting time. It was one of Tommy's favorites.

Harbor Boulevard south of Westminster Avenue is lined with used car lots with signs reading "Se Habla Espanol," RV dealerships, tire stores, auto parts stores, shopping centers and apartment complexes with no air-conditioning. For $39.50 a night Tommy, using the name Springer, got a plain, threadbare, but clean room away from the street on the second floor of the Harbor Air Motel; a run-down, pink stucco building with a stone front and two bedraggled palm trees surrounded by Spanish Bayonet plants gracing the entrance. The stout Mexican woman behind the counter promised him it was a quiet room. Tommy gave her an extra twenty bucks to keep it that way. Not many gringoes stayed there more than an hour with one of the local hookers, who could usually be seen strutting their stuff day or night along the Boulevard, so she didn't fail to mention that if he wanted company, to be sure to call room service. "Our room service delivers," her cigarette ravaged voice told him, her laugh degenerating into a hacking cough that made Tommy's lungs wince.

His arm throbbed dully, making it impossible to think. He had calls to make and had finally remembered to bring his Smith & Wesson .38 revolver out from under the seat of his car. He planned to clean it, but couldn't concentrate. He took one of the pills the doctor had left him and he lay down on top of the worn yellow bedspread to wait for the pill to kick in.

Two hours later he woke up shivering. With the sun on the other side of the building the noisy air-conditioner seemed to take the temperature down to that of a morgue icebox. The throbbing was gone, replaced by a more manageable sharp pain. After a shower and change of dressing he was ready to make some calls.

Cartwell had been in but was now out. The homicide investigator wanted Tommy to leave a number; Tommy said he'd call back. He wasn't telling anyone where he was, especially over the telephone.

Dialing again, he got who he wanted.

"Fumio!" Tommy said with enthusiasm. "I'm glad somebody's where they're supposed to be."

"Ah, Samurai Inspector Dalgliesh," Fumio said. "What the hell are you talking about?"

"Never mind. Did you see Dr. Jackson?"

"Yes, I did. Man, do they have a setup over there. I thought we had a good lab here but it's dark ages compared to their equipment. They have a—"

"Fumio, please, don't start. Maybe they'll offer you a job. Of course, then you might have to do some real work for a change, so that might not be such a good idea." He heard a chuckle from the other end. "What about the chips? What about DEX Four?"

"Okay, Tommy. Okay. But one day you will let me tell you about all the neat things you are missing."

"Fumio," Tommy said seriously. "If I'm still alive when this is over you can tell me everything you want and I'll buy the drinks while you do it."

"Is that a promise?"

"That's a promise."

"I will hold you to it, Tommy. Don't be stupid and get yourself killed before then. You'll miss a lot of good stuff." Fumio took a breath. "Okay. Caroline thinks the chips are theirs. She's going to test them, but does it really matter now, if they belong to them?"

"No. Not really, I guess."

"We talked about your problem with DEX Four. It's incredible what they've done, isn't it? That guy Brian had an incredible brain. Alife, fuzzy logic, chaos theory, all the bio stuff, he was into them all. And understood them, too. I wish I had met him. I think his theory involved a combination of theories. I am not sure how chaos fits in, but—"

"Fumio! Take it easy," Tommy interrupted. "Stop drooling. Later, remember?"

Enthusiasm still in his voice Fumio apologized. "Sorry. It is just so damned exciting. Anyway, we went over your problem and came up with a few ideas. We do not quite have a handle on where to begin. It's like we're missing an essential variable in the equation that will show us which equation we are dealing with, you know?''

''Yes, I know. I feel the same way, like I'm missing something that's right in front of me.'' He stretched the phone cord and watched it bounce back. ''Or, missing a question that I should be asking.''

They hung up soon after agreeing to relay anything important through Cartwell. Tommy sat in thought for a few minutes, hoping the elusive clue or question would come to him, but it didn't. And neither did something about the events of the night before that hid in the back of his mind.

Next he called Niles Von Joss.

''Yes, Mr. Case what can I do for you?'' Von Joss said.

Tommy listened for anything in his voice that might indicate surprise at his call or disappointment he was alive. But there was nothing except his slight German accent asking a polite question in a neutral tone.

''I'd like to talk with you sometime about Brian Chambers. Maybe this afternoon?''

''I'll be busy all afternoon. Why don't you come to my house at six for dinner? Go early if you like, my wife will be there. By the way, Mr. Case, I hired a private investigator to look into Dr. Cammillo's death. I expect a preliminary report this evening.''

Tommy agreed to dinner with some misgivings. He wondered if he should take a food-taster along. In any case he was going to take his gun. If they were going to murder him in the study with a candlestick, he wanted a chance to defend himself.

TWENTY

ON THE WAY TO the Von Joss house Tommy stopped at a Circle K convenience store and made another call. The same voice answered as the night before, "Wait."

Pat came on the line. "Mr. Case, I didn't think I would hear from you so soon."

"How's Salina?"

"She's very weak and in some pain, but with a week or two in bed she'll be fine." Her voice softened a little. "Sal is strong and heals fast. And she holds a grudge. As soon as she's up she'll be looking for your man with the cap. If you want to take him alive, you should find him first. We are making inquiries, also."

Tommy knew better than to ask the identity of "we."

He said, "At this point I don't think I care who takes him, as long as he's taken." Then, "Tell her thanks for saving my life."

"I will. She says thank you, also. As do I, again."

He thought about Salina as he worked his way through traffic toward Newport Beach. By rights he should have turned her in. She was a wanted criminal and he didn't think he liked her much. He supposed a case could be made that his promise not to turn her in was made under duress. A call to Cartwell with Pat's phone number would probably get her and who knew how many other criminals.

But, he knew he wouldn't.

TOMMY STOPPED AT the Newport Boulevard-Seventeenth Street stoplight. A red Ferrari F-50 stopped in the left-turn lane next to him. He glanced over and his heart thumped. Steve Langdon occupied the car. Either too preoccupied or intentionally ignoring Tommy he intently watched the light.

"Steve," Tommy called.

Steve's head snapped around, eyes wide with surprise. For a second Tommy thought he had made a mistake. The man he saw had not shaved, needed a haircut and had a nervous, haunted look. *He's sick,* was Tommy's first thought. *Scared,* his second. *Confused,* his third. The light changed and the driver behind Steve blasted his horn. Tommy and Steve locked eyes for a few seconds, then with a screech of tires the Ferrari raced away.

The uniformed guard at the entrance gate to Linda Isle passed him through after calling the Von Joss house to make sure he was acceptable company. There were no red-vested valets this time, so he parked in front of the garage door farthest from the entrance. At the last minute he decided not to wear his gun. It would be too uncomfortable and too obvious under the lightweight jacket he wore over a dark blue Hawaiian shirt and tan trousers. He didn't think he would really be in danger here, but just in case he had left a message for Cartwell about where he was going. Besides, it wasn't polite to show up for dinner wearing a gun.

He put the unsettling sight of Steve out of his mind. It had to be a business problem that bothered his old friend, nothing more. Tommy's heart just was not ready to accept what his brain was telling him.

A pretty Mexican maid in a gray uniform answered the doorbell. Tommy stepped into a wide entrance hall. The landing was blue tile, then a step down to a thick beige carpet. The walls were covered with white wallpaper patterned with dark blue anchors and seagulls, and hung with two large prints of old time sailing ships and photographs of modern day fishing boats and fishermen standing with big smiles by big fish. A broad, carpeted stairway with a polished wood banister led upstairs.

The maid motioned him to follow her. Tommy glanced into an open doorway and had to stop. As a beginning investigator some of his fantasies involved a room like the one before him. He'd dreamed of solving cases from a wood-paneled den with bookcases to the ceiling filled with leather-bound volumes; of sitting by a stone fireplace in a leather chair and contemplating the intricacies of exquisite models of sailing ships under glass cases, the notes for the solution of his latest case lying on the solid wood, leather-topped desk.

This was that room. He stood on the threshold and breathed in the smell of old leather and polished wood. His gaze took in gleaming brass fixtures and hardwood floors covered with Turkish carpets. He reached in and ran his fingertips over the detail of the paneling by the door. For a few seconds he felt a sadness at the loss of this room from his dreams.

The maid lightly touched his arm, *"Señor?"*

Reluctantly, Tommy turned away. The rest of the house was furnished in a conservative, yet elegant old-world, old-money style with plenty of polished wood and floral prints.

Sylvia Von Joss stood to greet him when he stepped out onto the patio. With her hair combed casually back and her white shorts and pink cotton blouse, she was a model of gracious hostessing. At her invitation he told the maid, Marguerite, what he wanted to drink and sat down across from her at a round, umbrella-covered table. At the far end of the patio Anne Sexton lay face down on a padded lawn chair, the top of her bikini undone and the bottom almost nonexistent.

"Are you still investigating Brian's murder, Mr. Case?" Mrs. Von Joss asked, her manner smooth and polite as if asking if he still collected first editions. "I heard that your boat sank and a girl was in the hospital? Is she all right?"

Tommy wished his drink would arrive. "She died a few days ago."

"Oh, I'm so sorry. Were you close, or...?"

Tommy forced a smile. "A friend," he said.

But, was Jessie his friend? Why had she asked him to find out about Brian? Curiosity? Or was there some other reason? Sigmund Freud said that sometimes a cigar is just a cigar. Maybe it was just simple curiosity. But why hadn't she mentioned the money? And who was the friend George had mentioned? Was any of it connected?

The drinks arrived and he took a long cool swallow of the excellent wine. His taste in wine ran mostly to gallon jugs bought in supermarkets but he knew a fine wine when he tasted it. Tommy moved his gaze from the water to his hostess.

"She was a friend of Brian's, too. Maybe he mentioned her, Jessie Padeski."

He watched closely for any reaction, but she simply said, "I remember the name from the paper, but I'm sure he never mentioned her."

"Well, I guess he probably wouldn't. After all, they had been engaged, but he dumped her." Casually, he continued, "About seven months ago, I think. You knew him then, didn't you? That was about the time he started working for your husband."

Out on the bay, a seagull screeched.

Mrs. Von Joss' face turned stony, the steel grey eyes gone cold.

Tommy had seen enough at the gun shop to know the shooter was a man, not a woman. However, his arm hurt and despite his long nap that afternoon he felt dead tired. He hated to come on like a Dashiell Hammett character, browbeating a dame for information, but his patience was wearing thin.

Sylvia said nothing; shock turned to bewilderment on her face. Tommy continued. "Did your husband know he used you to get the job? How long after he started working there did you stop seeing him?"

A minute passed, then Sylvia's shoulders started shaking and she covered her face with her hands. Tommy waited, wishing he had a handkerchief like in the movies, then he realized she was laughing.

Sylvia, still amused, shook her head and sipped her drink. "Very good, Mr. Case." She paused for a second. "May I call you Tommy?" He nodded. "Please call me Sylvia. I didn't know about the engagement, although I'm not surprised. Brian was a user of women. After his death, Niles told me all about him. He wasn't treated very well by the women in his life, so I suppose I can understand why he was like that, but he was being used, too."

She sipped her wine and with a sandal-clad foot hooked a cushioned chair and drew it close. Relaxing, she put her feet up.

"Surely Tommy," she continued, "you don't think I'm so far gone in my dotage, even though I don't think I'm unattractive, I would really think that when a poor, incredibly handsome young man is interested in me, love is all he's after, do you? And what makes you think he came on to me first? Well, he did actually, and I'll admit at first I didn't mind having my ego, among other things, stroked. Who doesn't? We found, though, we had something in common.''

"Computers," Tommy said.

Surprised, she said, "You've been doing your homework, Tommy." He just shrugged while Sylvia spread a generous helping of Brie on a Ritz cracker. "It didn't take long to realize Brian was a natural; his intuitive grasp was amazing. He'd had very little exposure to neural networks, yet he understood the concept and the fundamentals right away. I knew that given a chance, he could be great. And that's all he really wanted, a chance to prove himself. So I talked to Niles and you know the rest." She fell silent, lips forming a sad frown. Draining her glass, she watched a half-million dollar yacht ghost past on the dying breeze. "But my God, I never thought he'd really crack AI. And with DNA? He knew next to nothing about microbiology yet he solved the information extraction problem.''

"You think he really did it?"

"Yes, I do."

"Why?"

Without a hint of humor, she said, "His brain was wired right. If artificial intelligence is going to be any sort of reality in the next twenty or thirty years, it's going to be because somebody like Brian had an intuitive insight that bypassed decades of experimentation. I just wish I knew what the hell it was.''

"He never talked to you about it?"

"He barely talked to Niles about it."

"Who does your intuition tell you killed him?"

"Anybody who knew the value of his ideas. A sufficiently ruthless person could rule the world with them in fifteen or twenty years.''

"Would that include Dr. Madding?"

"Nicholas isn't ruthless; he's insecure and doesn't like people, except maybe Niles. They've been together a long time."

"He seems to have been nice to Dr. Jackson."

"Huh. I wonder what that got him."

"Did Niles know about you and Brian?"

"Oh, he might have suspected," she answered distantly, then turned and locked eyes with him. "But we have an arrangement. As long as we're discreet, we can have our own, shall we say, private friends. I love Niles, but workaholics don't make the best of husbands; they aren't around a lot."

"So you don't think he might have taken," he shrugged a little, "desperate measures if he found out?"

Sylvia laughed. "No, Tommy, I don't. I should be angry you even suspect him, but I know he couldn't kill anybody. He might rip your guts out in a business deal, but murder, never. Besides, someone like Brian is a great asset. A good businessman does not shoot his assets."

Tommy had thought of Sylvia as a cold and humorless rich lady interested only in keeping up her social status. Nevertheless, he believed what she said—and found himself liking her.

"Do you miss working with computers?"

Sylvia flashed him a hundred-megabyte smile. "Oh, I keep my hacker chops up."

Marguerite approached with a cordless phone. Tommy watched Anne stand up and stretch, then cover herself. He focused his attention back on Sylvia as she set the phone down.

"That was Niles. One of his new clients wants to meet tonight. You see what I mean about workaholic husbands. He won't be home until late. However, he's taking the boat out tomorrow at seven and he'd like you to join him. I hope you do. He rarely has time anymore, and except for Anne, who hates fishing, the rest of us aren't keen boaters."

Tommy wasn't wild about the idea of being here at seven in the morning, but said, "Sure, I'll be here. I think the marlin are still running."

"Oh God," Anne said as she approached them. "I hope Daddy doesn't want me to take home some stinky fish. Robert loves it, but I have to use a whole can of Lysol to make the place livable again."

"I believe you met my daughter, Anne Sexton, when you were here before?" Sylvia said.

"Yes, I did. Nice to see you again."

"I hope so," she replied with a mischievous grin. "When are you going to keep your promise and go sailing with me? Like Mother said, Daddy and I are the only boaters in the family and he's a stinkpotter. How about Saturday? Say yes," she pleaded. "I'm dying to go. Just for the afternoon. Okay?"

He looked down at her beautiful sailboat tugging gently at her dock lines. He hadn't been sailing since the day Jessie came to see him. He missed it and wanted to go; maybe a day of sailing would clear his head. "Sure, I'd love to. Doesn't your husband like sailing?"

Showing mock disappointment at Tommy's question, Anne replied, "Robert and I have an agreement—he doesn't try to sail my boat and I don't try to run his bank."

Sylvia looked at Tommy with an innocent smile and a raised eyebrow—like mother, like daughter. Then she said, "You will still stay for dinner, won't you?"

The dinner with Sylvia and Anne turned out to be quite pleasant. His weariness diminished as the wine dulled the pain in his arm. Sylvia kept them laughing with tales of gourmet meals gone wrong. Anne proved to be a match for her mother with hilarious stories at the expense of the Newport Beach social elite. The talk turned at various times to sailing and boats where Anne's depth of knowledge astonished Tommy. Throughout the meal he constantly had to raise his opinion of her. It remained to be seen, though, how well she could put the theory into practice. At one point, the subject of guns came up. The two women assured him that Niles Von Joss disliked guns and explosives, had none in the house or on his boats and as far as they knew had never fired a weapon or blown anything up in his life.

Tommy hoped they were right.

Just after eight o'clock, pleasantly stuffed with roast chicken, baked potato, string beans, fresh baked bread, melt-in-your-mouth blueberry pie à la mode and fresh-brewed Jamaican Blue coffee, Tommy drove past the gatehouse and turned left onto Bayside Drive.

The last time he'd had a real old-fashioned home-cooked meal like that was the last time he saw his mother alive, three years ago. She was an old-fashioned housewife, perfectly content to stay home and cook and clean and let her husband go out and bust his ass making a living. Years ago, in the early 'eighties, she'd assured Tommy she had no regrets about not being a modern woman. He hadn't understood then, but after the funeral, with his father and a bottle of Cutty Sark, he'd looked back on her life and come to realize his mother had led a happy and contented life. Which was more than could be said for most people he knew. She taught him the ways of the kitchen and he liked to cook, but he missed real sit-down dinners at a cloth-covered table in a cozy dining room. Somehow, his dinners with Steve and Suzanne never had that quality.

TOMMY CALLED CARTWELL, who told him to "Get your ass down to my office ASA and goddamn P, and no, the department will not fix any speeding tickets, but you'd better be here in two freakin' minutes."

On his way down Harbor Boulevard Tommy had the feeling he was being followed. Traffic was light and he kept his eyes on his rearview mirror but the glare of headlights made it hard to keep track of the cars behind him, although he did think one set of lights kept a fairly constant distance. A traffic light turned yellow and he punched the throttle; the light turned red as he passed under it. With an open street ahead of him he continued accelerating to the next light and turned right. He ducked into a gas station and parked with a good view of the intersection, but he didn't recognize any cars that passed. After five minutes he continued by a different route.

The instant Tommy sat down, Cartwell leaned over his desk, eyes hard on him, and said, "What do you know about a shoot out at Mike's Guns and Ammo two nights ago? If you say 'nothing', you're a liar."

Tommy had a hard time meeting the detective's unwavering stare. "Well, I don't know anything about it," he began, "I might have heard about it on the radio...or something," he finished lamely.

Cartwell's face turned a shade redder. "Cut the bullshit, Case." He came around the desk and stood over Tommy. "Witnesses say the man who came out the front looked like he'd been wounded on the left arm—let's see yours." Tommy flinched when the other man reached to touch his arm. "Damn it, Case, what the hell are you doing? Shooting up places isn't your style. Jesus H. Christ!" Cartwell raised his eyes to the ceiling, "Did you blow that guy's head off? No bullshit."

Tommy sighed, resigned. "No, it wasn't me."

"Yeah, I know it wasn't. You were the one blasting away with the nine millimeter. It was your pal with the cap and a thirty ought six who did the head shot, wasn't it? Christ! Is this guy an amateur, or what? He sure as shit doesn't know how to shoot. They found bullets in buildings across the street for Christ's sake." Cartwell stood in the middle of his office, head tilted back, taking slow, deep breaths. Tommy stared at the floor and said nothing. If Cartwell turned him in he'd be in deep shit, no question. And even if he told the headhunters about Cartwell and the missing money, he'd still be in it up to his eyebrows. He'd be lucky to see a glass of water, let alone open ocean.

"Who was the woman with you?" Cartwell asked the room in general. "She was shot too, wasn't she?"

"She's okay. Friends are taking care of her."

"I didn't ask how she was, I asked who the hell she was." He ran short thick fingers through his thinning hair. "Her friends or yours?"

"Hers."

"Well, that's something. It was the sister, wasn't it? Salina Chambers—a wanted felon, as you know. Why didn't you take her to the hospital? Or at least call me?"

Tommy raised his eyes from the floor to meet Cartwell's stare. Voice dead level, he said, "She saved my life; I promised not to."

"Promised not to?" The sergeant repeated to the room, incredulous. He sat at his desk, clasping his hands before him. He glared at Tommy for a full minute before saying in a matter-of-fact way, "Case, if there's even a hint that I knew you were involved in that gun shop shooting, and didn't report it, we'll end up being cellmates. You do understand that, don't you?" Tommy nodded. Cartwell slumped back in his chair. "There's a lot of heat coming down on this one. Mayors and police chiefs are getting involved—stop crime in the streets and all that shit. They haven't connected it with our case yet, but they will. Michael Petterman was known to sell explosives from time to time.'' Cartwell sighed deeply and rubbed his eyes. ''Christ, what a fucking mess. They're putting a special team together for all your shit—''

''My shit? I'm the good guy, remember?''

Cartwell waved him off, ''You know what I mean. Anyway, they're going to put all this stuff together. I don't know if I'm going to be in charge, but until they figure out who that's going to be, it's still my case.'' He set his feet on the corner of his cluttered desk. ''Tell me everything, and I do mean everything, that happened last night.''

Tommy did, leaving out only Pat's number. He asked about Cammillo's death.

''He'd either been hit on the head or hit his head when he fell on his own. Died of smoke inhalation. The fire was electrical, but they aren't officially ready to call it an accident. Everything in his home office was destroyed; no missing notebooks were found. He had been drinking, though. And get this, he called his wife who's visiting the old homestead in Italy, and told her they were going to be incredibly rich.''

''Goddamn it!'' Tommy blurted. ''That son of a bitch was going to steal Brian's theory. That bastard.''

''That notebook's really worth millions, huh?'' Cartwell asked casually.

Tommy stared hard across the desk. ''You didn't happen to find that damn book with the money did you?''

The Sheriff's investigator stared back just as hard. ''I didn't find any notebook, Case.''

THE PARKING LOT was almost empty. The Mustang sat by itself, a gleaming shadow at the edge of the lot. Every scene of every television show where someone is walking through a dark, deserted parking lot before being killed ran like coming attractions through his mind.

Tommy approached the car from the rear. A yell, a laugh, the rumble of traffic, the sounds of the city at night drifted to him on the smothering, hot air. A low-rider cruised by with its stereo turned up to favor the bass lines: BOOM BOOM BA BOOM. He checked the back seat for surprise passengers. Nobody was there.

Somebody close yelled, "Hey!" Tommy turned sharply. His hand brushed the car and he dropped his keys. The man who yelled waved to another man on the other side of the street and they walked away, ignoring him. The keys lay slightly under the car. Tommy stooped to pick them up. As he reached for them an unfamiliar shape caught his attention. Kneeling, he stuck his head down to look. It took a few seconds to focus his eyes in the dark but when he did he stiffened and muttered, "Oh, shit."

Tommy caught Cartwell leaving his office.

"What are you still doing here?" Cartwell asked him. "Got something else to confess?"

Tommy, not rising to the bait, said, "Remember I told you the gun shop guy said he sold three pounds of C-Four, and the bomb guys said about one pound was used on my boat?"

"Yeah, I remember."

"Well, I know where the rest of it is."

The bomb squad had no trouble removing and defusing the bomb. Lincoln, the explosives expert, told Tommy and Cartwell that it was a simple device really, rigged to be detonated by short range remote control. He said pointedly to Tommy, "There's only one pound here, Tommy. That leaves one to go."

TWENTY-ONE

NILES VON JOSS was effusive in his greeting and his apology for missing dinner the night before. The man didn't seem at all like the hard-eyed businessman Tommy knew. He wore tan pants with a torn pocket and fish bloodstains. The collar of a blue knit shirt stuck out of a burgundy-colored sweater with a hole in the elbow; his fine snowy hair peeked out from beneath a white tennis hat. He looked like a Norman Rockwell grandpa getting ready to take his grandson fishing down by the creek.

After a quick pancake breakfast in a kitchen most restaurants would envy, they walked down to the boat. The customized sixty-five foot Bertram was a work of art, designed and built for one purpose only: to catch fish. Every piece of burnished stainless steel, varnished teak and polished fiberglass was there to enhance the efficient catching of fish. In the center of the cockpit stood a fishing chair that looked like it needed a license to sit in. The interior displayed its owner's hand in the design: practical, with touches of tradition. A beautifully crafted teak navigation station housed state-of-the-art electronics. Deeply varnished mahogany racks exhibited gleaming high-tech fishing equipment. Blue, gray and burgundy fabrics were set off by stainless steel and hand-carved wood.

A carved teak panel caught Tommy's eye. On closer inspection he saw it was a cleverly concealed door. The carving depicted a man and a bear fishing for salmon on opposite sides of a stream that led to the ocean where whales played. Beside the man a rifle leaned against a tree.

"Exquisite, isn't it?" Von Joss said behind him. "I had it carved by an Aleut in Alaska."

"It's a door," Tommy said, sure he knew what was inside.

"Most people don't notice."

Von Joss pressed two of the boulders in the scene and the door clicked open. The green felt interior contained a well-oiled twelve-gauge pump shotgun, a 30.06 rifle and a .357 Magnum revolver.

"Don't tell my wife about these. She hates guns."

"Do you use them often?"

"Three years and they've never been fired," was the proud reply.

On the flying bridge, one of three steering stations, Niles introduced the skipper, John Piro. Piro appeared to be in his early thirties, but already had the squinty eyes, crows-feet and deeply bronzed skin of the veteran sailor. He wore wraparound dark sunglasses, a long billed cap and didn't smile. Tommy's impression was of absolute competence, with a hint of the sinister. The cap he wore, faded red, not black, was like the one worn by the shooter at Mike's Guns two nights before. Tommy reminded himself that Niles was still a murder suspect and who was to say that John Piro didn't help in the dirty work? He took some comfort in the fact that he'd remembered to bring his revolver in his sea bag.

The twin Caterpillar V-12 engines rumbled to life; the powerful vibration set his heart racing. The odor of diesel exhaust mingling with the smell of seawater in the quiet morning air made his nose twitch. Tommy and Niles prepared the gear and bait while Piro guided the boat down the bay toward the ocean.

"Sylvia said you were asking about Nicholas last night," Niles said. "Is he a suspect in Brian's murder?"

"Yes." They were silent for a minute, then Tommy said, "You don't seem very surprised about that."

Niles's smile held no humor. "I've known Nicholas for over twenty years but I am not sure what he is capable of."

"What do you mean?"

Von Joss was clearly troubled on the subject of Nicholas.

"You're not talking about his engineering ability, are you?" Von Joss shook his big square head. "His temper?" The man's frown deepened. "What then?"

With an effort Von Joss said, "His loyalty."

"What makes you think he's not loyal to Electrobotics?"

The intensity of the hurt and anger in his glare pushed Tommy a step back. "Not to the company, Mr. Case, to me."

"Isn't that the same thing?"

For an answer the other man said, "Nicholas has worked for me for twenty years. Before that he was with JPL, the Jet Propulsion Laboratory in Pasadena, in charge of one of their projects." He talked slowly, a faraway look on his face. "I forget the exact name but it had to do with robots in space. He lost his temper and struck a junior scientist for a silly, minor mistake. Nicholas had to resign. I was a small subcontractor with big ideas but no particular talent for designing them, so I took him on as long as he promised to never strike anyone again. To my knowledge he never has." He clipped a wire leader and coiled it carefully. "Nobody else would have kept him, despite his brilliance. I made him wealthy and respected. He is not an easy person to work with. He owes me everything he has. I expect his loyalty. As he has every right to expect mine. I owe him much of my success."

"What makes you think he's been disloyal?"

"We used to talk about projects, business gossip, now we only speak when necessary, phone calls are interrupted when I come into the room, information withheld. Little things. A gut feeling that things have changed."

Tommy guessed, "This all started when Brian came to work for you."

"Soon after. Nicholas did not want him."

"Why?"

"I have many brilliant people working for me. All have at least a Masters Degree, many have Doctorates. Nicholas did not want to be a 'nursemaid to an untrained boy.'"

"And when Brian proved to be better in some areas like neural nets and artificial intelligence?"

"Nicholas takes his job as Chief of Research very seriously, and personally," Von Joss said, pulling a knot tight with a jerk.

Tommy started to reply but the skipper yelled down from the flying bridge to hang on. They were past the end of the jetty and the five-mile-an-hour speed limit. The exhausts roared and the big boat leapt toward open water.

An hour and a half later the boat returned to trolling speed after Tommy landed a large wahoo, a fish similar to a barracuda, and fine eating. Niles had a marlin strike, but hadn't hooked up. Once the first lines were out Niles talked freely about his success and the contributions Nicholas Madding made to it.

"The buildings you're in," Tommy asked. "Did you build them?"

"Yes, I did." He laughed quietly as he remembered. "Nicholas insisted he be allowed to design the laboratories. He drove the architects crazy, but it ended well. Everybody is happy."

Tommy sat up quickly as an idea occurred to him. "Mr. Von Joss," he said carefully. "Who designed the security system for the lab?" Even as he asked he knew the answer.

"Nicholas. Why do you ask?"

"He designed the whole thing? Including the program that records who goes in or out?"

"Yes. I still do not understand... Ah, yes, the problem that Brian wasn't there when you think he was killed."

Excitement growing, Tommy said to himself, "That's it. Son of a bitch, that's it. The question we're missing." He turned to Von Joss, who watched him with a quizzical expression. "So, he would have all the access codes, if that's what they're called, to the system?"

"Yes, of course."

"Who else has those codes?"

Cautiously Niles replied, "I do. Plus I have a special code of my own that locks anybody else out of the system, even Nicholas."

Tommy couldn't sit still; he paced across the wide fishing cockpit. "Do you really think your code could keep him out if he wanted to get in? And do you know, absolutely, that you have the only codes?"

Von Joss didn't answer. He watched the wake; checked the lines with his eyes; swiveled his head to watch a seagull fly by. The sun broke out. He winced at the brightness and reached for his sunglasses.

Tommy continued to pace.

After some minutes John Piro called down. "Mr. Von Joss, get ready. Fish coming up."

The older man pulled his rod from the holder and settled into the fishing chair. Tommy stood by his rod, ready to reel in if Niles hooked up. They waited, eyes on a dark shadow following the bait. The bait vanished with a splash and the outrigger clip released the line with a snap.

"Shark, sir," Piro called out. "Looks like a big Mako. Do you want to take it?" Von Joss raised one hand to signal assent, then set the hook.

It took fifteen minutes to bring the shark up to the boat. The Mako put up a good fight. It was a big one, probably seven feet and over two hundred pounds. They were not planning to land the fish, although it would bring a good price at the fish market. Once it came up to the boat they'd cut it loose.

Tommy opened the fish door in the transom and made ready to step out onto a teak platform extending two feet out from the stern a few inches above the water. He wore leather gloves and carried a pair of wire cutters.

When the shark drew near, he stepped out onto the platform, holding tight to the stainless rail running along the transom. He watched the fish with fascination; its mouth opened wide, baring rows of pure white, razor sharp teeth; its small, black eye regarded him with undisguised malevolence. The Mako stayed quiet until Tommy raised his hand to cut the wire leader, then the shark thrashed wildly, trying to get to its perceived enemy. It shot past Tommy, pulling the wire leader against him, knocking Tommy off balance. He lost his grip on the rail and fell backwards, landing hard on his left side. He gasped as the pain from the bullet wound sent sparks out his eyes. One arm hung over the edge of the platform. The wire cutters sank out of sight into the clear blue water. Through the pain and shock he heard a voice cry out, "Pull in your arm. Pull in your arm."

Dazed, he tried to remember why he should move. A splash of cold salt water slapped him in the face, jolting him back to awareness. As he pulled his arm up, huge teeth-filled jaws erupted from the water and snapped shut inches from his face. Hands grabbed him, pulled him toward the transom door, but the boat lurched and the hands fell away. Tommy heard a grunt of surprise and a splash, then saw Von Joss's tan pant legs disappearing into the water.

Quickly, he rolled to his knees and reached to help the older man. One leg was still in the water, with Tommy's hand under it, when the shark's head burst out of the water. Its jaws clamped shut. Niles roared; blood swirled in the water; the Mako's teeth dripped red. The shark began to slide back into the water, dragging Von Joss with it. Tommy leaned forward and with the heel of his gloved hand smacked the shark's pointed nose. The jaws opened and sank away.

Piro grabbed his boss under the arms and pulled him into the cockpit. Tommy followed on his hands and knees. He heard the snap when John cut the shark loose; smelled the fresh blood that welled from Niles' ravaged leg.

Once again Tommy found himself covered with blood while tending a seriously injured person. *Damn,* he thought, *if this sort of thing is going to continue, I really need to take a first aid course.* He did what he could to stop the bleeding and prevent shock while the big sportfisher flew back to Newport at top speed.

The boat blasted into the jetty entrance, ignoring the speed limit signs and the curses from other boats, and didn't slow until it approached the Coast Guard docks. Within minutes of docking, Niles was on his way to the hospital. After giving statements to the Harbor Patrol and the Coast Guard and getting an extremely stern warning about entering the harbor at speed, emergency or not, John Piro and Tommy headed the Bertram toward the Von Joss house.

They sat on the flybridge, sipping beer, trying to calm frayed nerves as the sportfisher cruised sedately up the bay.

"What a stupid thing to do," Tommy said. "Go out on that platform with a damn mad Mako just waiting to take a bite."

"Yes, it was," Piro said.

"I didn't hear you saying 'don't do it. Don't do it.'"

"You were Mr. Von Joss' guest, if you wanted to do something stupid, that was up to you."

"Shit," Tommy said in a light manner. He wasn't up for an

argument with the man. "You're the skipper. You're supposed to keep guests from doing stupid things. What if Mr. Von Joss had gone out there?"

A slight smile creeped over Piro's face. "That would be different, I suppose."

Tommy sipped his beer. "How long have you worked for Mr. Von Joss?"

"Couple of years."

"Did you ever take out a Dr. Madding?"

"No. I met him once. Didn't seem the boat type."

"How about Brian Chambers?"

John thought, then nodded. "Once." He sipped his beer. "You're investigating his murder, aren't you?"

"Yeah."

"We almost had a murder right here, that day."

Tommy's eyebrows rose up. "Oh? With Brian as murderer or murderee?"

"Murderee. He and another guest were alone in the cockpit and the other guy was mad as hell about something."

"Do you remember the other guy?"

"Sure, Mr. Langdon. Usually he's pretty mellow but, man, he was pissed that time."

Not bothering to hide his interest, Tommy asked, "You know what they were arguing about?"

"Couldn't hear. Mr. Langdon was doing the arguing, though. Mr. Chambers seemed like he was trying to reassure him about something."

"What happened?"

"Mr. Langdon stomped off and went inside, but even I could tell he really wanted to reach out and strangle Mr. Chambers." Steve stood up. "Get the starboard lines ready, will you? We're here."

Tommy sat at the desk in the wonderful, paneled room. He called Caroline but she was unavailable, so he asked for Leon. Quickly, he related what happened to Niles and what he had learned about the security system.

"Leon, tell Caroline to be careful. If Madding is the man, she's in danger if he suspects she's poking around his security system. I'm going to call Cartwell and see if he can put a watch on her.''

"I'll keep an eye on her," Leon said, then added. "You be careful, too.''

Next, Tommy called Cartwell. After explaining about Niles and the security system he said, "Can't you pick up Madding and hold him? If he knows you're on to him maybe he'll confess. He might tell you how he did it just to show how smart he is. What about searching his place?''

"Case!" Cartwell interrupted. "Take it easy. Relax. Don't go over the edge on me." Tommy could hear the investigator let out a deep breath. He took several himself. Cartwell said, "Look, I agree he's the most likely suspect, but we still have no hard proof and no witnesses." He hesitated a moment. "What about your friend from the gun shop? She must have seen him.''

"I haven't talked to her since then, she's been sick you know, but I plan to.''

"She's the only chance for an ID we have at the moment. We still don't know for sure the robot was the murder weapon, or that Chambers died in the lab, although, I will admit, that if you can come up with a reasonable method for using the robot or prove Chambers was there, then we would have something solid to work with. The fact is Tommy, we really have nothing but a big pile of paperwork. Designing the security system is hardly proof of murder. We have no witnesses, motive, opportunity or murder weapon. We have zip. And you know it.''

"Yeah, I know it, damn it." His fist hit the desk top. "It's just so damn frustrating. What about your new team?''

"I've got two extra men checking out leads right now, and I've been ordered to assemble all the information we have in an orderly manner and bring everybody up to speed.''

"And how long will that take?''

"Tomorrow at the earliest. Unless you want to help.''

"No. Not really.''

"Hey, I'm sorry. If I get something solid, I'll move on it, but until then we'll have to plod along as best we can. In the meantime, talk to your friend. If she has something good we might be able to work something out.''

"We'll see," Tommy said, unenthusiastically. "Oh, I almost forgot, Caroline Jackson. Can you keep a watch on her? If he finds out she's helping on this she could be in real danger."

"Jesus, Case. What do you want? Twenty-four hour body-guards? I'll see what I can do, but don't count on much."

Tommy leaned back in the old leather chair, savoring its comfort and aroma. Again he told himself he could have had a room like this, but in the long run he knew it wouldn't have been worth it.

He also knew he was hungry.

He always meant to have something different at the Beach-comber but when he ordered it always came out Hampshire Pie. He was just finishing when Lucy appeared beside him.

"Tommy, I'm glad I saw you stuffing your face."

Her laugh was uninhibited and gay, the kind you hear coming from parties to which you weren't invited, but Tommy knew her well and thought it a bit forced.

"I just saw Suzanne Langdon. She and Steve really want to talk to you."

The smile faded from his face. "Oh?"

"Come on, Tommy. They're not mad at you; well, they are a little, but they understand what was happening. Steve especially has been anxious to find you. Damn, Tommy, he's your best friend."

Tommy had no comment. But he did begin to question if it really was Steve he'd seen on his way to the Von Joss house.

"They're going to have dinner at Cano's tonight. They'll be at my boat at ten o'clock. I told them you'll be there. You don't want to lose your second best friend, do you?"

He looked at her, then averted his gaze before she drew him into her bottomless, brown eyes. "I'll be there."

"There's something else," Lucy said quietly. "I got another call today. You're to 'stop investigating or else.'"

"Christ, Lucy, will you go away to someplace safe?"

"I told him to go screw himself."

"Shit, Lucy, this guy is serious."

Lucy clenched her teeth and said, "Nobody is going to run

me off, Tommy. I've been terrorized and brutalized by the best. I can take care of myself. And if I can't, nobody will miss me."

Shocked, Tommy said, "Lucy, what the hell are you talking about? I'll miss you. What made you say that?"

She waved him off. "Forget it. Just don't let me down. Be there at ten. I don't want to be alone with them."

She slid out of the booth and stalked out of the restaurant, leaving Tommy to stare open-mouthed after her.

TWENTY-TWO

TOMMY SWALLOWED a pill to stop the throbbing in his arm. He lay with his eyes closed and listened to the voice on the telephone say, "Wait."

He waited.

"I have to talk with Salina," he said when Pat came on the line. "She's the only one who's had a good look at the guy and survived."

Pat was silent for a moment. "You'll come alone?"

"Yes."

"Be at the donut shop, Seventeenth and Flower, at six."

Tommy agreed but Pat had already hung up. The pill kicked in and he dozed off.

At two-fifteen he drove past Mike's Guns and Ammo heading for Nicholas Madding's house in Anaheim Hills, a well-to-do area along the Peralta Hills in the northeast corner of Orange County. The top ridge, the part that so far had escaped the landscaper's shovel, was burned golden brown by the summer sun. Along the winding streets the lawns were green and some of the slopes were dotted with yellow and orange wildflowers.

He found Madding's house at the corner of Zircon and Coral. Zircon Drive was a short street off Coral Avenue that ended in a cul-de-sac that accessed eleven houses. Madding's house was similar in design to the others, but bigger. It sat on the north corner, commanding views of the valley below and west along the hills. Tommy saw that the garage faced away from the other houses, making its use undetectable from casual observation.

Tommy spent a couple of hours driving between the house and the shop, timing different routes. With the right traffic and some luck Madding might have been able to return home before Tommy called him the night he and Salina had been shot in the gun shop.

At six o'clock the same black van that whisked Salina away stopped next to him in the Donut Hut parking lot. A large black man growled at him, "Follow us."

The van took a roundabout route through a unique section of Santa Ana featuring homes of totally diverse architecture: mini-plantation mansions with columned fronts, to houses with steep, rounded, flowing roofs that curled under at the bottom edge, straight from a European fairytale. The van passed through an electrically operated wrought iron gate set into a high, vine-covered brick wall. Inside the compound stood a two-story brick house, with dark green shutters and an elaborate entrance way. Pat waited by the front door. She greeted him with a smile, but when he stepped inside she pointed behind him and said, "I hope you don't mind?"

Tommy turned to face a short, wiry, competent looking young man wearing jeans and a well-filled black T-shirt. The man motioned with his hands and Tommy raised his arms while being expertly frisked.

When he turned back to Pat, she said, "Sorry about that. I trust you, but they don't." She pointed to the back of the hallway where the black man and a thin older man watched him with untrusting eyes. Tommy smiled and waved at the men as he followed Pat up the stairs. He didn't think he wanted any of these men as enemies.

Salina lay in a brightly lit corner room. The white wallpaper had a pattern of stylized wheat stalks, the furniture looked like real antiques. An IV stand and rolling bed table were tucked into a corner. Salina looked lost in the big bed with polished-wood head- and foot-boards. Bright eyes stared out of her pale face as they followed Tommy to the side of the bed.

"Pat tells me you're going to make it. How do you feel?"

"Ask her." Salina indicated Pat with her chin. "She keeps me so drugged I can't feel a thing."

"If I didn't, she'd be running around trying to find the son of a bitch who shot her," Pat said, obviously used to her patient's complaints. "If she'd just relax and rest she'd be up a lot sooner."

"Maybe Tommy came here to tell me who I'm going to be after," Salina said.

Tommy sat on the foot of the bed. "Afraid not. You must have got a look at him. Do you think you could identify him?"

Salina closed her eyes. "Yes, no, oh, I don't know." Her eyes fluttered open. "I could identify the fake mustache and the cap and the yellow glasses, but the man...?"

"What color was the cap?" Tommy asked.

"Black, dark blue maybe. Why?"

"Just checking. And the glasses?"

"Yellow. Shooters glasses. Didn't you see him?"

"All I saw was the cap, glasses, mustache and a big gun pointed right between my eyes." Their eyes met. "If you hadn't had your pistol that would've been the last thing I saw. Thanks."

Salina glanced at Pat, then stared at her feet under the thin blanket. "Well, I vaguely remember you getting me out and Pat says you kept me alive and out of jail. So I'm grateful, too."

"I guess we're even then?"

"Yeah, I guess so."

After an uncomfortable silence, Tommy said, "I have some pictures I want you to look at." He took several photographs from his shirt pocket and handed them to her. "Do any of these people look familiar?"

Salina struggled to sit up. Pat moved to help but was waved away. She exchanged looks with Tommy and fluffed up a pillow anyway. Salina studied each photograph; Pat looked over her shoulder; Tommy waited.

She studied each one twice. "Sorry."

Tommy pointed to a picture of Nicholas Madding and Niles Von Joss he borrowed from Sylvia the night before. "Are you sure about both of these two?"

Salina studied the photo again but still shook her head no, then she pointed to Nicholas. "This guy's too tall, and the shooter's hair was dark and both of them are too old. The guy we want is a little younger. And this guy's chin is all wrong," she said, pointing to Madding again. "It's too sharp, too square. Our man's chin is rounder."

He looked at Madding's picture and tried to make it conform

to what Salina said, but it just would not change. He felt Nicholas Madding slipping away from him.

"Here." Salina slowly reached for a newspaper on the table beside her bed. Tommy recognized the Accent section of the *Register,* where the comics were. She folded the paper and pointed to a picture on the society page.

"I saw this and thought it was him."

Tommy recognized them, of course. He read the caption to make sure: "Steve and Suzanne Langdon enjoy the dinner benefit for Safe House, one of their favorite charities." He put his finger on Steve's frilly shirt front and said, "Are you saying this is the gun shop shooter?"

"No, only that it could be. The others couldn't." Tommy stared at the photograph. Salina asked, "Do you know him?"

"Yes," Tommy said uncertainly, wondering if he really did. "But he couldn't have killed Brian, he was out of town."

"You don't seem too sure."

Tommy stared at the Langdons' smiling faces. Distracted, he replied, "Yeah, I'm sure. He was in Boston at the time."

"You still don't seem too sure," Pat said.

"Boston?" Salina asked. "That's where Brian got himself kicked out of school by getting himself hooked up with some bitch in a whorehouse." Salina rolled her head side to side in disgust at what her brother had done. "So stupid."

"Do you know for a fact the girl was a hooker?"

"Yes. Brian told me."

"Hmm." An idea occurred to him but it would take some checking of dates and ages. Nicholas Madding might be almost off the hook, but the Von Joss family was not.

He was not good company at dinner. Even two glasses of excellent wine didn't break through his black mood. He didn't want to be thinking about Steve Langdon, but his mind wouldn't stop. As much as he wanted Nicholas to be guilty, he wanted Steve to be innocent. His conscious mind tried to convince itself that the idea of Steve as a killer was ridiculous, while his subconscious thought different. Tommy knew one thing: he would make damn sure Cartwell scrutinized Steve's alibi and subsequent movements very closely.

Pat's voice broke into his thoughts. "How well do you know this Steve Langdon?"

"His housekeeper knows what I like to eat," Tommy said, pushing the food around on his plate.

"Want to talk about it?"

"No."

Pat sighed. "Eat your steak, it's quite good. I cooked it myself."

Tommy took a bite. It was filet mignon, and excellent; nevertheless, he couldn't enjoy it.

They were seated in a small dining alcove off the kitchen. A perfectly manicured yard surrounded by Italian Cypress and lit by hidden lights was visible through the bay window. Pat rested her elbows on the arms of her chair and held her wine glass to her severe lips. She watched Tommy stare at his plate.

"When you were a cop we had something in common."

With little interest he said, "What?"

"We had to trust our 'associates' completely, and if for some reason we began to doubt that trust, we had to be ruthless in determining whether that particular person still deserved to be trusted, because if he didn't, it might cost you your life." She tilted her glass again, their eyes not breaking contact. "And even though we are both 'retired,' I think it's still valid advice to apply to friends as well. Don't you agree?"

Tommy looked deep into her ice lady eyes and reluctantly nodded agreement.

AT 9:50 THAT NIGHT, Tommy took a glass of wine from Lucy. She appeared relieved he was there. Tommy was nervous. He wore his gun in a shoulder holster and didn't care who saw it. Lucy refused to talk about her strange behavior that afternoon and didn't listen to his reasons why she should go some place safe.

At ten they sat quietly, not speaking. At one minute after ten the background noise of wind, water and traffic stopped in one of those coincidental silences that sometimes occur at parties or in cities. The quiet came so suddenly Tommy jumped. Their eyes locked. Lucy made to speak, but Tommy held up his hand, commanding silence. He listened. And heard. His heart pounded at the faint familiar sound. In the second he recognized that annoying high whine he saw again his boat in flames and Jessie's limp body.

He pulled his gun and clamored up through the companionway.

"Lucy, get out!"

From the cockpit he searched the rippling dark water for a familiar shape. Lucy appeared beside him, pistol glistening in her hands.

"What is it?"

A small point of darkness rounded the stern of a larger boat.

"There. Another goddamn boat bomb."

He fired at it. Lucy saw it and fired too, the boom of her forty-five drowning out the crack of his thirty-eight. They kept shooting. A bullet hit, leaving the little boat drifting in the middle of the channel. The explosives strapped on top were under water when they exploded. The blast knocked the two of them off their feet. Water rained down, soaking them.

Hours later, excitement over, Tommy and Lucy stood alone at the end of the dock.

"Where were Steve and Suzanne?" Tommy wanted to know.

"I saw Steve in the crowd. He didn't look very happy."

"Suzanne?"

Lucy didn't answer. Tommy saw she was trembling and biting her lip. He took hold of her shoulders.

"Lucy, are you okay?" he asked. "Did something happen between you and Suzanne?" She tried to turn away, but he didn't let her. "You two are my best friends. If something's going on I want to know about it."

Not looking at him, voice tight, Lucy said, "I tried to get you guys together because I thought it would help you. It didn't work out, so now it's your problem. I don't want anything more to do with that condescending bitch. Okay?"

"Condescending bitch? Suzanne? What the hell happened this morning?"

"What do you care? I'm just a burned-out whore you screw every once in a while." She pressed her fists against his chest. "Why did you tell her about me, Tommy?"

"Lucy, listen to me. I didn't tell Suzanne, or anybody else, about your past—hell, I don't know enough to tell anybody. Did she say specifically she knew?"

A tear ran down her cheek. Tommy wiped it away.

"No," she admitted. "But she knew. And she knew how to push my buttons, giving me all that upper class high society crap. Making like it was my duty to do what she wanted." She took a deep breath and rested her head on his chest. "It got to me. It just got to me."

Puzzled, he said, "That doesn't sound like Suzanne at all. She's always been pretty down-to-earth. When I first met her she was sleeping with anybody who'd show her a good time; the only contact she had with the upper class was in the bedroom. She would hardly be able to look down on anybody else." He held her tight. "I don't understand, Lucy. Nobody seems to be what they seem. I don't like it. I don't like it at all."

TWENTY-THREE

THE NEXT MORNING, after he dropped Lucy back at her boat, Tommy drove north on 405. A call to Jessie's parents that morning had elicited an invitation to a service being held for Jessie at St. Michael's Church in Pasadena. He hadn't been sure how the Padeskis would take his request to talk to them so he was pleasantly surprised at Mrs. Padeski's cordial greeting and her apology for their behavior at their last meeting. She sounded sincere when she invited him over to their house after the service.

He arrived at the stone church, which was surrounded by bright flower beds and a freshly cut lawn. The church hosted an Episcopalian Congregation. Tommy's parents were Episcopalian, but he'd stopped attending after the death of his sister from a drug overdose. The problem of a benevolent God letting horrible things happen to good people would have to be solved before he believed again.

After a short service, Tommy followed the Padeskis, and Jessie's ashes, to their home. Attendance had been light, mostly supportive friends of the senior Padeskis and a few old acquaintances of Jessie's youth. There weren't many tears shed. He had a chance to talk with several of them and hadn't had any more luck than Cartwell. None of them had seen or heard from Jessie for years.

TOMMY, FOR NO real reason he could think of, had expected a modest house with perhaps a small, slightly unkempt yard on a slightly rundown street. Jumping to incorrect conclusions seemed to happen with increasing frequency these days, he noticed. He found himself in an attractive middle-class neighborhood, parked in front of a white, two-story clapboard house that might have been finished the day before. Two big oak trees shaded the house, the area around the trees as well as the borders around the lawn were a riot of well-maintained color. The interior looked as neat and clean as the yard. It had a homey, old-fashioned feel to it, solid, welcoming, like the house in Pennsylvania he'd grown up in.

Mr. Padeski motioned with a crooked finger for Tommy to sit in a heavy, upholstered armchair.

"Would you like to have a beer with us, Mr. Case?" he asked, his eastern European accent easily understandable. "Emma and I don't drink so much anymore, and certainly not this early, but I think we deserve one today."

He shrugged his coat off thick shoulders and dropped with a sigh into a worn leather recliner, the coat ending up sprawled over the back of a couch opposite Tommy. The older man looked at the coat, then turned close-set brown eyes on his guest.

"I was a machinist for forty-one years," he announced. "Do you know what a machinist must be, above all else?" Tommy shook his head. "Precise. Precise down to ten thousandth of an inch sometimes. And clean. And neat. Precise, clean, neat," he repeated. "Forty-one years I was precise, clean and neat." He turned a solid grin on Tommy. "I retired one year ago, Mr. Case, and now I can be the slob I always wanted to be."

"Well, he's trying," Mrs. Padeski said handing each man a Carlsburg Beer and a glass. "But forty years of neat and clean is a hard habit to break."

Emma Padeski wore her age well. Dark hair streaked with gray framed a round face that came alive when she smiled. It was obvious where Jessie's looks came from and looking at her father, where her large feet and hands came from.

The elder man drank off half his glass. "Mr. Case—"

"Please, call me Tommy."

"All right, Tommy." He pointed a thumb at himself. "Call me Henry." He hesitated a moment before continuing. "As you may have figured out by now we were not close to Jessie."

"How is the investigation going?" Emma asked.

"Frankly, not very good. I have one good suspect, though now I'm not so sure. Did you know George Stanis was killed?"

"Yes. The Newport Police called us, but we had never heard of him 'til Jessie's accident."

"But we never heard precisely—there's that word again—what happened," Henry said.

Tommy gave a brief account of his short visit to Wash's house. "It's the mysterious friend we'd like to find. At first I thought Jessie asked this friend to kill Brian—" He stopped when he realized what he was saying.

Emma, pain evident in her voice, said, "It's all right. We've realized for quite some time that our Jessie was not a nice person." Her eyes met Henry's. "We'd like to know the truth."

Tommy nodded once and continued. "I thought this friend was asked to kill Brian for the fifty-thousand dollar insurance money. But Stanis knew nothing about that and said there was two hundred thousand dollars missing. So, three questions: where did the two hundred grand come from? Was the insurance a coincidence that has nothing to do with anything? And of course, who the hell was the friend? Is the friend responsible for everything or just the money? Are we dealing with one, two or three people? Which events are connected to which?" Tommy threw his hands in the air. "I know that's more than three, but questions keep coming up with no answers."

Emma said, "The police from Newport Beach and the sheriff's department asked us about her friends, too. We told them we haven't known her friends since she graduated from high school."

"Have you thought of anybody since then? Somebody from a company called Electrobotics? Anybody she's mentioned on the phone or when she visited?"

"We didn't talk," Emma said. "She did insist on coming for dinner on Christmas; why, I don't know. It was usually an uncomfortable time and a relief when it was over. She never talked about her friends." She fell quiet for a moment, a sad smile wrinkling her pale features. "She'd always remember Henry's birthday, though. She'd call him."

"But not your birthday?" Tommy asked.

"No," she replied, her voice small.

Tommy watched Henry's scarred hand squeeze his wife's pale slim one. "She never mentioned a name that you can recall?" he asked Henry.

"No. Never." He looked at something on the wall behind Tommy, and said, "She had two lives, you know. The nice polite one she lived around us, and you apparently, and another life that if I was one of those ridiculous bible thumpers, I'd call evil." The hand not holding his wife's turned into a fist. His body stiff, he leaned toward Tommy. "You have to understand: she was not a good person. She did not give a damn about anybody."

"Henry," Emma said softly, and slowly he relaxed. She collected the empty bottles and went into the kitchen.

Tommy broke the silence by asking, "Was Jessie involved in drugs?"

Henry shook his head slightly. "I don't think so, but you can never tell. On her visits she always seemed okay. Sex, I think was her interest."

"Sex? You mean—"

"I mean she liked it and used it. For money, power, fun? I don't know."

"You don't know what?" Emma asked as she entered the room with three full bottles.

Henry smiled affectionately at his wife. "I don't know how I could have managed without another beer, and you."

"The beer I believe," she answered, returning his smile.

While they filled their glasses, Tommy tried to assimilate what he had learned about Jessie. Some detective he was. His own secretary living a double life and he never suspected. Of course, with the usual 20/20 hindsight he could see how she offered him the chance to enter her other life, but he'd been so hung-up on his divorce she finally shut the door on him and excluded him from what was probably a far more interesting life than the one she showed him. Judging from the one night they spent together, who could say if that had been to his advantage or not?

"Tommy?" Emma said, breaking into his thoughts.

"What? Oh. Sorry. I was just trying to see the other Jessie in the one I knew."

Emma smiled sympathetically. "I understand. She could be so nice when she wanted to be." She sipped from her glass and said, "I think I do remember her mentioning a man once. Maybe three years ago, on the telephone. We were arranging for her

Christmas visit and, I think, she said she had met a man. I got the impression he was a client of yours. She said he treated her just like a daddy, and then she giggled. Lord, I hadn't heard that laugh since she was a little girl.''

Emma stared at a spot on the floor. Henry watched the same spot, a stoic frown on his heavy features.

Tommy waited a minute before asking, ''Are you sure she didn't mention any names, and that he was a client?''

''No. No names and it was just an impression I had that he was a client. I don't remember why.''

''Does the name Dr. Nicholas Madding sound familiar?''

Emma and Henry looked at each other, eyebrows raised. ''Dr. Nicholas Madding?'' they said together. Henry continued, ''Nicholas Madding, tall thin guy used to work for JPL, then Von Joss Machining and Engineering? Brilliant, but hard as hell to get along with?''

''Has to be the same guy. How do you know him?''

''I worked for Von Joss M and E when it was just starting.''

''Then you know Niles Von Joss?''

''Of course. I worked for him when he had only three employees. He didn't know anything about machining, but he had big ideas and knew how to get other people to pay for them. Is he involved in this?''

Tommy explained how Von Joss fit into what was happening, including the shark attack, about which he slightly down-played his own role.

''How awful,'' Emma said.

''How appropriate,'' Henry said. ''A shark bit by a shark.''

''Henry,'' Emma admonished.

''Did Jessie know Von Joss or Madding?'' Tommy asked, trying to contain his excitement. Could this be the connection he was looking for?

''She met Niles a few times,'' Emma replied, ''but he wasn't interested in kids. But she and Nicholas became friends, if you can believe it. She was about fifteen and for some reason they got along. Maybe because neither of them got along with anybody else?''

"When Nicholas moved to Orange County, did she stay in touch with him?"

"We have no idea," Henry said. "Electrobotics! Niles changed the name when he moved, I'd forgotten that."

"Why didn't you go with him?"

"We're too old to move," Emma said. The smiles she and Henry wore didn't make them look too old to do anything. "We love this house and our friends are here. We have no plans to move." She turned to Tommy, "You'll stay to lunch, won't you?"

CRUISING SOUTH back toward Orange County, Tommy stopped in Torrance at Danner Racing. The team was on the road but the secretary, who wasn't happy to be left behind, gave him the number of the hotel where the team was staying.

In Huntington Beach, the consensus at Tim's Gym was that Jessie was a quiet competent woman who did not mix with the other employees, except for George. A few people expressed vague suspicions about Jessie and George, but none said what they were suspicious of.

Cindy, who'd told George where to find Jessie that first day, had no problem expressing her dislike of Jessie.

"She always had such a superior attitude, you know, leading George around by the nose like that. She thought she was too good for the rest of us. I mean, like it was a terrible way to die but I don't miss her."

George was the assistant manager and considered an extremely knowledgeable weight trainer. However, his temper and jealousy held him back from being nationally recognized.

Tommy next went to the hospital. He knocked on the door to Niles Von Joss's room and entered. The room looked and smelled like a flower shop. Lavish floral displays of condolence filled half the room.

"Tommy," Sylvia welcomed. "Come in."

Tommy stood at the foot of the bed looking at Niles' bandaged leg. His own arm throbbed in sympathy.

"They tell me your leg will be okay. Not so pretty, but okay. I'm sorry it happened. I shouldn't have gone out on the platform.

It wasn't necessary, so I feel responsible. Also, thanks for coming out to help me. I appreciate it.''

Niles, speaking slowly but clearly, accepted the apology and said he should have thought to say something about being on the platform, so he deserved some of the blame, too. Then they chatted pleasantly about hospitals and injuries before Tommy asked Niles if he knew Henry Padeski.

"Henry Padeski? Yes, I do know him. He worked for me when I was just starting out. A wonderful machinist, I had great luck finding him.''

"The woman, Jessie, who died when my boat exploded, was his daughter.''

"Ah. I didn't realize that. I must call him.''

"Yes, we must,'' Sylvia added. "Emma and I spent many evenings together while these two worked late. We lost touch when we moved. How are they both?''

"They're well. They mentioned that Dr. Madding knew Jessie. Do you know anything about that?''

"Yes,'' Sylvia said. "I knew there was something between them. God, I remember it so clearly. I don't know who I told but at least twice when I saw them together I said to someone there was something strange about those two. And she was just a child at the time.''

"You mean they might have been more than just friends?''

"Oh my, yes. Trust me on that.'' She slipped Tommy a wink. "I know what I'm talking about.''

"Ridiculous,'' Niles stated.

"Oh, Niles,'' Sylvia chided fondly. "You don't know anything about anything unless it's business or fish.''

That evening, after a dinner of chili and fries at his favorite hamburger joint, he walked into his motel room, looked at the cracked ceiling, the stained rug and the chipped furniture, and thought: *what a dump.*

Somebody knocked on his door. He saw the manager through the peep hole. He opened the door but said nothing.

Peering around him looking for visitors, she said, "A man called on the phone today asking for a Tommy Case. Tha wouldn't be you, would it, Mr. Springer? His description of Tommy Case and his car was very accurate.''

"What did you tell him?''

"Oh, I said there was nobody like that here.''

"Did he believe you?''

"I'm sure he did. I was almost a professional actress once.''
Tommy didn't miss the stress she put on professional.

"I can believe it,'' Tommy said, reaching into his pocket. He peeled off two twenties. "I'm sure Tommy Case would appreciate how discreet you've been. I don't suppose this man left a number where he can be reached?''

"No, Mr. Springer. He did not.''

"I see,'' Tommy said peeling off two more twenties. "Well, I'm sure Mr. Case would appreciate your continued discretion and immediate word if somebody should ask for him again.''

He lay on the bed wearing only a towel, with the telephone and his pistol beside him. Both Caroline and Leon were represented by their answering machines. Cartwell was home and not happy to be disturbed.

"Case. Where the hell have you been?''

"I've been chatting with Henry and Emma,'' Tommy replied pleasantly. "Nice people.''

"Who the hell are Henry and Emma?''

"Jessie's parents. They had a service for her this morning. I learned some interesting things.''

Tommy paused until Cartwell, with bad grace, said, "Okay, okay. I'll bite. What?''

"Well, to be brief—''

"Please.''

"Jessie was two people. A quiet unassuming, competent woman and a selfish, sexually uninhibited woman who didn't give a damn about anybody. She knew Nicholas Madding; they were friends, and according to Sylvia Von Joss, they might have been lovers, this at a time when Jessie was probably fifteen, more or less.''

"And you think Madding's the friend Stanis mentioned?''

"Could be.''

"I think it's time to have an official talk with him.''

"Me too. Unfortunately, he's in San Francisco for the weekend."

"Shit. Well, it'll have to wait. How's Von Joss?"

"He'll be okay."

"We heard from the Simon Wiesenthal Center."

Cartwell was quiet until Tommy finally said, "Very funny. What did they say?"

"There was a war criminal named Edward Von Joss, your fishing partner's uncle. He died in prison almost twenty years ago. Seems he tried to get the kid to join the Hitler Youth, but the kid wasn't having any. He escaped to England, then came here. The usual immigrant makes good story. Doesn't mean he's not a murderer, though."

"I know," Tommy said. "But I don't think he's the man."

"We'll see. Caroline Jackson left a message that she might be on to something. I haven't been able contact her. Have you?"

"I just tried. What about some protection for her?"

"We'll do some extra drive-bys. That's all we can do. What about Chambers, she see anything?"

"The only thing she's sure of is that the chin of the man in the gun shop couldn't possibly be the chin of Nicholas Madding."

"Terrific. Why not? She's sure?"

"The guy's chin was round, dark. Madding's face is long, narrow and pale. She says no way it was him."

"So what you're saying," Cartwell said, "Is that Madding may be the mysterious friend, but is not the killer. Is that right? He was your main suspect, you know."

"I know," Tommy answered testily. He closed his eyes, took a deep breath and let it out slowly. "There's something else."

"What?"

"Guess who Salina Chambers picked as a model for the gun shop shooter?"

"Forget the damn games, Case. Who?"

Tommy opened his mouth to speak, and froze. When he said Steve's name he'd be committed to investigating him as far as it took to prove him innocent or guilty. Even if Steve turned out to be innocent the friendship would never be the same. Changes, too many changes.

"You still there?" Cartwell asked.

"Yeah, I'm here." He decided that their friendship was already irrevocably changed. "Steve Langdon. Picked his face right out of the paper. Said he could easily be the shooter."

"We're finally checking on the airline. His alibi was on your say so."

"I know, but I'm not so sure now. I think he should be moved to the top of the list." After a short pause he said, "By the way. I'm leaving here tomorrow. Somebody called looking for me. I'm staying someplace nice for a change."

"Don't forget to write. By the way, your friend Fumio called. Call him back. I'm not a answering service, Case."

Neither Caroline nor Leon were home yet.

At the sound of high heels clicking past his door, he rolled off the bed and opened the door. "Excuse me," he called to the girl walking away from him. "Do you speak Spanish?"

She stopped and looked at Tommy, expression guarded. She wore red spiked heels, dark stockings covering long thin legs and a tight, black miniskirt. Her midriff was bare up to a red halter top that prominently displayed her prominent breasts. Teased black hair stood out three inches around her oval face. She was pretty and except for heavy lipstick around her generous mouth, didn't wear much makeup. She looked Tommy up and down as he stood in the doorway with only a towel wrapped around him.

"*Si. Yo hablo espanol,*" she said.

"Good. I need a favor. It won't take but a minute and would be worth twenty bucks."

The girl's grin widened as she stepped closer. "Oh, *señor,* favors are my business."

Tommy laughed. "This isn't that kind of favor."

It took a couple of minutes to explain to Rosie that all he wanted was for her to ask for somebody on the phone. They sat side by side on the bed. Rosie's perfume was hardly subtle, but it was intoxicating. Tommy tried not to think about what another twenty dollars would get him.

He dialed a number and after two rings Suzanne answered.

Tommy nodded and Rosie said, "Please, may I speak to Ramona?"

Tommy leaned close to listen at the ear piece. He attempted to concentrate on listening and not on Rosie's cleavage. He heard Suzanne call for Ramona and after a long ten seconds she answered. Rosie started talking to Ramona in Spanish as if they were life-long friends. He couldn't understand any of what they said except for "gringo" and the looks Rosie gave him.

Finally, he took the receiver from her. "Ramona, this is Tommy. I don't want Suzanne to know it's me. Okay?"

"Okay. Who is your friend? She sounds delightful. She says you are one cute gringo."

"Just a passing acquaintance," he said. He took a twenty dollar bill off the bedside table and handed it to Rosie. She leaned against him and with exaggerated slowness tucked it deep into her top, exposing most of one breast that pressed against his bare arm. She gave him a breathy kiss on his ear and when she stood up placed a hand high up on his thigh and squeezed playfully. Tommy watched Rosie close the door, then had to remember why he called Ramona.

"Ramona," he said. "Is Mr. Langdon home now?"

"No," she answered. "He is at a race and will be back Sunday night. Thomas, it is not the same since you leave. Now they argue all the time."

"Ramona, do you remember if Mr. Langdon was home last Tuesday night?"

"Let me think." He heard her counting the days backward in Spanish. "He was out but then he come back about five minutes to nine. I hear the car arrive, very fast. I remember because of TV. I was watching a very boring show and I hope it will be over soon."

"Do you know what car?"

"The Mercedes, I think."

Tommy fell silent. The time was about right and the car behind the gun shop could have been a Mercedes.

"Tomas. What is happening? I am getting worried."

"I can't explain now, but it is important that you don't tell anyone you talked to me. All right?"

"All right, Tomas. Be careful."

After hanging up Tommy thought for a minute, then dialed the number of the motel where the Danner racing team was staying. When Charlie Alister answered and Tommy identified himself there was a long silence before Charlie asked, "What do you want?"

"About our conversation before."

"We had no conversation before."

"Yes we did, Charlie. The one where you lied to me."

"About what?"

Tommy didn't know about what or even, for sure if he did, so he said, "Steve Langdon is a first-degree murder suspect. If you help him, you're an accessory to murder and the only race cars you'll see will be on your cell wall."

"Case, get off it. I didn't lie to you. I don't have anything else to say to you. Leave me alone."

"You *are* lying to me, Charlie. I can hear it in your voice. But that's okay, because next week there's going to be some heavy duty shit come down on this and it will be the police you're talking to, not me. And they don't know how to keep their mouths shut like I do."

Tommy waited, hoping Charlie would tell him something he needed to know, but when he spoke Charlie said, "I have nothing to say to you or the police. Leave me alone."

"Okay, Charlie, but when the police start questioning you, it'll be too late. You'd better get your story right because if Steve arrived on a later flight the police will find out and you can kiss racing goodbye."

"What are you talking about?"

"You know damn well what I'm talking about. For the moment, though, I'll leave you alone, but let me tell you two things: don't tell Steve you talked to me. If he thinks you said the wrong thing, you might have an accident. Second, I'm going to give you a Sergeant Cartwell's telephone number. If you get smart and maybe want to save your life, call him."

Tommy gave him the number, twice.

Charlie said, with no real heat, "Leave me alone, Case," and hung up.

Charlie had more to tell, Tommy was sure. If they could prove Steve took a later plane that Friday the rest would fall into place. It would be nice to know about the argument on Von Joss's boat, too. Again, more questions than answers.

This time Caroline answered on the second ring. "Caroline," Tommy said, relief in his voice. "I've been trying to call you."

"HI, TOMMY. I just got in. Leon insisted on taking Fumio and me to the car races. It was exciting. I'd never been before."

"I'm glad you had fun. Leon's enthusiasm can be catching. You left a message to call you."

"Yes, I did. Actually there isn't much to tell, yet. I can tell you the security records have been altered. We can't tell exactly what changes were made, but something was done to them. Also, we always keep exact records of DEX's operating time and there appears to be ten minutes unaccounted for."

"Do you think you'll be able to find the changes?"

"Well, eventually, but..." In his mind, he could see her brush her hair back, feel her confusion.

"But what?" he prompted.

"The information I got," she said in short rushes, as if still puzzling over what she was saying, "it was almost like it wasn't there and then it was. I'd tried the same thing before and got nothing. Later I tried it again, and got nothing again. Then, it just appeared on the screen, all by itself."

"Is it right? Could it be a decoy or something?"

"Once I knew what to look for, it checked out. I don't understand where it came from. Unless it was a time delay of some sort, but that doesn't make sense. In any case, Leon, Fumio and I are going to the lab tomorrow morning. Nicholas won't be there, he's in San Francisco this weekend." She hesitated a beat. "Do you still think he killed Brian? It's hard to believe."

"To tell the truth, I'm not sure anymore. I think he's done something, but I don't know what exactly."

He told her about the extra drive-bys and after she gave him directions to her place, he reluctantly hung up.

He called Anne Sexton to cancel their sailing date for the next day, but she pleaded with him until he finally agreed to go one hour out from the end of the jetty, then turn around. He did want to go, he missed the feel and touch and smell of sailing and Anne's boat promised to be exceptional.

Fumio was home, too. "Fumio! Where you been? You get a real job?"

"Is this Bond, James Bond? Blown up any fish lately?"

"Not funny. You called me. What's up?"

"Gossip, my friend, about a friend. Caroline tells me Brian wanted Von Joss to blow twenty million plus on a teraflops computer. Guess who just ordered one."

"Twenty million? Who?"

"Autotronics. They ordered the cheap model."

It took Tommy a few seconds before he could ask, "Steve Langdon's company?"

"The one. And he's looking for brains who know how to use it and have experience with artificial intelligence." Kindly, Fumio said, "It looks like he is expanding big time."

"Yes. He said he was." Tommy's heart sank in his chest and he forgot to breathe.

"You don't need a teraflops machine for car electronics. Maybe he has a new notebook he needs to use."

"Thanks Fumio. I have to go."

For half an hour he lay on his bed convincing himself that the facts weren't adding up like they were. Finally, he got up, got dressed and drove over to Caroline's condo. He didn't go in, just drove by, then returned to the motel. He hadn't accomplished anything but he felt better.

TWENTY-FOUR

THE MARINE LAYER was lower and darker than usual; it felt like rain. Tommy woke early even though he had lain awake until after midnight. He checked out of the Harbor View motel, exchanging good morning greetings with a working girl who looked like she earned her money during the night. In the office of a cozy, clean, two-story motel, just off Harbor Boulevard in Costa Mesa, an enthusiastic Oriental lady assured him that after two o'clock he could check into a quiet room in the back. He paid cash for two days in advance.

After a big breakfast at the Buccaneer, Tommy walked to the Leeward Marina. Lucy seemed happy to see him, but was unusually quiet. Tommy didn't push it, uncertain himself what their relationship was. She told him she hadn't received any more threats. He said that was great but he needed her to do something for him. It took some persuading but she agreed.

"Whether I find out what you want or not, you owe me big for this Tommy. Big," she told him unhappily.

ANNE HAD THE SAIL and winch covers off and started the engine as he descended the dock ramp. She wore Topsiders, sky blue shorts, a dark blue yacht club sweatshirt and a red, no nonsense sun visor. She greeted him with a smile, a quick kiss on the cheek and an order to let go the bow line.

Forty-five minutes later they powered past the end of the jetty. The clouds had lightened and lifted, allowing a patch of blue to break through. Unusual for eleven o'clock in the morning, a fair breeze blew from the west-southwest. Anne turned off the engine and, leaving Tommy at the wheel, spent a few minutes trimming the sails. He had to admit he was impressed with her seamanship and for the next hour they talked sailor to sailor about the boat and the way it handled. Unhappy at the dock, FLASH was a boat born to sail. Released from shore, she glided with smooth power and grace through the water. She was fast and responsive, with an easy motion. Tommy remembered something he'd read about Ferraris crying when they came to America because of the fifty-five mile per hour speed limit. He had no doubt FLASH cried when she returned to the dock.

Tommy forgot he was only going to sail out for an hour and as the sun broke through, Anne went below deck. No other boats were close.

Anne came through the companionway wearing only her visor and the bottom of a minuscule string bikini. She made her way to the rear of the cockpit where she stood beside Tommy and scanned the sails.

"Think we ought to ease the Genoa a bit?" she asked.

Tommy felt Anne's bare arm burning against his. Looking up he said, "Ahh, sure."

Anne moved easily around the cockpit making the adjustment. She let out the mainsail and told Tommy to fall off a bit. Keeping one eye on the sails and one eye on Anne, he decided she was slender, not skinny. Her hips were wider than he remembered and her legs longer and he already knew about her breasts. He also knew she was married, not that it seemed to matter to her. When Anne came toward him she was ninety-nine and forty-four hundredths percent pure sex. Relationships didn't figure into it.

Anne examined the sail trim then slipped between Tommy and the wheel. He pulled her against him. Her hips slowly pulsed against his.

"You're the helmsman," she whispered into the base of his neck. "How does everything look to you?"

Tommy's eyes traveled from where their hips met to the top of the mast and back to her. Her tan was total, unmarred by tan lines; her nipples stood out proudly.

"Everything looks fine to me, Captain."

"Good," she replied, unbuttoning his shirt. Her lips left warm spots on his chest and neck. Soft palms caressed his nipples until they stood out, matching hers. His growing excitement was obvious and the motion of her hips became more insistent. She pushed down his shorts, twisting sideways to pull them all the way down. Her tongue left a slow, hot trail along his thigh and stomach as she stood up. Her hand brushed his erection, making it jump.

"One hand for the ship and one for the captain, Captain?" he asked, voice gone husky.

"Both hands for the captain on this ship."

She moved to her right and pressed rubber-covered buttons on a black electronics panel. When she came back to him the tiny piece of cloth she wore fell away.

"Now we're on automatic pilot," she announced, pulling Tommy from behind the leather-covered wheel.

Later, he lay on the seat with his arm over his eyes and let guilt wash over him like an old, smelly, but familiar, blanket, his thoughts on Lucy. What a bastard he was.

Anne teased, "You have to admit this is a lot more fun than spending the day with Caroline Jackson."

"What?" Tommy said, distracted from his guilt.

"She wouldn't be doing what I've been doing, not to you anyway."

Tommy's brain began to turn over.

"What do you mean?"

She slapped his thigh playfully. "I mean, dummy, that I'm more her type than you are."

His brain slipped into gear. "Are you saying...?"

"That Dr. Caroline Jackson is a lesbian. Actually she might swing both ways, but trust me, if she were here I'd be having more fun than you."

Incredulous, Tommy said, "Caroline is a lesbian?"

Anne sat on the opposite seat, arms spread out on the coaming. Naked, except for the visor, she watched Tommy digest the news.

Tommy sat up. Staring unseeing at Anne's legs, he muttered to himself, "She's a lesbian; son of a bitch—she's a lesbian."

Then, like switches turned on one by one, words, actions and reactions clicked into place and he knew Caroline was in danger, that Dr. Nicholas Madding was a murderer and that he was not the only one.

TWENTY-FIVE

"WE HAVE TO GO BACK," Tommy insisted. Anne protested but Tommy grabbed her arms tightly. "You may not think much of Caroline, but I like her and I think she's in danger. We have to go back now."

Anne met his glare, considered, then nodded once. "All right," she said, not bothering to hide her disappointment. She shrugged his hands off, stood up to get her bearings, stepped behind the wheel and called, "Ready about!"

With the motor fired up and carrying full sail it took less than two hours to return to the Von Joss dock. They didn't say much on the way. He couldn't call ahead because the VHF radio was being serviced, so all he could do was worry. By the time he jumped onto the dock Anne had picked up his anxiety and she yelled, "Go. Go," when he stopped to help tie up the boat.

Two quick phone calls told him Caroline had left the lab and that she either wasn't home or, if she was, couldn't answer. He raced through the Saturday traffic to her Irvine Condo. The tract was quiet, with few cars and fewer people about. The pink stucco buildings with red tiled roofs alternated two-story units with two one-story units between; six buildings, nineteen units long, identical but for pink or beige color. Carports lined the parking lots.

Caroline's car sat in the shade of her assigned carport. The sun beat down on him as he crossed the searing asphalt. Cheers floated in the stagnant hot air from the next two-story unit down from Caroline's. Somebody had hit a home run.

Her condo was on the end. A short concrete walk led to the front door. He rang the doorbell. The faint sound of the chimes held no welcome and the door was locked. He cupped hands around his eyes and looked in a window. He saw the usual tiled entry leading to a living room from which open sliding-glass

doors let onto a small fenced patio. A stairway on the right led
up to a landing with two hallways leading from it.

Tommy saw a dark stain on the carpet on the edge of the
landing. As he watched, a drop fell and spattered redly on the
white entry tile. He put a toe on the edge of the window and
pushed himself up. In the fraction of a second before his foot
slipped, he saw on the landing a single, bare foot extending from
behind a corner.

He ran around the end of the building and scrambled over the
wood fence enclosing the patio. Gun drawn, moving fast, he
raced up the stairs. Caroline lay on her side, one arm stretched
out as if reaching for help. She wore dark green shorts and a
man's pink, long sleeved shirt. Tommy knelt beside her and felt
for a pulse he knew wouldn't be there.

"Ah, Caroline," he whispered. "I'm sorry." His stomach
muscles spasmed and a tear escaped from his eyes. "I'm sorry.
I'm sorry."

He turned the body over. Wet blood covered the front of her
shirt. Three small bullet holes, right over the heart, could be seen
in the middle of the stain. Tommy closed her eyes and left the
body as he found it.

The larger bedroom looked little different from any woman's
bedroom he had been in; neat and clean with frilly pillows and
drapes; a hint of perfume. Rather bare and boring he thought,
until he looked behind the door. On the wall hung a photograph
blown up to poster size of two women naked, in bed. They
looked at each other and the love in their expressions was obvious to anybody. In the minute he studied it, Tommy couldn't
decide whether it was pornography or art. Then he looked closer,
studying the faces. "Son of a bitch," he whispered. One of the
women was Caroline. The other woman was familiar, too. He'd
seen her before, but in a more deadly pose. "Caroline, why didn't
you tell me?" he said, staring at the face of Lucia Smyth. Now
he knew who Lucia Smyth's secret lover had been. And who
made Nicholas Madding so jealous he followed the lovers one
night and, when Caroline left, murdered his rival. *I knew you'd
done something, Nicholas. Now I know what.*

The other room was filled with computer equipment. Two

bookcases overflowed with books, magazines and papers devoted to electronics, robotics and mathematics. More journals and papers were stacked on the floor. One of the two monitor screens was smashed. When he inspected it he realized the computer itself was still on. There were no disks in any of the disk drives. There were no disks at all. Tommy felt fairly certain the working copy should still be in the computer, and he really wanted to know what Caroline had been working on.

He found a telephone in the kitchen.

"Fumio! I need your expertise, right now." After explaining what he needed, he hung up before Fumio could ask about Caroline. It took three tries to get Cartwell on the phone.

Tommy could see the fourth unit down from his view from the front door. The game still seemed to be on. A pretty young woman wearing an Angels T-shirt and cap and holding a can of Budweiser answered the door.

"Do you live here?" Tommy asked.

Defensive, the woman answered, "Yeah."

"There's been some trouble in the end unit down there." He waved a hand vaguely in that direction. "The police are on their way, but I wanted to ask if any of you had seen or heard anything in the last hour or so that might help."

The woman looked past him, as if expecting to see some trouble right behind him. "At the lady scientist's place? Is she okay?"

"No, I'm afraid not. Have you seen or heard anything?"

"We've been watching the game. I don't think anybody has seen anything. What happened?"

"May I ask them? It's important."

"Sure, I guess so. Come on in."

She led him into the living room. Four men and two women sprawled on a large sofa and matching loveseat covered in smooth, dark blue material with a pattern of tiny red flowers. Sparse furnishings, tending toward darkly stained oak, dotted the room. Two of the men and one of the women wore Angel baseball caps or shirts. Judging by the number of beer cans it had been a long game.

The woman yelled at them to listen up. They listened, but most of their eyes focused on the big screen TV. Tommy looked as official as he could when he pronounced, "A woman has been killed." That got their attention, even the fidgeting ceased. "I need to know if any of you have seen or heard anything or anybody suspicious or out of place in the last hour or two."

Blank stares and negative head shakes answered his question. Two of the men lost interest and tried to focus on the game again. One man, with a blonde flattop, stood behind the sofa and raised his eyes up as if looking through the wall to the landing, then turned his head slightly to stare in the direction of Caroline's condo, indecision plain on his deeply tanned, long face.

"The police will be asking you the same question." Tommy pulled a wad of bills from his pocket, "But they won't be offering twenty bucks for answers." Flattop turned his gaze to Tommy, eyebrows raised in interest.

Tommy's eyes held Flattop's. He peeled off another twenty. "Or forty bucks."

Flattop shrugged. "Maybe half an hour ago I came down the stairs from the bathroom. I looked through the front window and saw an old guy get into a Mercedes. He seemed to be in a hurry and he was carrying something. I've never seen him before."

"What did he look like? Could you identify him?"

"I never saw his face. Tall, thin, gray hair." He stared at the beige carpet. "White, short sleeved shirt, tan pants."

Nicholas. *That was a quick trip to San Francisco, Doc.* "I don't suppose you got a license number?"

Flattop smiled without humor and held his hand out.

"Afraid not."

Tommy laid the bills in his hand. The others were quiet, focusing on the two men. A faint siren could be heard over the cheers of the TV baseball crowd.

"The police will be along eventually to talk with you," Tommy said to the room. "No need to tell them I was here."

Fumio arrived a few minutes after the Sheriff's Department and the Irvine Police. Tommy explained quickly to Cartwell how he came to find Caroline. At Tommy's suggestion, Cartwell had the crime scene people go over the computer area first. Fumio hooked up a new monitor he'd brought with him. When he turned it on it showed only a blank screen.

"Damn," Tommy said softly.

"Ahh, that would have been too easy," Fumio said. With tentative strokes he started working the keyboard.

Tommy waited impatiently for Fumio to work his magic. He wanted to race over to Madding's house. If Nicholas was there, he wanted first crack at him and if he wasn't, Tommy wanted to seriously look around the house, but first he wanted to see what, if anything, Caroline had come up with. He stood in the doorway watching the Medical Examiner when Fumio said, "Bingo!" In half a second Tommy stood at Fumio's shoulder staring at a busy screen.

"Did you get it?" he asked.

"Read for yourself."

Quickly they scanned through the information. Tommy could barely contain his excitement. "It's all there," he said. "It's all there, isn't it?"

"You were right, Tommy-san. It happened just like you said, and she has even figured out how." He pointed a stubby finger at the screen. "Look, here are the changes made in the security system, how they were made—everything."

"Madding had to have made those changes, didn't he?"

"Well, yes." Fumio leaned back in the chair. His ponytail bounced as he spoke. "There's no doubt he changed the security records and fiddled the video tapes. The murder was done from his house, too. It doesn't necessarily mean he did the actual killing, though. Anybody could have manipulated DEX."

"I know that. But he had to know about it, set it up. What time was the murder actually committed?"

Fumio scanned the screen. "Between five fifty-seven and six fourteen p.m., Friday, the seventeenth of August. He looked hard at Tommy, who was staring out the window. "You aren't going to tell me Madding did not kill Brian, are you? What about Caroline? I cannot believe she is dead. I only knew her a few days, but I liked her. She did not deserve this."

"No, she didn't."

"Dr. Madding sure as hell had a motive, but he's in San Francisco this weekend."

Tommy told Fumio to make some hard copies of Caroline's findings, then went to find Cartwell. He explained what they'd found and what it meant. He suggested they try to determine if Nicholas Madding really was in San Francisco and asked if he and Fumio could leave.

"Tommy," Fumio called from the computer room. "Come look at this."

"What is it?" Tommy asked, leaning over his friend's shoulder.

"I found some of Caroline's notes at the end of the file. Look here." He scrolled through text on the screen. "She says there is a void in the memory capacity of the computer hooked up to the DNA. Does that mean what I think it means?"

"I'll explain later," Tommy said. "So there's a void?"

"Yeah, about four gigabytes. But it's not really a void. The bits are there, just isolated. There is no access to them. Not even a request for an encrypted password." Fumio scrolled to the end. He pointed a stubby finger at the screen. "Here. She says now there are almost six gigabytes isolated. And here, eight."

"It's growing," Tommy said. "Is it one of those viruses?"

"She doesn't think so."

Tommy straightened up and looked around the room.

"Is this something we need to check out right now?" he asked.

"I don't know. Probably not."

"Good. Let's get out of here."

They took Tommy's car to the nearest phone, outside a convenience store in a designer mini-mall built to blend in so as not to offend any delicate yuppie sensibilities.

The same voice told him to "Wait."

When Pat came on Tommy said, "You said you owed me for Salina. That offer still hold?" She said yes and Tommy replied, "Good. I need to borrow a thief."

TWENTY-SIX

THE THREE-YEAR-OLD Chevrolet made its slow way through the landscaped streets of Anaheim Hills. The sun had set and the sky faded fast to a washed out, starless canopy. Rick, the borrowed thief, drove, Tommy sat next to him, Fumio in the back. Tommy had explained to Fumio what he had in mind, giving the chubby computer whiz a chance to back out, but Fumio replied, "I'm in. I want the bastard, too."

Rick, forty-five, medium height, medium build, plain brown hair thinning on top, was as inconspicuous as his car. According to Pat, he was a master of alarm systems.

Madding's house was dark. Tommy figured he was back in San Francisco by now. They drove past the house twice, then drove a quarter mile away where Tommy and Rick changed places. Tommy drove slowly toward the house while Rick concentrated on a rectangular black box with two switches, a plastic knob and a digital readout. He turned the knob slowly, glancing at the garage door at every click. Just as the Chevy reached the short driveway the garage door opened.

"Turn in," Rick said.

Tommy turned, then said, "What the hell, there's two cars in there."

"I thought he would be gone," Fumio said nervously.

"Park all the way to the left," Rick said. "You think he's here or not?"

"Not," Tommy said, almost positively.

"Okay, get out. Walk in like you belong here."

Once inside the garage, Rick flipped a switch on his box and the garage door closed behind them. He went to the electronic number pad by the door into the house, dug into a small, leather bag and started disassembling it. Tommy checked the cars, both Mercedes. The hood of the newer one, a 560 SEL, was still warm. The other car, a 220S Cabriolet, didn't look as if it had been driven since it left the showroom, thirty-five or more years before. Fumio watched and tried to find something to do with his hands.

After five minutes, Rick said, "Hmm, very nice. State of the art." Two minutes later he tried the door. It was locked. "Now for the hard part," he grinned. Pulling something from a little pouch, he fiddled with the door knob and ten seconds later pushed the door open. After consulting another black box connected to the insides of the number pad, he announced. "Okay, no silent alarms. After you."

Tommy pushed the door all the way open and stepped cautiously through.

"Wait!" Rick whispered loudly.

Tommy froze, then stepped backwards into the garage.

Rick stepped through the door carrying another black box and wearing a thick, heavy looking pair of glasses wired to the box. He took small, slow steps through the hall leading into the kitchen. Before he entered the kitchen proper, he stopped and fiddled with the box. Tommy thought he heard him chuckle. The thief took a couple of steps back then opened a folding door that exposed a washer and dryer. He inspected the closet with the flashlight before reaching in and flipping a light switch. He scanned the kitchen once more, then flipped the closet switch again. After another scan he turned on the lights, flooding the kitchen in fluorescent brightness.

"Shit," hissed Fumio.

"Relax," Rick said, taking off his electric glasses. "It's a lot less conspicuous than flashlights flashing all over the place."

"What the hell are those glasses for?" Tommy asked.

"Checking for laser trip beams," Fumio said.

"Among other things," Rick added. "You've been telling me what a genius this guy is supposed to be, so I figured maybe I'd better check everything. There're pressure pads in the kitchen, totally independent from any other system; the switch in the closet activates it. Neither alarm was set."

The kitchen was large, clean and ordinary with the usual oak cabinets, black-fronted appliances and neutral-colored counter tops. It smelled of disinfectant and looked like it had never been used.

Two doors led out. One to the right and one catty-corner from where they entered. Tommy went right, into a formal dining room. Light from outside reflected off a polished dining table. Pistol in hand, he moved to his left through an archway.

As soon as he pressed the silent light switch inside the room he heard a strangled, bubbling sound, like someone breathing through a straw stuck in water. He took a breath to steel himself and smelled blood. He looked over the couch on the left side of the living room. Too late again.

Madding lay on his back on the floor. Tommy heard the strangled breathing again. Bubbles formed on Nicholas's white shirt front. A "sucking chest wound," he remembered from his cop days. He knelt beside the man, ripped open his shirt and pressed hard on the hole in the dying man's chest. Nicholas coughed. Suddenly his eyes opened wide, staring right into Tommy's. Tommy flinched, but kept pressure on the wound.

"Dr. Madding, who shot you?" he asked.

Nicholas turned his head and coughed, spattering blood on Tommy's bare legs.

"Dr. Madding, Nicholas, tell me who did this. Was it Steve Langdon?"

The thin head moved slowly, left—right—negative. His breathing became a little quieter, a bit more regular. He spoke in a whisper. Tommy leaned close to hear.

"Caroline. I'm sorry," he rasped, "...didn't want to hurt you."

"Who shot Caroline? Who hurt Caroline?"

"I'm sorry Caroline...had to protect..."

"Who did you have to protect?" Tommy shook the man, just a little. "Damn it, protect who?"

"Why did...she do it?" Nicholas asked, his voice gone dreamy. "Why? I helped her..."

Frustrated, Tommy wanted to slap the pale face and make it talk, but as much as he disliked the man he couldn't do it. Yet, there were so many questions. The dying man's speech lapsed into uncomprehensible mutterings. Tommy shook him.

"Nicholas, did you kill Lucia Smyth?" He shook Madding again. The dull eyes seemed to focus. "You killed Lucia Smyth, didn't you? You stabbed her after Caroline left that night. Didn't you?"

Madding's voice was weak but understandable. "She took Caroline. Had to get her back...loved her." He stared through Tommy. "He made me do it... She didn't know. Sorry...sorry."

So many questions. "Where is Brian's notebook?"

Madding's eyes closed. "He has it. Genius. Finally respect me."

"Who killed Brian?" Tommy shook Nicholas. "Who killed Brian? Damn you. Who?" Tommy demanded through clenched teeth.

Tommy shook Madding again, harder, but it didn't matter. Nicholas wasn't answering any more questions. Tommy sat back on his heels. Frustration, anger and sadness all vied for space in his chest. Poor Nicholas. He may have been a genius, and a jerk, but in his heart he just wanted to be loved like everyone else.

"That the guy who wasn't supposed to be here?" Rick asked from behind Tommy.

"Yeah," Tommy answered, voice flat.

"Shot like the woman?"

"Yeah."

"He say who did it?"

"No."

"Looks like you got a problem. I'll stick to B and E, thanks." He pointed with his chin. "We found what we were looking for. Fumio's having orgasms over the stuff."

Tommy washed his hands in the kitchen, then followed Rick to a room at the back of the house.

"Holy shit," he said as he entered the room filled with computers, black boxes, telephones and other equipment he couldn't hope to identify. A disorderly pile of disks lay in a corner.

"Hacker heaven!" Fumio exclaimed. He acted like a kid on Christmas, moving from one present to the next, unable to decide which one to open first. "This guy is a major hacker. There is no place he could not crack with this setup."

Tommy had a thought. "Could he get into hospital records?"

"Are you kidding? Any hospital in the country, maybe the world." Fumio turned to the others, his face alive with excitement. "Tommy, you could start World War III with this stuff." He waved that thought off and went to a table. "Look at this." He picked up a jumble of wires and held it up. The tangle spread out into two long nets, like shirt sleeves. A flat multicolored wire ran from each into a black box. "A sensor net," he declared. "Put it on your arms and DEX follows your movements exactly, just like Caroline said. Patch into DEX's computer, get Brian close, reach around from behind and *sayonara* Brian."

"How did...whoever...see where to make DEX go?"

"Through the security system. There was a pre-recorded loop to show the security guard monitors; they've been doing it in the movies for years. At some point the check-out records were changed to show that Brian left earlier."

Fumio stopped to catch his breath. Tommy jumped in with a question. It had been his theory all along but he thought he saw a problem.

"What happened to the body? I assumed DEX carried it out to the dumpster; but doesn't he have to be attached by wires to the computer?"

"That is the genius part. See, he developed a remote control unit to run DEX. It plugged into the regular multiplug. The base already holds enough back-up battery power for about thirty minutes. He removes the RC unit in the morning before anybody else arrives."

"And cleans up any mess Brian was inconsiderate enough to leave while he was dying," Tommy finished.

"Yes," Fumio agreed.

"What about operating DEX? Could anybody do it?"

Fumio's gaze ran over the equipment. "Sure. Once you know how to activate the system all you need is some good hand-to-eye coordination. A kid could do it." He shook his head in admiration. "The man is good, Tommy. Incredibly good. They tell me he is a real son of a bitch, but what you could learn from him! Too bad he is a murderer."

Rick, leaning against an empty spot of wall, listening intently, said, "Fumio, I know you admire the guy, and I can see why." He swept a hand over the room. "But I don't think you'll be learning anything from him now."

Puzzled, Fumio asked, "Why not?"

Tommy said, "Because he's dead." He pointed toward the living room. "In there. Shot, just like Caroline."

Fumio sagged. "In there? Hell, why did you not tell me?"

"You were too busy coming in your pants over this equipment; I didn't want to interrupt."

"Shit. Then he did not kill Caroline?"

"Doesn't look like it."

"Then who did?"

Rick pushed off the wall. "That's a good question. Why don't we discuss it some place else? I'd just as soon not have to explain my presence here to the police."

They left the house quickly, taking Caroline's disks with them. Tommy made an anonymous call to the police finishing with, "Don't bother knocking. The door's open."

A few blocks from the house two police cars passed them in a hurry. All three men muttered relieved curses.

TWENTY-SEVEN

FUMIO DESCRIBED some of Madding's devices during their drive back to Pat's house. Most interesting to Tommy was an answering machine that automatically dialed Nicholas' car phone, so he could have been anywhere on Tuesday night. Not that it mattered now.

The big question was, who killed Caroline and Nicholas? Tommy was almost willing to bet that Steve killed Brian, with Nicholas' help, and took the notebook. If Steve was the gun shop shooter then he was the one who blew up his boat and Jessie, too. It would be easy enough to verify—or not verify—that Steve was at a car race back east.

The more Tommy mulled it over the more certain he became that there was a new player in the game. Someone who knew both Caroline and Nicholas. They were both shot at close range; the killer must be getting desperate.

At the compound, they all had a stiff drink and filled Pat in on the evening's events.

"Tommy, you have blood on you," she said as if it suddenly appeared as some sort of lower extremity stigma and hadn't been there for the half hour since the men returned. "There's a shower upstairs you can use. I'll show you."

Tommy was wiped out. The heat and emotion of the day and two large glasses of wine had planted him in this chair for the next twenty-four hours, as far as he was concerned. But Pat was insistent. He leaned forward and looked at the blood spots on his legs. Nicholas Madding's blood. A murdered murderer's blood. There really wasn't much, hardly enough to worry about. But he followed her up the stairs, anyway.

SALINA WAS READING when Tommy opened her door. Seeing him, she flipped her book to the foot of the bed and said, "Thank

God, somebody. Come in, come in."

He stood by the bed, a malicious smile on his lips. He said nothing, knowing it would bug her. The shower had revived him. For the moment, he was in a teasing mood.

"Well, say something, goddamn it, or did you come in here to finish off my death by boredom?" Salina asked.

"You've got your books."

"I'm read out."

He glanced at her book, "Science fiction. I would have thought true crime. Research for your memoirs."

"Well, if I write my memoirs the most interesting chapter will be when I throw the private detective out the window for being an asshole."

She tried to sit up, winced, and fell back onto the pillows, some of the color draining from her face. When she opened her eyes Tommy said, "Pat says you're healing fast."

"Not fast enough. What the hell did you need Rick for? What's happening? Nobody tells me anything."

Tommy pulled up a chair and told her. "And now you tell me: how'd you and Pat meet?"

Salina cocked her head to one side and waved a dismissing hand although her grin disappeared.

"I was being raped. Some jerk at school I let get out of control. About ten more seconds and he'd have had me. There was nothing I could do except think how I was going to cut his balls off afterwards." Her grim smile gave him goose bumps. "Pat showed up and saved my virtue. The guy spent a week in the hospital." She looked Tommy dead in the eye. "He came out singing half soprano. A regular little gentleman."

"I get the idea," Tommy said. Switching to another subject, he asked. "You said the woman who got Brian in trouble was a hooker. Do you know her name? Did she work the streets or a house? How'd he meet her?"

"Brian didn't tell me much. Her name was Annabelle. She worked part-time in a house. He said a lot of the students used to go there and party. She graduated and disappeared."

Annabelle? Anne Sexton? Could it be? "Graduated? She worked her way through college as a hooker?"

"You'd be surprised, but maybe she liked the work. It seems to me he said her father was rich. I thought about tracking her down, but I was busy at the time and later..." She shrugged. "I should have found her and fixed her so she sang half bass, if you know what I mean."

"I get the idea," he said again.

"This Steve Langdon is the one?"

"I think so."

"You're not sure? Or don't want to be sure? I know he was your friend."

"I'm sure, but I can't prove it, yet."

Salina lay still; the dark areas under her eyes stood out like a Halloween mask. She looks tired, he thought. His arm throbbed in sympathy and his own weariness settled over him like a lead fog. He reached out and touched her hand.

Her eyes fluttered open. "Sorry," she whispered. "Still get so damn tired."

"I have to go," he said.

Her hand closed over his. "Call me if you need help getting that son of a bitch."

Fumio and Rick had left. Pat saw him to the door.

"Thanks for Rick's help," he told her.

"We're even now. Come back when Sal is better."

THE NIGHT AIR captured the moisture from the surrounding trees and grass turning the private enclave into an oasis of coolness from the September heat. The smell of newly cut grass triggered memories of summer nights as a kid—chasing fireflies, roasting marshmallows over a fire on family picnics, lying out in the middle of a field with best friends David and Paul looking for shooting stars and wondering what they would do when they grew up. Murder had not been in any of his scenarios.

The gate opened for him. He stopped halfway through to shift mental gears from bucolic eastern summer nights to Southern California driving. The street held no obvious movement, but on the sidewalk there was a shadow in motion, more felt than seen. On the very edge of his vision a long, black barrel of a pistol gleamed under a streetlight. For an instant he stared into the deeper black center of the barrel. *Not again,* part of his mind screamed. The other part did the only thing that might keep a bullet from permanently disrupting his brain cells—slammed his foot to the floor. Tires squealing, the Mustang leaped through the gate. He fishtailed down the street and skidded around the first turn. He saw through his rear view mirror that there were two holes in his rear window. The dash had a new hole, also.

"Jesus Christ!" he cursed the night.

Circling the block, he gripped his gun on the seat beside him. Headlights out, he cruised slowly past Pat's house. The street was empty, quiet and still. He cruised the neighborhood, but found nothing.

TWENTY-EIGHT

LIGHT SEEPED AROUND the heavy drapes of his new motel room and forced its way under his eyelids. He knew he should get up but couldn't summon the energy. The events of the last few weeks crashed down on him. He couldn't think; he couldn't feel. Faces and names marched through his mind like characters in a book he was too weary to read. His mind kept wandering to a week spent in Mexico where the only thing he had to think about was what bar to watch the sunset from. He wanted that life again and the desire paralyzed him.

Unwanted, Lucy's words came to him: "Stop whining."

At ten o'clock he sleepwalked into the shower. At ten-fifteen he walked down the street to Denny's for a Grand Slam breakfast. By eleven he was watching ESPN's live coverage of an Indy Car race. In the pre-race commentary they showed an interview with Charlie Alister. Tommy hoped that Charlie would be around to enjoy the rest of the schedule. And, behind Charlie, plain as day, Steve Langdon talked with a crew member. The interview had been taped late Saturday afternoon. *Well,* Tommy thought, *being on national television was about as good an alibi as you can get.* The race turned out to be a good one. The Danner car led for ten laps, eventually finishing a solid third. In the brief interview with the happy driver, Steve, in cap and sunglasses, could be seen prominently in the background.

At one-thirty he called Lucy. She was waiting for a call, but took the time to remind him he owed her big for this favor. "I've contacted people I swore I'd never be involved with again. They'd love to get me back," she told him. "Walking away from the Life was the hardest thing I ever did. I don't know if I could get out again."

"Lucy, I'm sorry." He sighed and laughed without humor. "I

seem to be saying that a lot lately. I didn't know it would be such a problem for you. You should have told me to go to hell.''

Her voice softened slightly. ''Believe me, I thought about it, but we're, you know, friends, and you asked for my help.''

For an instant, Tommy wondered if he had been as selfish and unconcerned with his friends' feelings before Jessie's visit. He didn't think so, but remembered his first meeting with Salina, and was not so sure. ''If you ever need somebody to pull you back from the past, call me, okay?'' he said.

''Call you where? You won't trust me with your phone number. It would be better if we were together,'' she said, her voice fading into a hesitant whisper.

''I know,'' Tommy answered in the same manner.

Lucy paused a few seconds to let him feel guilty, then said, ''Suzanne was around here again this morning wanting to know if you were all right. Don't worry, I was nice. Talk to her, will you?'' Tommy said nothing. ''Call me later. I can't call you.'' Lucy hung up loudly. Tommy felt guilty for a minute to make Lucy happy, then called Cartwell.

''Case, damn it, why didn't you tell me where you were going yesterday?''

''Don't you ever go home?'' Tommy asked.

''Always the joker, aren't you? Not with two more homicides connected with your other mess, I don't.''

''My mess?''

''Hey, if it hadn't been for you sticking your nose in, Chambers' case would be lost in the back of a file cabinet by now. Instead it needs a cabinet of its own.''

''Well, excuse me, Mr. Homicide Investigator with a nice tidy retirement fund stashed away somewhere that he wouldn't have if it wasn't for my nose.''

''What happened at Madding's house?''

''I found Lucia Smyth's killer.''

''Explain,'' Cartwell ordered.

Tommy explained, leaving out Rick's part.

''Jesus,'' Cartwell said. Tommy pictured him rubbing his forehead with a pudgy hand. ''More questions. At least we know it was a man who killed Chambers.''

"And somehow he found out about the Smyth woman and blackmailed Madding to help him kill Brian and—"

"He was protecting himself and or the killer," Cartwell finished, then said, "What about 'Why did she do it?' Does that mean: why did Dr. Jackson poke her nose into it?"

"That's what I thought at first," Tommy said. "But now I'm not so sure. The more I think about it, I wonder if he meant: why did she shoot *me?*"

"She, who?"

"I don't know. Sylvia Von Joss? Who else is there?"

"What about Suzanne Langdon? She's the only one who backs up Steve Langdon's statements of his whereabouts."

"Forget it. She's not involved."

"That's what you said about Langdon. I don't suppose you know where he was yesterday afternoon?"

"Yeah, I do. He was on television."

With a loud sigh, Cartwell said, "Explain."

Tommy did, reminding him of the possibility that Steve took a later flight on the day Brian was killed. Cartwell said they already started checking on that and he would check with ESPN about that interview.

"And where was Suzanne Langdon?"

Tommy started to protest but had to say, "I don't know."

"Anything else you haven't told me?" Cartwell asked.

"Nothing I can think of at the moment."

"I bet. By the way, we're pretty sure we know who shot Stanis, though I doubt we'll ever prove it. Joe Delcake, a middle-level hit man from L.A."

"An anonymous tip?" Tommy asked, not that interested anymore.

"Correct. Be here tomorrow morning. I want to go over what we have before pulling Steve Langdon in," Cartwell said. It was not a request.

Tommy had to park in the far corner of the hospital's elevated parking lot. The day was hot and still, the cloudless sky its usual washed-out blue. The flag on top of the building fluttered listlessly in a light breeze. *Another Santa Ana coming,* he thought, and realized at the same moment how bored he was with the weather. On this same spot in the middle of January the weather might be exactly the same.

"What the hell is going on, Case?" were Niles Von Joss's first words when Tommy entered his room. "The police told me this morning that Nicholas and Caroline were murdered yesterday." Niles jerked his arm from Sylvia's grasp and shook it at Tommy, his face turning purple. "And they don't have a clue," he exploded. "Do you? And now Leon tells me there's a virus of some sort in one of the computer banks."

Tommy took a straight-backed chair from the wall and straddled it. Sylvia tried to soothe her husband, but his breathing remained quick and shallow while he glared at Tommy.

"No," Tommy said. "I don't. Someone new has entered the game and I don't know who it is."

An uneasy quiet filled the room. Perplexed, Niles said, "Is someone trying to ruin me by killing my best people?"

Tommy looked up sharply. He hadn't thought of that angle, but finally he said, "No, I don't think so. Brian just happened to work for you. I think there was a past connection between Brian and his killer. Once the killer knew Brian had seen him, his days were numbered."

"Who do you think killed Brian?" Sylvia asked.

Shaking his head, Tommy answered, "I don't want to say. I can't prove it yet." He took a deep breath. "What did the police tell you about Nicholas?"

"Only that he had been shot, in his home," Niles said. "They were very closed-mouthed about it. Will you tell us?"

"Nicholas knew who killed Brian—he helped him. The murder was done from his house using DEX Four as the murder weapon. He set up everything: the telephone link, the sensor net hook up, the remote control unit he designed and installed in DEX, the changing of the security records and video tapes. He did everything but the actual murder."

"Oh my God," Sylvia said. "I can't believe it. Why?"

"Because the murderer found out that Nicholas killed Lucia Smyth because she and Caroline were lovers and Nicholas was in love with Caroline."

"God, you're serious, aren't you?" Sylvia said, disbelief plain in her voice.

"I'm afraid so," Tommy said.

"I always wondered about those two," Niles said.

Tommy filled in some details before saying, "I have to go, but there's one question I wanted to ask you. It has nothing to do with anything," he lied, "but I wondered if you knew how Steve and Suzanne were getting along these days?"

TWENTY-NINE

ON THE WAY TO the marina Tommy thought about what Sylvia had told him. About a year ago Suzanne admitted to Sylvia she thought Steve was having an affair. Sylvia had, of course, said all the reassuring words you're supposed to say, even though she, too, thought Steve was having an affair. A month or so later she broached the subject again and Suzanne said everything was fine, just fine with, Sylvia thought, all the sincerity of a pit bull bitch in heat offering to take care of your first born child.

Sylvia had no doubt Steve was playing around, but wasn't sure what Suzanne was up to. Outwardly, they were fine, though Sylvia noticed an increased tension under their banter. Tommy asked why she hadn't told him this before. She simply replied, "You didn't ask; besides, maybe they had an arrangement, it's not uncommon."

"And what do you know about such things?" Niles asked his wife with mock anger.

"I've been around," she answered.

"I am sure you have, my dear, I am sure you have."

He took her hand and the look that passed between them told Tommy that whatever their arrangement they still cared deeply for each other.

Before Tommy left Niles said, "I'm going to the lab tomorrow, no matter what the doctors say. I can't let that black hole continue indefinitely. *Mein Gott,* almost twelve gigabytes."

"Are you going to turn it off?"

"If I have to," Von Joss said.

"Oh, Niles, don't," Sylvia said, gripping his arm.

Niles' face hardened. "I can't let it take over," Niles insisted. "Who's left that can figure out what Brian has done?"

"Leon," Tommy offered.

"Leon is good, but this is far beyond him."

Tommy pointed at Sylvia.

"Your wife?"

The couples' eyes met.

"I can help, Niles," Sylvia stated flatly. "I've kept my chops up."

"I have a friend who would love to help, too. Fumio. Leon knows him."

"All right," Niles conceded. He patted his wife's arm. "I am ordering extra security. I do not want more of my people killed."

Tommy didn't either. He had a tight feeling in his stomach. He had not been able to contact Leon.

LUCY WAITED FOR HIM, back straight, arms crossed in front of her, knees pressed together. She didn't greet him, flashed no dazzling smile. He noticed a sailor's duffel on the galley counter.

"Going someplace?" he asked, uncertainly.

"I found out what you wanted," she said, clipping off each word, "Steve Langdon owns seventy per cent of the Boston Guest House. Has for years. It's popular with students but caters to rich men, and women, with a taste for the kinky things in life. It's all there." She indicated a piece of paper on the table with her chin. Before he could reach for it Lucy jumped up. Fists clenched at her side, she said, "I wouldn't have done this for anyone but you, Tommy. I broke a promise to myself that I would never, ever, have any contact with the Life again. It was harder than you'll ever know to walk away. I was raised to it, damn you. It's like a siren call, always there, constantly tugging at me. I had to listen to the call to get what you want. They want me back."

Tommy's chest tightened as tears rolled down her perfect cheeks. He gathered her in his arms. Felt her shudder as she struggled to stop the tears.

He said, "Lucy if I had known, I never would have asked you to do this. I know that I sometimes take things...people for granted. I ask them to do things for me and assume they'll do it. But I have to finish this," he said firmly.

"I know. It's gone way beyond doing a favor for a friend, though I doubt Jessie was ever your friend."

Tommy sucked in a long slow breath for strength. "Yeah, I know." They hugged a long time. "Don't go back, Lucy. Please, I need a friend like you to set me straight occasionally."

She turned away from him and used tissues from a box on a shelf. She tried out a smile. "I'm not going back," she insisted. A laugh and a sob tried to get out at the same time; the laugh won. "Besides, who would be here to relax you when you needed it? Don't answer that. But I am going away for a while, by myself. I love the sea, but sometimes you need the mountains. You know what I mean?"

"Yeah, I know. I've been thinking about the mountains lately, myself. Where're you going?"

"Just away. I need to be where nobody knows me. And I'm leaving right now." She blew her nose and smiled a stubborn, tight-lipped smile. "I hope that information helps. Take care of yourself. I don't want you going away, either."

THE TRAFFIC ON Coast Highway moved slowly, but Tommy wasn't in a hurry, he was going to see Suzanne. He hadn't been much of a friend lately and he thought she was going to need one soon. He parked under the thin, late afternoon shadow of the lone Joshua tree. It seemed like a long time ago he had left the house, hurt and angry. He looked for changes but even in California, the landscaping doesn't change much in two weeks.

Suzanne opened the door. She wore pink bicycle shorts and a simple white blouse. Dark circles under her eyes and no makeup gave her a worn, tired look. One hand went to her throat, the other felt for support from the doorway. Her nails weren't done; they were always done.

"Tommy?" she said, question and statement.

"Suzanne."

"I didn't expect you." She visibly pulled herself together. Raising her arms she offered a hug.

He hugged back, the familiar smell of her clouded his thoughts for a moment. Stepping back, he forced himself to breathe slowly. "I'm sorry I haven't been around and I'm sorry about the last time I was here. I was out of line."

She put a finger to his lips. "Don't apologize, Tommy. We

understand what you were going through. Anyway, it was bound to come out eventually, about Brian.'' She took his arm and led him through the house to the pool. ''We were worried about you, and nobody would tell us where you were. And then the other night the police wouldn't let us through. What happened?''

He told her while she got two bottles of beer and sat on a lounge chair beside him. Tommy had never seen her with un-polished nails. They made her look naked and drew his attention like a red dress in a room full of black tuxedos.

''Now the police seem to be asking a lot of questions about Steve; where he was on certain dates and things like that and you disappear and there's rumors of murders and then poor Niles. Tommy, what's happening? What are you involved in?'' She grasped his arm. ''Is Steve in trouble?''

Her voice had grown plaintive, but in the back of her glittering eyes he detected a glint of hardness he had never seen before. Suzanne urged him to stay and talk with Steve, who would be home soon. He considered it until she asked casually if anybody knew he came to see her. Then, suddenly, he needed to get out of the house. He no longer felt safe. Had Steve corrupted her or was it his own growing paranoia? The thought of being alone in the house with both Steve and Suzanne frightened him, constricting his chest, making him fight for every breath. Quickly, rudely, he left, making an excuse he didn't care if she believed or not.

It was night. He breathed easier as soon as he cleared the Langdons' gate and immediately questioned his reasons for such a hasty retreat. The house had always been a welcome and safe place, a hillside sanctuary from the press of people below. Was it his knowledge that someone was trying to kill him or was it a true sense of danger picked up from Suzanne that scared him? He had calmed down some when a red Ferrari coming from the direction of the airport passed him. It looked like Steve's, but red Ferraris were not uncommon in the area, even in Orange County's lean economic times. Nevertheless, sure that a meeting with Steve would not go well, Tommy congratulated himself on his timing.

At his motel, after watching the end of an old movie he never learned the name of, Tommy lay uneasily in bed, gun inches from his hand. He lay awake for a long time, occasionally getting up to peek out the window from behind the curtains.

He woke once in a sweat, heart pounding. He had dreamt of driving a race car up a mountain with steep drop offs on both sides. It was an exciting, wonderful dream and he knew he'd win if he crossed the finish line just ahead. A man appeared on the track. Tommy tried to wave him away but he didn't move. The man became Steve Langdon, laughing and motioning for Tommy to stop. Tommy stepped on the brakes, but nothing happened. He had to decide whether to turn off the track and go over a cliff or drive straight over Steve and win the race. Suddenly, his speed increased. The brakes didn't work; Steve was still laughing; Tommy had to decide now. Now!

In the dead hours of the morning Tommy woke again, not because of a nightmare but from the sound of the window sliding open. Instantly awake, Tommy spotted the silhouette of a person pushing the edge of the curtain aside. He rolled off the bed at the same time two bullets from a silenced pistol hit the mattress with muffled thuds. Tommy fired three quick shots from around the end of the bed, shattering the window. The shadow vanished. Tommy raced to the door, slipped the chain and stepped outside, gun double-gripped in front of him. The shadow reached the bottom of the stairs and slithered over a high block wall, leaving Tommy time to snap off two quick shots. A stifled grunt told him he hit the black shape that swiftly disappeared into the trailer park next door.

Tommy stood on the outside walkway surrounded by the smell of ocean and gunsmoke. Wearing only shorts, he shivered slightly, not only from the chilly fog. Lights came on and voices questioned. A door opened behind him but slammed shut when he turned around. He looked at the gun in his hand, shrugged and went back into his room to wait for the police.

THAT AFTERNOON Cartwell was interviewing Steve Langdon in an interrogation room when Tommy arrived at the Sheriff's Department. Neil McCoy, a deputy assigned to the case, let Tommy join him behind the two-way mirror. Steve, unlike the last time Tommy had seen him, looked as if he stopped by on his way to be photographed for the cover of *Esquire* magazine—every hair in place, silk tie knotted just so. The crease in the pants leg of his gray suit looked as if it would cut flesh. His lawyer, Richard Johansen, was as impeccably dressed and at ease as his client appeared to be. Tommy had met Johansen once and thought he was as tricky a Dick as there ever was.

"Okay, one more time, Mr. Langdon," Cartwell said. "You took the four thirty-eight flight to Boston on the Friday Brian Chambers was killed, is that right?"

"Detective Cartwell," Johanson interrupted silkily. "We have been over this before. I will remind you that my client is here voluntarily."

"And I will remind you, Mr. Johanson, that the voluntary part could change at any time." Cartwell turned to Steve. "Is that right?"

"Yes, I took that flight. I've shown you the used ticket."

"Yes you have. The thing is, we've talked to most of the people on that flight in first class and none of them remember seeing you. You're a handsome man, Mr. Langdon. Two of the passengers were single women who admitted that if they had seen you, they would have remembered you. They didn't."

"Maybe they'd had too many cocktails," Steve offered. "I can't help it if they didn't see me. I have the ticket."

"That doesn't mean you used it." Cartwell made a show of checking his notes. "There's another flight to Boston at six forty-five. One of the first class passengers on that flight thinks he saw you."

"'Thinks he saw' means nothing," Johanson said.

"We'll see after we talk with the other passengers, including the attendant, who we are assured is very good with faces."

Steve's legs were crossed tightly, his right shoe, one of a pair of five-hundred-dollar Italian loafers with leather soft as Lucy's bottom, swung side to side with a nervous rhythm. Though Steve's cool grin never wavered, the shoe stopped for a moment, then continued its motion.

"Are we through?" Johanson asked, preparing to rise.

Cartwell ignored the lawyer and stared into a corner with a wrinkled brow as if he were all alone. He let the moment drag on. Just as Steve and Johanson exchanged quizzical looks, Cartwell looked right at Steve and spoke. "How did you meet Kim Freeland?"

The shoe stopped.

Johanson stared at his note pad, waiting for Steve to say he'd never heard of her. When he didn't hear it, his eyebrows raised and his head turned toward his client.

The shoe started up again, quicker than before. "I didn't meet her," Steve said, cool and uninterested, though his knuckles were white. "I don't know her."

"You contribute to Safe House, don't you?"

"Many people do."

"Yes, we are talking to them. Where were you the night of August twenty-first?"

The interrogation continued, but Tommy didn't need to see or hear more. He stepped back and leaned against the wall, distancing himself from his friend. Steve was arrogant enough to rarely be nervous, yet Tommy knew his man. He could feel the tension in him.

It occurred to Tommy that Steve's arrogance was really suppressed cruelty. *What must his childhood have been like?* Time enough to delve into that later. Proof is what they needed now.

BY THE TIME Cartwell finished with the questioning, Tommy knew—without reservation—that Steve was guilty of murdering Brian, Jessie, runaway Kim Freeland, and Michael at the gun shop. Tommy knew Steve had the notebook, too. He didn't need a teraflops computer for automotive electronics. At that moment all feelings of loyalty and duty to friendship drained away, leaving a cold hollow in Tommy's chest.

"You know the guy," Cartwell said back in his office, "What do you think?"

"He's guilty. He did them all, except Caroline and Madding."

The detective gave him a questioning look, "He's your friend. Are you sure? Why do you think so?"

"He's not my friend. He's a murderer who needs taking down. I suppose you heard about last night?"

Cartwell wearily held up a file. "I got the report. Anything to add?"

Tommy reached into his pocket and dropped two bullets on the desk. "Somebody tried to kill me Saturday night, too. These will probably match the ones that killed Dr. Jackson and Dr. Madding. They're twenty-twos."

Cartwell picked up the two small lumps of lead and poked them with a finger. Shaking his head with frustration and resignation he said, "Christ, Case, you've got some dumb luck. I know you're not that good." He threw the bullets on his desk like a pair of dice. "Did you hear me ask how many of his fancy target pistols he had? 'Four,' he said. His wife only gave us three. Without using these exact words he called her a stupid bitch and promised to bring in the other one. I assume by your expression that that's out of character for him."

"Totally." Tommy rested his head in his hands. "I'm getting awful tired of people not being what they're supposed to be."

"You and every cop there is, Case. I think we need to have another talk with Mr. Langdon." Leaning back, he tiredly placed his feet on the desk and said, "Now tell me all about it, then tell me what they found at your latest little party."

Over lunch, Tommy told Cartwell, Neil McCoy and two others on the team that an insomniac resident of the trailer park had seen a small dark car speed away. The bullets in the mattress were .38 caliber.

They discussed Steve Langdon. They had plenty of circumstantial evidence but not enough to make an arrest. Owning a whorehouse in Boston, assuming they could prove it, wasn't illegal in California. They were still trying to locate stewardesses on later flights Steve might have taken after killing Brian. Someone suggested calling the IRS. It wasn't ruled out, but it would be admitting failure and nobody was ready to do that, yet. They needed a break.

There wasn't a clue as to who killed Dr. Jackson and Dr. Madding. On Sunday, Suzanne let the police take Steve's target shooting pistols for ballistics tests but preliminary tests, to no one's surprise, were negative.

By six that evening Tommy had checked into another anonymous motel on Newport Boulevard, showered and was lying on his bed trying to figure out where the big break they needed was going to come from.

He considered turning Salina in, then working a deal where she identified Steve at the gun shop in return for her release. But she had made him promise not to let the police get her. Besides, Pat would have his balls.

Michael Petterman had been the only lead to Jessie's and *No-morr*'s death, but unfortunately he had no mouth left with which to testify.

Tommy called his father, just to have somebody above suspicion to talk to.

"Are you still in danger?" David Case asked.

"Well, Dad, in the past few weeks I've been strangled, beaten up, blown up and shot at a few times. What does that tell you?"

"Don't be flip with me, Tommy."

"Sorry," Tommy said, meaning it. "I'm just getting tired of this. It's not what I wanted."

"Nobody says you have to keep at it, son. The police can take it from here."

Tommy laughed through his nose, "*I* say I have to keep at it, Dad. Steve knows he's under suspicion and he knows it's mostly my doing. Whatever happens to him he won't stop until he stops me. That's the way he plays, no loose ends."

"Is it worth your life?" his father asked seriously. "It sounds to me as if Jessie is responsible. She got you involved for no other reason that I can see except vindictiveness. Revenge because you closed your office."

"That may be true, but I still feel responsible, and that's what counts."

"Well, I wish you'd come up here now, tonight, and stay with me 'til it's all over, but I guess you won't. You're just as stubborn as your mother used to be. So what now?"

"Try to find the one thing that'll tie it all together. Something that links Steve to actually working the robot."

"You know," Tommy's father said, "when we had a problem toward the end of a project, sometimes the only way to solve it was go back to the very beginning and work it through. You'd be surprised at how often overlooking something minor at the beginning prevents a tidy ending. Chaos Theory, they call it now."

Tommy's thoughts raced. Where had it all begun? With Brian's murder? No. With a phone call to Brian. Mr. Neat-and-tidy himself. Neat and tidy; something overlooked. "Yes, it's definitely worth a look," he whispered softly to himself. "Dad, you've given me an idea. I have to go. I'll call you."

The records showed that Brian received a telephone call at five minutes to six on Friday afternoon. It came from Madding's house, but he did not make the call. If Brian took it in his office why did he go into the workroom with DEX 4? Tommy pictured the room. Workbenches, tools, electronic equipment. In the corner, where DEX stayed, were notebooks...and a telephone. So somebody, Steve, calls Brian, asks him to look up something in a notebook in the corner. While Brian does this, Steve is manipulating DEX.

But wouldn't Brian write down whatever he was supposed to look up? There wasn't anything on the big pad, which sat precisely in the middle of his neat and tidy desk. Neat and tidy. How many times had he heard that about Brian? His desk as always, neat and tidy. Even in a drawer a small note pad not in its proper place would not be tolerated.

"Bingo!"

Tommy sat up, excited. He stared at himself in the mirror on the far wall. If Brian was in a hurry, he did have a plane to catch, he might not have noticed the little yellow pad not being in its proper place. What was written on that pad might just be the break he was looking for.

Tommy looked at the clock on the television, *six-thirty, seven maybe, by the time I get there.* Then how do I get in? Niles, who else.

Before he called the Von Joss at home, Tommy left messages at three other numbers. Anne answered, "Oh Tommy, I'm so sorry about Caroline. I feel bad about dragging you out to go sailing. She might still be alive."

"Anne, it's not your fault. If it's anybody's it's mine, but that's not what I called about. I need to talk to your father. However, seeing as I have you on the phone I wondered if you've ever heard of the Boston Guest House. You went to school at Wellesley, didn't you?''

After a long silence Anne said, ''Sure, I've heard of it. It's no big secret. Why do you ask?''

''I don't suppose you worked there when Brian was a student and maybe took up a bit too much of his study time?''

Another silence. Anne said, ''Tommy if you were here I'd slap your face for that.'' But she didn't sound angry.

''I've never been slapped by an Annabelle before.''

''Maybe next time we go sailing we can make it slap and tickle.''

''You didn't answer my question,'' Tommy said.

Anne laughed, ''Oh Tommy, you must allow us our little family secrets. You're one of them now, you know. I'll get my father.''

Against doctor's orders, Niles Von Joss had gone to his office, but around three had been forced to admit he was not as strong as he thought and went home where he entertained some well-wishing friends. Of course he could get in, Niles told Tommy, and gave him his security codes and said he would tell the guard to expect him.

THIRTY

TOMMY PULLED INTO the parking space marked N. Von Joss next to a faded green Toyota pick-up, a perfect 1975 Corvette, and Fumio's Volkswagen van. The marine layer had moved in early. Low and gray, it brought the temperature down to the low sixties. Tommy shrugged on a light jacket to cover up the .38 snug against his back, which Cartwell had unofficially given him to replace the gun the Costa Mesa police took from him.

Stanley the guard, a gaunt, fifty something man, missing a tooth from the upper left of a too-wide mouth, greeted Tommy like an old friend. Tommy returned the greeting and asked about the Corvette.

"That's Mr. Flakee's car," Stanley replied. "It's a beauty, isn't it?"

"That it is. I didn't know he had a car like that. Is he in his office?"

"Yes sir, with a visitor. I believe he owns several cars, sir."

"This visitor. Is he a Japanese guy, about thirty, chubby, with a ponytail?"

"That's him."

"Okay, thanks. I'll see them when I'm finished here."

"All right. Have to do my rounds now. I'll tell Mr. Flakee you're here."

The door into the restricted area opened easily. The hallway and offices were dark, hushed. A single light from the computer room cast a pale glow through the windows in the double doors. He turned on the lights in Brian's office, his body coiled tight, ready for...nothing. What had he been expecting? Brian, come back to life? DEX, waiting for another victim? Tommy shivered. "Spooky," he whispered to the room.

The office and desk had not changed. Gingerly, Tommy picked the Post-it pad off the top of the stack. He held it up at an angle to the light and saw the imprint of writing. His pulse picked up a beat. Carefully laying it on the desk he took a pencil from the Orange Coast College mug and, holding it at an angle, lightly darkened the paper. Letters and numbers appeared: "arm accur. 2' arm Vol. 3?"

Mumbling to the empty room, Tommy tried to make sense of his find. "Vol. 3" was Volume 3; "2' arm" was probably a two foot long arm; "arm accur." was most likely arm accuracy. Okay, easy enough. Now to find Volume 3 and see if there was anything about "two-foot arm accuracy," whatever that meant.

The light from the computer room cast dim shadows on the workroom floor. DEX hulked malevolently in the corner. Tommy turned on the light for the far end of the room and DEX was just DEX, waiting innocently in his corner. Tommy spotted the notebooks and went to them. He stopped to look DEX in his video eyes.

"Is anybody in there?" Tommy asked.

DEX didn't answer.

Tommy took out volume three and opened it to reveal pages of graphs and tables that made no sense. Turning the pages one by one brought him to a table titled Arm Accuracy. It seemed easy enough to read and he soon found that a two-foot arm had an accuracy of plus or minus five thousandths. Well, shit. What the hell did that mean? What arm? Whose arm? How the hell did this point to Steve?

Tommy heard a rustle behind him, a footstep. When he turned around he expected to see Leon or Fumio. It wasn't them. It was Steve Langdon, ten feet away, with a gun pointed at Tommy's chest.

Tommy froze; his heart thumped dully. "I see you got my message to meet an hour from now at your house, after I left here."

"Your message? I've been looking all over for you," Steve said in a jovial voice, full of menace. "Then, not twenty minutes ago I got a strange call on my cell phone. The voice was distorted, mechanical, and said you would be here. And here you are." He motioned with the gun. "Move away."

Tommy moved along the workbench, not trusting himself to speak. He hadn't been able to get through to Steve's cell phone.

STEVE WALKED to the book and glanced down.

"Very good. It took you long enough to think of it, not that it would have done you any good." A superior smile marred his handsome features. "I just made it up."

Tommy found his voice. With an effort he kept it neutral. "Yeah, I figured you killed him, and the others, and destroyed my boat. Damn it, why *Nomorr?* We were friends."

"We were friends, weren't we?" Steve said. "I am sorry about your boat, Tommy. Really. She was fine and you did a great job on her. I wish you were out sailing now, with a couple of beautiful young native girls to crew for you. But poor Kim failed to do the favor I asked her," Steve shrugged unsympathetically, "So..."

"Jesus, Steve, she was just a kid."

"Yes, she was, wasn't she, but you know how kids are with secrets. It's no good if they can't tell anyone." He smiled wistfully. "We did have some fun, though," he said offhandedly.

The two men watched each other while Tommy handled the shock of learning the truth he'd only suspected before. Tommy spoke calmly, his revulsion limit overloaded.

"How many other girls did you use from the Safe House— your special charity?"

"I never touched any of the girls from Safe House."

"Kim stayed there."

"Yes, she did, but I didn't know it 'til I read it in the paper. Believe me, Tommy, I didn't know."

"Why should I believe you?" Tommy shot back. "You've been lying all along. Our friendship was a lie. Your marriage is a lie. Us, damn it, us. My best friend. A lie."

"You're right, but Tommy, you have to believe me," Steve pleaded, "I never touched any girls from Safe House. That's why it's called that. It's a place for kids to get off the street and be safe from, from—"

"From people like you," Tommy finished quietly.

Steve gripped his gun with two shaking hands. Cords stood

out on his neck. He advanced on Tommy, his body quivering from the effort to either pull the trigger or not pull the trigger.

"Damn you, Tommy. Damn you. Why couldn't you leave it alone?"

Tommy stood his ground, held by the anger that blazed in Steve's bright eyes. Time passed. The fire in Steve's eyes faded and he stepped back. More time passed and a wistful smile returned to Steve's lips. He said, as if Kim had never been mentioned, "I almost didn't do it, you know, but when I saw Jessie on the boat with you I couldn't pass up the opportunity to take out that greedy little bitch, too."

Tommy's thoughts came together. "You and Jessie were lovers, weren't you? She got the two hundred grand from you. A little blackmail on the side?"

Steve shrugged, "Too bad she was such a child in some ways, she never got to enjoy her money. What happened to it, anyway?" He paused for a few seconds, shaking his head a bit as if remembering something enjoyable, but weird. "I wouldn't say we were lovers in the usual way. We had sex, a lot of sex, but there was no love involved." He sighed. "That girl didn't love anything, including herself, except money, fucking, and fucking people over. And she was very good at the second two."

"Goddamn," Tommy spat, taking a step forward. He wanted to strangle the man with his bare hands. Another step. The gun in Steve's hand jumped and Tommy felt a sting on the outside of his right thigh. The sharp report reverberated around the high-ceilinged room. Tommy looked through the ragged tear that had appeared in his pant leg. The wound was only a scratch, but for the first time he really felt the fear. He knew the bullet hit exactly where it was aimed and that Steve was going to kill him when he was ready.

"Tommy, you should know better than to interrupt a man when he's remembering past pleasures."

Disgust and revenge filled his mind. "Insane," Tommy said through clenched teeth. "You're insane."

Steve nodded in agreement, eyes gone dead. "Yes, maybe. Maybe." Steve looked through Tommy to a past Tommy couldn't begin to imagine. "My father was a cruel man," Steve said, with a voice as dead as his eyes. "Did I ever tell you that?"

"No," Tommy said, curious now, despite the situation.

"People feared him, and I wanted to be just like that. Have that power. My mother was cruel, too, in her way. She enjoyed punishing me when I acted like my father. Then I met Miranda. There wasn't a hard-hearted thought in her." His eyes turned glassy as he said, "Then she died, and there was nobody to stop me."

"Jesus, you've been waiting all your life to be a monster?"

"Not me, Tommy." His shoulders lifted and his hands spread out in a what-can-I-do? gesture. "My parents installed a dated virus in me. Its time to run arrived when Miranda left."

"A virus manmade for murder. No wonder you never talked about your parents. Give it up, man. Viruses can be deleted."

Steve's face came alive and he flashed a mirthless grin. "But I'm rich, Tommy, and when you're rich you can afford to be a little crazy. Eccentric, it's called."

"You've gone way beyond eccentric."

"That's because you look at it from the poor point of view, like I used to, seven years ago, before Miranda left me. You'd have liked Randy. She was a good woman. Strong. She knew me so well. Knew when to hold me back and when to let me go, then she left me and suddenly I was rich and she wasn't there to tell me I couldn't have what I wanted."

"Like whorehouses and teenage girls?" Tommy watched the gun, ready to jump if the opportunity came.

"You know about that too, huh? Like I said, you can have anything you want with enough money, and soon I'm going to have more than you can imagine." His face lit up at the thought of his coming wealth. "I have Brian's notebook," he announced barely able to contain his excitement. "It's real, Tommy. It'll work and I control it and it'll be worth billions, Tommy, billions and it will be mine and I won't let anybody keep it from me. Not even you," he finished, eyes suddenly cold and vicious.

"What about Suzanne? Doesn't she mean anything?"

Steve shook his head. The gun stayed steady. "No, not any more. At first she was fine. She had a hell of a body, ready and able to do anything I wanted.'' He shrugged. ''But she got older and I wanted younger and I can have whatever I want.''

''Why not just divorce her?''

''And give her half my money? Besides, now that you'll no longer be a problem, I think in a month or so she'll have a fatal accident and then I get to keep all the money. Much neater than a divorce, don't you think?''

The swinging doors crashed open. Caught off guard, the two men swiveled toward the noise as Suzanne burst through the doorway. She wore jeans, a dark blue, long-sleeved blouse and black leather driving gloves. Blonde hair trailed behind as she stalked toward the men, fury in her eyes and a black semi-automatic pistol in her hand.

''Yeah, I think that's a great idea,'' she shouted, ''only you're the one who's going to have the accident.'' She stopped fifteen feet away from Steve, ignoring Tommy. ''You were going to kill me,'' she stated. ''That's the thanks I get for keeping you out of jail all this time? Oh, don't look so shocked. I know all about Brian and that slut Jessie. You're slime, Stevie. As sick as they come and all your precious money doesn't make it any different.''

''Don't call me Stevie, you bitch,'' Steve snarled. ''I took you out of the goddamn gutter where you were sleeping with anybody with the price of a drink.''

''Yeah, and I was with your son down there in that gutter. He's ten times the man you are.''

Steve's eyes grew wide. He started to raise his gun, but froze when Suzanne stiffened and commanded, ''Don't do it, Stevie. This isn't one of your playtoy twenty-twos that take three shots to kill somebody.''

''Don't call me Stevie, damn it,'' he demanded in a high, whiny voice.

Tommy sagged against the bench as the meaning of Suzanne's words sank in. *She* killed Caroline. Why? Without thinking, he asked out loud, ''Why kill Caroline?''

Suzanne flicked a glance at Tommy. ''To save poor Stevie's ass, I'm sorry to say. I am sorry about the woman, Tommy. I made a mistake. I should have let the police have him. However, this way will be quicker than a divorce. Just like you said, Stevie.''

''Goddamn it, don't call me Stevie,'' Steve cried, raising his gun. Tommy heard the boom of Suzanne's pistol and saw Steve slam backward against DEX 4. A dark hole appeared in his otherwise immaculate shirt. His feet went out from under him and he slid to the floor, leaning against the robot's base. The acrid smell of burnt gunpowder reminded Tommy of the gun shop. Suzanne took two steps forward and fired two more bullets into her late husband. The body jerked twice, rolled onto its left side and lay still.

Suzanne stood over the body, kicked it once, picked up Steve's gun, then turned to face Tommy. Her eyes were still wide with the killing anger. She leveled the shaking gun at his chest. They looked at each other, Suzanne calming herself and Tommy mentally kicking himself for not drawing his own gun.

Suzanne spoke first. ''So, Tommy, here we are.''

''Yes, here we are. How did you know I was here?''

''I was visiting Niles when you called. I tried to call Stevie to tell him, but his cell phone was off. Then I saw his car and followed him here. I don't know how he knew where you were. I'd hoped he would get rid of you. Now I'll have to do it. You've really been a pain, Tommy. You should have just said no to Jessie. It would have saved a lot of trouble, and lives. Including yours, I'm afraid.''

Tommy decided to ignore that, maybe it would go away.

''How did you know about Steve?''

She chuckled smugly to herself. ''I've been recording all the phone calls at our house for the last year or so. I also bugged his office,'' she said proudly. ''I've been through all his private papers, including the ones in his private safe. I know all about his business and personal dealings, including his private playpen in Boston and the five million dollars stashed in a Caribbean bank.''

''Did you know he was going to kill Brian?''

Furrows appeared on her brow, ''Unfortunately, no. I knew he and Nicholas Madding were up to something at the lab, but I didn't think he'd kill Brian. I should have, though, and arranged an accident for him.''

"You and Brian were lovers for more than a few hours."

Suzanne smiled fondly, "Oh yes. While Stevie was out playing race car and screwing his whores, I was at home, screwing Brian, who was a good man, actually, if not exactly faithful.''

"Why *did* he kill Brian?"

"Stevie thought he might tell somebody about their meeting in Boston when Brian went to school there. It was one of Stevie's girls who got Brian into trouble. It was so stupid. They had a big argument and Brian only wanted to forget about it, but Stevie wouldn't let it go. Of course, there's the notebook, too. Nicholas was crazy jealous when he found out about it. Stevie already controlled him, but when Brian made that breakthrough his fate was sealed. Now it's mine. What do you think I can get for it, ten, twenty million? I'm not as greedy as poor little Stevie.''

They stared at each other. *Keep her talking,* Tommy told himself. *Leon or Fumio will come looking for me eventually.* She seemed comfortable with the pistol, although she had never showed any interest in guns.

"When did you learn how to use a gun?"

"About six months ago. The same man who taught me about bugs and recording telephone calls. When Steve started getting crazy about Brian, I thought some self-defense training might come in handy. Stevie was right about one thing: if you have the money, you can have anything you want.''

"This man wouldn't happen to have been hanging around my motel room early this morning, would he?"

"He followed you last night. You got him good in the arm, by the way. A lucky shot, I imagine." She let out a big sigh. "I will say one thing for pretty Stevie: he taught me some things in bed that would drive you wild. At one point I thought maybe you and I would get together.'' Suzanne tightened her grip on Steve's pistol and leaned back against DEX to steady herself. "But I guess now I'll have to teach somebody else.''

Tommy tensed. He had to move. Think it through and do it. Jump. Grab his gun. Roll. Shoot. Ready... Ready... Wait. Did DEX move?

Time slowed.

DEX's head had tilted forward when Suzanne's first bullet drove Steve against him. In his mind's eye Tommy saw DEX shedding oily tears. Dex's arm slowly began to rise. Leon and Fumio!

"Sorry, Tommy, I have to go," Suzanne said. "I'll leave you two here to shoot each other."

Tommy, eyes wide, watched both Suzanne and DEX's arms. Blood pounded in his ears. Suzanne tensed. His heart hammered against his chest. Dex's arm continued its slow upward movement. Faster! Move faster! Suzanne pushed the gun out, away from her body, eyes narrowed at the expected noise. Tommy shook, the adrenaline in him crying out: Move! Move! The metal hand touched the flesh arm. Forced it up. Crack! The bullet left a small puff of smoke by the barrel, then passed through the space Tommy's head had occupied a few milliseconds before.

Suzanne cursed.

Tommy rolled. He snapped off a shot from a prone position. Missed.

Suzanne disentangled herself from DEX and fired. Tommy rolled again. Her bullet ricocheted off the concrete floor and put a small hole in the computer room window.

Coming to his feet in a hurry, Tommy slammed his hip against the bench. A wave of pain took his breath away. Realizing he had no cover, he threw a wild shot that creased DEX's chest. Suzanne flinched, then steadied the gun with both hands for the final shot.

Suddenly DEX lurched forward, knocking Suzanne off balance. Her shot went wild. Another hole in the window. DEX's movement stopped the shot but also gave her cover. Tommy fired twice as he backed along the bench toward the doors opposite the pair he had entered. He stumbled through. A bullet followed him. It splattered against the wall, stinging his face with pulverized cement.

On his feet, he chanced a quick look through the heavy glass window. Suzanne ran across the open floor, heading for the other doors. She fired once. Tommy ducked back, avoiding flying glass from the shattered window.

He called through the window, "It's over Suzanne. Everything was recorded," he lied. "You have no place to go."

She stood by the doors, her face a mask of pure fury.

"Go to hell, Tommy."

She punctuated her words with bullets. Two of them thunked into the heavy metal door, swinging it against him.

He darted a look in time to see her blond hair disappear through the security door. He followed at a run. As he crossed the workroom he shot a glance at DEX, and came to an abrupt halt. The robot had moved away from its corner. The thick bundle of wires that connected it to electric and computer power stretched taut. One arm reached out to Tommy, palm up in an unmistakable gesture: Help me. DEX's video eyes caught Tommy's. Tommy saw deep into the glass and metal tubes and like the first time he saw the robot, thought that behind those lenses lurked more than inanimate blankness. His mind's eye supplied more tears to the robot's face as DEX inched forward against his tether.

A muffled shot came from the lobby. Still riding the adrenaline high of near death, Tommy jerked his head toward the sound. Then snapped it back to DEX.

"Shit. I can't help you now, DEX," he said quickly. "Thanks for saving my life."

He spun through the doors, his thoughts switching to pursuit of Suzanne.

Stanley had sunk to his knees, hands red with blood, clutching his stomach. The front door swung shut. The color drained from Stanley's face but his eyes were bright.

"I'm all right," he said.

Tommy eased the wounded man against the wall, picked up the telephone and dialed 911.

"Shooting at Electrobotics Labs in Irvine. One dead, one wounded. This is Tommy Case. Tell Sergeant Cartwell, Sheriff's Department." He handed the receiver to the guard, "Talk to them, Stanley."

Tommy limped through the front door just in time to see Suzanne's red Ferrari blast past. Suzanne held a purple spiral bound notebook triumphantly in the air. He fired after her. He couldn't tell if he hit the speeding car. It didn't explode like in the movies, so he figured not.

THIRTY-ONE

TOMMY FOLLOWED the Ferrari through the darkness down Alton Parkway to Sand Canyon Avenue and onto the 405 Freeway. The relatively light traffic allowed them to make good time and Tommy thought maybe Suzanne didn't know he was following her. At the usual slowdown through El Toro the two cars closed up. Keeping another car between them, Tommy wondered, now what? There were too many people around to force her off the road or risk shooting.

When the road opened up south of Mission Viejo, a puff of exhaust appeared behind the red car. Its rear end squatted and before Tommy could get clear opened a half mile gap. She had seen him all right. Tommy gripped the wheel, narrowed his concentration and slapped the accelerator to the floor. The Mustang leaped in pursuit, pressing him firmly into his seat.

A few miles later he caught up enough to see if she exited the freeway. If he lost her in the night she would disappear for good. Where the hell was the Highway Patrol? If he had been driving this fast for fun, the CHP would have been all over him like bugs on a just washed windshield. Suzanne was born in San Diego, he remembered, surely the CHP will notice us before that.

Traffic slowed Suzanne down and Tommy gained on her fast. Too fast! Brake lights flashed. The Ferrari turned slowly sideways, trailing tire smoke. It stopped in the middle lane. Tommy stood on the brakes; cars skidded around him. The nose of the Mustang rocked to a stop inches from the Ferrari's door. Suzanne's wild hair glowed white in his headlights, her head rocked, urging the stalled engine to start. It did with a high revving blast of power. She tossed her head, flashing him a victorious sneer. Tires screaming, she raced down the shoulder and back onto the highway.

Tommy followed and with a clear road they accelerated up to

a hundred and twenty within seconds. Just as he came within a few feet of her in the middle lane, Suzanne swerved to the right onto an exit ramp. "Son of a bitch!" he shouted. Out of the corner of his eye, before going under the overpass, he saw a gloved hand snake out of the car's window, its middle finger extended.

"Son of a bitch," he repeated, stomping the brakes. He glanced to the right. The on ramp was clear. He darted the Mustang across lanes and up the ramp. Shaking fists and swerving cars showed him what direction Suzanne had gone. East. Tommy blasted his horn as he weaved through traffic across the overpass. Then he realized where they were heading—the Ortega Highway. Despite the circumstances, a small smile forced itself onto his tight lips as the Ferrari disappeared ahead. Ignoring the pain in his leg, he set himself firmly into the seat, flexed his hands and gripped the leather-covered steering wheel firmly at nine and three.

The Ortega Highway. He knew this road, a driver's delight. A narrow two-lane, thirty-mile-long road that twisted up San Juan Canyon, over the Santa Ana Mountains, then dropped precipitously down to Lake Elsinore. Tommy had driven it many times, but never with such urgency. Nevertheless, his grim smile remained as he chased the speeding red car through a short residential neighborhood and into the first section of relatively level road. The cars plunged through the darkness. Trees formed tunnels with their overhanging branches, spelling disaster for the least mistake.

They stayed even for fifteen miles. The Ferrari had the edge on power—Tommy knew Steve made some modifications, emissions standards be damned—and their suspensions were about equal, but Tommy had the experience. He knew the curves and what lay beyond, how to set up for a turn and exit at maximum speed. Suzanne's driving was erratic, sometimes fishtailing under braking when she went in too deep, sometimes leaving a dust cloud where she skidded off the road. Her superior power, and perhaps desperation, kept her a couple hundred yards ahead.

The character of the road changed when they entered the canyon. The road allowed no mistakes, as many would-be racers, especially motorcyclists, found out every year. On the right, solid rock, straight up. On the left, a hundred-foot-plus drop, straight down. Tommy remembered the rhythm of the road and closed the gap quickly, the nose of the Mustang coming within inches of the Ferrari's twitchy rear end. Suddenly, the lead car slid to the right against the granite face; sparks lit up the night. The Mustang rammed its rear end. More sparks flew as Tommy lost control for a second, scraped the rock face. Immediately he backed off, regaining control.

They came to a hundred-eighty degree turn that dipped down, then up, where the bottom of the canyon rose to meet the road. Tommy knew that not far ahead were some wider straight sections where he might be able to get beside the other car and force it off the road. He checked that his reloaded pistol was at hand and pushed hard to catch up. Ninety-five, a glance at his speedometer told him. The same glance also told him of the rising engine temperature. He came even with the other car, made contact and started to ease to the right.

He barely heard the gunshot, but saw its effect. Through the spiderweb hole that appeared in his passenger window he saw Suzanne, wisps of hair whipped by the wind, trying to get a shot at his front tire.

Tommy jerked the wheel and both cars spun onto the wide dirt shoulder. The Ferrari came to rest fifty feet away. His first shot raised a swirl of dust under the car, the second left a hole in the body by the rear tire. Suzanne returned fire. Two shots thumped into the Mustang. Tommy fired again but the other car darted away spewing out a dust-and-gravel rooster tail.

They blasted past the campground at El Cariso, heading for the eastern face of the mountains where the road dropped two thousand feet in three miles.

The Mustang's temperature hit two-ninety. *We'll be going downhill soon,* Tommy reminded himself, *but if I can't stop her by Lake Elsinore, I'll lose her. There're too many places to go and this engine won't last.*

He pictured the road ahead and an idea came to him. It would truly be a last ditch effort and possibly Tommy's last effort, ever

The road turned south, descending along the steep mountain

face. The town of Lake Elsinore glittered serenely below. Tommy pushed hard, in two miles he had to be right on the Ferrari's rear bumper. More vehicles used this portion of the road, going to El Cariso or the restaurant on the mountain's edge. Take a blind corner in the wrong lane and it might be the last. The temperature gauge nudged red, the smell of his overheated engine swirled around him.

Tommy had two chances, two hairpin corners with decreasing radiuses. If he could get on the inside of the other car, in the correct position against the left rear quarter, and if Suzanne did not know the curves, as the turn became tighter, she would have no place to go, except over the edge, most likely with Tommy following right behind.

They started into the first turn. Tommy darted into the left lane, the inside track. He just made contact when headlights appeared, blinding him. On the brakes, he ducked behind his quarry a split second before a minivan, horn blaring, rushed past. Even over the roar of his engine he heard the children's screams.

He tried the same maneuver into the next corner but Suzanne darted into the left lane ahead of him. The temperature gauge needle disappeared into the red zone and Tommy felt the loss of power. He bulled his way between Suzanne and the bank with his foot to the floor. The clatter of rocks striking the underbody drowned out the scream of his dying engine. The rearview mirror vanished against a rock.

As the turn tightened, both cars edged toward the outside. The Ferrari's rear end slid away; Tommy kept his foot down. In T-bone formation they slid off the road together. Suzanne's car dropped away under the Mustang. In the air, in the sudden silence, he heard the solid crunch and felt the whoomp of flame as the red car stopped permanently in a brush-covered ditch.

The Mustang sailed over the gully, dipped its nose into the dirt, flipped upside down, and jolted to a stop against a massive boulder. A headlight flickered and went dark. Steam rose languidly into the night, quiet now except for the cooling tic tic tic of the ruined engine and the crackle of flames.

EPILOGUE

LOUNGING IN his usual place by the pool, Tommy heard some-body enter the kitchen from the garage. He listened to the rustle of paper bags and quiet voices as groceries were put away.

The voices came closer.

"He is by the pool," Ramona said.

"How is he?"

Ramona didn't answer, but Tommy, in his mind's eye, saw her raise her thin shoulders and throw up her hands: who can tell?

TOMMY LEFT the hospital ten days after the crash. His fractured left arm and leg forced him to obey doctor's orders and rest. Harry Langdon, having matured greatly since his trip to Las Vegas with his future stepmother, persuaded Tommy to use the house as long as he needed it. Ramona, of course, could also stay. To the families of his parent's victims he promised what help and support he could provide. After all, he had suddenly become a very rich man.

After his release, Tommy turned taciturn and lethargic. He told Ramona he was unavailable to everybody and spent his time by the pool, staring at, but not always seeing, the ocean. Wash came to see him one day; Ramona let him in and Tommy allowed him to stay.

Occasionally he talked of the last months, like when Wash asked him, "Why did Jessie go to you?"

"I think my Dad had it right, vindictiveness," he said, unin-terested. "She just wanted to make me do something she knew I didn't want to do. She didn't gain sexual control of me when we first met, although at the time I wanted her to, so this was her last chance to prove she could do it."

"And she did."

"Yes, she did."

"What about Brian?"

"Oh, I think she loved him, as much as she could love anybody. She probably saw him as her last chance at a normal life. Of course, he was pretty screwed up too, so when he saw his chance, through Suzanne, he took it."

Another time he asked, "How did Steve get Madding to help him?"

"Blackmail, mostly. As far as the police can figure out, Jessie told him about her underage affair with Nicholas. Also, when Steve was questioned about Lucia Smyth's murder he saw a picture of the body and recognized a pattern. Nicholas was prone to doodling when he was thinking. Also, Nicholas was extremely jealous of his job, so it was no trick to convince him Brian was after it."

"And Suzanne knew all this?"

"Most of it. She was interested in the money. She didn't care what Steve did, but when he started getting really crazy she panicked. She killed Caroline and Nicholas in a last attempt to stop the inevitable, instead of being patient and letting him get caught. If she had just waited, she was covered."

HUGH CARTWELL stopped by on his way to Mexico.

"I just came by to see if I was going to be looking over my shoulder the rest of my life."

"You have nothing to worry about from me," Tommy said. "Buy yourself a good hat. The sun can be killer down there."

"Thanks for the advice. Look, Case, the Department lost a good man when you left. I thought you should know that."

For the rest of that day Tommy rose out of his blue funk and was actually pleasant to Ramona.

TOMMY ROLLED HIS HEAD to watch Lucy step onto the patio. She tugged her sweater tight around her and sat next to him. The sun, bright orange from the day's pollution, hovered over Catalina Island. As the lower limb touched the horizon, Lucy said, "I talked with Fumio today. You should see him. He's worried about you.''

"Doesn't he have enough to worry about already?''

Fumio and Leon swore they had nothing to do with DEX saving Tommy's life. But they did, by chance, record a transmission stream from the ever-growing black hole in the Electrobotic's computers at the same time Tommy said DEX moved. Fumio, a new Electrobotics employee, thought he had managed to isolate and limit the growth of the hole at about twenty gigabytes, but the empty space in another computer had begun to fill up, attempts to foil phone line connections were intermittently successful at best and DEX kept moving on his own. There was no doubt in anybody's mind that the void would keep trying to expand. Yet, so far, the new presence had not destroyed any data, so Von Joss had not pulled the plug. Not to mention that deciphering the half-burned notebook recovered from Suzanne's car was a full-time job in itself.

Yeah, Fumio had plenty to worry about.

"Sure he does,'' Lucy answered her own question. "God, what if 'it' did get loose? What would it do, do you think? Well, anyway, he's your friend. You should talk with him.''

"He's probably loving every minute.''

"Probably, but he needs a break. Call him.''

"Okay, Mom.''

"Tommy, I am not your mother. I'm your friend. If I'm anything else, I don't know.''

Tommy struggled to sit up and face her.

"How'd you like to be my traveling companion?''

Her expression turned puzzled.

"Where to?''

"How about Colorado?''

"Colorado? You can't sail to Colorado, Tommy.''

"Yeah, well, I guess, for the moment, sailing has lost some of its appeal.'' Tommy lowered his head and inspected the signatures on his cast. "What happened with Steve and Suzanne hurt a lot. He destroyed my boat and I'm just not ready to have another one, yet.'' He took Lucy's strong hands in his and forced a smile. "I'm going to meet my dad there. We have time to get

in some good fishing and hiking. It's beautiful in the San Juans.''
Their eyes met and Tommy let himself fall into the warm liquid
of her gaze. "Come with me. I...I need you. Please.''

"Oh God, Tommy, I was hoping that... well, hoping that we
might go cruising together. Still...''

Tommy leaned forward and kissed her. It was a light, tender
kiss that nevertheless set his heart pounding and his body quivering like a puppy when it hears its master approach.

Inside the house, the telephone rang. The sun had retired for
the night, leaving a fast fading sky and a few clouds on the
horizon blazing red and black. A leftover breeze with a hint of
autumn stirred, chilling the two lovers.

"Tomas," Ramona called. "Telephone for you. I think it is a
Mr. Dix something. You come in now. Dinner is ready.''

Tommy and Lucy stared at each other.

"Dix?" Lucy said. "DEX?''

"It couldn't be," Tommy said, though he was not at all sure.

"Christ, Tommy, if it is, then you were right. Fumio does have
a lot to worry about.''

"Let's go find out.''

Tommy hopped on his good leg while Lucy readied his
crutches. She took his good arm as they made their slow way
toward the house.

Lucy asked, "So if this artificial intelligence has really taken
over DEX the robot, does that mean it, DEX, has emotions, too?
Isn't that one of the tests for humanness?''

Lucy held the screen door open. Tommy hesitated and turned
to her.

"I don't know about that, Lucy," he said. "But don't let anybody tell you that robots don't cry.''

The Girl at the End of the Line

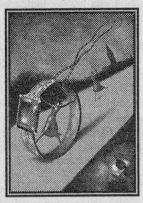

Charles Mathes

A MOLLY & NELL O'HARA MYSTERY

When Nell O'Hara and older sister Molly discover that their grandmother died under suspicious circumstances, they decide it's time to find out why sudden death seems to run in their family.

An old Broadway playbill leads them to secrets of their grandmother's scandalous past. The sisters follow a trail of adventure and mystery that sweeps from America to England, and finally to a secluded island on the Atlantic coast where a chilling legacy of murder awaits....

Available March 2000 at your favorite retail outlet.

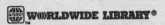

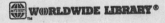